BY EMILY STONE

Love, Holly
One Last Gift
Always, in December

Love, Holly

Love, Holly

A NOVEL

EMILY STONE

DELL BOOKS
NEW YORK

A Dell Trade Paperback Original

Copyright © 2023 by Emily Stone
Book club guide copyright © 2023 by
Penguin Random House LLC

Published in the United States by Dell,
an imprint of Random House, a division of
Penguin Random House LLC, New York.

DELL and the D colophon are registered trademarks
of Penguin Random House LLC.
RANDOM HOUSE BOOK CLUB and colophon are trademarks
of Penguin Random House LLC.

Published in the United Kingdom as *The Christmas Letter*
in 2023. Published by arrangement with
Headline Publishing Group Limited.

LIBRARY OF CONGRESS CATALOGING-IN-PUBLICATION DATA
Names: Stone, Emily, author.
Title: Love, Holly: a novel / Emily Stone.
Description: New York: Dell Books, 2023.
Identifiers: LCCN 2023014899 (print) |
LCCN 2023014900 (ebook) | ISBN 9780593722114
(trade paperback) | ISBN 9780593722121 (Ebook)
Subjects: LCGFT: Romance fiction. | Christmas fiction. | Novels.
Classification: LCC PR6119.T6743 L68 2023 (print) |
LCC PR6119.T6743 (ebook) | DDC 823/.92—dc23/eng/20230407
LC record available at https://lccn.loc.gov/2023014899
LC ebook record available at https://lccn.loc.gov/2023014900

Printed in the United States of America on acid-free paper

randomhousebooks.com
randomhousebookclub.com

2 4 6 8 9 7 5 3 1

Book design by Alexis Capitini

serendipity
(noun) finding something good without looking for it

Love, Holly

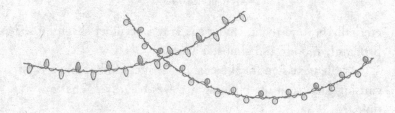

Chapter One

Holly kept her eyes peeled as she drove along the main road that led through North Devon, her sister resting her head on the window, eyes closed. Which was not helpful, being as how Lily was supposed to be keeping Holly awake on the long drive from London to the little holiday cottage in the middle of bloody nowhere that their parents had rented for Christmas. And right now, Holly was flagging. Despite the cold, damp air, it was toasty warm inside her parents' little Fiesta, the Christmas songs on the radio were now making her sleepy with their repetition, and her and Lily's car game of *Who Am I?* had long since been abandoned.

And what kind of main road was this, anyway? All these winding turns made it impossible to go safely above about forty miles an hour. All Holly wanted right now was a coffee, but there hadn't been any sign of a petrol station for miles. It was beautiful down here, though, she'd give it that. There were hedgerows lining each side of the road, slightly bare at the moment but no doubt full of life in spring and summer, with fields stretching out eternally beyond them. Under the gray December sky, it looked brilliantly moody and almost ethereal.

At the next sign for the nearest village, Holly hung a right, causing Lily to sit up, blinking her eyes blearily. "What are you doing?"

"I need caffeine; I'm finding somewhere to stop."

Lily wrinkled her nose, but that was the only sign of protest she made as they drove into the village. It was buzzing with life—more life than Holly would have expected. Maybe that was because it was Christmas Eve: Everyone was out doing their last-minute shopping here too, just like in London. There were Christmas lights hanging up on what Holly presumed was the high street and a giant Christmas tree stood on the green, opposite a clock tower. A mini version of Big Ben, Holly thought, snorting quietly to herself.

When she saw a café, just past the clock, she flicked the indicator and swung over to park on the road outside it, earning a beep from the car behind her.

Lily frowned. "You can't stop here—there's no parking."

"I'm not going to last the remaining forty-five minutes without caffeine," Holly said, by way of contradiction.

"You wanted to drive all the way," Lily pointed out.

"I'm not saying I don't want to drive; I'm saying I need a coffee. Besides," she added, "you can't drive, in your condition." She patted Lily's tiny baby bump, which was only just beginning to show.

"I'm pregnant, not an invalid," Lily muttered.

"Can't you be both?" Holly asked sweetly, and Lily hit her lightly on the arm.

"Be nice. I'm funding this."

"Only until I pay you back." Not that she was totally sure how she was going to do that. She'd forgotten her bank card, leaving the house in a last-minute rush, because she *never learned,* according to Lily. But really, that was beside the point. She couldn't afford this family trip. After two years of trying and failing to make money as an artist—something she'd wrongly thought would be straightforward, since she'd graduated from one of the best universities for art in the country—she'd caved and got her PGCE, qualifying as a teacher and earning a nod of approval from her parents and sensible sister. However, until she actually got a teaching job, she was back to living with her parents, and living off their goodwill.

"You can't park here," Lily was saying again, barely holding back a long-suffering sigh. "Your front tire is on a double yellow."

"Oh no one will notice that, come on."

"Holly," Lily said firmly, using her responsible "big sister" voice. But Holly switched off the engine.

"Come on, we'll only be two minutes. Plus, look at how Christmassy this place is!"

And it was—there was a blackboard outside with the Christmas specials, including a delicious-sounding camembert and cranberry sandwich, with a hand-drawn chalk snowman to the side of the menu. Mistletoe hung above the entrance, and the windows were decorated with silver tinsel. Fairy lights were draped around the low thatched roof, giving the place a delightfully rustic appearance: somewhere you'd want to curl up with a hot chocolate and a good book. Christmas had always been one of Holly's favorite times of year—perhaps because she'd felt the need to live up to her Christmassy name—but the Christmassy vibes weren't the reason Holly was feeling increasingly drawn to the coffee shop. Quite aside from wanting to get her coffee and be done with it, she was now intrigued by the name of the place: Impression Sunrise Café. It had to be a nod to Monet's famous painting, and any coffee shop named after a piece of art had to be good.

Relenting, Lily got out of the car and followed Holly onto the pavement, sticking her hands in her coat pockets as she walked and making Holly wish she'd grabbed her coat from the trunk. Side by side, they looked so similar they could almost be twins, even with the six-year age gap between them. It was the red hair that did it—twin little redheads. Holly's hair was wilder than Lily's, though that was probably because Lily tamed hers religiously with all kinds of fancy products, whereas the most Holly ever did was stick it in a bun when it annoyed her. *I'm owning my wild mane of red,* she'd said when Lily tried to get her to brush and straighten it before leaving today. *I'm like Ariel in* The Little Mermaid.

Not all redheads can be Ariel, Lily had said with a sigh—no doubt because both of them had been subjected to more than enough Ariel comments while growing up. *And anyway, Ariel brushes her hair. She's literally always brushing it with a fork or whatever.*

Well, like you said, not all redheads can be Ariel.

But it wasn't only the hair. They had the same cheekbones, same pointy jaw, same arched eyebrows (even without plucking them obsessively like Lily did). Only their eyes were different—Lily's were brown, whereas Holly's were a bold green.

Holly pushed through the café door without really concentrating on what she was doing because she was distracted by an absolutely gorgeous painting hanging inside the doorway, the kind of art that demanded your instant attention. It was a rainforest, depicted in a way she'd never seen before—bold and abstract, with vibrant colors that shouted life. She wanted it. That was her first thought. She wanted to hang it opposite her bed so she could wake up to it every morning and take in some of its vibrant energy. Her second thought was that she'd been right about the café—not just an arty name but real art inside and that was—

Her second thought was cut off as she slammed straight into an alarmingly solid chest. She noticed the crisp smell of a freshly washed and ironed shirt, along with a darker, woody scent, before heat seared down her arm. She yelped and yanked her arm back.

She swore, loudly, at the same time as a deep voice said, "Jesus Christ!" Something heavy thumped to the ground, along with two takeaway coffees.

Holly shoved back from the stranger, which caused her to slip on the liquid that was now coating the wooden floor, flailing her arms in the air but then catching herself, just managing to stay upright. She swept her hair back in one angry motion before looking up into the man's face. And Jesus, that *face*. She wanted to sculpt that face. Bring it to life with clay, capture the impressive contours of it, the sharp jawline, the dark eyes, the nose that was slightly off-center in a way that made it all the more perfect.

But hot embarrassment was curling in her veins. "What the hell!" she shouted, causing a few people to look over at her, including the woman behind the counter, who was peering over the metal jug of milk she was frothing. "You could have burned me!" It was only her sweater—a Christmas one, black with sequined writing on the front saying let Christmas BeGin—that had protected her skin from the scalding coffee.

"Are you kidding?" the man exclaimed. "You're the one that walked into me! Try looking where you're going, why don't you?" That impressive face tightened as he sucked in a breath, looking down at the mess on the floor, where two coffees—one milky, one black—were definitely beyond rescue. His briefcase was also there, one of the clasps sprung open. A briefcase, really? Who carried a briefcase around on Christmas Eve? He was wearing a suit, too—a suit that fitted him perfectly, she couldn't help but notice.

Holly scowled and opened her mouth to snap back, an automatic response, but felt a light hand on her arm. She glanced at Lily, who was giving her a *look*. A look she'd seen many times before.

Holly forced herself to take a calming breath. Lily was right. "I'm sorry," she said gruffly. "I wasn't looking where I was going." Her words were stiff and awkward.

"Clearly," he muttered.

Though her temper flared and the words *Well, I said I was sorry!* were trying to fight their way out, she could still feel Lily watching her. So she made herself look up to meet the man's gaze instead. Which was a mistake, because his brown eyes—like black coffee, she thought, though maybe that comparison was because of where they were—were impossible to look away from. They had a slightly unreadable quality, unlike hers, which she'd been told time and time again always gave all her emotions away.

Right now, his jaw was held tightly, as if he, too, was biting back words he wanted to snap at her. And as he reached up to run a hand through his hair—dark brown curls that set off the rest of his features—she noticed that his white shirt was stained with coffee. Oops.

She wrinkled her nose. "I really am sorry. I got distracted." She waved a hand to the painting she'd been looking at and his expression softened.

"I like that one too. It makes me think of . . . life." He made a face, like he thought that sounded stupid, and opened his mouth as if to say something else, but Holly cut him off.

"That's exactly right. It's so vibrant." She gave a helpless little shrug, feeling Lily's stare burning into her back. "I couldn't look away and . . ." She gestured to encompass both him and the coffee now spilled on the floor.

"They're for sale, you know. The paintings." He waved a hand around the café—which was buzzing, she realized belatedly—and noticed more paintings hanging on the walls.

She doubted she could ever afford any of them. But still, a coffee shop that doubled as a gallery—that was pretty cool.

Next to Holly, Lily cleared her throat. "I'll get us some drinks, shall I?"

"No," Holly said, "you sit. I'll get them."

Lily scrunched up her face. "I told you, I'm not a—"

"*Sit,*" Holly repeated firmly, and Lily sighed, going to perch on the nearest empty table—of which there weren't many. There were tiny little Christmas trees on each of the tables, Holly saw now, each with a wooden star on top. Cute.

"She's not a what, exactly?" asked the man.

"An invalid."

"Oh. Well, that's good to know, I suppose."

"Look," Holly said, over the sound of "Last Christmas." "Let me buy you another coffee." She glanced down at the mess on the floor. "Or another two, I should say. As for your shirt . . ." She wrinkled her nose again as she looked at it. "This is the one and only time I wish I was one of those girls who had cleaning supplies tucked into her handbag or knowledge of some kind of secret stain remover, but I have neither of those things, so in all honesty I think all hope might be lost for the shirt." She grimaced. "Sorry."

He laughed, and the sound was open, those deep brown eyes warming so that their depths weren't quite so unreadable. "That's OK, I have another one hanging up in the car."

"You carry a spare shirt in the car?"

"Well, I was right to, wasn't I?"

She couldn't imagine ever packing a spare of something, just in case—it required a level of organization she wasn't capable of. She wasn't convinced she even had enough clean underwear for the Christmas mini-break—she had thrown pants in at random while shouting downstairs to Lily that she was coming.

She wondered what was so important that he had thought to

come prepared with a spare shirt—a wedding, maybe? *His* wedding? No, surely not—if it was his wedding, he wouldn't be standing here with her; he'd be all flustered and running off to get to the church on time. He did have two coffees, though. Off to meet someone? It shouldn't bother her. She didn't even know his *name,* for God's sake: What right did she have to care if he was off on a date?

He picked up his briefcase and they headed to the counter together, where the woman serving was surprisingly calm and friendly, given how busy it was. Was this what life was like in the countryside? No London barista had ever beamed at Holly like that before.

"What can I get you?" She tucked a strand of her honey-blonde bob behind her ears, showing off sparkly earrings.

"Ahh . . ." Holly glanced at the man.

"A black Americano and an oat milk latte, please."

The woman looked at Holly expectantly. "And, umm . . ." She caught sight of the specials. "A cinnamon spiced latte and a mint tea." Not that she saw the point in paying for mint tea, but Lily was drinking it by the bucketload these days, refusing to even drink decaf coffee in case it was bad for the baby.

Holly glanced at the man. At five foot ten she considered herself pretty tall, but she felt small next to him. It wasn't just his height—it was the way he was standing there all broad-chested in his black suit jacket, confidence somehow radiating from him. "Um, can I get you a cake or something too? To make up for almost knocking you over?"

"You don't have to."

"I want to."

"All right, then . . ." He ran his gaze across the display of cakes behind the glass. "The chocolate-and-ginger star looks pretty good." It *did* look pretty good—and perfect for Christmas. It's exactly what she would have gone for—and it was the only one left. He let out a little chuckle. "You want that one, don't you?"

She realized she must have been looking at it a little longingly, was probably one step away from drooling. *Nice one, Holly.*

"No, no," she said quickly. "It's all yours." She ordered it, along with a lemon torte for Lily, who was going through a lemon craving phase.

"That'll be £16.80 please," said the woman, smiling again.

It was only then, after a quick pat of her jeans, that she remembered. She slapped her forehead. "Oh God, I don't have my card. I forgot it when I was leaving the house and I . . . Look, wait here," she told him. "I'll go and ask my sister. Hang on."

She turned, feeling her face burn—*not* a good look for a redhead—at the mortification of having to go and ask her big sister for money, but he caught her arm, his fingers resting there. Only lightly, but enough that she felt the pressure of them through her sweater, felt a little thrum of heat at each point of contact.

Stop it, Holly.

"It's fine. I'll get them," he said, his eyes meeting hers.

"But I—"

He handed over his card to the woman before Holly could argue, and she felt her face burn even more.

"I'm sorry," she said, almost a groan. "I left my card at home; I've had to borrow money from my sister for fuel, and I—"

"It's fine. Honestly."

The barista handed over their coffees and cakes, saving Holly from trying to explain further. They shuffled to the end of the counter to separate out the drinks and get out of the way of the queue behind them. After peeping into one of the brown paper bags, the man brought out the chocolate-and-ginger star and held it up. "Looks pretty good, doesn't it? And it smells *delicious.*"

She tried not to bristle at the teasing—he had just paid for her drinks, after all.

Then, his lips curving into a small smile, he split the star down the middle, and handed half to her.

She looked at it. "I can't—"

"Sure you can. You're saving me from an overload of sugar and caffeine." He held up his two coffees.

"They're both for you?" Was that relief she was feeling? *Get a grip, Holly!*

"Afraid so. I need the hit today, so I'll down the Americano, then enjoy the latte."

"Wow. That's a lot of coffee."

"Exactly. So I don't need any more stimulants—it would send me over the edge."

Holly silently snorted at the idea of this very solid man going over the edge, but she took the offered cake. "Thank you."

There were more people moving to their side of the counter now, so Holly backed out of the way—and in doing so, stumbled straight into the man's briefcase, knocking it over. The other clasp sprung open, and a few papers fell out.

Holly groaned inwardly. There was clumsy, and then there was *her*. "I'm so sorry," she said, bending down to help tidy the papers up.

He laughed, the sound warm, a little infectious. "I'm beginning to see a pattern here."

Holly handed over a pen that had rolled away, then picked up a card off the floor. She stared at it for a moment. It was beautiful. A painting of the sea, but like she'd never seen before—a swirling mass of blue and gray and green that gave life to it, somehow making each wave look distinct while capturing the vastness of the ocean. The boldness of the colors, the shapes, reminded her of the rainforest painting hanging inside the café door.

"This is so cool," she said to him. "Is it hand-painted? An original? Did *you* paint it?" He laughed again, and she shook her head. "Too many questions, sorry."

"Yes, yes, and no," he said, ticking off her questions on his fingers. After a beat, he added, "It was given to me, a while ago . . . It was painted by a local artist. There are a few of her things hanging up here, actually." He gestured around the café.

"What's their name? The artist?"

"Mirabelle Landor."

"Mirabelle Landor," Holly repeated, trying to commit it to memory,

The man cocked his head. "An art lover, are you?"

Holly gave a noncommittal shrug. She didn't feel bold enough to call herself an artist. Because if she'd never made any money doing it, could she really own that title? Lily told her that she could still follow her dream, could still work toward becoming a *real artist,* whatever that meant. But for Holly, she sort of felt like she was already giving it up and changing her course in life by going down the teaching route. *No,* she told herself firmly. She mustn't think like that—who knew what the new year might bring?

Holly looked at the card again, tracing one of the waves. She glanced up to see the man watching her, a smile playing around his lips. But there was something more, something deeper, in those dark eyes of his. "Sorry," she said quickly, thrusting it back to him.

"Don't be." He hesitated, then reached into his briefcase and slipped out another card. One of a forest this time—more golden and brown than green—but still the same style. "Here." He pressed it into her hands. "It's by the same artist. I can't give you this one"—he held up the waves—"because . . . Well, just because—"

"You don't have to justify that!" Holly exclaimed, feeling mortified. Did he think she'd been trying to take it? And for god's sake, *why* could she not stop blushing? "And I wouldn't take it. I didn't mean . . . I wasn't *asking*—"

"I know you weren't," he said, his voice, unlike hers, perfectly level. Level—and gorgeous. Could the sound of someone's voice be gorgeous? She decided right then that it could be—all deep and low and smooth, like liquid chocolate. But dark chocolate—rich and alluring. "But I bought this one on a whim," he continued, "at a shop on the way into town—and maybe this is why I did. So I could give to you." It was a stupid, romantic notion, what some might call fate, which Holly did *not* believe in. But even so, she couldn't stop her heart from fluttering ever so slightly.

It felt churlish to keep protesting, so she took it. "Thank you," she murmured. "I don't . . . I'm not being weird. It's just, that's what I want to do—I want to be an artist, and it's cool when you see people who aren't super-famous or whatever making it work, and I . . ." She broke off, sure that she was only sounding more crazy, not less.

"Then all the more reason for you to have it," he said simply. He slipped the other card back into his briefcase. It was worn, she noticed now, the edges well-thumbed, and there was writing inside. She wanted to ask who it was from, but she didn't—she had *some* sense of what was appropriate, after all.

"I'm Holly," she said instead.

He smiled. "And I'm Jack."

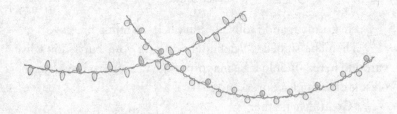

Chapter Two

The way Jack was looking at her right now made Holly glad she'd applied a wash of color to her lips, put in the dangly star earrings. She tucked a strand of hair behind her ears. "Ah, so, where are you off to today in your suit and with your briefcase then, Jack?"

His face tightened a fraction. "Oh. It's a . . . family thing."

Before she could ask anything else an alarm went off on his phone, making them both jump. "Sorry," he said as he switched it off. "I've got to go—my parking ticket is about to expire."

"You set an alarm for that?"

He smiled a little sheepishly. "Just to be safe."

Holly laughed, somewhat delighted.

"Sorry," Jack said again. "I might risk a parking ticket to keep talking to you, but I can't miss this . . ."

"Family thing?"

"Right." But he hovered for a moment longer. "So, I think it's your turn to buy the coffee next time."

Holly cocked her head at him. "Or, actually, four coffees, plus half a biscuit."

He grinned, and Holly couldn't help grinning back.

Then she sighed. "I definitely do owe you, but I don't live around here." Would it be inappropriate to move to Devon as the result of a single conversation?

"Great. Me neither."

"I'm in London at the moment," Holly said, her eyebrows raised.

"Well, that works, because so am I." OK, she knew what it looked like but this was *not* fate. *Fate* wasn't real.

Jack took a pen from his briefcase and reached for her takeaway coffee cup, which she handed over to him. He wrote his number on it, passed it back to her. "There. Now you've got to call me—this is what all those rom-com movies start with, right? Next thing you know we'll be caught in the middle of a montage."

Holly just stopped herself from snorting—snorting was not attractive. "I love a good montage."

"Me too," Jack said, and though he added a wink to make it jokey, Holly couldn't help it—she blushed again.

Jack turned to leave and Holly made her way back to the table where Lily was sitting.

"Well, that took longer than expected," Lily said, looking up and giving Holly a knowing look.

"He was just being polite," Holly said primly. Though she couldn't help the glance over her shoulder to where Jack was now leaving the coffee shop. He had a nice back, she decided. A back she really wouldn't mind seeing without that jacket on. *Stop that, Holly!*

"This might just be me," Lily said mildly, "but I don't make a habit of handing out my number when I'm just being polite to someone."

Holly glanced at the number scrawled on her coffee cup. "It will probably come to nothing. I mean, I can't *actually* call him, can I? I'm about to start a new job and I'll have to move and—"

"And?"

"And it's complicated," Holly finished with a shrug.

"Look," Lily said, taking a sip of her mint tea, "I never thought I'd meet Steve the way I did, but when I bumped into him outside that club—"

"Your eyes met across the smoking area and you knew he was the one. I know, Lils, I was there."

"I'm only saying . . . sometimes fate steps in and you have to—"

"Yes, yes." Holly didn't like it when Lily started playing the "fate" card—it was a way for people to justify the bad things in life, in her opinion. "Come on, let's go—aren't you worried about the parking?"

Lily rolled her eyes but got to her feet. Holly knew it was ridiculous—Lily was only a few months pregnant after all—but she couldn't help watching her extra carefully as she did so.

She glanced at Lily's stomach. "How's my little Talula doing? Soaking up all this Christmas atmosphere?"

Lily gave her a look. "She's not going to be Talula. I've told you that."

"Well, I'm calling her that," Holly said, as they walked out the café.

"Even if she's a boy?"

"Yes, even then."

"I'm sure you'll get *tons* of auntie points for that."

"Pfft!" Holly waved a hand in the air. "As if I have to worry about that—I'll obviously be the favorite auntie."

"You're the *only* auntie."

"Yes, exactly—that's why it's obvious." She made it into a joke for Lily, but Holly couldn't disguise it—she was very excited about becoming an auntie. She was so far off even *thinking* about kids of her own, but she loved the idea of having a little niece or nephew to play with—and to buy copious amounts of art supplies and coloring books for, of course. She'd actually already started working on a little sculpture to give him or her on the day they were born. It would be a little giraffe, she'd decided, because Lily loved giraffes, and small enough that the baby could clutch it in their little hands—and she'd paint it with bright, bold colors, like Elma the elephant, whom both Holly and Lily had loved growing up.

Holly switched on the ignition and cranked up the heating the moment they got into the car—it was definitely colder down here than in London. It wasn't yet four P.M., but it was already getting dark, and small misty droplets of rain were clinging to the windscreen. Holly wrinkled her nose—not exactly ideal driving conditions. Still, it was only forty-five minutes; she could manage that in the dark and rain.

Lily was strapping herself in and looking at the coffee cup Holly had put down in the cup holder. "Seriously, Holly, this guy could be the one—you should send him a message now."

Holly rolled her eyes. "Yes, because that wouldn't come across as overly keen."

"Those games are ridiculous—if you like someone, you like them."

"Says the happily married woman who doesn't have to worry about it anymore."

"At least save his number then."

"Lily!" Holly adjusted her rearview mirror. It was only seeing the headlights on the car behind them that made her remember to switch her own on.

"I'm just saying . . . You're always complaining that you never meet anyone. This is why—you don't take chances, even when they're offered up to you on a coffee cup."

"I take plenty of chances," Holly said, trying not to sound defensive. And she did—she usually said yes if someone asked her out, didn't she? Fine, she wasn't on all the apps, but Lily hadn't done that either—really, what chances had Lily taken? Met her husband aged twenty-one, stayed together five years, got married, two years later she was pregnant and on the way to a 2:4 lifestyle. And though she knew her sister was genuinely trying to be supportive, it did sometimes feel like Lily was telling her to hurry up—meet someone, follow the same pattern. But she kept quiet—it would only turn into an argument if she said more.

Holly pulled out when the road was clear, belatedly realizing that she had no idea where she was going. She fumbled for her phone, which she'd stored next to her coffee cup, and brought up Maps, entering in the last known postcode before propping it on her dashboard. As she drove, the raindrops grew heavier—though actually, now that she looked closer, it looked more like—

"It's *snowing*!" Lily exclaimed. "It's actually snowing—on Christmas Eve!"

Holly turned on the windscreen wipers. "I'd say that's more sleet than snow."

Lily flapped her hand. "Stop ruining it. Mum and Dad are going to *love* this."

"I doubt they'd like it if they had to drive in it," Holly muttered, but low enough that Lily could pretend not to hear her. She turned left at the end of the road and Lily frowned.

"You're going the wrong way."

"No I'm not. I'm following the blue line on Maps."

"Well, maybe you entered the postcode wrong, because I looked at the map just now in the café and you're going the wrong way."

"Lily! For God's sake, just let me drive, OK?"

"I'm not telling you how to drive, I'm telling you you're going the wrong way. Look, I'll show you." She reached over and snatched Holly's phone from the dashboard.

"Hey!"

"All I'm saying is that your sense of direction is hardly brilliant, Holly. Better I just—"

Holly snatched for the phone with one hand, glaring at her sister when she moved it out of reach. "Give it back!"

"I'm *checking*, Holly, that's all."

"Well, there's a junction coming up. Am I supposed to turn left or right?"

"Hang on for a minute, will you?" Lily lowered the phone, zooming in on something.

Holly made a sort of growl noise. "Why do you always have to interfere like this every time I'm in charge of something? Why can't you just let me sort it myself?" There was a car coming up from behind now, practically tailgating. *For God's sake!* She was going the speed limit, even when it was sleeting; couldn't they back off a bit?

"I think that's a touch dramatic."

"No it's not! You always think you know better, don't you?" On some level Holly did realize she was overreacting, but it was so *annoying*.

The junction was coming up fast now, and she pressed on the brake. With a car right behind her, though, and on a main road, she couldn't just stop completely.

"Give it *back*," she said again, snatching and this time grabbing the phone. Victory!

And in that moment, that tiny moment when she was concentrating on the phone, a car swerved around the junction ahead of them, far too quickly. So quickly that it missed the turning, had to over-compensate, and sped over into their lane. Holly dropped the phone and gripped the steering wheel with both hands.

"Shit!" she swore, at the same time as Lily yelled, "Brake!" her hands coming up protectively over her stomach.

So Holly braked.

But the car behind them did not brake. Not in time. And so instead of avoiding the oncoming car, their own car was thrown forward a few extra meters—straight into harm's way.

Holly felt it—the moment of impact. Felt her body lurch, heard a sickening crunch of metal. Felt her seatbelt cut into her, her breath being stolen from her. Saw Lily's face, her eyes wide, the hair she'd so carefully styled this morning flying out in front of her.

That was it. That was the last thing she registered, before something hard smacked into her head. Before the pain, shooting across her skull. Before her whole world went dark.

Three Years Later

DECEMBER

Chapter Three

Dear Stranger,

This will be my third Christmas alone. By the time you get this letter, it will be three years since I drove my sister headfirst into another car. Three years since we were taken to hospital, both unconscious. Three years since my sister disappeared from my life.

Every year, I think it will get easier—but it never does.

Christmas will always be the anniversary of that day, a reminder of the crash. Christmas Eve will always be the day I wonder, what if? What if I hadn't insisted on driving? What if I'd powered on through, hadn't stopped at that café? What if we'd enjoyed our drinks there, instead of taking them on the road?

I started taking part in this Dear Stranger club to feel less alone. Well, if I'm being totally honest I started it because my friend Abi made me do it after she heard about it on some radio program, but the reason I went along with it was because I hoped it might make me feel less lonely. And I suppose it does. Knowing that you, wherever you are, whoever you are, are out there, somewhere, knowing that you will read what I write, listen and understand what it feels like, is a comfort. So thank you for that.

But Christmas is supposed to be a time for family and friends, isn't it? And it still is in some ways for me too, I suppose. I still find myself looking at things in a shop window, and thinking they would be a good present for Mum or Dad. For my sister. Even if I'll never spend Christmas with Lily again, I still manage to find the perfect gift for her, every year.

I'm sorry: this letter is more morbid than my letters usually are. It isn't all bad, I promise. And soon enough, the festive period will be over and I can look forward to term starting and the distraction that brings. I hope that you, too, have some distraction to look forward to.

Anyway, I'm glad you're out there, Stranger, and I hope that, like me, it gives you comfort to know that even if you are alone, even if you are lonely, you are not the only one feeling like that. We will both get through this Christmas, I promise, and there will a bright, shiny new year waiting for us. At least that's what I'm telling myself. I'm telling you too, and I hope maybe you'll believe me.

I am sending love and good thoughts out into the world as I send this. I was never one for fate—that was always my sister's style—but good thoughts can't hurt, can they?

Love,
Holly

"What are you doing right now? Are you sitting around on the sofa doing nothing?" Holly held the phone away from her ear as Abi practically shouted at her down the line. She had a tendency to do that. Holly was convinced it was the drama teacher in her—she got so used to telling all her students to *project* that she'd forgotten what it was like to speak at normal volume. "You are, aren't you?" Abi pressed. "You promised me you wouldn't."

"I'm not sitting around doing nothing," Holly said obediently, though she was, in fact, currently sitting on her second-hand green sofa, staring into space because switching the TV on felt like too much effort.

"Lies," Abi said, calling her bluff. "But I'm seeing you tomorrow, right? For Christmas Eve drinks? I've sent James to London to see his brother, so it's just the two of us."

Holly sunk deeper into the sofa. Christmas Eve. She'd done nothing to decorate the flat this year—that had always been Abi's domain, before she'd moved out—so there was no sign of impending Christmas in her little flat. The flat itself wasn't terrible—it was small, yes, but had been done up nicely before Holly had moved in, and it still had a sleek, modern feel, even if the kitchen cupboards did have a tendency to fall off their hinges. But right now, it seemed danker than usual—the gray winter light giving the living room a dreary feel, making it obvious that the beige carpet had seen one too many spillages over the years. It made Holly wonder if she'd done the right thing, continuing on the lease after Abi had moved in with James, her gorgeous Irish fiancé—but where else was she supposed to have gone?

She'd met Abi just after the crash, when she'd moved to Windsor, running away from London and her life there, unable to face the grief and the guilt. She'd managed to get a job at a secondary school and she had been thankful every day since then

that Abi had been one of the other teachers there—because
though it had felt like her very world had been imploding on
her, Abi had been there to help her through it. And when Abi
had moved to the creative arts college to become assistant
head, Holly had managed to get a job there too. She'd even let
Holly move in with her, which had proven to be a godsend, because Holly hadn't factored in quite how expensive rent was in
Windsor and had been struggling in a random houseshare at
first.

Abi had moved out two months ago, finally caving to the pressure to move in with James, and leaving Holly feeling a little be-
reft. She'd meant to get a new flatmate, advertise on SpareRoom or
whatever, but hadn't got around to it. Plus, she had a vague notion
that she might ask Daniel to move in with her—because isn't that
what you were supposed to do in your late twenties when you'd
been with someone a while?

"Do you want to get dinner or just drinks?" Abi asked, bringing Holly out of her reverie.

"Umm, dinner? We should probably eat, right? Though will
we get a table anywhere this last-minute?"

"I'll sort it," Abi said simply. And she would—Abi always
mysteriously "sorted" things.

Holly's phone beeped at her and she checked the screen. "I've
got to go, Abs, Daniel's trying to call."

"Good. Do something with him so you stop sitting around.
Go and have some fun!"

Holly didn't bother trying to deny it this time. "I can't. He's
off to Prague, remember?"

"Oh yes, how could I forget." There was disapproval in Abi's
voice.

"He's allowed a life, Abs."

"Yes, he is. I just think maybe he ought to invite you along
with him every now and then."

"We have a healthy relationship," Holly said, aware that she was going on the defensive but unable to stop herself. "We respect each other's space." It was one of the things she liked about being with Daniel—he wasn't on top of her all the time, didn't make her feel claustrophobic.

Abi rang off and Holly took a moment to make sure her voice was bright before answering Daniel's call. "Hey!"

"Hey, listen, can we talk?" He sounded stressed. He did have a tendency to talk that way—had, in fact, been nicknamed Stresshead by some of the students at school, and could be heard losing his cool during his music lessons at least once a week—but generally that was limited to teaching, so this was a little odd.

"Sure," Holly said. "What do you need to talk about?"

A cyclist in the wrong lane? He really didn't like that. Or maybe he couldn't find something he needed to pack for Prague?

"Are you at home?" Daniel asked, his words tumbling into one another.

"Err, yes . . ."

"OK . . . Look, I'm five minutes away. Can I come by?"

"Aren't you supposed to be packing?" It was the reason he'd given for not wanting to see her earlier, when she'd suggested they meet up before he left for Prague. His flight was going out first thing tomorrow—Christmas Eve was cheaper, apparently.

"I know, I just . . . Look, Holly, I really need to talk to you."

"OK, well, come on over!" She didn't like his tone, but she kept hers optimistically bright. There was no reason to freak out, none at all.

A few minutes later, Daniel let himself in the front door. She'd given him a key and the code to the block of flats about six months ago—another of those steps she'd thought she ought to take. She stood up as he shut the door behind him, noticing the letters stuffed through the letterbox, ones she hadn't got round to sorting yet. Some of them must be Abi's—she still hadn't changed her address, though not through lack of organization, but rather, Holly knew, a worry that things wouldn't work—that however much she loved James, living together would uncover some incompatibility that they'd never noticed before.

Holly conjured up a smile for Daniel, who was wearing that oversized expensive black coat he'd bought two years ago. It didn't fit him very well and the black made him look washed out, especially in winter, but she'd never said anything.

"Do you want a cup of tea?" Holly asked. "I've got those lemon and ginger teabags that you like." She headed for the kitchen—kitchenette, really—which joined onto the living room. But he didn't follow her.

She turned back around. He was patting his blond hair, the way he did when he was nervous, making it even flatter and highlighting the fact it was thinning out on top—something he was self-conscious about, she knew, but which she'd told him, repeatedly, didn't bother her.

"Daniel? What's up?"

He took a breath, his chest expanding with the motion. "Holly." His voice was a little strangled. "This isn't working."

Holly frowned. "What isn't working? The tea?"

He shifted from foot to foot. He hadn't taken off his shoes, Holly noticed—still in those chunky walking boots that were his go-to in winter. "Us."

She looked at him blankly, genuinely baffled. "What do you mean, us?"

He closed his eyes briefly—a pale blue. "Sorry." He patted down his hair again. "God, sorry, I didn't mean to blurt it out like that."

"Blurt what out?"

"I don't think . . . That is to say, you and I . . ."

She stared at him—at the thinning hair, the eyes that wouldn't quite meet her gaze, the crooked nose from breaking it as a child after falling out of a tree—and felt a dawning realization. "Wait, wait, wait . . . Are you . . . Is this a breakup?"

His grimace was enough to confirm it.

"What the hell, Daniel!" She took a breath, tried to take the snap out of her voice—that was unlikely to help anything. "Where has this come from?"

"It's . . ." He swallowed. "It's been coming awhile."

"For a *while*?" And there she'd been, postponing looking for a flatmate under the assumption that sooner or later they'd be living together. "Well, thanks a lot for clueing me in on that." She pulled both hands through her hair, only realizing then that she hadn't brushed it today. "Why?"

"I . . ." He dropped his gaze to the beige carpet. "I don't think your heart's in it."

"Are you serious?" She felt her temper rising again. "You're showing up here, the day before Christmas Eve to break up with me and you're blaming *me*?"

"I didn't want to wait to talk to you about it," Daniel said, his words rushed. "I mean, I was going to wait until the new year, but I was talking to my mate and he pointed out we'd do all the presents, the whole shebang, over Christmas and it didn't feel right to go through that, when I knew . . ."

She could only stare at him. How had she not seen this coming? How had she not even had an *inkling*?

"And at least this way," he continued, "we have a few weeks before we'll see each other again at work."

"Oh yes," Holly said bitterly. "Very considerate of you." She turned from him, heading for the kitchen to get herself a glass of water. She didn't know what to do. What were you *supposed* to do in this situation? She'd never actually had someone break up with her before—all her relationships before Daniel had been short-lived, and they'd just sort of . . . fizzled out.

"I'm sorry!" Daniel called behind her, following now. "I

don't know what to say—it feels like there wasn't a right thing to do, a right time to say it."

Holly got a glass down from the kitchen cupboard, swearing to herself when one of the hinges dislodged, and filled it with water, playing for time while she tried to sort out her thoughts. Then she faced him, over the countertop that separated kitchen from living room. "I just don't get it, Daniel. What's changed?"

Daniel took a step toward her. "Look, when we got together, you were . . . Well, you were going through some stuff."

Holly winced. By the time she'd met Daniel, the crash had been a year in the past, but she still hadn't got over it. And when Daniel had asked her out, Abi had encouraged her. *You need to start looking forward, babe. You can't live in the past—it will kill you.*

"And I got that, I did, but I thought maybe . . ."

"You thought *what*?" Holly asked, her tone biting.

He shook his head, and the action looked weary. Seriously? Now he had the audacity to look *weary*? "I don't know."

"You thought I'd get more fun as time went on. Is that it?"

"No! You're plenty of fun." But the assurance sounded placatory, like he didn't really mean it. *Was* she no fun? Was that the problem? "It's just . . . You don't seem really . . . in it. It was like you were doing things because you thought you should, not because you actually wanted to. I thought maybe after some time you'd talk to me more."

She scowled. "I talk to you all the bloody time."

He sighed. Like *she* was the one being unreasonable here. "I want someone to build a life with, Holly."

"So do I!" The words were automatic—the right thing to say. But they were also true. Weren't they?

"Do you?"

"Yes." She stuck her chin in the air, and the action reminded her briefly of arguments with Lily. *Do you really want to wear that, Holly? Yes. Do you really want to drive the whole way? Yes.*

"Maybe you do," Daniel conceded. "But not with me. You haven't even introduced me to your parents, for Christ's sake."

Holly flinched but refused to let him make her feel bad. "You're telling me what I want now, are you? Telling me how I feel? How fucking dare you! And my parents, my family . . . That's—"

"Holly, calm down, I'm not—"

But Holly shook her head, talking over him. "Do you know what? I don't want to deal with this right now. Get out."

He didn't move. "See, this is my point—you never want to actually have a conversation, open up about how you're feeling."

"Oh, you want me to open up, do you? Tell you how heartbroken I am so you can pat me on the back and console me, the whole time having a little ego boost, is that right?"

"That's not what I meant." He pulled a hand through his hair again. "Shit, I'm not doing this right."

"No, you're bloody well not."

"I'll go."

"Yes, please do."

"I'll call you later, once you've . . ."

"Once I've *what*?"

"We need to talk this through properly," he said calmly.

Holly sighed. "Just leave, Daniel." Her anger was fading now, something more tiring coming to take its place. She'd rather be alone when that feeling settled in properly.

He hesitated, but then turned to leave. He paused in the open doorway, looked back at her. "I'm sorry, Holly. I'm not doing this to hurt you."

Holly gave a humorless laugh. "Well, it feels a lot like that to me."

"I'll call you," he repeated, then closed the door behind him. The action dislodged the letters that had been stuffed into the letterbox. Holly walked toward them, feeling a little numb. She bent down to pick them up, her movements stiff.

And there, right on the top of the pile, was this year's *Dear Stranger* letter.

Chapter Four

Dear Stranger,

I don't really know how to start this letter—it's the first time I've done it and it feels a bit ridiculous. But I'll give it a go. I suppose there's something about knowing I'll never meet you that makes it easier, to be honest. Pam was right about that—I'll give her that.

You see, I'm alone. Have been for years. My son, Richard, died in a car crash eighteen years ago. Almost eighteen years to the day, as I write this. There's something about the Christmas period that puts everyone in a rush, isn't there? The rush to get home or get out to see friends. The rush to start having fun or relax, in whatever form that may be. Did you know that you are up to four times as likely to be involved in a car accident around Christmas than at any other time of year?

When Richard died, that was it. My husband, Charles, couldn't cope with it, and it tore us apart. We stayed to-

gether, and I still loved him and I like to think he still loved me, despite it all. But he was a shell of himself, and when he died, seven years ago, I felt almost relieved. It's awful to say that, isn't it? I wouldn't say it to anyone I know, but writing this letter doesn't feel like talking to a real person. I suppose that's what Pam was on about when she suggested it. Don't get me wrong, I didn't want Charles to die. It cut me up, and of course I would rather he was still here. But I can't deny the relief I felt, at not having to pretend anymore.

Charles blamed me, I think. He never said anything, but I know he blamed me. Not so much for Richard's death, but for the fact that when we lost Richard, we lost our grandson too. His mother took him away from us, told us they never wanted to see us again. I loved that boy, so much. He had his mother's steadiness and his father's passion—I wonder if he still has both, or if one or the other has been eroded away over time.

I suppose there is no point in lamenting what we have lost—at some point, you just have to accept it. But as I write this, sitting in my local cafe—it's called Impression Sunrise and it's got lovely coffee, you should stop in if you ever chance upon it—and staring at a painting of a rainforest, wishing I was there, I can't help but wonder what life would have been like if Richard hadn't got in the car that day. Would I have someone to lean on now?

Because I quite wish I had someone this year. I've just been diagnosed with cancer. Pancreatic cancer, to be exact. And I suppose there's something about confronting your mortality that makes you take stock of your life. Of your regrets, the mistakes you made. And right now, I'm not only facing the possibility of death—I'm facing it alone.

Do you know what? I'm not sure writing this has made me feel much better. I'm not sure it will make you feel better, either—so clearly I'm doing it all wrong. But maybe it will? Because aren't you alone too? Isn't that the whole point of this—that we know we're not the only ones? Perhaps there's a kind of comfort in that. I wish I had inspiring words of wisdom to give you, but that's somewhat difficult, given I don't know anything about you, and good advice should be tailored to the individual, don't you think? I'm not sure you'd want to take advice from me, in any case—I'm hardly an example of how to live your life.

So I'll leave you with a "Merry Christmas" and be done with it. Merry Christmas—and good luck, whoever you are. I hope that you find joy in the next year, somewhere—even if that is just in looking at a painting of a rainforest and imagining the taste of the air there.

With regards,
Emma Tooley

Holly pulled the duvet up around her shoulders and read the letter for the third time. She'd been holed up in bed since Daniel left, the obligatory chocolate on her bedside table, next to the lamp, which had a tendency to flicker every now and then. It was easier to keep reading the letter, to absorb this stranger's—Emma's—grief and loneliness, rather than contemplate her own. Because she didn't want to face the fact that Daniel had left her, that she had proven herself to be unlovable yet again. She didn't want to face the fact that she was truly alone at Christmas, especially while her family were together, without her.

She also didn't want to face the fact that she should be feeling worse. Shouldn't it feel like a part of her soul had been torn away? Wasn't that what you were supposed to feel when someone broke up with you out of the blue like that—if you really loved them?

I want someone to build a life with, Holly.

So do I!

Maybe, but not with me.

Was he right? The answer sat too uncomfortably in her chest, so she pushed it away, concentrated on the letter. Maybe it was because of what had just happened with Daniel, or maybe it was because this letter was different, more frank in its grief and loneliness, but it spoke to her more than any of the others ever had.

A car crash. This woman, Emma, had lost her son in a car crash. If anyone could relate to that, it was Holly.

Then the words about her local café. The Impression Sunrise Café. It gave her a jolt every time she read that bit. Because she knew that café. She'd *been* to that café. And she'd even googled it to be sure—there was only one coffee shop in the whole of England by that name, as far as she could tell. The one in Devon, where she and Lily had stopped on that fateful day.

She knew what Lily would say, if she was here with Holly now. *Maybe it was fate, you receiving this letter. Maybe you were* meant *to get it.*

But the only reason Holly was reading this letter was because Lily was no longer in her life, and so it couldn't be fate. It was too damn depressing if it was.

This was the third Dear Stranger letter she'd received, and she'd never met any of the senders. She never would have been able to—there were no return addresses on the letters, no contact details. But this time . . . If she was right, and it was the same café, then she knew the village where this woman lived. And she knew the woman's full name. Not everyone signed off with a surname, but this woman had. She could find her, with some well-placed googling, she was sure of it.

Her phone buzzed on the bedside table. Daniel. She scowled and turned it face down. And that was what decided it. She didn't want to sit here alone, lamenting her failed relationship. She didn't want to spend the next few days jealous of all those with family to share it with, remembering her past Christmases with her sister and her parents in a way that made her heart hurt. Didn't want to remember the years before the crash, when she would have been cooking with her dad in the kitchen, listening to her mum tell more and more elaborate stories after one too many mulled wines. And didn't want to remember the night that had changed it all.

No, instead she'd do something productive. Whether or not she was "meant" to get this letter, she had decided to act. To throw off the duvet in one fluid movement and grab her phone, ready to look it up, to test her theory.

Then she saw the time. Somehow it had got late without her realizing. OK, she'd sleep first. She'd sleep and wake up early, and *then* she'd track this Emma Tooley down—find her and make her realize that there was someone out there who cared. That she was not as alone as she believed.

"So, don't hate me, but I'm not going to make drinks this evening." Holly flicked her indicator on, turning left, out of Windsor, and toward the M4.

"What? Why?" Abi's voice came through the Bluetooth on her car. It had taken two years for Holly to work up the courage to drive again, and she'd made sure to invest in a built-in GPS as well as a Bluetooth connection so that she'd never again have to touch her phone while driving. "And please bear in mind while answering that I will only accept a limited number of excuses, such as the flat burning down, you've contracted something contagious, or you are currently ill with food poisoning."

"Daniel broke up with me last night."

"Oh shit, babe. I'm so sorry."

"It's fine," Holly said with a sigh. There was already so much traffic on the road, even though it was barely light, the gray morning dull enough that she'd needed to switch the headlights on. She supposed that made sense on Christmas Eve, everyone was on their way to families for the day itself. She remembered Emma's statistic about traffic accidents at Christmas in the letter and slowed down a fraction, checking her sideview mirrors.

"It's OK to say you're not fine, you know. So you don't feel like going out?" Abi continued. "Totally understandable. I could come round instead? Pick up Thai from that place you like or something?"

"Er, well, actually . . ." Holly explained her impromptu trip quickly, bracing herself for Abi's inevitable reaction.

"For God's sake, Holly!"

"You were the one who told me to join the club in the first place!" Holly protested.

"I told you to write the letters, because I thought it might be cathartic and help you to come to terms with it all, alleviate your guilt or whatever. I did *not* tell you to go off hunting for a stranger you've never met with some ridiculous mission in mind!"

"Look," Holly said, "I need to do this. I need to help this woman."

"Why?" Abi asked—her voice stubborn rather than curious. Proving a point rather than actually asking.

"Because . . ." How could she explain it? The fact that she felt she *should* do this—because maybe, even if she couldn't stop herself from being lonely at Christmas, she could stop someone else from feeling that way instead. And fine, OK, maybe she also wanted the distraction. But what was wrong with that?

"Holly, I know you think what happened to Lily that day was your fault, but—"

"It was my fault, Abi," Holly said flatly. "I was driving."

"It was the other car who was wrong," Abi said gently. "You have the court case to prove that." Holly shuddered a little, remembering. The driver of the oncoming car had been given a year's prison sentence. Only a year. And Holly wasn't even given a slap on the wrist. She was a victim of someone else's dangerous driving, they'd all said so—the barrister, the judge. Her dad had said so too, as the verdict was announced—her dad, not her mum, because her mum had been sitting separately, on the other side of the courtroom with Lily.

There was nothing you could have done, Holly. But if he'd really thought that, then why had her parents suggested that it was better, all things considered, if she didn't spend the Christmas after the accident with them? That it would be better if she gave Lily some space?

Holly took a breath. "Look, the point is, I can do something about this. This woman is alone, and dealing with a cancer diagnosis, and I can help."

"How, exactly, are you planning to help? Are you just going to show up and throw your arms around her as if you're a long-lost friend? You don't even *know* the woman, Holly—she could be anyone! She might not *want* you to find her."

Holly said nothing. Admittedly, she hadn't thought much further than just getting to Devon, but she was pretty sure the answers would come to her once she was there.

"I'm going to go now," she said instead. "I need to concentrate on driving. I am sorry for ditching you, though. I promise to make it up to you."

"It's fine," Abi said on a sigh. "James has been trying to get me to go to this drinks thing with his brother for the last two days; he'll be thrilled I can come along now."

Holly tried not to feel put out by the fact she was so easily replaced—she was the one ditching Abi, after all, not the other way around.

"But actually, do you know how you can make it up to me? By coming on this drama trip next term—if I don't get one more member of staff the whole thing is off and I've been banging on about Barney Norris's plays to my second years long enough that I'm going to have to put my money where my mouth is."

Holly hesitated. "Is Daniel coming?" He taught music, but they all helped across the board.

Abi's pause went on a beat too long. "Noooo."

Holly sighed. But then, what kind of friend would she be, if she refused to go just because he was there? What kind of teacher would she be? And yes, teaching hadn't always been her lifelong dream, but that didn't mean she didn't care about the kids. "You're a terrible liar, but it's fine, I'll come."

"You're the best." Abi said it confidently, like she'd always known Holly would say yes.

"Yes, yes, I know. I'll see you soon, yeah? Have fun with the Irish duo tonight."

"I will. And Holly?"

"Hmm?"

"Just be careful, OK? Just because you might be able to find her, that doesn't mean she wants to be found."

"She's lonely and worried about dying alone—of course she wants to be found," Holly said airily. "She'll want the company, I'm sure of it."

"Yes, but sometimes, it's not about having other people's company. Sometimes it's about coming to terms with your own company instead."

Holly rolled her eyes, even though Abi couldn't see her. "Get that out of a Hallmark card, did you?"

"Just be careful, that's all I'm saying. I don't want to see you get hurt, especially not on Christmas." But she was hurting anyway at Christmas, wasn't she? The time of year she used to love was now the time she dreaded.

So as she drove, she tried to block all thoughts of Christmas from her mind, switching the radio off so she wouldn't have to listen to Christmas music and ignoring the decorations on passing houses. She also tried to block Abi's words from her mind. *Sometimes it's about coming to terms with your own company instead.*

Because she felt sure that Abi hadn't been talking about Emma. That no matter how hard Holly tried to pretend that she'd moved on and built a life after the crash, Abi could tell that the fractures were still there, inside of her—and that, sometimes, she feared those parts of her were broken for good.

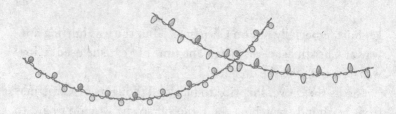

Chapter Five

Dear Lily,

I'm about to do something crazy. You would definitely tell me not to do it, if you knew. But then again, you were always the one banging on about fate, so maybe you'd tell me to go for it? I'm going to choose to think that's what you'd say. And I'm going to choose to be optimistic. This is a good thing; I know it is. I feel sure that meeting this woman—Emma—is going to change things for the better. I am doing something productive, and helpful, and not sitting around wallowing. You always did tell me not to wallow.

There are a TON of cyclists in Devon, even on Christmas Eve. It must be miserable, cycling in this weather. I don't think we noticed that last time we were here, did we? I can't remember the last time I went cycling. But do you remember when Mum and Dad bought you a new bike for your tenth birthday? It was bright purple with *silver stripes, and I thought it was the most beautiful bike I'd ever seen. I was jealous, but you knew that. We went to the park together, and Dad wasn't really watching when we cycled off. I couldn't keep up, do you remember? I was on my first little training bike and it didn't have gears or anything, like yours. Not that I would have known how to actually use the gears, I'm sure, but that wasn't the point.*

I remember giving up and throwing my bike down and crying because you were too far ahead. And you turned around and came back. You were so annoyed with me—because it was your birthday and I was making it about me—but you still came back. And how did I repay you? I pushed you off. I remember it exactly— getting off the ground and shoving you, hating the way you were frowning down at me. I didn't expect you to fall, though. I was so much smaller than you and I promise you, I didn't think you'd actually fall. But you did, and the bike fell on top of you, and you screamed, and then Dad came running.

I was so upset when I was sent to my room, afterward. I lay there for hours, crying—not because Mum and Dad had shouted at me, but because I thought I might really have hurt you. There was blood on your shin, and you were hugging Dad and wouldn't look at me, and I thought maybe you were really, really hurt. And maybe you wouldn't ever forgive me.

But you came into my room later to sneak me some birthday cake—I wasn't allowed any, after what I'd done. I told you that you could have all of my My Little Ponies, and you told me I could ride the bike when I was tall enough, and that was that.

For a while, after the crash, I thought maybe it would

be like that. That was stupid, I know. I wasn't minimizing what happened, or what I'd done. It was just hope, and it was something I clung to.

I've stopped hoping you'll forgive me, but I still can't help hoping that someday you'll speak to me again. Because as much as I tell you I'm sorry in these letters, it would be nice to tell you in person one day—I never really got the chance to do that.

But I am, you know. Sorry. I hope you know that.

Love,
Holly

Holly sat inside her car, staring at the Impression Sunrise Café.

After a four-hour journey, here she was. Her palms felt clammy on the steering wheel and she flexed her fingers, one by one. She hadn't thought of how to find Emma, exactly, but the café had seemed like a good place to start. It looked the same as it had three years ago. Fairy lights around the top of the building, silver tinsel along the windows, and a blackboard outside, the chalk still visible despite the increasingly heavy rain, this time with a reindeer drawn on it. An impressive reindeer—more like a sketch than a cartoon, with big, detailed antlers. It had been a snowman the day of the crash. Amazing how much detail came back to her whenever she allowed herself to think about it.

But then, this was the last place she and Lily had had a proper conversation. And if it hadn't been for her pitstop here, she never would have crashed.

My fault, my fault, my fault. The words echoed around her mind, even as she closed her eyes against them.

Get out of the car, Holly.

Her legs were stiff as she got out and locked her car behind her. She paused for a moment outside the café, staring at the wooden OPEN sign.

A man approached the door from inside, holding a takeaway coffee cup. He opened the door, holding it for her. Feeling like she'd look like an idiot if she backed away now, she stepped through, and they exchanged cursory smiles. She couldn't help but be reminded of the last time she'd stepped into the Impression Sunrise Café, the last man she'd bumped into—or barreled into, more accurately. Jack. She still remembered his name. Remembered those depthless brown eyes, the dark curly hair, the polished, tidy essence of him. The woody scent on first impact. Remembered the way he'd grinned at her later, when he'd broken the chocolate-and-ginger star in half. How he'd given her a Mirabelle Landor card, written his number on her coffee cup. She'd lost the coffee cup in the crash, along with any chance of contacting him again.

She still had the card, though. She'd tucked it into her pocket, and for whatever reason it had stayed lodged there after the moment of impact, in all its forest glory. It had been lying on her bedside table when she'd woken up in hospital—she'd never found out who took it out of her jacket and put it there. She'd found herself picking it up in comfort during those first twenty-four hours when she was waiting to be discharged, the doctors telling her how lucky she was to have no serious injuries. She'd taken the card home with her when she snuck out to pack up her things from her parents' house, leaving them in the hospital, talking to the doctors with grave faces. And then she'd taken it to Windsor, to her new job, her new life, and kept it with her, safely stored in her bedside table drawer.

Her legs felt stiff as she walked to the counter, getting in place behind a woman with perfectly blow-dried platinum-blonde hair, a long red coat and impressive red heels. Her mouth felt a little dry as she waited to speak to the woman behind the counter. She'd gone over what she might say on the way down, but attempting to plan it in any kind of depth had felt vaguely ridiculous, so she'd ultimately decided that winging it was probably the best option.

"Yes?" The woman behind the counter was smiling at her expectantly—Holly hadn't noticed that it was her turn to order.

"I, ah, I'll have a mint tea, thanks," she said, ordering the first drink that came to her, thinking of Lily. "And, umm, I also wondered if you knew where I could find Emma Tooley?" The woman gave her a curious look as she paused in the action of ringing up the till.

"Emma Tooley?" For some reason, the woman behind the counter looked at the woman with platinum-blonde hair, who had stopped on her way past Holly, coffee cup in hand.

"Are you the artist, then?" the platinum blonde woman asked, giving Holly a quick glance up and down. She was in her seventies, at a guess, and was holding a brown handbag that looked expensive. Her nails were painted bright red, to go with her coat and shoes, and Holly saw the glint of more than one ring on her hand. Could this be her? Emma? She was nothing like the woman Holly had pictured in her head.

"I, ah . . ."

"You were supposed to meet her here yesterday," prompted the woman behind the counter, also looking at Holly in a rather assessing manner. All this scrutinization was making her glad she'd at least made an effort today. Not only had she brought out her best handbag—a crocodile-print one she'd bought in a charity shop—but she was wearing her pale green coat, which had been an impulse purchase but which fitted her perfectly, and her long brown boots, which had been dubbed "wicked" by one of her second years. She'd tried her best to tame her hair and had put on a light touch of makeup, just to smooth out the shadows under her eyes and take away some of that winter paleness.

"I'm afraid you're out of luck now, love," continued the woman behind the counter. "She was waiting for you for an hour yesterday, then she left."

"Put her in quite a foul mood," the platinum-haired woman said. "I have you to thank for that, do I?"

Holly glanced between the two women. "I . . ."

The platinum-haired woman frowned. "You *are* the artist, aren't you?"

Holly thought of the Dear Stranger letter, sitting in her bag. Then, she went on impulse. "Yes," she said firmly. Because who-ever this artist was, she had an in with Emma. "Can you help me find her? Emma?"

"I'm sure Pam will take you," the woman behind the counter said. "Won't you, Pam?"

"Are you sure you want to just show up at her door?" Pam asked, giving Holly another once-over.

"Ah . . ." Holly swallowed. "Maybe you could ring her, get her to meet me here instead if you think that would be better?" Because now that she thought about it, it might be a bit overly bold to show up at her house unannounced.

"No use," Pam said briskly. "She never answers the phone these days. Says the only people who call her are those blasted telemarketers. And she wouldn't come down here to meet you anyway, not after you stood her up yesterday. No, you'll have to do some serious begging if you want to get an audience with her now."

And why would the artist want an audience with her? Holly wondered.

"And I'm afraid I can't walk up with you," Pam said, a small, genuinely apologetic smile crossing her face. "I've got to do the rest of my Christmas shopping before the shops close in an hour or my husband will not be impressed."

"That's OK—if you give me the address I can find my own

way there." Better that way anyway, Holly thought—fewer awkward questions she'd have to make up answers to. After a moment's hesitation, Pam told her the address, and she put it into
her Maps app.

"Thank you," she said, working up a smile for both women.
"Thank you both so much."

"Don't forget your mint tea," the woman behind the counter
said, handing it over to her. When Holly tried to pay, the woman
shook her head. "On the house. You'll need it, trust me."

It took her ten minutes to walk up the hill to Emma's house. The
cool air hissed between her teeth as she climbed, the wind biting
her face and bare hands. The sky was gray above, threatening
rain, and with each step her pulse seemed to race.

When she reached Emma's street, her heart did a funny kind
of spasm, into her gut. This was it. There was a line of cottages,
all beautiful old stone. The street felt quiet, even though it was
lunchtime on Christmas Eve. A few of the cottages had been
decorated: One had a big showing of Christmas lights, including
a flashing Santa, which didn't quite fit with the cozy English vibe
of the place.

It was too cold to stop and think about what she was doing,
so she shoved her phone into her handbag and headed for number twenty-seven. The outside of the cottage looked a little more
run-down than the others—white paint was flecking off the windowsills, and the garden looked as though it hadn't been tended
in years; the lawn was overgrown even in winter, with grass and
moss coming up to hide the stone-slabbed path which ran to the
front door, old leaves giving it a discolored and rather treacher-
ous look.

Holly picked her way carefully to the front door, which, like
the window, clearly hadn't seen a lick of paint for years, pale blue
giving way to white underneath. She took a breath and knocked.

It took such a long time for anyone to answer that Holly wondered if she was ever going to come. But then the door opened.

The woman standing there was thin, with long, wavy gray hair that lay flat on her head, wrinkles creasing around turquoise eyes which, though tired-looking, still managed to be striking. She was wearing a white cardigan with holes in the sleeves, and old slippers that looked like they had seen better days. The biggest thing Holly noticed, however, was her scowl. An impressive, all-encompassing scowl that pulled together the wrinkles around her lips and made her eyebrows almost disappear into the flesh surrounding them.

"Yes?" she snapped, her voice louder and sharper than Holly would have expected, given her appearance. "Can I help you?"

"I, umm . . ."

"Spit it out, girl, I have better things to do than stand here and watch you sputter." The woman—Emma—folded her arms, and Holly felt heat travel up her spine. This was not the welcome she'd been expecting.

"I'm Holly," she blurted out.

"Good for you," Emma said.

"I . . ." Holly fumbled in her bag, pulling out the Dear Stranger letter, which was folded in half and a little creased from the journey. "This is yours," she began again. "Your letter, I mean. I received it. I'm the one you wrote to, in the Dear Stranger club."

Emma's face paled. "What?" The word came out a little strangled. "It can't be." Her gaze flickered from the letter to Holly's face and back again. "They told me they didn't give out contact details!"

"They don't," Holly said quickly. "It's just . . . I recognized the name of the café, and I thought it sounded like you might . . ." But she trailed off, because Emma's expression had hardened—

not a scowl now, but something worse, something that made Holly stumble back a step, the letter still clutched in her hand.

"You were not supposed to find me," Emma said sharply, turquoise eyes cold. "No one was. You were not supposed to even really *exist*—you were a fiction in my mind, do you hear me? An invisible stranger." Holly winced. "That's the whole point! How could you possibly think it was OK to . . . ?" She closed her eyes, blew a breath out through her nose. "I want you to leave."

"What?" No. This wasn't what was supposed to happen. Emma was supposed to *welcome* her, maybe feel a little shocked initially, but ultimately be *glad* of her arrival. This was all wrong. "But I—"

"You wanted to come here and comfort an old, sick woman, did you? Get your Good Samaritan badge? Well, I don't want to be comforted, and I don't need some stranger sticking her nose in where it doesn't belong. So I'll have this"—she snatched the letter out of Holly's hand—"and you can be on your way."

With that, she slammed the door in Holly's face, barely a hair's breadth away, leaving her standing alone outside. And as if the world had decided to seal her fate, at that very moment, it started to rain.

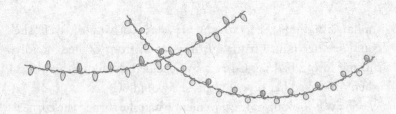

Chapter Six

Holly stared at Emma's front door for a solid two minutes, the rain beating down on her head. But it did not reopen. Stumbling on now slightly numb legs, she headed back down the path, walking quickly in case Emma was peering out the window, checking to see if she was gone.

She would not cry. She would *not* cry. But why the hell had she decided to *walk* here? She was going to be soaked to the bone before she got back to her car.

She wrapped her arms around herself, breathing quickly as she practically ran back down the hill toward where her car was parked, outside the café. And she'd probably have a ticket by now, wouldn't she? That would be just her luck.

She felt the cold rainwater dripping down her neck, underneath her coat. This was all wrong. She wasn't supposed to be spending any time outdoors. In her head she'd arrive, be welcomed in out of the cold and given a hot chocolate almost immediately, after which she and Emma would bond over their similar situations. She thought of what Abi would say if she could see her now, breath misting out in front of her, rapidly turning into a bedraggled rat, and decided then and there that when Abi asked her how it went, she would lie.

She was looking at the pavement when she turned the corner, staring straight at her feet and not looking where she was going, so that she collided straight into someone.

"Whoa, there."

Holly looked up and saw it was the woman from behind the counter in the café.

"Oh, it's you. How did it . . . ?"

Holly let out a sob. She hadn't realized it, but she had started crying—warm salty tears mixing with the rain, making her regret the makeup she'd put on this morning.

"Come on then, my love. Let's get you a cup of tea."

Holly stemmed a hiccup. "I really should . . ." But she trailed off. Because what else was she going to do? Get back in the car, soaking, and drive straight back to Windsor? So she followed the woman back toward the café and watched as she unlocked the doors, switched on the light.

"Oh, you're closed," she said, biting her lip. "It's fine, honestly, I can just—"

"Nonsense. I'm not letting you get back on your way until you've dried off a bit and had something warm. Not on Christmas Eve. Now, what did you say your name was?"

"Holly."

"Holly. Well, I'm Mona, and don't you worry about Emma. She's all bark, and I'll be having a word with her next time I see her, making someone cry like that."

"Oh, no, it's—"

"Sit down, love. I'll get your tea."

And with that Mona left Holly to perch on one of the window tables, feeling awkward in the silence of the café. She stripped off her sodden coat, cursing herself for not wearing a waterproof one. This had been a stupid idea.

Stupid, Holly.

She got her phone out to distract herself. There was a message from Daniel. *Let me know when you're ready to talk.* She scowled at it, then closed the conversation and brought up Facebook—though she almost immediately regretted that. There was a notification from a family friend.

A festive catch-up with the one and only Helen Griffin!

There was a photo to go with the caption—a photo of Holly's mum, brunette hair cut short, her smile a little tired, face perhaps a little too thin, with her dad's arm around her. It was him who she and Lily got their red hair from—though it was thinning on top, it was definitely still hard to miss. And Lily. Wearing a slightly formal-looking smile. The three of them, a happy family—without her.

Though Holly looked, there was no sign of a baby bump underneath Lily's black-and-gold dress. She kept hoping she'd see one—that somehow, if Lily got pregnant again, she would forgive Holly. Holly could still see Lily's face, her eyes red rimmed and swollen, as she'd looked up from her hospital bed the day after the crash. Could still hear the sound of Lily screaming at her to get out, voice hoarse. Broken.

Holly knew Lily hadn't been able to get pregnant in the first couple of years after the accident because her mum used to keep her updated. But she'd stopped asking some time ago—it only seemed to make things worse, causing a thick layer of tension down the phone line.

She could remember the day Lily told her she was pregnant. She'd come into Holly's room at their parents' house on the outskirts of London—the same one Holly had slept in as a teenager. Holly had been reading but put the book aside when Lily pushed the door shut behind her with a quiet click. Lily had come to perch on Holly's bed covers—the caterpillar duvet cover she'd picked out as a thirteen-year-old—had taken a deep breath, then blurted it out in a whisper.

"I'm pregnant."

Holly stared at her. "For real?" Her voice was only a murmur too. She'd known Lily had been trying to get pregnant—that it was taking longer than either she or Steve had expected, that there had been a few false hopes. And no matter how many times Lily had told her that she *wasn't worried*, the worry was evident all the time, in the set of Lily's eyebrows whenever the topic of children came up.

A sheepish smile had crept to Lily's face. "For real."

"Oh my God!" Holly moved into a kneeling position, launching herself at Lily for a hug, but Lily stood up and flapped her hands.

"Sssssh! I haven't told Mum or Dad yet." She glanced at Holly's bedroom door. "I can't face Mum's disappointment on top of my own if something happens, and I'm not supposed to tell anyone until twelve weeks, but, well, I wanted you to be the first to know."

Holly clambered off the single bed and threw her arms around her sister. "I'm so, so happy for you." She hid her face in Lily's perfectly smooth hair, partly to hide the tears that had sparked in her eyes—because she knew how much this meant to Lily. She'd wanted to be a mother for as long as Holly could remember.

Holly stepped back, and Lily gripped her hands. "You're going to be an auntie."

"I'm going to be the *best* auntie."

Lily sniffed and pulled a hand back to wipe away a tear. When Holly frowned and opened her mouth to ask what was wrong, Lily shook her head. "Happy tears, I promise." She blew out a breath. "It'll be the hormones, I'm sure."

Holly had grinned—at the fact that Lily had clearly been desperate to say this for some time. "Is that going to be your excuse for everything for the next eight months?"

Lily had given a little watery chuckle. "Count on it."

"Pam?" In the present day, Mona's voice carried over to Holly. "It's Mona. Are you at home? Good, now . . ."

But Holly didn't want to listen to the gossip she knew she'd be causing—a bedraggled woman sitting alone on Christmas Eve in a café in Devon, far from where she belonged. Though, in all honesty, she wasn't actually sure where she *did* belong.

In the aftermath, she'd tried to get in touch with Lily multiple times, but Lily had made it clear she wanted nothing to do with her. She still spoke to her parents. They'd said they didn't blame her, that they weren't taking sides. But it had felt like it. *Give her some space,* her mum had said—and Holly had done just that, leaving London to give Lily as much space as possible. And despite Holly's attempts to reach out, that space had grown and grown until it felt uncrossable.

Her parents had invited her to spend Christmas with them, last year.

"Will Lily be there?" Holly had asked her mum.

"Well, yes, but I thought that maybe—"

"Then it's probably better if I don't come." She didn't want to force her presence on her sister—and she couldn't stand the blame in her eyes.

A sigh down the line. "Well, if that's what you think is best." And that was that.

Holly folded her arms on the high table in front of her and stared at the rain on the window. The tears came again, then. Silent tears. Stupid, pointless, self-indulgent tears. But tears she couldn't stop, once they'd started. Tears at how royally she'd screwed everything up—and at how she was wrong and Abi was right, because Emma hadn't wanted to be found. Holly hadn't been able to fix it—because maybe it wasn't something someone else could fix. She should have known that, shouldn't she? Because Daniel had thought he could fix her and had left when he hadn't been able to—and what kind of person did that make her? A broken person, that was what.

"Here you go, love," a gentle voice said, and Holly started, blinking up at Mona. "You just drink that, and I'll bring you some cake too, shall I?"

Holly started to say thank you, but Mona was already walking away. It was ridiculous, that the kindness of a stranger should make her want to cry even *more*. She took a sip of the tea to stop herself, looking out the window as a car pulled up behind hers. She watched as the passenger door opened. As a woman, wearing an anorak with the hood pulled up around thin, wavy gray hair, stepped out into the rain. As she turned, a scowl on her face, and looked toward the café with turquoise blue eyes.

Holly only caught a glimpse of platinum-blonde hair in the driver's seat before the car pulled away and Emma walked stiffly toward the entrance of the café.

Holly felt her heart pounding as she clutched her tea tightly in her hands, glancing at Mona, who was back behind the counter pretending not to notice a thing, and then at the front door, through which Emma now stepped.

Emma gave her a long look as the door closed behind her, and the silence in the café became even more pronounced.

"The usual, Emma?" Mona called, as if this was nothing more than a customer coming in on a busy day.

Emma tsked, then walked right up to where Holly sat. Holly flinched back, and Emma gave her a narrow-eyed look. "This is the café I wrote about in that damned letter," she said, without preamble.

Holly hesitated, then nodded. "I know."

Emma sniffed. "You know it too, then?"

"I've only been here once before," Holly said carefully.

"And it made such an impact, did it?"

Holly wasn't sure she wanted to tell Emma about the crash just yet. "I like art," she said instead.

"Well, that's something, I suppose," Emma muttered. "So are you really an artist or was that just a lie to get to me?"

Holly winced again. "I am really an artist," she said, the words out before she could think better of them. "But I don't think I'm the one you're looking for."

"No. Nor the one I've just been told off for treating so harshly. *That* one never showed up. Doesn't have any interest in her work being on display in a café, apparently."

Holly looked at Emma, considering her in a slightly different light. "That's what the meeting was for? You're the one who decides what goes on display in here?"

Emma huffed out a breath. "Something like that."

"And on that note," Mona called, abandoning pretense that she wasn't listening, "we've sold another Mirabelle Landor—can you see if she'll—"

"I doubt it," Emma said, a snap to her voice. "She's having a break."

Mona raised her eyebrows. "If you say so."

Mirabelle Landor, Holly thought, the name of the artist coursing through her. But Emma was now giving her a very direct look, and she thought it best not to ask about that right now.

"I don't know why you thought it was a good idea to come down here from . . . Where *have* you come from?"

"Windsor," Holly said. And OK, yes, it seemed ridiculous when she put it like that, but it hadn't *felt* ridiculous at the time.

A sigh. "Windsor. Well, there is no use you sitting here looking miserable and crying into your tea. You'll make it all salty, for one." Holly didn't know if that was supposed to be a joke and if she ought to laugh, but Emma was already waving a hand to Mona, who looked up. Emma held up two fingers and Mona nodded, and, clearly trying to hide a smile, turned to grab a paper bag from behind her.

"We'll take two of the cakes from here—the carrot cake is the only way to go—and two Earl Greys, and you can come back to mine. Only for an hour, do you hear me?"

Holly bit her lip, not wholly convinced.

Emma huffed impatiently. "Come on, now. Isn't this the whole reason you came down here? To come and talk to me? So come, talk. It's Christmas Eve, after all, and this place is closed— Mona wants to get going with the festivities."

"Well, if you're sure," Holly said slowly, earning yet *another* sigh.

"You didn't give me the chance to be sure, did you?" Emma said, as Holly got to her feet. "But it's too late now, so come on. We might as well see it through."

Chapter Seven

Emma swore under her breath when her key got stuck in the lock. She tried again, shoving her shoulder against the door. The rain had only got heavier—big sheets of it that hid the surrounding view of the countryside.

Holly was well and truly sodden now, her socks squelching inside her boots, her coat heavy with the water it was absorbing—even the tank top underneath her sweater was damp. She bounced on the spot to try to keep warm, but the air was icy and unforgiving. She spoke through chattering teeth. "D . . . do you want me to . . . ?"

"I've got it," Emma snapped. "Damn door, always does this." She managed to get it open, practically falling over the threshold, and Holly rushed in after her. She only realized quite how loud the wind was once she was out of it.

Emma stripped off her dripping anorak to reveal a long-sleeved gray dress with black flowers on it, over black tights. The dress had certainly seen better days—the sleeves were frayed at the edges and it was starting to wear through in places—but it had the look of a classic, suggesting Emma had once been more stylish than she seemed now. Holly studied her, while trying to look like she wasn't. She wondered just how the cancer was affecting her, if it caused her pain day-to-day. She didn't feel like she could ask.

Holly took off her coat too, shivering as she did so—the house wasn't exactly warm. She couldn't work out whether it was better or worse to keep her sweater on, given how damp it was, and in the end decided to keep it on in the hope it would dry quicker that way.

"You can hang it up there," Emma grunted, indicating the coat in Holly's hand and a coat rack to the left of the front door.

Just below the coat rack was a small wooden table, and Holly did a double-take when she saw what was on top of it. A beautiful glass sculpture—two thin waves rising out from the bottom, one blue, one silver, twining together. She'd mainly worked with clay herself, but she loved the look of glass sculptures. *Togetherness*, the little plaque said—and though it must have once been bright and shiny, ready to capture the light, it was now gathering dust. She reached out her forefinger to touch it, to sweep away the layer of grime, but felt the back of her neck tingle with warning. She retracted her finger quickly and looked over her shoulder to see Emma watching her.

"My husband gave that to me on our twentieth wedding anniversary," she said, and though she had the same brisk tone, the way she held herself—stiff, unmoving—hinted at the emotion under the surface. A brittleness Holly herself knew well. "It's had pride of place since that day, and I haven't been able to bring myself to put it away since he died. Sentimental fool," she added in a mutter—though "sentimental" wasn't exactly the word Holly would use to describe her.

Emma shuffled through the house and jerked her head to indicate Holly should follow. There was a surprising lack of clutter—weren't you supposed to accumulate stuff as you moved through life? But though Emma's house had all the usual furniture, though the carpets and curtains were all intact, though there were paintings hanging up on almost every wall, the place seemed somehow . . . empty.

"What kind of artist are you, then?" Emma asked, leading Holly into a small kitchen, complete with an Aga cooking range, tiled floors, and rustic wooden cabinets.

Holly glanced at Emma. "What?"

"Are you a sculptor or painter or . . . ?"

She cleared her throat. "I'm not, I mean, I am, sort of, but I don't . . ." Emma raised her eyebrows and Holly bit her lip. "I don't really do it anymore." She could help *others* with it, could find a way to describe how the clay should feel beneath your palms, and had found there was a certain kind of joy in seeing one of her students bring something to life, in seeing that elation that came from taking something that exists only in your imagination and giving it life. But she couldn't do it for herself, not anymore.

"No talent?" Emma asked bluntly, dumping two teabags unceremoniously on the kitchen counter and reaching for the kettle. She'd asked for the teabags only from the café, telling Holly that the teas would only get cold by the time they got back otherwise, and Mona had given them over free of charge, along with a discount on the carrot cake.

"No, I—"

"No time?"

"I . . . Well, sort of." Teaching took up most of her time, after all—not just the hours in the classroom, but the preparation, the marking.

Emma snorted. The sound wasn't unkind, not exactly. More like . . . disbelieving. "Sounds like an excuse to me."

Holly said nothing to that—she wasn't sure how to explain.

How what had driven her to sculpt, to create, had disappeared after the crash—after what she'd done to Lily. She'd tried a few times in recent years, feeling that she should practice what she preached, but she'd all but fallen apart once the clay was in front of her. So she'd decided that part was done with, along with her chances of seeing her work in a gallery. No, she was content with helping *others* to create art they loved—that was her calling now.

Emma didn't pry anymore as she waited for the kettle to boil. Holly shivered in her damp sweater and stepped instinctively closer to the Aga. She looked out of the back door, leading to a big garden. She couldn't help but admire the wildness of it, something that was only highlighted by the brewing storm outside: the way the wind battered the bare branches, the way the grass, long and overgrown, quivered in the unrelenting rain. But the wildness was also sad, somehow. Because it didn't seem wild on purpose: Like the front garden, it had signs of once having been lovingly tended.

"It used to be a hobby of mine," Emma grunted, following the direction of Holly's gaze and shoving a cup of steaming tea into her hands. Holly flicked a glance at Emma in question, and she elaborated. "My husband and I used to get out there together, sunhat and shovels and muddy knees and all. I tried to get my son into it, but he never quite got the green fingers. My grandson did, though. He and I . . ." Her face tightened. "Well. I couldn't face doing it, after I lost them both."

Holly looked out again at the wild, abandoned garden and felt a lump swell in her throat. She blinked and looked down at her tea instead. "I have to say," she said, relieved to find her voice was steady, "I know nothing about gardening. I bought a tomato plant and tried to keep it alive in my bedroom while I was at university, but I failed."

"Love and time," Emma said simply.

"I gave it love," Holly said, wrinkling her nose. And she

had—she'd cried when she'd had to admit defeat and throw out the dead plant, even though Lily had laughed and said she was being silly.

Emma grunted, taking a sip of her Earl Grey. "And knowledge—each plant is different, needs different things. Some are stronger than others and do just fine even if you make mistakes and are best left mostly alone—get one of those next time. An aloe vera or a spider plant—they make good houseplants."

Maybe she would get one, Holly thought. She could call it Fred, have a little spider plant pet. She didn't know what they looked like, but they *sounded* cute.

Emma took Holly through the living room, which smelled a little musty and had an old fireplace in the corner that looked barely used. There was a pile of newspapers on a glass coffee table in the center of the room, one sofa, a faded red with a multicolored blanket lying on top of it, and a single armchair. As with Holly's flat, there was no sign of any Christmas decorations here.

Emma took a seat on the sofa, pulling the blanket up around her knees, so Holly went for the armchair, though she found herself sinking too deep into the squishy cushion and having to try to pull herself back upright, looking quite the fool.

Quiet descended on the room, so that the only sound was the wind howling, the rain battering the windows. The curtains had been drawn already, and the light was low—it would be homey, in another situation, but the awkwardness felt thick in the air and Holly cleared her throat to try to dissipate it. "So, umm, you live alone now then?" She regretted it immediately—she already *knew* that—but she was floundering for small talk.

Emma gave Holly a wry look, as if she knew exactly what she was thinking. "No point looking all disgruntled, my girl," she said, confirming her mind-reading abilities. "You were the one who decided to act on the letter and lord only knows why. But yes, I live alone. I thought about getting a dog, but it felt cruel—what if the dog outlived me?" She glanced at the mantel above the fireplace—at the photos there.

Holly followed her gaze. The first frame held a photo of Emma and a man that must have been her husband. It had a yellowing edge to it and had clearly been taken about forty years ago. In it, Emma was smiling—her hair was brunette with only the slightest tinge of gray and was more bouncing curls than lackluster waves—but she had the same angular chin, the same turquoise eyes. Her husband looked softer—warm brown eyes that crinkled in the corners, a deep tan giving him a weathered look, despite the fact he wasn't old in the photo. The next one was of a man that Holly presumed must have been Emma's son, standing alongside the husband, both of them with the same brown eyes, both smiling awkwardly into the camera. The last photo was Emma again—an older Emma but still clearly many years ago—with a small boy on her lap, around seven or eight, with curly brown hair, and the same brown eyes as the other two men, only deeper somehow. He was grinning a toothy grin, full of open childhood innocence.

"Three generations." This time, her voice wasn't a snap. It was brittle, vulnerable. And it made Holly's heart constrict. "All taken from me."

Holly looked at Emma's face, at the pain etched there, along with the lines of laughter and sadness, accumulated over the years. She wanted to reach out, lay a hand on Emma's in comfort—but she suspected that would not go down well.

Emma shook her head. "And here I am, sounding bitter when I promised myself I wouldn't spend whatever time I had left being so."

"Is that why you signed up to Dear Stranger?" Holly asked tentatively.

"No, I did that because my ridiculous neighbor forced me to. It's easier just to say yes, to get her to go away."

Holly hesitated. "Do you want to talk about it? About them?"

"No, not really. Does no good to go over the past."

Holly took a breath. "I was in a car crash a few years ago." She felt a need to explain, to give more of a reason as to why she'd showed up out of the blue. "I was driving." She usually left that part out, if she was ever forced to tell the story, but Emma's frankness made it easier. "My sister miscarried as a result—and she hasn't been able to get pregnant since."

Emma didn't ask whose fault it was, whether someone had crashed into her or the other way around. She only nodded slowly—an acceptance of what Holly was offering, of the mutual connection they shared.

"Where did it happen?"

"Just around the corner, on the A39."

Something dark flashed across Emma's face. "Horrible road. Too many idiot drivers coming too fast. Twenty-eight fatalities in the last three years." It was said quickly, a statistic pulled from thin air. Maybe it was where Richard had crashed too.

"We were lucky Lily wasn't a fatality," Holly said softly. *Her baby was,* a voice inside her mind whispered. The same voice that told her, repeatedly, that it was her fault. It was a voice that sounded a lot like Lily's voice, tearstained and broken, as it had been when Holly had seen her in the hospital after the crash.

She'd crept around the corner into Lily's room, following the nurse's directions on where to find her. Their parents were standing beside Lily's bed.

She remembered rushing in, pushing in between her parents to see her sister. "You're OK." Her voice was a wobbly breath. Because the bruises, the cut on her face, the dark purple line from where the seatbelt had cut in above her collarbone, were nothing, surely, because her sister was alive, was here, awake, and—

"No, I'm not OK," Lily said. Her voice was numb, and she wouldn't look at Holly. Holly felt her heartbeat rise as she looked over her sister, looking for some damage she hadn't noticed right away. She felt a trembling start up in her core—as if her body knew what was to come.

"You're both alive," her mum said, giving Holly's arm a squeeze, before reaching for Lily's hand. Her face was still tearstained, but she was clearly trying to control her voice, to make it calm, bolstering. "Let's focus on the good things. That's what matters most right now. Isn't it, Harry?" She shot a look at Holly's dad, who ran a hand through his red hair and nodded silently, his eyes scanning over Lily as if he, too, was looking for signs of further damage. "And the other drivers are OK too," her mum added. Holly felt the words cut into her, the reminder of the other car, spinning around the corner and coming straight at them. And then the one behind—too close behind. But relief slid through her. No one had died. It would be OK.

Holly's dad glanced at her then, watching her a little too carefully, Holly thought. "Yes. We should be thankful everyone survived," her dad said, his voice gruff.

"That's not true." Lily's voice—quiet and numb and lost. "Not everyone survived." Holly's stomach lurched as her gaze searched for Lily's. But her sister's eyes stayed closed, even as tears leaked out, tracing twin paths down her pale face. "I lost the baby."

It was a sob, and Holly's whole body went tight. *I lost the baby*. No. It couldn't be true. She looked to each of her parents, hoping one of them would contradict Lily. Her mum teared up, and her dad looked at the floor.

"I lost the baby," Lily said again, her voice a little stronger. "Because of you." Her eyes snapped open now. There was angry fire there—enough to make Holly take a step back. "Because you were more interested in getting your fucking phone to prove a point than concentrating on the road."

Holly was crumbling, unable to take her eyes away from her

sister. Away from the burning anger there. The *blame*. "No, I . . ." But she couldn't think of what to say. The car had come at them, but she'd reacted too slowly. She had tried to take the phone back, and she hadn't been looking, and it had lost her precious seconds. And now, Lily's baby . . .

"I'm so sorry," Holly whispered.

"Lily, love," their mum said tentatively, "maybe we ought to—"

"Get out," Lily said sharply. Her face lost some of the paleness as heat flooded her cheeks. She looked to their mum. "I want her out!" Her voice was scratchy, painful sounding. But it was full of a certainty that hit Holly like a physical force.

Her mum turned to her, her eyes carefully shuttered. "Holly, why don't you—"

But Holly was already backing away, already turning to flee from the hospital room, unable to bear the grief and rage on Lily's face, unable to face up to the reality of what had happened, the consequences of her mistakes.

"How is your sister now?" Emma's question brought her back to the present.

Holly hesitated. "I don't really know. She doesn't speak to me."

Emma nodded, no judgment in the motion. "Happens." She looked at the photos on the mantel again. "That's the last photo I have of him." She nodded toward the most recent photo, with the little boy. "Of my grandbaby. I didn't lose him the same way I lost his father, but I lost him in all the ways that count."

Outside, the rain sounded as though it was getting heavier, if that was even possible. "Why doesn't he talk to you anymore?"

"That's between him and me."

"Have you . . . Did you ever try to get in touch?"

Emma sniffed. "He's made it clear he doesn't want to see me and I have no business stepping into his life now. It's too late. It would do more harm than good, and it's a selfish desire of mine to see him again. It's not what's best for him. That's why I wrote the damn letter in the first place—so I could get it off my chest without having to put the weight of it on him. And so that I didn't have to have a conversation with anyone about it." She leveled her eyes at Holly as she spoke the last sentence.

She didn't have any right to argue with that, so Holly went quiet, listening to the howling wind. She imagined children tucked up in bed on Christmas Eve, the excitement of being warm and cozy with a stocking waiting for Santa, while it was cold and wet and wild outside. What would *Santa* feel, if he were real, having to go out in that? Would Rudolph just refuse point-blank to come out of the stable?

"And . . . how are you handling . . . the cancer?"

"You like to pry, don't you?"

"It must be your warm and open nature," Holly said dryly.

Emma snorted, and this time, the noise sounded almost approving. "Yes, well, the cancer. I'm dealing with it."

"Are you having treatment? What will you have to . . . ?" But she didn't finish that sentence, realizing belatedly that this was going too far.

Emma took advantage of Holly trailing off and rubbed her hands together in an efficient manner. "I think that's enough of story time for one night, don't you? Especially since, as we've just established, I'm an old woman with ill health. I need my sleep."

"Right," Holly said quickly. "You're right. I'm sorry." She got to her feet, glancing at the crack in the curtains. It wasn't only stormy now but pitch black. She grimaced as she fished around in her crocodile-print handbag for her keys. Driving home would not be fun in this.

"Many people wouldn't find the courage to drive again, if they went through what you did." Emma was staring at the keys in Holly's hand with an odd, twisted expression.

Holly shrugged, unsure of what to say. She was unwilling to admit that it had taken her a full two years to get back behind the wheel. Not to mention that the first time she'd done so, she'd had a full-blown panic attack.

Emma huffed out that small, impatient breath. "Well, you can't drive in this."

Holly glanced out at the crack in the curtain again. She was probably right—especially because she'd be a state of nerves, driving so close to the place where she'd crashed before. "I'll get a hotel, I guess."

Emma scoffed.

"An Airbnb?"

Emma rolled her eyes. "You're expecting to find somewhere to stay at this hour on Christmas Eve, are you? The only accommodation you'll find is the camp site, and they'll expect you to bring your own tent." She gave Holly an appraising scan, and for a moment she thought Emma might actually pack her off with a tent. She had a vision of spending Christmas Eve and Christmas morning in the car on the side of the road—a new low even for her.

Then Emma sighed. "I've got a spare room. It's not much, but you can stay in it for the night."

Holly hovered in the middle of the living room as Emma got to her feet. "But it's Christmas," she said blankly. It was Christmas, and she couldn't impose on a stranger, despite the fact it was exactly what she'd set out to do this morning.

"Indeed." And with that, Emma gave her a smile that suggested she hadn't always been so spiky, that maybe there was warmth buried there too. "It's Christmas."

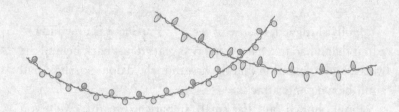

Chapter Eight

Dear Lily,

I'm writing to you from Devon right now. It's a long story, but I'm staying with a woman I'm pretty sure might be more fun than she's letting on at the moment. Though I'll hold judgment on that until the end of the day, I suppose.

It's hard, being here, not to think about the crash. I drove right by where we had the accident. I remember Mum telling me it could have been worse. There was a car a little behind us that saw the whole thing, called an ambulance—it's why we got to hospital so quickly. Did you know that? I'm sure Mum and Dad told you at some point, but we've never talked about it.

Are you spending Christmas with Mum and Dad? I presume so, because if you and Steve were doing something else, I think Mum would have tried harder to get me to go to theirs. I don't think I would have gone *though. It's almost easier not to be asked—because then I don't have to explain anything, don't have to hear Mum try to pretend that she's fine with the fact that you and I aren't speaking to one another. If you are with them, I hope you have fun. I hope Dad makes his epic mulled wine and Mum doesn't fall asleep before 9 p.m. Even though I know I shouldn't, I also hope you'll all miss me, just a little.*

Because I miss you, Lils. More than you know.

Love,
Holly

Holly woke while it was still dark. Dark—and quiet. She blinked a few times, listening. She could no longer hear the howling of the wind or the battering of the rain. She shivered as she pushed the duvet off and got up out of the little single bed. She reached for the back of the bedroom door, where the dressing gown Emma had lent her hung. A dressing gown, to go with the flannel pajamas Emma had also given her—ones she claimed she hadn't worn in approximately fifteen years.

Holly checked her phone, smiling a little when she saw a message from Abi.

Happy Wednesday babe! I'm sending this message for no particular reason because as you know there's nothing remotely special about today but thought I'd let you know I was thinking about you and I love you and I'll see you very soon. Xxxx

Then another one, just underneath.

P.S. Can you please update me on how your
quest went? I've constructed about a million
different narratives, and I want to see if any
of them are right.

There was also a message from her mum.

Happy Christmas, Holly. I hope you and Abi
have a lovely day. Thinking of you, as always.
Xx

She stared at the message, feeling an all-too-familiar lump. She'd told her mum she was spending Christmas with Abi, when she'd asked. It had been easier than the truth—she hadn't wanted her mum to feel guilty about her spending Christmas alone.

Deciding that she needed a beat to compose the right reply to her mum—and that updating Abi would need a phone call rather than a text—Holly shelved the messages for later. As quietly as she could, she opened the bedroom door and started down the stairs. She hissed when, halfway down, she stubbed her toe on the banister, but she refused to swear out loud, not wanting to wake Emma.

Christmas morning. When she was growing up, she used to think life felt *different* on Christmas morning. She'd creep into Lily's room every year, so that she and Lily could find their stockings and then go and wake their mum and dad together. She remembered one year in particular. She'd been eight; Lily was twelve and had decided she was too cool for some of the things Holly still wanted to do. Neither of them believed in Santa by this point—Holly had cottoned on, even though Lily had tried, along with their parents, to keep the ruse going as long as possible—but that didn't make things any less exciting.

"Lily?" Holly had whispered, creaking her sister's door open and tiptoeing inside. Her sister's room always smelled funny these days—full of those perfumes she insisted on wearing to school, which Holly thought smelled disgusting.

Lily groaned, not opening her eyes. "Really, Holly? It's too early."

Holly shifted from foot to foot. Their stockings were downstairs, waiting for them above the fire. Lily still had one every year, even though she did that eye-rolling thing when their dad asked them what they wanted from "Santa" this year.

"But it's Christmas," Holly said, still whispering.

"And it will still be Christmas in an hour."

Holly had stood in silence. She'd known this would happen. Known there would be a day when Lily decided she was too *cool* for Christmas morning, like she'd already decided she was too cool to spend Saturday mornings with their mum in the café, which Holly loved doing. And she knew she complained to her mum and dad about Lily being so *bossy,* but she missed the way she used to be, when they'd play together.

Then Lily had opened one eye. "Do you think Santa might have bought me a mobile phone this year?"

Holly giggled. "Maybe."

"And you? What will be in your stocking?"

Holly thought about it. "Maybe the painting of the horse. You know, from that shop with all the clay stuff."

"Pottery," Lily corrected automatically.

"Pottery, right."

Lily threw off her duvet. "Come on, then. We better go and find out."

And Holly had grinned as she bounced down the stairs after Lily, because she knew that Lily really was excited about Christmas still even if she pretended not to be, because Holly knew her better than anyone. And the painting she'd hoped for wasn't in the stocking—because it was under the tree, a present from Lily. Because Lily knew *her* better than anyone, too.

Holly tried to shake the memory away as she crept into Emma's kitchen, wincing at the cold of the tiles on her feet and heading straight for the Aga, stumbling in the darkness. She eyed up the kettle but decided she couldn't just start helping herself to things in the kitchen. Instead she took a seat at the small wooden kitchen table, pulling across one of the newspapers that had been left there, still not switching on the light in case it woke Emma. The pale morning glow, unique to winter, was starting to make itself known now, but it was still nowhere near light enough to read. So she pulled out one of the adverts from inside the paper, allowing her mind to drift as she folded and twisted the paper in her hands absentmindedly.

The kitchen light flicked on, causing Holly to jump and drop the paper. She turned on her chair to see Emma standing in the doorway, wearing a pale-blue dressing gown, the twin to Holly's pale-pink one.

Emma blinked a few times, bleary-eyed. "What are you doing sitting here alone in the dark?"

"I didn't want to intrude."

Emma laughed, but the sound wasn't unkind. "You're already intruding, my girl. Might as well make yourself at home while you're at it." She padded into the kitchen in thick, fluffy socks. "Come on, let's have a hot drink."

Holly stood awkwardly. "I can leave, if you want me to."

Emma waved a hand at her while she filled the kettle. "You might as well stay for a bit, then head off when you're ready." She turned to give Holly a narrow-eyed look. "I won't be cooking some big Christmas dinner, though, so be warned. Cooking was never my thing, and I don't have much food in the house." She gave a little sniff. "Pasta, that's about all I can stretch to—and even then, better you make it. You can cook?"

"Ah, I guess so. I'm not the next MasterChef or anything, but I get by." Though the local Thai takeaway did know her name, so perhaps that said something.

"I'm sure it'll be better than anything I could whip up."

Emma looked down at the paper Holly had been playing with, lying on the kitchen table. She'd twisted it into a little giraffe—an old habit of hers, creating little paper animals when she was bored or restless. She hadn't been thinking of what she was doing, really—wouldn't have made a giraffe if she *had* been thinking about it, it being Lily's favorite animal.

"Sorry," Holly said quickly, reaching for the paper. "Habit."

Emma made a clicking noise. "Impressive habit." Then she glanced at Holly's feet—bare on the kitchen tiles—and grunted. "Socks."

"Huh?"

"Hang on," Emma said, shuffling out of the kitchen. "Make us a tea, will you? Earl Grey for me, and whatever you can find for you. There's instant coffee around somewhere too."

Holly busied herself in the kitchen and had just managed to find the coffee when Emma reappeared, holding a pair of multi-colored fluffy socks in one hand and a card in another. She thrust both into Holly's hands at the same time.

Holly looked down. "What's this?"

"Well, traditionally you put socks on your feet, but if you have other ideas I'll try not to judge."

Holly held up the card—a cliff edge, which managed to look both majestic and powerful, and . . . lonely. She recognized the brushwork, the distinctive boldness of the landscape. She lifted her gaze to Emma.

"You said you like art," she said simply. "So there you are. Happy Christmas and all that. It's by a local artist. The one I mentioned in the café. Mirabelle—"

"Landor," Holly finished, her voice barely a murmur.

"You've heard of her?" Emma's eyebrows shot up.

"I . . . Yes. Yes, I've heard of her."

Emma gave her a long look, then sniffed. "I imagine she'd be happy to hear that." She picked up her steaming Earl Grey off the counter and cupped it between her hands.

"Thank you," Holly said, her voice still low as she took in the painting—perfect, in miniature form. She remembered, so clearly, the first card she'd seen—and with the memory of that came the memory of Jack's face: his dark eyes, his off-center nose, the striking cheekbones. It was a disturbingly clear memory, given they'd had no more than a brief conversation three years ago. But still—that was two of Mirabelle Landor's cards she'd been gifted now, both in the same place. *Fate,* a voice whispered in her head, though she shoved the voice—definitely her sister's—aside. It had been her own damn decisions that got her here.

She shook her head helplessly at Emma. "I don't have anything to give you."

Emma waved that away. "You can make me one of those paper animals. A dog, to make up for not having my own. Or a tiger. I always did like tigers."

The two of them sat for a while at the kitchen table, sipping their hot drinks in companionable silence. Holly had been right—the storm from last night had burned itself out, and the sun was now shining over a garden that looked a little bedraggled. Even knowing nothing about gardening, she could see how beautiful it must have been once—could imagine it in full bloom in summer, with insects buzzing around, the smell of flowers filling the air.

As she drank her coffee, she couldn't help glancing at Emma, who was flicking through the newspaper, now two days old. She didn't *look* ill. At least not obviously. She was a little thin, perhaps, her face a little pinched. But she was there, sipping her tea, looking so . . . normal. Holly didn't have enough experience with cancer to know what to look for, though—if there even was anything to look for. It must be different for each person, mustn't it? But this could be a good sign. Maybe the cancer wasn't that bad?

Holly cleared her throat. "Can I make you something? Toast?" Because surely food was a good thing, if you were ill?

"Think I'm out of bread," Emma grunted. "Might have some Weetabix somewhere."

But as Holly got to her feet to find said Weetabix, there was a knock at the front door, then the sound of that door opening.

"Helllloooooo!"

Holly jumped at the sound of the slightly shrill voice.

"Emma? Are you up?"

"Damn woman," Emma muttered, getting to her feet. "Need to remember to lock the door."

When Emma left the kitchen and headed for the hallway, Holly hesitated, then followed, a little tentatively.

"There you are, my darling," the voice continued. "Jim's starting with all the chopping and whatnot already, so I wanted to pop round and—" The woman broke off, raising her perfectly arched eyebrows, when Holly came into view. It was the same woman Holly had met yesterday in the café—the one who had given her Emma's address. Pam—platinum-blonde hair perfectly blow-dried, wearing a red dress and big gold hoop earrings, along with a wash of red lipstick. "Ah, so it worked out OK in the end? You *are* an artist, then? I thought that might be a lie, though I couldn't figure out why on earth you'd be lying about it."

Emma let out a snorted *Ha!* and Pam turned to look at her.

"Holly was the recipient of that Dear Stranger letter you made me write."

Pam's red lips pursed. "I thought that was supposed to be anonymous."

"It was," Emma said on a growl. But this time, Holly refused to wince, and straightened her back. If Emma had wanted her gone, she would have booted her out by now.

Pam gave Holly an overtly curious look, then shrugged. "Well, Merry Christmas to both of you!" She held up a bottle of champagne, plus two glasses. "You have a third, yes, Emma?"

"I'm not sure I should," Holly said quickly. "I'll be driving soon."

"Nonsense," Pam said. "It's Christmas—you must. She can stay another night, can't she, Emma?"

Emma shrugged but didn't contradict the statement, and when Pam poured out the champagne, Holly took the glass she was offered and followed the two women to the living room, claiming the armchair again, while Pam and Emma took the sofa.

Pam sat forward on the edge, sipping her champagne and studying Holly over the rim of the glass. It made her feel self-conscious—like she ought to be wearing something more glamorous than a dressing gown, like maybe she should have bothered to brush her hair when she woke up this morning. Not that she'd brought a hairbrush with her, but still.

"So, Holly. What's your story?"

"My story?"

"Yes, yes, your story. What brings you here?"

"I, ah . . ." She couldn't help it: She glanced at Emma, though whether it was for help in avoiding the question or permission to answer it, she couldn't quite be sure.

"Holly's an artist; that much is true."

Presumably Emma said it to help, so that Holly didn't have to talk about the crash, but Holly grimaced all the same—at the fact that she wasn't, not even close. And despite what she told herself, the failure of that still hurt.

"Speaking of which, where's my tiger, hmm?"

Pam looked questioningly at Emma, and she lifted the paper

giraffe Holly had made earlier in the air. Holly hadn't even noticed Emma picking it up. "Oh, how brilliant—can you make me one too, Holly? A lemur, I think—my soul animal."

Emma was already handing her another newspaper, and with both women looking at her like that, Holly saw no choice but to take the paper and crack on with it.

"So that's what you do, is it? Paper animals?"

Holly couldn't help a small chuckle—at the fact that making paper animals sounded like a perfectly reasonable career choice when Pam said it. "No, I'm an art teacher."

Pam sat back, nodding serenely and sipping more champagne. "Ah, filling young minds, a valuable career. I always thought I would have made a good teacher."

Emma snorted. "I beg to differ."

"Ignore her, Holly," Pam said loftily. "She gets like this sometimes, but you just have to drown it out."

Holly decided not to comment on that and focused on Pam instead. "What do you do?"

"*Did,* my darling. I'm a lady of leisure these days."

Holly grinned. "What *did* you do, then?"

"Oh, this and that," Pam said, with a casual hand wave.

"She never gives me a straight answer either," Emma muttered.

"So are you good at art then, Holly?" Pam pressed.

Holly gave an awkward little shrug. "I'm all right, I suppose."

"All right." Emma huffed. "Don't be self-deprecating. Either you're good or you're not."

"Well, I am, I suppose." Holly swallowed. "Or used to be. I lost it, after . . . Well, I just lost it."

"But you're making art now, aren't you?" Pam said, gesturing at the tiger that was coming together between Holly's fingers. "You can't have lost it all."

Holly was so stumped by the way she said it, the simple *fact* of it, that she couldn't think of anything to say in response. Because on some level, she supposed this *was* art. Nothing grand, nothing special, nothing more than silly little entertainment—but art, nonetheless.

"It's either in your soul or it's not," Emma said, matter-of-factly, "and I'm going to take a bet and say it's the former for you, my girl."

"Emma's an art expert," Pam said, nodding her head impressively.

"I am not."

"You bring in all the art for Impression Sunrise, don't you?"

Emma took a healthy glug of champagne. "I wanted to do it more seriously, at one point," Emma told Holly. "I went back to university in my forties, after Richard had grown up and moved out and I had the time. Did Art History, then a master's degree—all part-time. But then . . . Well . . ." She didn't need to finish, because Holly understood all too well—a car crash had derailed Emma's dreams, just as it had her own.

Pam reached over to the other side of the sofa and gave Emma's hand a squeeze. Then she finished her champagne, putting her glass down on the table. "Time for some sherry, I think. Emma—you have sherry, don't you?"

"About the only thing I do have." Emma got up and shuffled out of the room, leaving Holly feeling a little baffled. They hadn't even finished the champagne yet—and now on to sherry? It seemed like Pam was angling for a very merry Christmas indeed.

Pam was getting out her phone, putting on a Christmas playlist. "There's no speaker in here, unfortunately," she told Holly. "But even so, it lifts the atmosphere, don't you think? I'm afraid starting a fire's a little beyond me, though," she added, eyeing the fireplace suspiciously.

She folded her hands on her lap and gave Holly a very direct look. "So, Holly," she continued. "How's the love life?"

Holly wrinkled her nose. "Nonexistent, as of the day before yesterday." Though she hadn't thought of Daniel since she'd walked into Emma's house. The realization caused a flare of guilt. Which was ridiculous. *He* broke up with *her*. She shouldn't be the one feeling guilty.

"Hmm. Well, I had to go through four husbands to meet the right one—maybe you're doing the right thing, choosing to be single."

"My boyfriend broke up with me," Holly said flatly. "It was hardly a choice."

Pam pursed her lips. "Well, there's always another one around the corner—young people today are too picky, in my opinion." Despite the fact that Pam had just directly contradicted herself, Holly felt a little lurch in her stomach. Because it hadn't been her being picky, had it? She would have quite happily ticked along with Daniel—was all ready to move in with him, for Christ's sake. But *he* hadn't picked *her*.

"Where is your husband now?" Holly asked, moving the subject along.

"Oh he's next door, cooking Christmas lunch. He likes to sneak a glass of wine or two while I'm not there and pretend to open the first bottle of the day over lunch, and I like to pretend I don't notice because that way I get dinner cooked for me. Speaking of which," she said, looking up as Emma walked back into the room, a slightly dusty-looking bottle of sherry in hand, "Emma, what are you feeding this girl for Christmas lunch?"

Emma scowled, and Holly cleared her throat. "I think pasta's on the menu. Which I love," she added quickly, because Pam was looking almost comically shocked.

"No, no, no," she said. "That just won't do." She held up a finger as she picked up her mobile, causing the Christmas music to stop and earning a "Thank God for that" from Emma. "Jim?" Pam said into the phone. "We'll have two more for lunch." A pause. "Emma and her friend . . . Don't be silly, we have plenty of Brussels sprouts. . . . Neither of us even *likes* Brussels sprouts, for God's sake. And it'll do you good to have one less roast potato and you know Emma barely eats anything . . . Yes . . . Yes, exactly . . . Don't worry, darling, I have every faith. We'll see you shortly." With that, she hung up the phone, and nodded brightly to Emma and Holly.

"That's settled then. You'll both come round."

"Oh, I couldn't—"

"Oh, nonsense. We'd love to have her, wouldn't we, Emma?"

"Who said I even wanted to come?" Emma grumbled.

"Ignore her, Holly, she doesn't mean any of it."

Emma sighed but shot Holly a look. "I suppose you could help entertain Pam over Christmas lunch, if you were to stay, so I don't have to."

"Right, well, both of you go and get dressed, then," Pam said, making a shooing gesture with her hands. "You're not coming round unless you make some sort of effort."

Emma slouched out first, leaving the sherry on the glass coffee table. Holly got up more slowly, glancing again at the three photos on the mantel.

"It's a sad story," Pam said, a gentleness coming into her voice now.

Holly looked back, saw Pam watching her.

"Do you know what happened—why her grandson doesn't speak to her anymore?"

Pam looked at Holly for a long moment before shaking her head. "It's not my story to tell. And to be honest, by the time we met it was already in the past, so I'm not even sure I have the details I'd need to do it justice."

"Where is he now?"

Pam hesitated. "Last Emma told me, he was in London, working at one of those management consultancy thingamajigs."

Holly's heart gave a little jolt. He was so close to her. Windsor and London were different worlds—she knew that well enough, having escaped from one to go to the other—but they were just a short train ride away from one another. And she'd even be in London in March, for the school trip with Abi.

But she turned away from the photos, took a step toward the living room door. It was not her business. It was up to Emma to tell her about it, up to Emma to get in touch with her grandson if she wanted to.

"Germain & Co.," Pam said from behind her, her tone mild, almost incidental.

Holly frowned as she turned back to Pam. "Huh?"

"I think that's the name of the company Jack works for. Just in case you're interested," she added with a little shrug.

Holly paused, letting the knowledge settle into her, trying to read between the lines of what Pam was saying.

"Jack?"

"That's his name," Pam said with a little nod. "Emma's grandson. Jack."

And though Holly told herself it was ridiculous, that it couldn't be, there was no possible way that *Emma's* Jack could be the man from the café all those years ago, she felt a tug, deep inside her. *Stupid,* she told herself again. But still, she couldn't deny it. That tug inside her—it felt like a thread, being pulled tight.

MARCH

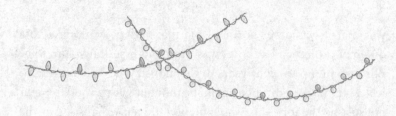

Chapter Nine

Jack sat at his desk, his back to the office window and the view of the city that it offered, the email on his computer screen going blurry in front of him even as he blinked to try to draw it into focus. He reached for the coffee next to him, only to find it empty. Probably a good thing. It was coming up to lunchtime now, and he'd already had four cups this morning—which was a lot of caffeine, even for him. But he'd been in the office until gone ten P.M. last night and had started again at seven A.M. this morning, and caffeine was sort of necessary in that situation. Only now he was starting to get a headache, and it was hard to know if it was because of the coffee or all the blue light.

He rolled his shoulders, read the email again. They were a team member down at the moment—Jenny having left for bigger and better things—which meant he was working on more projects than usual, and next week he'd be up in Scotland with a new client—a startup that had done pretty well for the first three years and was now floundering—so he was trying to get ahead of the curve. If there was one thing that could be said of his job, it was that it was never boring—and that variety, working across different projects all at once, was what had first drawn him to it. But coming up to eight years in the industry, he was starting to feel a bit knackered. Then again, he thought with a sigh, it might not just be the job—his whole bloody life felt exhausting at the moment.

His desk phone started to ring, the red light flashing. Reception. Jack stared at the phone for a moment, wondering whether to bother answering. They'd hired a new receptionist—young, just out of university, who wore a baffling combination of a T-shirt and tie—and he definitely hadn't got the hang of things yet. He was frequently ringing the wrong person or directing client emails to the wrong team. Though it wasn't that he wasn't making an effort—he'd learned the name of everyone who worked here, as far as Jack could tell, and always tried to greet them with some sort of personal reference, trying, no doubt, to establish camaraderie.

Jack picked up the phone—who was he kidding? He'd never ignored a work call in his life—and switched the speakerphone on. "Hi, Mike."

"Jack! Looking forward to Scotland next week?"

"It'll be a ball." Frankly, he couldn't imagine anything worse right now than trekking to Glasgow in mid-March, but there you had it.

"Totally. Look, I've got a George Ham . . ." He trailed off on a cough. "Err, well, he's from Create Construction, says he's got a meeting with—"

"You want Sophia." Jack did his best not to sigh. "She's the project manager for that one."

"Oh right, sorry, I thought it was you, because—"

"No worries." There was a knock at Jack's office door and he looked up, signaling for Ed to come in. "Got to go, Mike.

Good luck." He wasn't really sure why he'd said that—luck just always seemed appropriate when it came to Mike.

Jack sat back in his swivel chair—he'd spent hours choosing it from a catalogue and it was arguably the best in existence—and nodded at Ed, who was now leaning against the inside of the glass door. How Ed always managed to look so put together was beyond Jack—he knew for a fact that Ed had been out in Soho until late last night, but there was no sign of baggy eyes or sallow skin, as Jack knew there would be if he'd been out drinking.

"All right?" Jack asked. He reached again for his mug, stopped his hand halfway and wrinkled his nose. Right. No more coffee.

Ed grinned. "Looks like this is good timing—I was coming to see if you wanted lunch. Or coffee, apparently?"

Jack sighed. "I'm not supposed to have any more caffeine."

"Says who?"

"Me."

"Well, tell you that you're ridiculous."

"Tried that," Jack said with mock seriousness. "I didn't believe me."

Ed snorted. "Come on. Let's go get food—I'm sure that bowl of granola feels a long time ago now."

Jack got to his feet. "It's odd that you remember my breakfast of choice."

Ed put on a serious face. "It's that kind of attention to detail that means I'm the one sent champagne from the clients, mate."

"You only get champagne? I get champagne and flowers and those little truffle things—I'd say you need to up your game."

Ed smirked. "Flowers, hey?"

"Peonies. They're my favorite—surprised you didn't know that what with all your attention to detail." Peonies were not, in fact, his favorite flower: That would be a ghost orchid, one of the

UK's rarest plants, which, unlike most, didn't use sunlight to produce food but relied on a special kind of fungi. Which, you had to admit, was pretty damned cool. A rebel plant. Not that he'd spout that kind of thing out loud: Not only would Ed scoff at him, albeit fondly, for such knowledge, but it always gave him a pang of regret, thinking about his childhood dream of finding a way to work outside—something he'd given up on when he'd moved to London straight out of university.

Jack turned to get his winter coat off the hook by the window. He deliberately kept his desk facing away from the window—mainly because facing the door meant he could see who was approaching and wouldn't be caught off-guard, but also because there was something a little depressing about the City of London. Though some of the skyscrapers of Canary Wharf were, he supposed, majestic in their own right, looking out at all the concrete and glass, with no sign of any green, made him feel a little trapped, like he couldn't breathe quite easily enough.

"Shall we grab something from the canteen?" Jack asked, turning back to Ed, who held the glass door open.

"Nah, I'm sick of it there. Let's go to Caravan." It was one of the cooler eateries in the area—complete with a terrace that was always crowded in summer. Jack stole a quick glance out the window. He doubted they'd have that problem today, given the gray sky, the way it made you feel cold just by looking at it.

"Reckon I could get away with a beer before my client meeting this afternoon?" Ed asked, as the two of them headed through the office and toward the lift. They were up on the sixth floor, and though Jack routinely told himself he'd start taking the stairs, it was a habit he hadn't managed to properly get into.

"Ah, no."

Ed wrinkled his nose. "You're the wrong person to ask, aren't you?

Jack offered a sort of helpless shrug. "Sorry."

Ed pressed the button for the ground floor. He gave Jack a look out of the corner of his eye as he did so. Jack knew that look, the not-so-subtle assessment. "Heard you were in the office late last night," Ed said. His voice was casual, but Jack wasn't fooled.

He shrugged. "Par for the course here."

Ed hesitated. "Have you talked to Vanessa recently?"

Jack rubbed a hand across his face, the tiredness that seemed like a constant companion these days flooding through his body. "No. She's called a few times but I just don't have the energy." He could feel Ed's eyes on him as the lift arrived and they both stepped in. He sighed. "What?"

"Nothing," Ed said, a little too quickly. "I just wondered, maybe if you talked to her, you'd get some—"

"Ed," Jack said, his voice a warning.

"Right. Right, sorry, not my business."

"No, sorry, it's not that." And really, he appreciated having a friend who looked out for him. Given the long work hours and what had happened with Vanessa, he'd let some of his friendships slide—and it wasn't like his family was nearby. Wasn't like he talked to them all that much, anyway. So he was grateful that Ed was looking out for him, even if he'd rather not talk about what a fuck-up his life was right now.

"So," Ed said, his voice becoming brighter, obviously trying to lighten the mood, "you're back on the twenty-third, right?"

Jack looked at him blankly.

"From Scotland?"

"Ah right. Yeah, the twenty-third." He frowned. "That would make it the fourteenth today, is that right?"

"Yeah. Quick math. Why? What's important about the fourteenth?

"Nothing. My mum's birthday's soon, that's all." He ought to send flowers. A card and flowers. Jesus, when did he last call her? Christmas, probably. He'd chosen to spend Christmas alone

this year—the first one in nearly five years now—rather than opt-
ing to be with his mum and her family. It had never felt right, ever
since she'd got remarried after he'd left for university. Derek
seemed like a nice enough guy, and Jack was glad his mum had
eventually found something after the awfulness of what had happened to his dad—but it still just felt . . . odd, at these kind of
traditional family get-togethers. He had two half-siblings too,
though they always treated him with a faint air of curiosity and
suspicion, like they weren't quite sure what to do with him or
whether to trust him. Though maybe that was just because they
were teenagers.

"Hello? Earth to Jack?"

Jack blinked at Ed, who was now getting out of the lift. "Huh?"

Ed shook his head. "If I didn't know any better, I'd say you
think I'm boring, mate."

"Sorry," Jack said as he followed Ed onto the ground floor.

"I was just asking when you're next going to see your mum.
Maybe I can come, convince her to leave her husband for me."
He put a hand over his heart and Jack snorted quietly. His mum
had come to visit him in London around a year ago, braving the
city even though she hated it. He'd had to work some of the time,
meaning she'd come to the office and met Ed, who had then decided she was the best thing since sliced bread.

The two of them used their office key cards to swipe through
the electric glass barriers and into the main reception area, which
was much classier than the office at large. There were armchairs
dotted around, seemingly haphazardly, though Jack knew for a
fact that they'd had an interior designer in to position them all
just so, along with the occasional beanbag. Seriously, who the
hell wanted to wait for a meeting on a beanbag, for Christ's sake?
They were trying way too hard to be cool, in his opinion.

"I think you have tough competition there, mate. What with
her husband and two kids and all."

"Ah well, a man can dream, can't he? But anyway, what I was going to say is that if you're back on the twenty-third, my mate is having this party in Soho on the twenty-fifth, if you wanted to come along."

"A party in Soho, hey? For what?"

"His birthday."

"And you don't think said friend would mind me gate-crashing his party?"

"Course not. The more the merrier." It was said in a bolstering tone, but Ed had been doing this rather a lot recently, springing invitations to random events on Jack.

Jack smiled a little. "Mate, you don't need to worry about me—I'm fine." He glanced at the reception desk as they approached it. Mike was there, manning it solo, wearing a red-and-black spotted tie today. He was talking to a woman who had her back to Jack, a whole lot of red hair cascading over her shoulders. Jack realized that's what had made him look over. The woman was saying something, gesturing emphatically to Mike, who was nodding in earnest. She had a fancy handbag sitting at her feet, with a kind of print that made it look like it should have teeth.

"Who's worried?" Ed was saying. "All I'm saying is, rather than sitting around in that awful flat on your own every weekend, or working just for something to do, you could . . ."

But Ed's words slid away somewhere in the space between them. Because the red-haired woman had turned, and Jack had seen her face. The face he'd thought of too much in the years since he'd seen it—a face that would sneak into his dreams, where it had no place being, given he'd spoken to the woman all of once. She'd never called, and he'd spent an embarrassing number of days trying to remember if he'd written his number down right.

It was one of his *what if* moments. What if she'd called?

What if they'd gone out? Would he still be working here, in London? Part of the reason he was still in London was because of Vanessa, after all, and maybe he never would have made the leap from being friends with her, if he'd been dating someone else. Stupid, to pin it all on this woman, who he didn't even know. It was only because she was here that he was thinking about it. *Here,* in his office. He couldn't help the jolt to his stomach—at the *serendipity* of it.

His imagination had not done her face justice—the slightly crooked mouth, high cheekbones, green eyes that you couldn't help but get lost in. They reminded him of the outdoors, of the green of grass and forests, where there was space to run, space to breathe. He'd come to a stop. Only realized it as Ed was now looking at him in question. But he was frozen there like an idiot as she jerked her head toward him. No. Jerk was the wrong word. She wasn't graceful—he remembered that clearly enough—but she had such *energy* in everything she did. It was that energy that had drawn him to her at the time, had made him want to linger. He'd been at that café on a day when he'd felt depleted of it, and he'd left feeling like, maybe, he'd be able to face what was coming.

She was looking at him now. So he saw it—that spark of recognition in her eyes. She remembered him too.

Ed was speaking to him, asking what was up. But Jack moved away, walking across the reception, toward her, like his feet were on autopilot. He'd long since given up on the idea that he might just bump into her one day—London was not the kind of city where you just bumped into people. She watched him approach, her gaze flickering over his face, quick assessment there. Her body was very still, held taut. He felt it, the same spark of something he'd felt when he first saw her, when their gazes finally collided.

He couldn't help it. He let out a small, incredulous laugh. "It's you."

Chapter Ten

It's you.

His words echoed for a moment around Holly's mind.

And it was *him*. Jack, Emma's grandson, was actually Jack from the café. She'd dismissed the possibility of them being one and the same—because, seriously, what were the chances? But it *was* him. Out of all the Jacks in the whole of London, Emma's grandson was *this* Jack.

And right now, she was staring at him like a catatonic idiot.

Get a grip, Holly!

"I . . ." But no words would come out. Because what was she supposed to say? She'd had this all planned out . . . sort of. She'd come to Germain & Co., ask for Jack, be shown up to his office. Then she'd take a seat and calmly deliver the whole speech she'd prepared. About Emma, about the fact that she had cancer and didn't want to get in touch because she didn't want to burden her grandson with it after so much time apart. About the fact that Emma was sad, and lonely, even if she wouldn't readily admit it, and that going through a diagnosis of cancer without any family by your side was something no one should have to do, if there was any other option available. She would do that all levelly, with an air of professionalism, and say it all so *reasonably* that Emma's grandson would see that he should pick up the phone and call his grandmother right away.

But now . . . How was this possible? Something tightened in her throat—because Lily would have *loved* this.

If this isn't fate, Holly, I don't know what is.

They were imagined words, of course, but Holly could hear her sister's voice, could imagine her clapping her hands, beaming delightedly. Nudging Holly right now, to *talk to him*.

He looked the same as she'd imagined him, whenever she'd brought out the Mirabelle Landor card to look at it. Curly dark hair to go with his dark eyes, eyes that were currently looking at her in a way that made her face heat. A jawline that was an artist's dream, covered in a light layer of stubble, and an ever so slightly crooked nose that offset the whole thing perfectly. He smelled the same, too—that woody scent which reminded her of somewhere deep in the countryside, rather than a sleek London office surrounded by city types. Though here he was, in a posh skyscraper office, wearing a long, sensible black coat—and hadn't he been wearing a suit and carrying a briefcase last time? Most definitely a city type.

"What are you doing here?" he asked—but his words weren't accusing; they were more said in wonder.

"I . . ." But again, no words would come out. *Think, Holly.* She should ask if there was somewhere they could talk. Sit him down, redress the balance. Remind herself that she didn't *know* him. Maybe he wasn't even Emma's grandson—maybe there were multiple Jacks working here, in a big office like this. But even as she had the thought, she knew he was Emma's Jack.

"Ah, Hellie?" The receptionist, wearing a black-and-red spotted tie over a black T-shirt—quirky, and more interesting than what most office workers wore—was hovering on the other side of the desk.

"Holly," Jack corrected.

It was stupid—*stupid*—for her heart to jump like this at the fact he'd remembered her name. She'd remembered his, hadn't she? It didn't mean anything.

"Right," the receptionist said. "Did you still want me to . . . ?"

"No," she said quickly. She'd asked him to look up a Jack, claimed she was here on behalf of her new jewelry company and wanted to have a talk about some "consultancy." It had sounded like a lie even to her, but the receptionist had gone along with it just fine. "No, that's OK, thanks." She moved away from the reception desk, stumbling over her handbag as she did so and flailing her arms to catch herself. Because of course, now was a great time to fall flat on her face.

Jack bent down, picked the handbag up, and handed it to her.

She took it with as much dignity as she could muster. "Thanks."

"Snazzy," he said, indicating the bag.

"Yeah." Her lucky charity-shop crocodile-print bag. Although she wasn't sure if this was good luck or bad. She shoved at her hair. She should have brushed it, for God's sake. She dropped her hands to her sides awkwardly.

There was a man looking at them from over Jack's shoulder, in a slim-fitting suit, with neatly cropped brown hair and a clean-shaven jaw.

Jack saw her looking, and gestured toward the man, who came up to join them. "This is Ed."

Holly squashed down a bubble of laughter that *had* to be coming from nerves. "Right. Hi."

"And this is Holly." Jack's gaze scanned her face again. Then, without warning, he burst out laughing. And that was it—enough to set her off so that she collapsed into giggles too, not particularly caring that it was earning them a few curious looks—because really, the *chances* of this.

Ed glanced back and forth between them with raised eyebrows. "I often pride myself on my sense of humor, but I have to admit I'm missing the joke this time."

Jack cleared his throat. "Sorry."

Holly straightened, pressed her lips together. "Yes, sorry. It's just . . ." She trailed off, gesturing at Jack, and had to stop herself from collapsing into laughter all over again. Seriously, what was *wrong* with her?

"I know," Jack said.

"If you leave me in any more suspense I think I'm going to keel over," Ed said.

Jack pulled a hand through his dark hair, ruffling it in a way Holly couldn't help thinking was a little sexy. *Stop it, Holly.*

"Holly and I sort of . . ."

Ed turned a hand in the air to encourage Jack to keep going. "Know each other?"

"I wouldn't say that," Holly said quickly.

"We met," Jack amended.

"Right, we met," Holly agreed. "Met" was better than "knew," for a number of reasons.

"Once," Jack added.

"You met once," Ed repeated, still looking between them as if trying to connect the dots.

Jack sighed. "It's a long story."

Holly cocked her head. "Is it? Because I think that about sums it up."

"Ouch," Jack said, putting on a mock-hurt voice. "What about you knocking into me?"

"Or you scalding my arm?"

"I think that was still you, actually," Jack said mildly. "As was the lack of payment device and the envy over some biscuit."

"A chocolate-and-ginger star."

"Still upset about it, are you?"

Holly shook her head seriously. "I never forget a biscuit."

"Clearly." His eyes hadn't left hers the whole time, and Holly felt her cheeks heating at the intensity there—so much so that she had to look away.

Ed held up a finger. "So, let me get this straight. You met once, and now you're here to see Jack again, Holly? Is that right?" He turned to Jack, his lips quirking with amusement. "So you *do* have friends! Where have you been keeping this one hidden?"

She could *feel* herself flushing—why did she always do that? "No, I . . ."

A slight frown creased Jack's forehead. "Yes, what exactly *are* you doing here? Not to be rude or anything," he added quickly.

She hesitated. "I came to find someone." And, apparently, was not quick enough on her feet to deal with the unexpected hitch.

Jack smiled. "And instead you found me."

She nodded slowly. She supposed both were true—she *had* come to find someone and she *had* found him.

In her handbag, Holly's phone buzzed, and she drew it out, thankful for the distraction. A WhatsApp from Abi.

How's it going? I still say this is a terrible idea and you should talk to Emma about it first, so if you get this before you find the elusive grandson then consider yourself warned. If not, then I hope it's all going swimmingly. Either way, I need you back in an

```
hour, stat. No one is staying in their
assigned room and it's a total disaster and
I'm considering sending up the security guards
to scare them.
```

Oh God. Abi was going to have a *field day* when Holly told her about this. Though come to think of it, she didn't think she'd ever told Abi about the man in the café that day—because it would have meant recapping the accident in more detail than she was willing to. Besides, it hadn't felt important to mention him— why bother telling Abi about a man she'd spent five minutes with and was never going to see again? Now, that felt like an oversight.

"Err, I don't mean to hurry this reunion along," Ed said, "but do you still want to get lunch, Jack? Or I can grab something for you if you want to, ah, catch up?"

Jack looked at Holly. "You could come?"

"Come where?"

"To lunch?"

Lunch? He was inviting her to lunch, now?

"I mean, we've only got about thirty minutes, but you could come. You wouldn't mind, would you, Ed?"

"Fine with me," Ed said easily. "You can both fill me in on your one and only previous meeting. I love a story about chocolate biscuits—you can never go wrong. And any friend of Jack's is a friend of mine and all that."

Holly laughed, the sound a little high pitched. "I can't, I—"

"Oh right, you're here to meet someone," Jack said. "Who is it? Maybe we can help?"

What a complete fuck-up. "No, I . . ." She swallowed. "Actually this is totally embarrassing, but I think I'm in the wrong office. This part of London always confuses me. I was actually looking for, umm . . ." *Think.* What was the name of a company?

Any company will do, Holly.

Both Ed and Jack were looking at her expectantly. "Cecelia Appleby," she blurted out. She'd gone to school with a Cecelia Appleby, and it was the first thing to come to mind.

Jack frowned. "Don't think I know her, sorry."

"No," Holly said quickly. "I think I got confused about where she works." And now, she looked like a total idiot. Great.

"So . . . does that mean you *are* coming to lunch?" Ed asked.

Holly bit her lip. "Sorry, I can't. I'm on this school trip and I—"

"School trip?" Jack asked, his eyebrows shooting up.

"I'm a teacher," she explained. "And we—"

"A teacher?"

Ed chuckled quietly. "Not very with it today, are you, mate?" He glanced between them again. "Did that not come up the first time you met?"

"No, well, we had other more important things to talk about," Holly said, putting on a lofty air.

Ed nodded seriously. "Like biscuits?"

"Well, exactly," Holly said, with a little incline of her head.

"I thought you were an artist?" Jack asked.

She couldn't believe he remembered. She wanted to feel warm with that, but instead something hard lodged itself in her throat. She forced herself to keep smiling, an alternate version of Dory's theme song from *Finding Nemo* popping up into her head. *Just keep smiling, just keep smiling.* "Not anymore. I teach art, though." She glanced down at her phone. "And I've got to get back, apparently the students are causing chaos at the hotel. We're taking them to see a play this evening, but until then they are running wild."

"And after?" Jack said.

"After what?"

"After the play. What are you doing after the play?"

"Ah, hanging out at the hotel, I guess."

"You're not on teacher duty, whatever that entails?"

"Well, teacher duty is sort of split, so—"

"Good—meet me for a drink then, after you're done."

Holly stared at him, unable to keep up. She noticed Ed looking at Jack too, though he smoothed out the slightly incredulous look when Holly glanced at him. "Ah . . ." she began.

"Just a drink." He schooled his face into a mask of sincerity. "For old time's sake."

Despite herself, Holly laughed, though stopped when it sounded *just* a touch too hysterical. "Fine, yeah, OK." She needed to see him again anyway, didn't she? Maybe it would be easier, to bring the whole thing up over drinks. Plus, it gave her a little time to figure out a new, more appropriate way to deliver the information.

Jack's face brightened. "OK?"

"Don't act so surprised, mate," Ed stage-muttered. "She'll think you're out of practice at this."

Holly forced herself to keep her face straight. "Yes, OK."

"Brilliant. Where's your school play?"

Holly huffed out a laugh. "It's not a school play, it's a play we're taking the students to. But it's in Hackney."

"Hackney? Weird but we can work with that. Meet me at the Nightjar. It's in Shoreditch, so not too far."

"I'll find it," Holly promised. She hadn't heard of it before, but then again, Shoreditch hadn't really been her area when she'd lived in London.

He smiled—not a full smile, the one that Holly was sure would transform his face, but something soft and kind. "Good. Well, see you then." He jerked his head at Ed to indicate they should get going, but Ed stood still. "What?" Jack asked.

"Aren't you guys forgetting something?" Holly and Jack both frowned at Ed, whose lips twitched. "Don't you want to set a time or something?"

Jack slapped himself on the forehead. "Time!" He dropped his hand, looked at Holly in question. "Your call?"

She did a quick calculation in her head as she worked out the timings of it all. "Make it nine?" It was impressive, really, how casual she sounded. Look at her, taking all this in her stride, cool as you like.

"Nine. Perfect." He glanced at Ed. "Anything else I'm forgetting?"

Ed clapped Jack on the back. "Nah, reckon you're good. And clearly a *total* player, too." He winked at Holly. "Nice to meet you, Holly. Maybe see you around."

"Yeah. Yeah, maybe." Holly stood there, allowing the two of them to get ahead of her as they left the office, so that she didn't look like some kind of stalker as she followed. She heard Ed speaking to Jack as they stepped out through the revolving glass doors: "What the hell was *that* about?"

Well, quite, Holly thought, as she blew out a breath through her nose. It felt like her head was spinning. A drink with him. Was it supposed to be a date? A nervous fluttering started up in her stomach. Which was silly, it was just a drink with a man, for God's sake. A man who happened to be Emma's grandson. Who she had to convince to reunite with her after some kind of family feud that she still hadn't got to the details of.

Which was fine, she told herself firmly. She'd figure it out.

She started toward the glass door herself, felt her phone buzz in her hand again, and looked down to see another message. Think of the devil . . .

Check out the Maureen Paley Gallery in Bethnal
Green if you have the chance. And I can
probably get you an appointment at Kate
MacGarry, which is well worth a visit. How
long did you say you were there again? And are

you still coming for lunch on your half term?
Pam keeps asking me about it and she's driving
me mad.

Holly felt a squirming in her gut. Emma had said she'd send
over a couple of art gallery recommendations—conveniently ignoring the fact that Holly had lived in London for many years
and had, in fact, *studied* art in London, because, as Emma put it,
*You've been out of the game awhile, my girl, and you have to
have an ear to the ground for these things.* So yes, Holly had told
Emma—and they had been staying in touch on a regular basis,
though which one of them that surprised more, Holly couldn't
say. So in one of their conversations, Holly had let slip that she
was heading to London for a few days as a chaperone on Abi's
school trip.

She hadn't told Emma about the other task she was planning
to accomplish while she was here, however. Partly because she
wasn't sure if she *would* track Emma's grandson down—it had
only been an idea, that was all. But mainly because she knew
Emma would disapprove. In her head, though, Emma would get
over that and be thrilled once said grandson picked up the phone
and a tearful reconciliation followed. Because Holly knew that,
whatever Emma said, she would love nothing more than to connect with him again.

And that could still happen, Holly told herself firmly. Jack
being the man from the café changed nothing. Nothing at all.

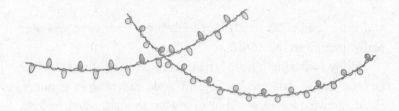

Chapter Eleven

She was late. *She* was the one who had named the time, and she was late. Which was wholly predictable, given her awful time-keeping skills, but still.

What if he'd left already? What if he'd never shown?

Holding her phone in front of her she hurried down the pavement, her leopard-print heels clacking noisily even over the early drunken shouts of Shoreditch. When she reached the bar, she shoved the phone back into her handbag and fluffed up her hair before stepping inside and being greeted by an onslaught of welcoming heat, the hum of chatter, and jazz-style piano music. She let out a slow breath and tried to ignore the way her stomach would *not* stop churning with nerves as she did a quick scan of the bar. It was too dark in here: Trendy mood lighting was all very well and good until you wanted to find someone. Candles flickered on each of the tables, occasionally catching one of the low-hanging glass lampshades and sending off a glint around the room. There were leather-backed sofas crammed full of people, and little square red stools that looked cool but were probably really uncomfortable to sit on.

Holly walked in a little farther, trying not to stumble in her favorite heels—favorite because of style rather than comfort. She'd agonized for a solid hour over what to wear, which had left her with less time than she would have liked for hair and makeup. She had at least managed to tame her hair a bit after washing it, though she drew the line at borrowing Abi's straighteners. Still, she was pretty sure she looked OK, having settled on a dark-green off-the-shoulder top with skinny black jeans.

She headed past the gorgeous wooden bar, with high stools that were currently all occupied, clocked the piano in the corner, a real live pianist playing with deft fingers. And there, a few tables back, in one of the leather booths that ran along one whole length of the wall, was Jack. He waved her over. God, he was attractive, wasn't he? Why did he have to be so damned attractive? And yes, this place, with the candles and the moody lighting and the music, it would probably make *anyone* look attractive, but there was no denying that this man was sexy, from the stubbled jaw, to the broad, muscled back, to the slightly rumpled hair he was currently running a hand through.

Focus, Holly. She worked up a nice, polite, *appropriate* smile, as she walked over to him. She thought of Abi's advice, which she'd delivered in hushed tones under the chatter of the students as they waited for the bus to take them back to the hotel.

Try not to blurt it all out without thinking, won't you? But also don't leave it too long, otherwise it will get awkward. And Holly, have you really thought about what you're—

Abi! It's too late now, so words of encouragement, please, rather than concern.

Sorry. Sorry. Well in that case, keep it professional. Aim to tell him approximately halfway through the first drink, after a brief exchange of small talk, and do not let things get too per-

sonal before you do. Make it clear that Emma does not know you're here, but that you just thought it was worth a conversation with him, and do not, whatever you do, put any sort of pressure on him.

Super-specific, thank you.

It's always better when you have a set plan.

Yeah, and you know me and planning . . .

She pushed the conversation with Abi out of her mind as she reached Jack. He stood, leaned over the table to kiss her cheek. Formally, she thought, as a posh acquaintance might do. Not that she had many of those, but she imagined it was the type of thing they did.

"I got here early—thought I should nab us a seat," Jack said with a wave at the table. And sure enough, almost every other seat in this place seemed to be taken.

"I'm sorry I'm late," Holly said quickly. "I got held up at the theater." Only partly a lie—but he could hardly blame her if she referenced her teacher duties as the cause of lateness rather than her poor planning.

"No worries." He was still in a suit, she noticed, with his shirt unbuttoned slightly, jacket slung on the red stool. "Shall I get you a drink?"

"I'll get them," Holly said, waving him down when he tried to insist. She could feel Jack's eyes on her as she headed for the bar, making her feel that she should have gone with comfort over style with regard to the shoes. Why couldn't she be like Abi, who had mastered that somehow *efficient* way to walk in heels? She ordered a pint for him and a cocktail for herself—asking for the strongest one they had, paying no attention to what was in it. She figured that it wouldn't hurt to have her tongue a bit looser and her nerves a bit steadier, with what she was planning to say.

Jack had moved to the red stool by the time she got back, and he indicated for her to take the comfier-looking sofa, in between two women at neighboring tables. Holly sat, took a sip of her drink. Jack mirrored her. They both put their drinks down, looked at each other.

"So," Jack said.

"So," Holly agreed. Then she laughed a little, still not quite over the strangeness of meeting him again.

He smiled across the table at her. Seeming to read her thoughts, he shook his head and said, "I still can't believe you're here. That you're real." Then he grimaced. "Sorry, that sounds stupid. I mean—"

"No, I know what you mean." And he only knew the half of it.

He sat back in his chair. "So how was the play?"

Holly took a sip of her drink. "Oh, it was great. Well, *I* thought it was great, but some of the students didn't agree. There may have been one or two comments on how they could have done a better job than the actors onstage."

Jack laughed softly. "And could they have?"

"No idea, really. You'd have to ask my friend Abi—she's their drama teacher. But to hazard a guess, I'd say no. Especially as they're all sixteen . . ."

"Ah, the confidence of a sixteen-year-old."

"I remember it well." She'd thought she'd had it all sorted, back then. Yes, there had been the arguments with her parents, the impossible hormones, the stress over whether her crush at the time would text her back, but really, she'd been full of hope and a certainty that things would just work out. She knew she wanted to become an artist, and she felt sure she'd get there, that it was only a matter of time.

Jack gave a rueful head shake. "I don't. My teenage years were not kind to me."

Holly raised her eyebrows. "I doubt that very much."

"It's true. I was the only one not with a girlfriend at sixteen—

or, at least, the only one not *bragging* about having a girlfriend, real or fake."

Holly laughed. "And you didn't consider making up an imaginary girlfriend, just to fit in?"

"Oh, I considered it. I had her name picked out and everything. Francesca," he added, when Holly gave him a questioning look.

"Francesca, hey?"

"Yeah, and she was a looker, I'll tell you."

"I'm sure."

There was a brief pause, in which Holly had time to remember why she was here—not to talk about imaginary girlfriends, but to talk about *Emma*. She took a gulp of her drink, felt Jack watching her.

He cleared his throat, and the sound was a little strained— like he'd picked up something in her body language. "Ah, so, if you could hop on a plane right now where would you go?"

Holly raised her eyebrows at the abrupt change of subject.

"What?" Jack asked innocently. "OK, fine, I may have googled 'good conversation starters' before you came in."

Holly couldn't help laughing again. "Always do that before a date, do you?" Damn it, she'd said date. She didn't *mean* date—it had slipped out.

He didn't seem to notice, though. "Well, it's been a while," he muttered, barely audible—so much so that she wasn't sure she was meant to have heard. He picked up his beer, gestured with it. "Plane, go."

"Umm . . . São Paulo, probably."

"Curveball, love it."

Holly cocked her head, felt her hair spill to the side. "Why, what did you expect?"

"To be honest, I'm still trying to figure out what to expect from you."

"I suppose that's reasonable, given you've known me for approximately ten minutes in total."

"Or three and a bit years, depending on how you look at it." It was a jokey tone, but there was something deeper in his eyes, something that sent licks of flame across her skin. And those eyes: They looked a darker brown than usual in the dim lighting, perhaps because his face was half in shadow, the other half bathed in flickering candlelight. She could see it in that moment—the sculpture. Two sides of the same man. She didn't know him nearly well enough to be making the assumption that there *was* that light and shade in him, but that wasn't really the point. She could imagine it, the way the sculpture would come to life, the story it would tell. And resting on the table, her fingertips pulsed, like they wished there were clay here, now.

"So why São Paulo?" Jack's voice, the normality of it, made her jolt.

"Ah." She forced herself back to the bar—to the real man here, and not the clay version she was conjuring up in her mind. "There's a good art scene."

"Really?"

"Yeah. Most people think of Paris or New York for art—or London, I guess—but the Museu de Arte Moderna is supposed to be amazing, and it has a garden where there are these cool sculptures and—Sorry," she said, noticing the way he was looking at her. "Talking too quickly." And she'd been gesturing emphatically, hands going every which way. She took a sip of her cocktail to give them something to do—sweet, with enough sour taste that it wasn't overpowering.

"No, you're not," Jack said. "It's just . . . I remember you like this—at the café." His voice. Had she thought it was light? Because it wasn't. It was gorgeous, all smooth and sensual, liquid dark chocolate. "When you were talking about the painting, and then looking at the cards. You had the same kind of . . . expression, and it took me back for a moment." Her face heated at his words, and she hoped it was dark enough that he didn't notice. He picked up his drink, made a face. "Sorry. That sounds bizarre." Before she could contradict him, he spoke again. "You're not an artist anymore, then?"

Holly felt the flinch run through her, even if she didn't let it show on the outside. *I never was.* But she didn't want to sound sorry for herself, so instead she said, "Well, I teach it."

"What's that like?"

"It's . . ." Holly chewed her lip as she thought about it. "Difficult, sometimes. I teach teenagers, so there are obviously ups and downs in terms of how they're feeling, and that can have a real impact. Plus, there is a lot of work to do for not much money, but, well, it's also pretty cool. It's a specialist arts school, which is amazing because the kids all want to be there—and some of them are so talented. And you get to come up with ways to challenge them—like, I set this task where they had to build a sculpture out of the materials I provided them at the front of the class, or where they had to do a real-life drawing but only in green, which got them thinking about all the different shades of green." She gave a small, self-deprecating shrug when she realized she was babbling. "I really like green."

"Why wouldn't you? Green is great." Only then did she remember that she was currently wearing green. And that her eyes were also green—eyes he was currently looking at. She decided the safest thing to do was to take another sip of her drink.

"Sounds like you kind of love it," Jack said. "Teaching, that is, as well as green."

"I guess I do," she said slowly.

"You guess?"

"I don't know." She reached up to toy with the hoop earring. "I sort of fell into it, I suppose. And it's not what I imagined myself doing." It had felt like a stopgap at first, something she needed to do to have an income while she figured out her next step. But somewhere along the line, she'd stopped thinking of next steps. Stopped thinking of anything too far into the future, come to think of it.

"Doesn't mean you can't love it."

"No. No, I suppose that's true." And she was lucky, wasn't she, to have that? Despite that little niggle, the one that came out to play whenever she stared at the clay for too long, or caught sight of something that really inspired her, when she wished she could be *doing* as well as teaching.

"What about you?" Holly asked, setting her near-empty glass down on the table. "Do you love what you do? Management consultancy, right?"

Jack made a face. "That's not fair—I gave you an easy in with the plane."

Holly grinned. "OK. Umm . . . Would you rather sit in front of a fountain or a fire?"

Jack blinked at her. "That is so random."

"Well, some of us don't check out the best openers on Google beforehand." She flicked her hair back overdramatically, saw him follow the movement.

"Very true. I'd say fire," he said firmly. "Definitely fire." It wasn't just her face that heated this time—she felt the warmth spread through her whole body. Jack gestured to her empty glass. "Another drink?"

"Yes, please."

"What was it?"

"No idea. Anything is fine."

"Whatever?" He frowned at that, like the concept baffled him.

"A cocktail. Or wine. Anything," she repeated, waving her hand.

"Right." He took the two empty glasses with him, which Holly couldn't help but find endearing. She didn't realize she was watching him—and the impressive muscles in his back—all the way to the bar until someone, a skinny guy in his early twenties maybe, wearing tweed trousers came over to her.

"Anyone sitting here?" He indicated the stool Jack had just vacated.

Holly looked up at him. He had one of those tiny little beards that she'd never fully understood the point of. "Yes."

But he'd already picked up the stool, started dragging it back to his table.

"Hey!" He didn't turn back, so Holly got to her feet, calling after him. "Hey, I said—" But Jack was back now, and the sight of him cut her off midsentence.

He raised his eyebrows. "Who are you shaking your fist at?"

"I'm not . . ." She looked down to where she was gesturing—with a closed palm. She immediately dropped her hand. "They stole your seat," she said by way of explanation.

"Yeah, that happens," Jack said with a grin. "Room for me on your side?"

Holly did a quick assessment of the sofa—there was probably enough space for the both of them. "Ah, sure, yes."

He handed her a cocktail—a red one this time—and Holly noticed he had the same. She looked from the drink to him. "She thought I said two," he explained, "and I didn't want to correct her."

He came around to her side of the table and sat down next to her. This close, she could smell that aftershave or whatever it was he wore that reminded her of the outdoors—different types of wood, all mixed together. His leg briefly pressed against hers, and even though she shifted away to give them both space, she felt the warmth linger on her skin. They reached for their cocktails at the same time, their arms bumping into each other. Holly snatched back her cocktail so quickly that she sent some of the liquid sloshing over the rim.

She cleared her throat. "So, there's something I've been meaning to ask you."

One corner of Jack's mouth crooked up as he looked at her, shifting so he was facing her. "Really? Well, consider me intrigued."

Holly took a breath. "Why were you in that café three years ago?"

"What do you mean?" But his tone was too careful—he knew exactly what she meant.

"Well, you live in London."

"So do you."

"Not anymore. But my point is, I was stopping off, on the way to a family holiday." She swallowed down the dull throb of pain that hit, using her drink to cover it up. "But why were *you* there?"

"I was . . ." He frowned down at his drink, as if deciding whether to tell her something, twirling the glass round and round in his fingers. And it didn't feel right, because she was probing into a life she already knew so much about. She almost reached out to lay a hand on his, to stop him, but he started speaking again before she could. "My dad . . . It was the anniversary of his death. The fifteen-year anniversary, to be precise." He kept looking at the cocktail, rather than her. And I was . . . Well, I was holding a kind of memorial. To celebrate his life, I guess, and to remember him— because it's something you do less of as time passes."

Holly couldn't help the little spasm in her gut. He was talking about Richard—Emma's son. But Emma hadn't mentioned anything about seeing Jack three years ago, she had made it sound like she hadn't seen him since he was a kid. So maybe she hadn't been invited? But to not invite Richard's mother . . . What could be so bad, to make Jack do that?

"What happened, with your dad?" Holly asked quietly. It's what she *would* say, if she didn't already know—but she also wanted to hear it from him, to see if he mentioned Emma at all. Was hoping it would be somehow easier to say what she needed to, if he offered her a way in.

"He . . . There was a car crash. When I was ten. He didn't make it."

"I'm sorry," she said. She shouldn't be doing this, shouldn't be forcing him to talk about it this way. She couldn't help it—she reached out, laid a hand on his. He looked up, met her gaze. And her hand stayed there, resting on his.

He shrugged, smiled sadly. "It was a long time ago."

"I'm not sure that kind of thing ever goes away," Holly said gently. She certainly didn't think it would for her—and she hadn't actually *lost* Lily. At least her sister was still alive, still healthy. Happy? She was never sure about that. She always thought she saw a tightness in her smile, whenever she got up the courage to check her out on Facebook—Lily hadn't removed her as a friend, though Holly wasn't sure why, when she'd cut her out of her life so completely in every other way. And maybe Lily would never totally get over the life she'd lost that day, either.

"Yeah," Jack said with another shrug. "Maybe." He was looking at her like he was reading something more into what she was saying. She knew what he was going to ask—but she didn't want to tell him. She didn't want to talk about her own crash. She drew her hand back, slowly, as he started to speak again. "You say that like you—"

But at that point, someone from the table next to them slid out of the booth, bumping into her so that she was pushed toward Jack. So that the small gap that had separated them was closed, his thigh pressing firmly against hers. Her whole body went taut, suddenly very aware of the clothing separating their legs.

"Ah, sorry," she said, tilting her head up to look at him. He was so close now—she could count his eyelashes, if she'd wanted to. And that stubble—she wondered how it would feel if he— *Stop it, Holly*. It was the cocktails. It was the bloody cocktails, making her lightheaded and infatuated. She looked away from his gaze and toward the piano, needing a direction to aim for.

"No worries, bound to happen on a Friday night," Jack said easily. So, clearly he wasn't as aware of their legs pressed together as she was.

"Right," Holly agreed. "Right," she said again, reminded of the fact that it was Friday and she had to be up in the morning to help Abi get the students on the bus and see them off like a responsible adult. "And actually, on that note, I'd better go." But she made the mistake of looking at him again, and he caught her gaze with his own. She swallowed, pulling her bottom lip between her teeth. She saw him follow the movement with his gaze.

"OK," he said.

She blinked. "OK?"

"OK, you need to go?"

"Right. Right!" She stood up with such force, determined not to sit there like an idiot for one moment longer, and lost her balance. Swearing slightly, she pressed a palm into his shoulder to catch herself, then took her hand back quickly. His hand just missed hers as he reached to steady her, their fingertips grazing.

"Sorry," she said. She wasn't usually this apologetic, was she?

He only chuckled as he got to his feet.

They both slung their coats on and Jack handed Holly her handbag, then placed a hand on the small of her back to guide her out of the bar. OK, she needed him to stop touching her. Or touch her a hell of a lot more—she couldn't quite work out which.

The latter, she definitely wanted it to be the latter.

Outside, the cold, biting air was a relief, cooling her insides and offering some sanity from all the sexy lighting and seductive music. Their breath misted out in front of them under the streetlamps, and where she'd felt overheated a minute ago, her hands immediately felt freezing as she shoved them in her pockets. *Surely* it couldn't stay this cold for long—wasn't it supposed to be spring? Though in all honesty, she was never quite sure where the line between winter and spring actually was.

Jack and Holly turned to face each other at the same time. Now. She should tell him now and get it over with, come what may.

"If I give you my number again, will you call me this time?" Jack teased her lightly, with a smile in the corner of his mouth.

"I lost it," Holly said quietly. "The cup with your number."

"Yeah, yeah."

"I did!"

"That's what they all say."

"All the girls you chat up in coffee shops?"

"Who says I was chatting you up? You must have misinterpreted."

She laughed, hit him lightly on the arm. So quickly she barely noticed him move, he caught her hand, his thumb grazing the inside of her wrist, where her pulse responded. "Will you?"

"Will I what?" she repeated dumbly.

"Call me."

"Oh. Well, yes, I suppose, but I . . . Jack, I live in Windsor." *I live in Windsor—and I'm friends with your grandmother. You know, the one you won't talk to?*

He frowned, still not letting go of her hand. "How long are you in London for?"

"Until Monday." It was half term next week, so she was sending the kids off in the morning with Abi and staying for a long weekend, but a few days in London was more than enough for her. Especially as she was aware of how close she was to her family. Her parents lived on the outskirts of London, and Lily . . . Well, she was pretty sure Lily still lived in west London somewhere.

"Tomorrow, then?"

"Tomorrow?"

"Jesus, Holly, you don't half make it hard," he said, his face lighting up with laughter.

She let out a huff of laughter to match his. "Sorry, I'm not usually this dense." But it was becoming hard to concentrate, because all her awareness was zoning in on his thumb, resting lightly against her wrist, and that forest scent of his was wrapping around her, and what she'd really have liked to do was step into him, tilt her head up and . . . She took a breath, stepped safely out of reach. He let her go, dropping her hand. "I'm doing a kind of art gallery tour tomorrow—going to different ones in the morning and afternoon." *Art galleries that your grandmother—who has cancer, by the way—recommended.*

"Ah, right. A good way to spend a weekend, I reckon."

"You could come?" The words were out before she could think better of them. "Unless it'd be too boring," she added quickly.

Something that could have been relief flashed across Jack's face, though his tone was still light, easy. "Nah, I like art. I'm not an expert or anything, but it was kind of part of my childhood in a way. Enough that I think a day trip to a few galleries sounds grand."

"Who got you interested? Your parents?" *Come on,* she thought to herself. *Say her name.* Because she knew who must have given him an art education as a child—whether he'd liked it or not.

"No." The hesitation was so brief, she might not have noticed it, had she not been looking for it. "No, my grandmother—she was big into art."

Say it, Holly. Tell him. Ask him what happened between them. She was holding her breath, her heart picking up speed as she tried to work out a way to broach the topic. But before she could get any words out, he smiled at her.

"So, tomorrow?" And just like that, the moment was gone.

She let out her breath on a whoosh. "Shall I meet you there?"

She got out her phone, brought up a new contact—nearly adding his surname before she realized she shouldn't yet know it—and handed it to him.

"I can't lose it this way." She contemplated that as he typed. "Well, knowing me, I *could,* because I could lose the phone or something—but I'll do my best not to." Her eyes met his as they flicked up from her phone, his crinkling at the corners from his smile.

"Somehow I believe that. So how about you put yours in mine too—because I will definitely not lose my phone." He said the last bit so seriously, like he'd never misplaced anything in his entire life.

Numbers safely exchanged, Holly kept her phone out and opened Uber.

"Will you be OK getting back?" Jack asked.

"Yeah, I'm just getting a taxi."

He insisted on waiting until the taxi arrived, and Holly had never been so aware of another person next to her, every movement he made. When the cab finally arrived, she turned to him. "See you tomorrow?"

He nodded. "Until then." He leaned in to kiss her cheek again, the way he'd done when she'd arrived. Only this time he lingered, and though his lips were barely a whisper on her skin, the touch of them sent a shiver down the back of her spine.

She let out a slow breath as she got into the car. It was a good thing, she decided, that they were heading in opposite directions this evening—it stopped her from doing anything impulsive. This way, she could get back to the hotel, where Abi would no doubt be waiting up, and give herself a damn good talking to before she saw Jack tomorrow.

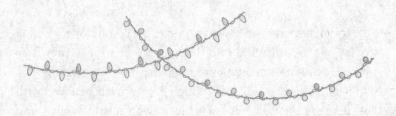

Chapter Twelve

Holly stood by the window of the hotel room, looking out at the London skyline. It was a relatively low-budget hotel, so the room itself was rather plain and boring, but it had a good view. She could see the London Eye from here, along with Big Ben, if she looked out to the left far enough. The sky had brightened today, and against the backdrop of the blue, it was really quite stunning. She didn't usually miss London but today it gave her a pang, looking at it, at what she'd left behind.

She had her phone pressed to her ear and was listening to Emma as she reeled off the names of artists she'd "discovered" in the gallery she was sending Holly to. She'd even managed to get artwork from them for the Impression Sunrise Café, she said, her voice taking on a rather grand air. "Before they got too important for the likes of Devon, that is."

Meanwhile, Abi was sitting on one of the twin beds behind Holly, propped against the pillows in her sensible red-and-white pajamas as she talked to James, her usually calm teacher voice becoming increasingly higher pitched.

"And make sure you say my name at the second one," Emma was saying, "because I've told them to expect you, so they'll be sure to let you in—sometimes they can be snobby about that."

"Right," Holly said, even though her stomach spasmed with that. Because she was going with Jack, who would surely think there was something strange, if Holly mentioned his grandmother's name.

She was going to have to tell him. Today.

"Holly?"

"Yes, sorry. Yes, I'm here."

Emma huffed out a breath, sounding annoyed. But Holly was learning not to take that too seriously—that was sort of Emma's resting sound, and Holly was pretty sure she didn't even realize she was doing it sometimes. "Well, anyway, you'll have a great time—is anyone going with you? That friend of yours?"

"Abi," Holly said automatically, glancing over her shoulder to where Abi was now hugging a pillow to her, her mouth a tight line as she listened to whatever James had to say. Uh-oh. "And no. Abi's not going with me." Not quite a lie, but not the whole truth, either.

"Well, good. Art is best appreciated alone, I always find."

"Totally," Holly said. *Oh, but actually, I won't be alone— I tracked down your long-lost grandson and have been fantasizing about making out with him so I invited him to the art gallery with me. Hope that's all good with you?* Jesus, this whole thing was a terrible idea. She never should have got involved in the first bloody place. Though, really, she still thought it was ridiculous that Emma wouldn't pick up the phone to call Jack. Well, the theoretical phone. Emma didn't actually have his number, but she could have *tried*. She knew where he worked, after all, she had to have been the one that told Pam the name of his company in the first place.

Now Holly had his number, but she couldn't very well hand it over without an explanation, could she? Besides, she didn't want Emma to get mad at her—she didn't want a repeat of Christmas, of the door being slammed in her face. And it would feel worse if Emma did that now. Because Holly had got to know Emma, because she *liked* her, and wanted Emma to like her too. Because she felt she could talk to Emma, in a way that she'd lost with her parents and her sister, since the crash.

She gave herself a little mental shake. She had to explain things calmly to Jack, that was all. He seemed like a reasonable guy and surely anything Emma might have done couldn't have been *that* bad.

"When's your doctor's appointment?" Holly asked.

"Hmm?"

"You heard me." Emma often did this when it came to talking about her health—she liked to pretend it wasn't happening, as far as Holly could tell, and often went temporarily deaf. But pretending it wasn't happening wouldn't help anything, would it? "They were going to talk to you about chemo, weren't they? Surely they need to get started on that?"

"Oh, they're across it, don't worry."

"But I *am*—"

"Holly. I can handle my doctor, thank you very much, I've been doing so for years without your help."

"But this isn't a head cold, Emma."

"I'm well aware of what it is, my girl," Emma said, her voice low, almost soft—or as soft as Emma got, anyway. The sound made Holly swallow. She didn't like it—the admission of vulnerability from a woman who normally seemed so implacable.

"So surely you need to start the chemo, need to—"

"I am still talking through the various options," Emma said, and though she didn't raise her voice, it cut through Holly's protests. She would have made a good teacher, Holly thought dryly. "Besides, I'm fine, aren't I? A bit tired, and the cramps aren't fun, but nothing worse than when I used to have my periods."

"Hmm." Holly was learning she had to pick her moments with Emma, and this was not one of them.

"Anyway, you'll see me next week, so don't wear yourself out now. Pam is making us a 'curry feast,' apparently."

"You mean her husband is."

"Well, she's decided on the recipes—doesn't that count?"

Abi's voice, higher still, rose from the single bed. "What do you mean I don't care about the flowers? Of course I care about the bloody flowers, but you didn't like the ones I picked, so I just said . . . Well, it's *my* wedding and . . . Our. That's what I said, our . . . Oh for God's sake, James, stop being difficult."

"I'd better go, Emma."

"So I can hear."

"Thanks for the recommendations."

"Remember to—"

"I'll remember," Holly said firmly.

"Good. Well, have fun then. Try not to pretend you don't love it—if you're alone then there's no one there to pretend to."

Holly decided to ignore that and hung up, knowing Emma would appreciate the drama and probably have a little chuckle in her kitchen, where Holly could imagine her sitting and reading a two-day-old newspaper now.

Abi had hung up too and was sitting with her arms wrapped around her knees, resting her head there and staring at nothing. Her chestnut curls—curls which, coupled with her heart-shaped face, made her look a little doll-like, hiding the no-nonsense exterior beneath—hung sort of limply.

Holly crossed the room and sat down on the end of the bed. "Abs?" she asked tentatively. "Are you OK?"

"He thinks I don't care about the flowers," she said, still staring into space.

"Oh."

"But I do." And then, to Holly's alarm, a tear fell down Abi's cheek.

"Hey," Holly said, climbing onto the bed and crawling toward Abi. She didn't usually cry. Holly had always admired how together her friend was, and that stability had been something she'd leaned on over the last three years. It made Abi look even more vulnerable now, with her lip quivering, because Holly just wasn't used to seeing it. "What's happened?" she asked gently.

"Nothing," Abi said, swiping at the tear.

"Abi?"

"He's a dog person," Abi blurted out.

"OK . . ." Holly said slowly. Of all the things she could have guessed, this would not have been one of them.

"He's a *dog* person, Holly, and I've always thought of myself as a cat person."

Holly frowned. "But you love dogs."

"And cats," Abi said, her voice rising to near hysterical levels.

"Ah, right." Holly tried to keep her voice soothing, but she couldn't really follow the logic.

"But that's not the point."

"No," Holly agreed, still bewildered.

"The point is, I didn't even *know* he was a dog person until I moved in. How could I not know that? I'm engaged to him and that is a serious thing—something you should know about someone, something that comes up on the first date, for God's sake."

"Well, I wouldn't say—"

"And what if there are all these other things we don't know about each other? What if it turns out he doesn't like wood lice? Because I *love* wood lice, Holly, they are cute and little and I had a pet one called Woody growing up and—"

"Abi. Breathe."

Abi took a shuddering breath. "Breathing."

"This is normal."

"It is?" Abi frowned. "What is, exactly? Woody?"

"No, not Woody, as adorable as I'm sure he was. Though, by the way, I'm pretty sure I saw James rescuing a wood louse from a café once. I remember it because he cut me off midsentence to do so, so I'm pretty sure you're safe there."

An almost-smile flittered across Abi's face. "He cuts me off midsentence to do stuff too, sometimes." Her eyes softened with it, like it was the *cutest* thing and not actually rather annoying.

"Right, well, what I meant was that this is just pre-wedding anxiety or whatever. When Lily was . . ." But she trailed off, because it hurt to think about Lily in the run-up to her wedding: the swings of emotions she was going through, the need for everything to be *perfect,* how she'd given Holly and her best friend from school *very* explicit instructions on what the bachelorette do should look like, how she'd even written Steve's speech for him. Lily had grabbed Holly's hands after the ceremony, squeezed tight. "You know I love you, right?"

Holly had laughed. "Of course."

"Right. It's just, I know I've been a total demon."

"A bridezilla, one might say."

"Only if one were being unoriginal." But Lily had smiled. "I just wanted to say . . . Thank you. It was totally worth it."

Holly had wrapped her arms around her big sister, careful not to put her face, adorned with more makeup than she would have gone for herself, anywhere near the dress. "Yeah. It was. The one and only time I'd say all the fuss *was* worth it, in fact."

Lily tossed her head back dramatically. "You just wait. I'm sure you'll make even more of a fuss than me—and it will be worse with you, because you'll leave everything until the last minute. Your wedding day will be *chaos.*"

"Who says I'll ever meet someone I like enough to get married to, hmm?" And although Holly had said it jokingly, although she brushed it off, playing up to her role as the baby of the family, it was something she was more insecure about than she let on.

Lily had looked at her, like she knew Holly wasn't completely joking. "You're still so young. You have ages."

"You met Steve when you were twenty-one," Holly pointed out.

"Well, you're not me."

"No," Holly agreed—she was nowhere near as sorted as her big sister.

"I mean that in a good way," Lily said quietly, giving Holly's hand a squeeze. "I wish I could be more like you sometimes."

Holly laughed, a little incredulously. No one ever said Lily should be more like her—it was always the other way around. "You do?"

Lily curled an errant curl, done so perfectly by the hairdresser, behind her ear. "Well. Only sometimes. Anyway, I know you'll find someone."

There was a beat before Holly asked, "How?"

Lily smiled. "Because you're too special not to. And because big sisters are always right."

Holly pushed the memory aside, brought her attention back to Abi. "All I'm saying is, you are blowing this out of proportion. You love James?"

"Yes," Abi said without hesitation. What must it feel like, to love someone like that—with absolutely no doubt in your mind? And she gave a sniff before she added, sounding much more like the Abi Holly knew, "You think I'd have said yes if I didn't love him?"

"And he loves you?"

"All signs would point to yes."

"And you want to marry him?"

"Yes." Again, no doubt.

"Well, there you go then," Holly said, giving her friend's arm a little squeeze.

Abi nodded, swallowed, then gave Holly a narrow-eyed look.

"What?" Holly asked defensively.

"I don't like it when you're the sensible one. It feels off-balance." It was probably because she'd just been thinking of Lily that Abi reminded her of her sister in that moment. They had a lot in common, she thought, not for the first time. Both so sorted, both knowing exactly what they wanted from life—today's little blip notwithstanding. They would have liked each other; she was sure of it.

"Come on," Holly said, forcing brightness to her tone. "Let's rally the troops, get them all safely back to parents."

"Yes. So you can get off to your *gallery viewing.*"

"You don't have to make that sound suspicious—it is in no way suspicious!"

"It *wasn't* suspicious, until you came home last night all energetic and . . ." Abi waved a hand in the air. "Floaty."

"Floaty?"

"Yes. Floaty. In a weird, ungraceful way."

"Whatever." Holly prodded Abi in the ribs. "I'm not going to take this from someone who had a pet wood louse growing up."

Abi snorted and got to her feet. "Hol?"

Holly looked at her.

"Thank you."

Holly shrugged. "Always."

"And—"

"I know," Holly interpreted, her voice low. "Be careful."

Abi came up to where Holly was still on the bed, ran a hand down her hair in a friendly gesture. "It's only that it feels a little like you're playing with fire here." She gave Holly a small smile. "And I just don't want you to get burned."

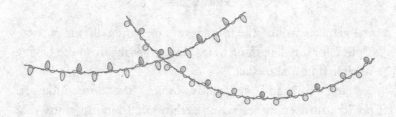

Chapter Thirteen

Holly and Jack walked around the gallery—a bright, open space with paneled wooden floors and white walls—the type of place that was both an artist's dream and nightmare, Holly thought. A dream because there were no distractions for the gallery-goers, the artwork very much front and center stage, and a nightmare because there was nowhere to hide. No dim moody lighting, no corners where shadows could play in your favor; if there were an imperfection somewhere, it would be well and truly on show.

Jack had stopped by an abstract sculpture: different rings entwined out of wire, nearly a meter in height. He was frowning at it like it was a particularly difficult puzzle. "I don't get it."

Holly felt a smile pull at her lips. "You don't necessarily have to get it."

Jack gave her a sidelong look. "Is that what you say to your students?"

"Sometimes." He started walking and she stole a look at him

as he glanced around the room, eyes not resting on one particular piece for any length of time. "Does that mean you're having a terrible time?" she asked.

"No!" His head jerked back to look at her. "Sorry. I like art. I *do*," he insisted at her raised eyebrows. "I kind of think that people who say they *don't* like art are a bit stupid, because there are so many different kinds of art and even, like, a birthday card can be art, right?"

Holly thought of the Mirabelle Landor card, sitting on her bedside table back home. "Right," she agreed with a nod.

They stopped at another piece—clay, this time, a man hunched over, folded in on himself. *Betrayal,* the label read.

"It's just," Jack continued, scratching his chin as he studied the man, "I feel like an idiot sometimes, like I should be seeing some sort of higher meaning when sometimes all I see is"—he glanced back over his shoulder at the wire sculpture—"hoops."

Holly swallowed down the laugh—because the gallery was the kind of place where you had to talk in low tones. "I think everyone feels like that sometimes."

Jack gave her a little smirk. "So wise."

She gave him a friendly shoulder bump. "I'm serious. I *teach* art, and even I'm not sure I 'get it'—whatever the 'it' is—sometimes. I think people who say they do are mostly making it up. Because how can you ever be sure—really *sure*—that you understand exactly what the artist was trying to say?"

Jack grunted in acknowledgment as they moved on, and she took that as a win. "Besides, it's not about understanding everything—it's not even about *liking* everything. Certain pieces will just. . . . call to you, if you're lucky." She tucked her hair behind her ear, unsure whether that sounded daft.

"Did you ever hope to see your art on display, somewhere like this?"

She didn't answer for a long beat. "Yes," she said eventually, allowing the truth of it to slide through her. "But it wasn't meant to be. I'm not an artist—I'm a teacher."

"Can't you be both?"

"Maybe. But I'm not."

Jack raised his eyebrows. "Well, not if you talk like that. If you don't take yourself seriously no one else will either." He winced, just as she opened her mouth to object. "Sorry," he said quickly. "That made me sound like a dick."

"Only a lot."

Jack laughed, though stopped immediately when a couple ahead of them both looked back, their disapproval obvious in their glares. "It's just something we say to clients—you know, take yourself seriously, go after what you want, have a plan, that kind of thing." He sighed. "I guess it's kind of become entrenched in me, to say stuff like that."

"I get that," Holly said slowly. "But art isn't . . . You can't just *become* an artist—it is so dependent on so many things. Talent, timing." She paused. "Luck."

"But surely if you're doing it then you are an artist—as in, you can call yourself one." Holly made a face and Jack shrugged. "Does art need to be seen by others to have value?"

"Yes," Holly said automatically, sticking her chin in the air. "It's about making other people feel something, about bringing joy or clarity or evoking an emotion or—"

Jack held up a hand. "OK. But don't you feel those things when you . . . *create*?"

Holly hesitated. "Yes," she admitted. At least she used to.

"Well, there you go then," Jack said, leading the way to the next room. There weren't any other people in this one, just three sculptures.

"You're acting like you've won that argument, but you haven't," Holly whispered behind him, feeling even more need to be quiet now they were on their own.

"You're just being stubborn," Jack whispered back.

"And you're being—"

"Go on," he said, and she didn't have to look at him to know he was smiling. "What am I being?"

But before she could answer, he turned in to her and she stumbled, backing up toward the wall. Her heart gave a huge lurch—at the unexpectedness of it, the *speed* of the move, and his sudden closeness. She took another step back, and of *course* she managed to nearly fall into the nearest sculpture.

She righted herself, resting her hands behind her on the white, cool wall to stay steady. "You'll make me trip if you keep that up!" she said, her voice a tad too breathless to be properly scolding.

Jack raised one eyebrow. "There's nothing to trip over."

"That's beside the point."

He was smirking slightly as he looked down at her, as he reached out and placed his hands on either side of her shoulders on the wall, boxing her in. "Go on," he repeated. "You never said. What I am being?"

"Ah . . ."

Jesus, could her heart just calm down? There was no reason for it to be overreacting like this—none at all. But despite herself, she couldn't stop looking at his mouth, curved into a little smile, barely a breath away from hers. How did he do this? Turn from all calm and affable one minute to . . . well, *this,* the next.

She cleared her throat. "Inappropriate. You're being inappropriate."

His smirk only grew bigger.

"Stop looking at me like that," she snapped.

"Like what?"

"Like *that,*" she said, gesturing at his face. Trying not to look *too* hard at the contours of that face. "That *smile.* You're—"

"You don't want me to smile?"

Did he mean to do it—to speak like that, in those dark chocolate tones?

"Not even if I'm having a good time?" The smile grew, lighting up his face as it did so.

"You said you wanted to come to see art," she said, as firmly as she could.

His eyes swept her face. "Sorry. I'm a little distracted."

She rolled her eyes, making it an overly dramatic gesture, trying to hide how much he was getting to her. Then she shoved lightly at his chest. He backed away immediately, giving her space to step away from the wall, as much because of her push as because a group of three had just entered the room.

Well, that wasn't embarrassing at all. What would they say, if those strangers knew this was only her and Jack's second . . . *encounter*? Because the first, let's be honest, didn't count. But the thing was, it didn't feel like they'd only just met. She felt . . . easy around him, the way she'd only ever had with very few people. It didn't come around all that often—that instant feeling that this was it, you were going to be friends—and that it was fine that you didn't have a shared history, because you'd make one. Though that could just be the bloody *chance* of it all—of bumping into a man in a café, and then, three years later, somehow winding up in his path again. Yes. She was sure it was just that, playing tricks on her mind.

She gave him a sidelong look as he shoved his hands in his pockets and went back to his easy stroll, out of this room and into the last one. What was this all to him? When he'd given her his number in the café all those years ago, what had he been hoping for?

A montage, he'd said, and it was pathetic—*pathetic, Holly*—that she even remembered that. But what was he hoping for now?

It was impossible to tell—and irrelevant, she told herself firmly, because she was not here for him. She was here for Emma. Who she *still* hadn't mentioned.

"What about you?" she asked, feeling the need to say *something*. She picked up the previous conversation. "Do you love what you do?"

He wrinkled his nose. "Not really."

"Do you have something you *do* love?"

He hesitated for a beat too long. "Not really."

"Come on . . . you can tell me. I won't laugh."

But he said nothing.

"You didn't always want to do what you do now?" she prodded—refusing to let it drop, now that she knew there *was* something to drop.

"Does any six-year-old in the playground look around at their mates and declare that they want to be a management consultant when they're older?"

"No, but most six-year-old dreams are based on no knowledge whatsoever." She'd wanted to be an artist, though—for as long as she could remember. And Lily? Lily had wanted to be a mum. She could remember Lily coming home one day—she couldn't remember when, exactly, but they were both still in primary school. She'd been crying, because the teacher had said being a mother wasn't a viable career option. Holly could still see their mum's expression, her lips pressing into a thin line, and she understood more now—understood how that must have stung, because she'd chosen to be a stay-at-home mum, and only later had started working again.

"I think she meant you can be a mother *and* be something else," their mum had said diplomatically.

"I want to do what you do, though," Lily had said through sobs. "You look after us. I want to do that."

Their mum had smiled, her expression softening as she sat at the kitchen table and pulled Lily onto her lap. "It's stupid, any-way," she said. "They can't expect anyone to know what they want to be at this age."

"*I* know," Holly piped up, earning a scowl from her sister. She produced a drawing from her bookbag—different-colored birds above a forest of green. "Miss Cully said it was the best she'd ever seen in our class," she announced grandly.

"Did she now?" their mum asked, struggling with a smile. And though Holly had meant to give it to her mum, though she wanted it on the fridge where all the visitors could see it, she held it out to Lily instead. "It's for you," she said. "Because you like birds." And because maybe it would make Lily smile. Lily took it, her eyes drying up as they flickered across the page.

"I like the blue one," she said eventually, and Holly nodded, her job done.

"Hey, where'd you go?" Jack asked in the present. Holly glanced up at him. Was it unnerving, that he'd seen her mind drift? Or maybe it was just her face, refusing to allow her any privacy, as per usual.

"Sorry. But some people want to be management consul-tants, right?" she pushed. "It's, like, a big deal—one of those high-flying careers."

"Well, yeah. My friend Ed—you met him."

"I remember. The stylish one."

Jack grinned. "Right. God, he'll love that, when I tell him. Anyway, he loves it—and he's good at it."

"And you're not?"

"No, I am." It didn't sound boastful, just honest. "It's just . . . I don't know. It's not exactly fulfilling."

They both came to a stop simultaneously in the middle of the final room, in front of a bronze sculpture. It was made up of many partial faces, all turned away from one another. And in the center, one full face, which none of the others seemed to notice.

It was eerily beautiful, and Holly felt something swell in her throat. Because she could imagine being that face in the middle—could feel the loneliness there. She supposed that was the point—everyone had felt like that, at one point or another, whether it was a fleeting moment or something more.

"It makes me feel sad, somehow," Jack murmured.

"I know," Holly said simply.

Jack took his hand out of his pocket and lifted it toward the bronze face, then dropped it to his side, the edge of it brushing past Holly's own hand and settling so that their little fingers rested together. It was barely even a touch, just the smallest point of contact—but Holly felt all her concentration flood there.

She wasn't sure how long they stood there, neither of them moving, staring at the sculpture, their little fingers a small point of connection between them. After a time, Jack cleared his throat. "Should we . . . ?"

"Yeah," Holly said, and she drew her hand away.

She couldn't be sure, but she thought she heard a soft whoosh of breath from Jack as she turned and led the way out of the gallery.

They had time to kill before heading to the second gallery, so Jack suggested Hyde Park, which, Holly had to admit, was pretty gorgeous on this kind of crisp, clear day. She'd never spent much time here while she lived in London, and now she was wondering why. They were walking under a tunnel of trees, their branches bare, but somehow *hopeful,* as if they knew it wouldn't be long before they'd come to life again. The longer they'd walked around the park, dodging endless runners and dog walkers, the looser Jack's stride had become, and the more relaxed his posture seemed.

They took a right at the end of the path, and Jack looked around at the grass and the lake that stretched beyond it. "It's just so impressive, the design of this place," he said, his voice sounding satisfied, like he himself had something to be proud of. "It's something people take for granted," he continued. "But the serpentine—the lake, I mean—it's actually one of the first artificial lakes that was designed to look natural."

Holly's phone buzzed and she fished it out of her bag. Her stomach lurched when she saw who it was.

Does your silence mean that you hate the galleries, or that you're having too good a time to update me on your thoughts?

"And the trees . . ." Jack continued, oblivious to her inner turmoil. "Everything has been thought out so it works all year round."

Holly made a noncommittal noise as she slipped her phone back into her bag. And she had a flash, then, of Emma, telling her that she used to love gardening—that she'd done it with her grandson. She glanced at Jack, opened her mouth to say something, then snapped it shut again. Instead, she latched on to something up ahead—an ice cream van. She nodded toward it, sped up.

"Are you mental?" Jack asked, though he lengthened his stride to keep up with her. "It's too cold for ice cream."

"It's never too cold for ice cream."

"*No one* gets ice cream in March."

"Then why is the van here, hmm?"

Apparently stumped by that, Jack didn't say anything as Holly ordered two cones, then handed one to him. He looked at it for a long moment, a wisp of his dark messy curls falling over one eye.

"Come on," she said, fighting to keep her face straight. "Live on the wild side."

He muttered something inaudible, then licked his ice cream.

They headed for the edge of the lake, eating their cones as they walked, coming to a stop when they arrived there, a peaceful quiet settling between them.

That was, until a brisk breeze curled around Holly's neck, making her shiver. "Jesus, it's freezing," she muttered, doing a little jump up and down and making Jack laugh.

"That's because you had the ice cream, oh wild one."

She made a face at the nickname, then continued her little hop, wrapping her arms around herself. She felt him come up behind her, felt her body go motionless. He reached out, put his hands on her arms, and started to rub them up and down over her coat. "Better?" he asked, a smile in his voice.

"Hmm." But even though she made the noise disapproving, she couldn't stop the pinpricks of heat sparking on her skin as his touch traveled through the layers of clothing. Couldn't stop herself from leaning back into that touch. Into him. She felt his hands slow, more of a caress now. And even knowing that it was a bad idea, she couldn't stop herself from turning to look at him.

His hands stayed on her arms as she lifted her gaze to his, and she felt his fingers tighten, digging into her skin. His gaze dropped to her mouth in a way that was so *focused* it made her breath catch. He moved his hands up her arms and down her back, where they rested, his fingers curling there, bringing her closer. The rest of the world dropped away, the park becoming blurry, the sounds of toddlers crying and people chattering dropping into nothingness, so that all she could hear was the two of them breathing.

She ran her hands up the front of his coat, spread her palms on his chest, wishing there was less material between them. She kept going, settling with placing her hands on either side of his neck, on the bare skin there. The tiniest of shudders ran through him, and her whole body tightened.

Oh God. She wanted to kiss him. She wanted to sink her teeth into that mouth, wanted to taste him. His dark eyes were level on hers as he bent his head toward her.

But she didn't meet him halfway, the way she wanted to. Instead she took a low, shuddering breath. "Wait." Her voice scraped over her frayed nerves. His fingers tightened on her back one more time, then released. She dropped her hands too, took a step back.

"Right." He ran a hand across the back of his neck. "Sorry."

"No. No, it's not that. It's . . ." She pulled her hands through her hair. "Look, before this goes any further, I have to tell you something."

"Tell me something?"

His expression went carefully neutral, though his gaze flickered to her left hand.

"I'm not married or anything," she said quickly, though that only made his face tighten all the more—expecting something worse, no doubt.

"I . . ." God, why was this so difficult? "I really don't know how to say this, so I'm just going to spit it out. Jack, I know your grandmother."

He stared at her for a long moment. "What? What are you talking about?"

"Right, so, I met her this Christmas and we're . . . Well, we know each other. Emma Tooley. That's her name, right? She lives in Devon, near the café where we first met."

It was Jack, this time, who moved back—away from her, still looking at her with that same, unreadable expression. "OK. So you know my grandmother," he repeated, his voice calm. Too calm.

"Yes. She's . . ." She swallowed. "She is the reason I came to find you."

Chapter Fourteen

Jack was still staring at her like he didn't believe what she was saying and possibly a bit like she was off her rocker. "She was the reason you were in the café?"

"No," Holly said quickly. Where before the park had faded into oblivion, now it came rushing back into focus—the joggers, the dog walkers, the business types on their phones. No one was watching them, no one *cared*, but she felt suddenly on show, and the previously gentle noise of them all suddenly felt cacophonic. She took a breath of the crisp air to steady herself. "No," she repeated. "I only met her in December."

"I'm sorry, I still don't understand. Why would you know her? And why would that make you look for me? And why wouldn't you tell me any of this until just now? I mean, don't you think you should have opened with this? You can't be serious."

She grimaced.

"This is absurd. *Absurd*," he repeated. He turned, paced a couple of steps away, back again.

"Jack, I—"

"She told you about me?" he bit out.

"Well, yes, she—"

"So she got you to track me down, did she? To befriend me, convince me to go and see her—is that it? Because that's . . ." He shook his head. "I don't know what that is, Holly, but it's not right."

Shit, she was doing this all wrong. All this time she'd had to plan, to think, and here she was, blurting it out at the worst moment imaginable. This was why she should have listened to Abi. "It's not like that. I—"

"Jesus fucking Christ, Holly. I was about to kiss you! Here I was, thinking all of this was fate, but it was just a lie the whole time!"

"I know, I should have told you sooner!" She dragged a hand through her hair, felt it catch in a mat that hadn't been there this morning. "I'm sorry. I wanted to tell you, but I wasn't expecting you to be *you*, and—"

"What's that supposed to mean?"

"Nothing," she said quickly—because she didn't know exactly what she meant either, and everything she was saying just seemed to make the situation worse. She tried again anyway. "Nothing, it's just . . . I recognized you, and then you invited me out and—"

"So this is my fault," he said, deadpan. It reminded her enough of what she'd said to Daniel when he broke up with her that she winced.

"No, I'm explaining this all wrong." She forced herself to take a very long, very slow breath. "Emma has cancer."

"What?" Holly hadn't thought it was possible, but she saw his face close off even more as he said it.

"She has cancer," Holly said, her voice level at last, "and

it's . . . Well, I don't know exactly how bad it is because she won't tell me—but the point is, she's ill, and she has no one, and I thought that maybe you would . . ."

Jack folded his arms, his jawline tight. "Would what, exactly?"

"I don't know," Holly huffed impatiently. "Want to call her? Talk to her? Go to see her?"

"Well, thanks for delivering the very unsolicited message, but no. I won't be calling her."

She looked at him incredulously for a second. "But she has cancer!"

"Yes, I heard you the first time. And I don't appreciate you trying to make me feel guilty or inserting yourself into a situation that you clearly don't seem to understand. I haven't spoken to Memma in nearly twenty years—she is not part of my life anymore."

Memma—a childhood name, no doubt. She should have known Emma wouldn't be granny or grandma. Memma. It sounded like Emma. She could imagine a child's voice saying it, and the thought of that was enough to send a splinter through her too-soft heart.

"Jack," she said, her voice pleading.

"No," he said sharply. "Don't 'Jack' me. You have no business trying to drag me back to that—to something I've left behind." He scraped a hand through his hair in a way that looked painful. "And *she* has no business trying to manipulate me into getting in touch. Jesus, of all the ways—"

"She didn't send me," Holly said quickly. Shit, maybe she should have led with that—because OK, yes, that looked really bad. "She doesn't even know I'm here. Here with you, I mean. She didn't send me," she repeated. "I sent myself."

He stared at her, then shook his head. "That's worse."

"How is that worse?"

"I don't know, but it's certainly not better!"

And just when she thought she'd been doing well, had been keeping so calm, something about his tone made her temper snap, the energy that had been building within her needing an outlet. She threw her hands in the air. "For God's sake, why are you being so unreasonable about this?"

Jack made a choking sound. "Unreasonable?"

Holly tilted her chin in the air. "Yes, unreasonable."

"*I'm* the one being unreasonable?" He laughed, the sound pure, bitter cynicism. "Yeah, right. You *knew*, didn't you? You knew about the crash, even as I was telling you, and you acted like it was brand-new information. You already *knew* my dad had died. You were manipulating me, Holly."

"I was not!" But even as she said it, there was a part of her whispering, *well, you sort of were*. But she shut that voice down—*Lily's* voice—because she was doing it for a good reason, wasn't she? So maybe she could have done it better, but she was just trying to *help*.

She fought for patience. "I knew about the crash, yes, but I was just trying to find a way to—"

"Did she tell you she was the one driving?" Jack interrupted, and his eyes darkened—still unreadable, but somehow *more* so.

Holly went very still. "What?"

"Did she tell you she was the one driving, the night my dad died?"

Holly said nothing, and Jack had his answer.

"She was driving," he said, his voice too calm again. "My dad was in the passenger seat. My mum, my grandad, and me in the back. She crashed into a tree. We all survived. He didn't."

Emma was driving? Emma had crashed the car? But . . .

"She is the reason my dad is dead," Jack said. "And then, after making my mom a single parent, she just disappeared on us, left us to figure out how to go on all on our own."

Holly opened her mouth to speak, but she couldn't.

"She didn't tell you that part, did she?" He laughed again—that same ugly, cynical sound.

Holly was still frozen, her mind refusing to catch up with what Jack was saying. Rocks fell, one by one, into the pit of her stomach.

Emma had been driving.

Emma had been driving, just like Holly had been driving. Holly had told Emma that, opened up to her. Been vulnerable. And Emma had not reciprocated. She knew how it felt better than anyone, and yet Emma had elected not to say anything. The next breath she took tasted acrid on her tongue.

But . . . Richard had died. He had *died*. And Lily . . . She'd miscarried, so a life had been lost, but Lily had survived. Maybe Emma couldn't face admitting what had happened. Because *this* was what had torn them apart—Jack and Emma. Not the death itself, but the blame. And apparently Jack was still blaming Emma—just as Lily was still blaming Holly.

Holly's mouth was dry, but she managed to speak. "You should still talk to her."

"Why? She's not part of my life anymore." She saw Lily, like she was saying it too, as he said the words. "And it's not like she's tried that hard, either, that's half the problem—so don't go casting me as the bad guy here, Holly."

She gritted her teeth. He narrowed his eyes. "And don't go looking at me like a . . ."

"Like a what?" Holly said, a bite to her voice.

"Like a petulant child."

Holly opened her mouth, a snarl starting to come out, but he cut her off.

"For God's sake, Holly! You come here, springing this on me out of the blue after leading me on, and expect me to . . . what? Say thank you? Go and call my dear old grandmamma? You think *you* can fix this with one little conversation in the park? She killed my dad. Don't you get that? My entire life changed that day."

Holly winced.

She killed my dad.

I lost the baby. Because of you.

"It was an—"

"How would you know? You weren't even there! Just . . ." He turned away from her, scraped a hand down his jawline. "Just get out of my face and leave me be, OK?"

The dismissive tone, the disregard for what she was trying to do, acting like it wasn't her place, to be talking about his grandmother when she was the one being there for her now tipped Holly over the edge. And it felt good, to be angry. Everything was happening so fast, her plans unraveling so quickly, that she couldn't take it all in, she needed to focus on one thing, so she focused on her anger. Accidents *happened*. Did he not get that? Did *Lily* not get that? Emma had not *meant* to crash. Holly had not *meant* to slam into that car. And fine, yes, maybe that didn't excuse it; maybe she and Emma both deserved to be outcasts. But she did not want to feel that right now. Not here.

"Do you know what?" Holly said, and Jack, clearly sensing a change in her tone, jerked his head back around to look at her. "Fuck you."

He looked so stunned, it almost made her want to laugh— a cruel laugh, one that did not feel like her. "What?"

"You heard me," Holly said, raising her chin. "If you are so incapable of even the *thought* of forgiveness, if you find it impossible to even *try* to consider another point of view after all these years, then fuck it. Maybe she's better off without you after all."

And with that, she spun on her heel, narrowly avoiding a nearby jogger, and only just catching herself before she faceplanted on the path. She didn't let that stop her. She stormed away, keeping her head high, listening to the pulsing in her veins.

It took her a full hundred meters before she stopped listening out for the sound of her name behind her. Before she accepted that Jack was not going to call her back.

And it was only then that she realized her eyes were damp with tears.

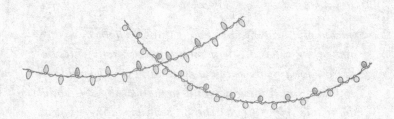

Chapter Fifteen

Dear Lily,

I'm in London at the moment. I'm so close to you—Mum told me you still live near Tunbridge Wells. I tracked down Emma's grandson this week. I told you about Emma, didn't I? Well, she and I are sort of friends now, believe it or not. She's kind of spiky, but not as spiky as she'd have you believe. I think she does it because she's worried about letting people get close, in case she loses them—and that's something I can relate to. I was so hoping that when I found Jack, I'd be able to fix things between them.

You'll love this twist—do you remember the man in the coffee shop? The one we ran into that day? Well, turns out he's Emma's grandson—Jack, that is—and if anyone can appreciate the irony there, it's you. He's still just as attractive, in case you were wondering. I should have told him right away, about Emma. But I got dis-

tracted and I didn't, and now I think I might have only made things worse. Sorry, I'm rambling, aren't I? It's because I don't really know what to do. I wish I could call you, ask you. I imagine you'd say what Abi says about the whole thing—that I should stop meddling—but it's different somehow, hearing it from a big sister.

You used to tell me to fix things, to own up to what I'd done and put it right, because I was always trying to pretend I hadn't done anything wrong. Like Mum's vase, do you remember? The one with the purple flowers on it. I knocked it over and it shattered everywhere. I can't really remember why. I was probably playing with it. Anyway, I refused to own up to it, even though it was obviously me and even though Mum was really upset, because Dad had given it to her on a birthday—and it was one of the only presents he'd picked out for her himself that she actually liked. You kept telling me to fix it—I think you meant I had to say sorry, because I doubt you meant I had to glue it back together. You did the same when I was eighteen and spilled red wine on the carpet when everyone else was out—only then you meant to actually fix it, clean it up before Mum saw.

I didn't listen to you back then. Maybe that was a good thing, because as it turns out, I'm not very good at fixing things. But I'm trying, Lily. I might not be able to fix things with you, but I'm going to try and fix this, ok?

Love,
Holly

On Monday morning, Holly woke with a new determination—something which only intensified as she packed her suitcase, baffled at the way everything no longer seemed to fit when she'd managed to get it all in in the first place. And yes, she could have done this before she was trying to rush out the door to catch her train, but instead she'd spent Sunday in her hotel room, ordering room service and watching Netflix, stewing over what Jack had said. She hadn't expected such a strong reaction, and she had therefore felt perfectly justified in what she'd said—he *was* being unreasonable.

And as though she didn't feel bad enough, she'd spent a solid hour cyberstalking her sister and then she'd called her parents. Her parents were almost the only people she knew who actually still had a landline, and she didn't really know why but she always called them on that. Habit, she supposed. And, these days, something about the anonymity of it, the fact that they wouldn't see her name on the screen.

Her dad had answered. "Holly! Helen, it's Holly!"

"Holly!" She could hear her mum's name down the corridor, picture them in their little house in Hammersmith, the same one where she'd spent time after her teacher training. Some of her things were still there, she knew—she hadn't packed properly when she'd bolted for Windsor, and she'd never really planned a trip to pick everything up.

"How are you, love?" Her dad's voice, deep and gravelly, brought a wave of emotion in her fragile state.

"I'm OK."

"Are you sure? You don't sound OK. Helen, she doesn't sound OK."

Her mum spoke down the receiver then, clearly having had the phone shoved into her hand. "What's wrong, love?"

"Nothing. Nothing, I'm fine. I just . . . I just wanted to see how you were."

"Well, we're fine. How are you? Are you still with that chap? What was his name again?"

God, Daniel. She hadn't even told them that she and Daniel had broken up, evidence of how long it had been since she'd spoken to them properly.

"How are things at that school? And when are you next in London? We'll come to see you if you don't want to come to the house." The way her mum barely paused between questions, ever so familiar, made Holly smile a little. And then there was the slight spasm of guilt at the suggestion that Holly wouldn't want to visit them there—or maybe it was that they didn't really want her in the house either.

She could tell them she was in London now, though. Could get the tube, let her dad cook for her, listen in detail to her mum telling her about the latest novel she was reading and inevitably give away all the spoilers, even though she tried not to. She was almost going to, until she heard a voice. Lily's voice.

"Hi, Mum! Steve's got the rest of the shopping, where do you want it? We went for chicken rather than lamb, that OK? Oh, sorry, you're on the phone."

There was a pause, minute, but still there. "It's Holly."

Another pause, and Holly found herself holding her breath.

"Do you want to say hello?"

Holly could imagine it, the way her sister would be backing out of the living room, where the phone was kept. "No. No, that's OK, thanks. I'll just . . ."

After that, Holly told her mum she had to go, made some excuse or another, promised to call soon. Because it was a reminder, as if she needed one, that though her parents might not entirely blame her for what happened, her sister certainly did.

She remembered trying to see Lily, a few weeks after the accident. She'd come all the way to London, gone to the Hammersmith house where she knew Lily was staying, back with their parents, Steve there too, until she recovered. Her mum hadn't let her in past the threshold. *You need to give it time, Holly. I think you'll only make it worse, seeing her now—she's not ready.*

Her own mother hadn't allowed her back into her own childhood home.

So Holly gave her time. And that time had stretched on and on.

Stop it, Holly. She had to focus. All of that was yesterday. Today, she had a plan.

She checked out of the hotel, pulling her little suitcase—purple with light-blue polka dots—behind her as she headed to the nearest tube station, aiming for the Jubilee line and Canary Wharf. One of the wheels on the suitcase was broken—it didn't turn properly so kept getting stuck, causing her quite a few annoying moments as she wrenched it on its way, earning disapproving looks from passersby.

She found the office more easily than the last time and headed through the glass revolving doors into the reception area. She walked past the beanbags, which she had to admit looked pretty comfortable, even if everyone here was too uptight to sit on them, and past the boring-looking magazines on the glass coffee tables. The same receptionist who had been behind the desk on Friday greeted her. He was wearing a blue T-shirt with a black-and-yellow tie today—and when she looked more closely, she realized the yellow bits were actually feathers.

He smiled at her, flashing brilliantly white teeth. "Hello, can I help?"

"I'm here to see Jack," she said, filling her voice with a confidence she didn't feel. "Jack Tooley."

"Wait, I think I remember you. You were here on Friday, right? About the jewelry company?"

"Yes, that's right."

"And you're here to see Jack? Again?"

"Yes," she said, her voice a little shorter than usual. But

really, did he have to sound so incredulous? Who did he think she was, a stalker? Though, to be fair, maybe she was sort of acting like a stalker.

The receptionist didn't push anymore, picking up his phone. "Jack, my man! You're here—thought you might be in Scotland."

Holly frowned—he hadn't told her he was going to Scotland. And why the hell would he? It was proof of how little they knew each other—she'd been attracted to him, yes, but it had all just been surface level.

"Oh, tomorrow, yeah, I remember. I've got a Hellie here, says she's got a meeting with you?"

Holly made a face at the wrong name. Though, actually, maybe that was a good thing—it meant Jack couldn't refuse to see her. She'd deliberately shown up rather than called him so he couldn't ignore her, and she was prepared to sit in reception until he came out of his office to leave for the day, if necessary.

"A jewelry company," the receptionist was saying. "Oh. Huh." He put his hand over the receiver. "Are you sure it's Jack you're after?"

"Yes," Holly said firmly. "It's definitely him. It's really important; I have to see him." She wasn't sure what could qualify as this urgent in management consultant land, but surely there was something.

"Ah, she says it's really important," the receptionist repeated, a little hesitantly. "OK, OK. Sure." He put the phone down, flashed her another smile. "He said to take you up."

Holly nearly said, "Really?" but stopped herself and managed to nod, trying to put on an air of self-importance. She followed him, dragging her case behind her. The receptionist glanced at it as they got in the lift.

"I like your suitcase," he said.

"Thanks. I like your tie."

He smiled. "My brother designs ties."

Ah, that explained it.

They got out of the lift on the sixth floor and Holly followed him through a lot of busy-looking people at adjoining desks, many of them with headphones in, all typing frantically or frowning at their computer screens, a few of them laughing into phones while clicking their mouses with a slightly panicked air. Holly had never really considered going down this route. Not management consultancy, per se, but this kind of corporate office environment. Right now, she was exceptionally glad of that.

Holly saw Jack before he saw her. In his very own office—one of only a handful as far as she could tell—staring at his computer screen, the city skyline sprawling behind him through the glass window in a way that looked vaguely futuristic. She couldn't help it, that nervous little lurch in her stomach, even as she tried to breathe through it.

The receptionist knocked at his door, and Jack looked up, frowning. He didn't even glance at the receptionist—his gaze settled on her immediately. And though she thought she saw something flash across his face, his face went smooth, everything hidden behind that damn neutral expression. She wished she could control her expressions like that. Even as she tried not to let them show, she was pretty sure her nerves were plastered across her face right now.

The receptionist pushed open the door. Jack's gaze flickered toward him. "What's going on?" he said, standing up behind his desk. His very neat, organized desk.

"This is Hellie," said the receptionist.

Jack's jaw tightened. "It's not Hellie, it's Holly, Mike. And I said I'd come down to see her."

The receptionist tugged at one of his earlobes. "Oh, I thought you said—"

"Never mind," Jack said briskly. "Come in, *Hellie,* take a

seat." He gestured toward the chair opposite him, his voice perfectly formal. This was what she'd imagined when she'd first thought of tracking Emma's grandson down. Maybe, if that's how it had played out, she wouldn't have screwed it up so badly.

Mike hovered for a moment. Then, when Jack said nothing more to him, he backed out of the office silently, closing the glass door behind him.

"Posing as a client, now, are we?" Jack said, sitting down slowly.

Holly caught herself biting her lip, stopped it. "Seemed like the best option. I thought you might hang up on me, if I called."

"I wouldn't have hung up," Jack said mildly. "I just wouldn't have answered." Even though she'd vowed to think only of Emma, it still stung. "That's what you were doing when you came here on Friday, wasn't it?" he asked. "Trying to track me down?"

She decided not to answer that, because it would inevitably lead to questions about why, exactly, she hadn't told him what she was doing here right away, and though it had all seemed to make sense at the time, it now seemed very poorly thought out. Sort of as poorly thought out as this entire weekend had been.

Instead, she took a breath. "Look, Jack, I think I went about things the wrong way."

His eyebrows twitched upward. "You think?"

"Would you just let me *finish*?"

"Do you know what, Holly? I don't think I will."

She'd opened her mouth to continue but now she snapped it shut, dumbfounded. He'd seemed so *reasonable* during the time she'd spent with him, that she'd convinced herself that Saturday afternoon was just a blip. That once he'd had time to think it through, to calm down and get over the shock of it, he'd be willing to hear her out.

"Look," Jack continued. "You've known Emma"—*Emma*.

Not *my grandma*, not *Memma*—"what, all of three months, if what you're saying is true? And you think you can just come swanning in and fix something that's been broken for twenty years? That's not how life works."

"But she's *ill*," Holly said, and she hated the pleading note that had crept into her voice.

"Her being ill does not change the last twenty years," he said, totally level.

She stared at him. "How can you be so callous?"

He closed his eyes briefly, so that she couldn't catch whatever emotion might have flashed there. "This isn't . . . Forgiveness takes work. And generally speaking, it also takes an apology, which Emma has not given. You don't just turn around one day and decide to forgive and forget and have some sort of cuddly Hallmark reunion."

Rocks slid into her gut. Because she realized that's exactly what she was hoping for with Lily. And if Jack wouldn't—*couldn't*—forgive Emma, would it be the same for her sister?

"Jack . . ." And now when she spoke, her voice was a little wobbly. "I—"

But his office phone started to ring, cutting her off. He pressed a button on it, answering on speakerphone. "What is it, Mike?" His voice sounded a little weary.

"Ah, sorry, Jack, I know you're in a meeting, but it's just your wife is here to see you."

Jack's gaze snapped to the phone. Holly's heart lurched.

"She says she hasn't been able to get through to you—she wanted me to call up, wouldn't take no for an answer, actually and . . . well . . . Do you want me to send her up, or—?"

"No," Jack said shortly. "Just tell her to wait." He pressed a button on the phone.

Holly was staring at him. Very slowly, he lifted his gaze to meet hers. His *wife*.

"You're married," she said, her voice barely a whisper.

He said nothing. But he'd asked her out. Twice! And he'd been about to kiss her—he'd said so himself. But now, he wasn't speaking, and with every growing second of silence, her throat became more and more clogged.

"You never . . ." She shook her head, the action a bit frantic. "You didn't say anything!" It was a demand for information, anger and hurt lacing her voice.

He dropped his gaze. "Well," he said, his tone clipped. "I suppose we were both hiding things, then."

She gave it a second longer—waited a second for him to contradict that statement. Then she stood and spun away, nearly tripping as she pulled her suitcase along.

She opened the door, rushed through it. She heard him get to his feet behind her but she wouldn't give him the satisfaction of looking back. He might have said her name—once, quietly—but she couldn't be sure, because she couldn't hear properly over the pounding of her heart, her now frantic breathing.

This was all wrong. Fucked-up. This was so fucked-up.

There was a giant wrench inside her, one that felt out of place—too intense.

She was the one driving.

Not everyone survived.

Get out of my face.

I lost the baby. Because of you.

She killed him.

Your wife.

She wasn't concentrating, was hurrying to get to the lift, to get *away,* and so she didn't see the woman until she nearly ran her over. The woman took a step back—and even in the state Holly was in, she could admire the beautiful pointed red heels. She looked into the woman's face. Blonde, blue-eyed. Perfect hair and neatly manicured nails.

"Whoa there, honey," the woman said with a smile.

"Sorry," Holly muttered, and dragged her suitcase around her. Her eyes were stinging. God, she was going to cry. She needed to get out of here—out of this office, and out of London.

"No problem," the woman said, even as Holly was already moving away. "Hey, were you just coming out of Jack's office? I didn't mean to cut your meeting short—"

"No, I wasn't with Jack," Holly said quickly, and left, practically at a run, managing to catch the lift just as the doors were closing.

Was that her, Jack's wife? Either way, it wasn't on Holly to explain. To explain *what*? she wondered. Nothing had happened between them. Nothing. So why did she feel like this, after two days? Why did she feel like something was tearing at her insides?

Because of Emma. Because she'd messed it up, again—and now, any chance of reuniting Emma and Jack was lost. And what if Emma got worse? What if there wasn't another chance? What if . . . ? But no, she wouldn't let her mind go down that road.

She reached the ground floor and tore through the reception, heading out to the gray and the cold. And then she fled, away from this mess and toward the safety of her home and Abi. Abi, who had been right, as usual. Because it had been wrong of Holly to get involved. Wrong of her, to think that *she*, of all people, could be the one to fix what was broken.

JUNE

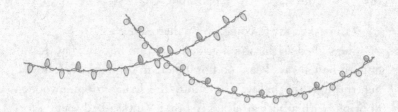

Chapter Sixteen

Jack stared at the front door. At *his* front door. This should not be difficult, for Christ's sake—he still owned half the damn flat. Though they'd bought in Balham because that's where Vanessa had wanted to live, compromising on the space—and the garden—that they could have had if they'd gone for somewhere on the outskirts of London, as he'd suggested. But still.

He squared his shoulders and knocked. He had a key, but after nearly nine months not setting foot in the place, it felt kind of rude to use it.

Vanessa opened the door. Wearing a blue dress to match her eyes, her blonde hair neat as always. She seemed to wake up with that hair—in two years of marriage, he'd never seen it anything other than perfect, and honestly, he didn't know how she did it.

She smiled—and it was only because he knew her so well that he saw the tentativeness of it.

"Well, hi there, stranger."

"Vanessa."

Her lips twisted. "So formal."

"You asked me to come, so I'm here, OK?"

She sighed as she stood aside to let him into the flat. It was hot—it had always been too hot in here in summer. He followed her through the hallway and into the living room—wooden flooring, with a big patterned rug that Vanessa had spent a fortune on in the center of the room, two leather sofas he didn't recognize at its edges. It was weird, to see the flat looking so *hers*, with no sign he'd ever lived there, even though it shouldn't have come as a surprise—he'd moved his stuff out six months ago. Not that he'd had a lot of stuff, but the painting they'd bought together, the one which made him chuckle—of a man looking totally baffled as he turned in his seat to see who was there—had been taken down, and, of course, none of his books were shelved in the bookcase anymore. The few photos he'd put on the top—initially at Vanessa's insistence to make the place feel "homey"—were also gone, still in boxes at his rental flat.

Vanessa headed to the square wooden coffee table in the middle of the living room. She bent down, picked up a few papers, then held one out to him. "I wanted to show you these," she said, and though her body language was calm, he could hear the tightness in her voice. Well, good. At least he wasn't the only one who felt uncomfortable and strange.

He glanced down at the paper she was holding and felt a little jolt. He didn't need to take it to know what it was, but he did anyway, staring down at the county court stamp, his and Vanessa's names printed at the top. She'd never taken his surname—neither of them had been bothered about it—but somehow the different surnames, Tooley and Fox, seemed to jump out at him, announcing the fact that they were completely different entities now. That maybe they always had been.

He glanced at Vanessa. She was watching him, her hands twisting together in front of her. "It's official?" he asked.

She dropped her hands to her sides. "It's official."

He looked down again. The final divorce order. Proof that the marriage had been "dissolved," nine months after filing. He put the paper back on the coffee table. He didn't want to hold it, this document that proved how epically he'd managed to fail.

"You could have just told me this over the phone," he said with a sigh. All the paperwork was sent to this flat, because he hadn't had a permanent address when they'd separated. Which they'd done after she'd arrived home late one night and told him that she'd cheated on him.

"I know, but I wanted to see you. Thought it was the kind of thing we should do in person."

He couldn't think of what to say to that. Do how, exactly? he wondered. There was nothing to sign this time.

The last time he'd seen her was when she'd come into the office because she needed a signature on one of the forms that they'd missed the first time around. He'd been ignoring her calls and so she'd taken it upon herself to just turn up. He still cringed at the memory of Mike's voice, on speaker. *Your wife's here.* Still remembered Holly's expression, shocked and hurt. He shouldn't have let her believe he was married. It was cruel, something he'd done only because *he* had felt hurt, angry that she'd tracked him down and hadn't told him why, then thrown it on him like that, asking for something he couldn't give. He'd told Mike a dozen times to stop calling Vanessa his wife. Vanessa herself had stopped when they began the proceedings back in October—and in March, they'd already had the divorce papers. But while Mike had many good qualities, following directions wasn't one of them.

"Want a drink?" Vanessa asked, heading for the kitchen.

Jack raised his eyebrows. "Are we celebrating?" But he followed her anyway—it felt weird, to be standing in the living room alone.

Vanessa gave a sad little headshake. "Whatever you may

think of me, Jack, I do not deem a failed marriage to be a cause for celebration."

He blew out a breath. "Fine, yeah. Let's have a drink." He leaned against the granite counter as she opened the fridge— a fancy, bloody expensive one that had a wooden door to make it look like a cupboard.

She opened two beers—the light stuff—and held one out to him. He took a sip more for something to do than because he really wanted one. He wasn't sure how he was supposed to feel. He'd never thought he'd be the type to get divorced. If there even was a type. But he'd assumed he'd keep following the right trajectory—he'd landed the right sort of job, was successful in his career, made a good salary, lived in London in a nice flat. It was all supposed to lead on from that—marriage, kids, move out to the suburbs. Not the most exciting of lives, maybe, but secure, and comfortable, and you couldn't ask for more than that, could you? But now . . . He no longer felt the gut punch he'd experienced at first, but he was still a bit lost, unsure what to do or where to go from here.

Was this how his mum had felt, after his dad's death? This, times a million? He *knew* she'd felt lost, because even after they'd moved to the other side of Devon, she'd had this sort of . . . vacant look about her. He'd catch her sometimes in the kitchen, with the fridge door open or the tap on, just *staring,* as the fridge started beeping or the water ran so hot it turned scalding, and he'd have to snap her out of it.

He had a memory, then, of the night itself. Of waiting downstairs, nervously twisting his tie—one that had been bought just for this occasion—and wondering if they were going to be late. He'd heard his mum's voice upstairs.

"Come on, Richard, you knew we had to leave at six."

"I'm ready, I'm ready."

"You're not. We'll just go without you."

"Of course you're not going without me—I want to see Jack play."

Emma had come into the hallway then, her gray hair all curly in the way she did it for, as she put it, "occasions that are worth the effort." She'd winked at him. "Ready, my boy?"

"Umm . . ."

She'd waved a hand. "Course you are. You were born ready."

His dad's voice had got a bit louder. "Where are my damn keys?" There was a pause. "Come on, Rose, where are my keys?"

Emma's smile had turned a bit fixed then. "I'll just go up and chivvy them along, shall I?"

It had been the school concert—he'd been learning the trumpet, which he'd later given up when he and his mum moved house. He'd never really been that into it, but his dad had loved the idea that he would be a "performer" one day, so he'd stuck with it for a bit.

"What would you have played, Richard?" his mum had asked once, with raised eyebrows.

His dad had grinned. "The triangle." It had made his mum laugh, and his dad had swooped in, across their little kitchen, and twirled her around. "You'd have liked being married to a musician, wouldn't you? Much more glamorous."

"I'd prefer a bit of help with the washing up—I'm not a glamorous sort of person."

"How about a glass of wine instead?" His dad had winked at Jack, who was hovering in the doorway, wanting a biscuit but unsure as to whether he'd be told off for asking.

"Jack? Are you listening?" Vanessa was staring at the side of his face.

He cleared his throat. "No. Sorry. I am now." He needed to stop doing that. He'd been thinking about the crash, and his dad, more and more since Holly had shown up in March. He hadn't called Emma, though. He didn't know how to get ahold of her, even if he wanted to. Actually, that wasn't true—he could text Holly and ask for Emma's number. He was sure she'd be only too delighted to give it to him. But what would he say? He'd meant what he said to Holly—you couldn't just kiss and make up after this length of time, after something like that. He'd dealt with what had happened, had moved on from it as best he could. But that didn't change the fact that things would have been different, if Emma hadn't been driving that day. And it didn't change the fact that she'd not been there for him, after it had happened.

"So," Vanessa said, "I've been trying to figure out a way to say this."

Jack studied her face for clues. He knew that face so well—knew the dimple that would wink out when she smiled, the one she hated but which he'd told her was cute; he knew the frown lines that would pull together when she scowled, the slight pigmentation on her forehead, which she'd spent a goddamn fortune trying to get rid of, no matter how many times he'd told her that no one noticed it but her. Right now, though, he didn't know what she was thinking. Maybe he'd never known what she was thinking, in fact—after all, he'd never even suspected that she was cheating on him.

"Say what?" he asked eventually.

She took a sip of her beer. "That I'm sorry."

Jack's eyebrows shot up. It didn't sound to him like that should have taken much figuring out.

"I realized I never said it," she continued.

"No," he said flatly. "You didn't."

"Well, I am. Sorry, that is. I'm sorry for my part in it."

"You've waited until now to say that?" He frowned. "And what do you mean, your part in it? You slept with someone else, Vanessa. It was all your part."

"I did do that. But I did not destroy our marriage single-handedly."

"I'm not sure I need to hear this."

"You left, Jack," she said, and though her expression was smooth, there was a wobble in her voice.

"After you told me to! After you announced you were bloody cheating on me! What the hell did you *expect* me to do?"

"But you left *immediately*. I told you I'd slept with someone; you didn't even ask their name." The wobble was stronger now. "You just walked out."

He stared at her. "What did you want me to do?"

"I wanted you to talk to me! I wanted you to fight, for me or *with* me, just a little." She blinked furiously, and looked away, down to the tiles, and then to the near-empty beer bottle in her hand.

"You were cheating on me," he repeated, his voice frostier now. Because seriously, what was she doing, trying to put this on him?

"*Was*. I slept with someone three times. It was a mistake. But it wasn't ongoing."

"So you said," Jack muttered, taking a deep swig of his beer. "I don't know what you want me to say here, Vanessa. You cheated. Then you asked for a divorce. What did you expect to happen?"

"I only asked for one because you'd walked away so easily." She pressed her lips together, lifted her gaze to his. "Because it was like . . . It was like you'd been looking for a reason to end it. It doesn't excuse what I did," she said quickly. "I'm not saying that. But I . . ."

"Why *did* you do it?" he asked quietly. He hadn't asked before—hadn't wanted to know the answer.

"I was lonely," she said, her voice barely more than a whisper.

"You had me!"

"Did I?"

He let out a low whistle. "That's harsh."

"I know." She let her breath out on a whoosh. "I'm sorry."

"So you've said." He put his beer bottle down on the counter next to him. "Well, it's done now." He pushed away from the counter, not sure he wanted to be here, hashing it out when it didn't matter anymore. But he couldn't help hesitating, couldn't help looking at her again. His friend, who had grown into something more, who had become his wife. It felt like so long ago, when they used to sit up talking about everything and nothing, lamenting all the bad dates they'd been on, the bad sex they were having. Until one day, she'd looked at him with those baby blues and cocked her head. "Do you think maybe *we* should have sex? You know, just to try it?" And they'd just fallen into a relationship, as easily as they'd fallen into being friends. Where, along the line, had that gone wrong?

"I wasn't looking for an excuse to end it," he said. For a moment, though, he allowed himself to consider the possibility. He wouldn't have ended it, not without a reason—you didn't end things just because they weren't perfect. And he certainly wouldn't have risked the instability, just for the sake of it. But would he have wanted to end it? He'd never really thought about it—would never have asked himself that question. Even now, he wasn't sure he knew the answer to it. He'd agreed to a divorce without much of a fight, yes: If she wanted one, then he wasn't going to stand in her way. He didn't want to be married to someone who didn't want to be married to him. It had felt like the right option. It had felt like the *only* option.

"I kept thinking of how I pushed you into it," Vanessa said. "Getting married, I mean. After a while, I started to wonder whether that was the only reason you went along with it."

He frowned. "I asked you to marry me."

"Because I dropped the hints."

He nearly smiled. "Yeah. But I wanted to marry you, Ness. I wouldn't have asked you if I hadn't. Surely you know that."

She nodded firmly. "I do. And I wouldn't have said yes if I hadn't believed you did—I have too much self-respect for that."

"Then . . ."

"You were always so level," she said, with a huff of what might have been a laugh. "So difficult to rile. I loved that. But then I got thinking—maybe you were so level with me because you weren't really . . . in it. Because you didn't really care. So I lashed out. It was wrong," she said sadly. "I should have just asked you."

They looked at each other for a long moment.

"Are you still sleeping with him?" Jack asked.

"No. No, I'm not sleeping with him—as I said, it was over by the time I told you."

He hesitated. "Are you sleeping with anyone else?" She didn't answer right away and he winced. "Scratch that. I don't want to know, and it's not my business anyway."

She laughed then—not her usual bright laugh but a laugh nonetheless. She pushed away from her side of the kitchen, met him in the middle. "Forgive me if I'm a little bit glad, seeing you squirm like that."

"Jesus, Ness."

She patted him on the shoulder. "Shows you care."

"Of course I care."

"I'm sorry. That was a low blow."

He met her gaze. "I loved you, Vanessa." It felt important that he say it—that she knew. He'd loved her, and no matter that things weren't perfect, it had felt like something ripping inside him, when she'd made the announcement. Because she'd been his friend, first and foremost, and she wasn't supposed to hurt him.

Something flashed in her eyes, and it took a moment for him

to realize what it was. He'd put it in the past tense. Without even thinking about it.

With a sad sigh, he rested a hand on her shoulder, and she moved toward him, coming into his arms and laying her head on his chest, the way she'd done so many times before. They knew exactly how to stand with their arms wrapped around each other like this, knew how to position themselves just right.

"I'm sorry," he said into her hair.

"Me too. That kind of got lost there."

He paused. "Maybe you were right. Maybe I was too ready to walk away." He hadn't really considered it. But he realized now that she was right—he'd fled, the moment she'd told him, and he'd barely had a conversation with her since.

"We are doing the right thing, aren't we?" Vanessa asked, her voice slightly muffled.

"What, hugging or getting divorced?"

Vanessa huffed out a laugh. "Either. Both."

He didn't answer that. It was too late to change things now—and he knew he wouldn't, even if he could.

She didn't press him for an answer. Instead she eased back, and he dropped his arms away from her. "I saw a woman coming out of your office," she said, her voice careful. "Back in March, when we last spoke."

"Nothing happened." He said it too quickly, and it earned him a look. But it was true—nothing *had* happened. So why did it feel like it had? He'd wanted something to, that's why. He'd forgotten in those stolen hours with Holly that he was a divorcee, that he was only thirty-two and already had a failed marriage behind him. He hadn't really been thinking of much at all, while he was with her—for those few hours, she'd swept him away.

"Is that so?" Vanessa said wryly. "Because she was in a bit of a temper, the way only certain things can fire you up."

"It wasn't like that," Jack insisted. Maybe it would be easier for Vanessa, if it were—even the balance, somehow even though the divorce was already well under way by then. Maybe she was just curious, the way he'd been curious about her. "I kind of had a go at her," he admitted.

"You had a go at her?" Vanessa repeated, her voice going up at the end.

"Yeah. I was a bit 'unreasonable' some might say." *Holly* might say, he thought.

"Is that so? Unreasonable how?"

"Does it matter? I shouted at her, said things I shouldn't have and things I didn't mean." Things he'd replayed in his head constantly since she stormed somewhat ungracefully from his office, her red hair flying behind her.

"Hmm. Have you seen her since?"

"No. I sent her a message," he admitted. "She didn't answer." He'd only said he was sorry, and that he hoped she got back home safely—he hadn't asked a question or anything. But still, no answer. And really, who could blame her?

Vanessa was looking at him in a way that felt assessing.

"Why are you staring at me like that?"

"Because you never had a go at me, Jack," she said, smiling sadly. "Even after I told you I'd slept with someone else."

They looked at each other for a long moment, then Jack took a step back from her. "I'd better go. I appreciate you trying to be my friend here, but I don't think we're there yet."

"But maybe we will be?" Vanessa asked. "One day, I mean. Maybe we'll get there?"

"Yeah. Maybe." He felt a pang, then, for the friends they'd once been. He hadn't realized how much he'd missed that friendship—not just in the last nine months, but before then.

He headed for the hallway, turning to face her when he got to the door. What did you say to someone, in this situation? "Thanks for the drink," he said. Probably not that, he admitted to himself. But maybe there wasn't a right thing to say.

"I . . ." She looked up at him out of those blue eyes, then looked down at the floor, blinking. "Never mind." She gave his shoulder a squeeze, still not looking at him. "Goodbye, Jack."

"Yeah." He opened the door, looking back at her one last time. "Bye, Ness."

His phone rang as he headed out onto the street.

"Why aren't you in the office?" Ed demanded when Jack picked up.

"Vanessa wanted to meet," Jack said, his voice more tired than it should have been for the middle of the day. "So I took the day off." And she was a social media manager who worked from home, meaning her hours were of her choosing.

"Ah. How'd that go?"

"Well, it went." Jack headed for the train station automatically. "Anyway, you need me?"

"Nah, mate, it can wait."

"Ed," Jack said sternly.

"Jack," Ed said just as firmly. "I am not asking you about work when you've just gone and seen your soon-to-be ex-wife for the first time in nine months."

"I suppose work can wait. And it's just ex-wife now. It's official."

"Is that so? How are you feeling?"

"I don't know. Weird."

"Are you on your way back home? Why don't you take a detour? We can meet for a pint or two, and I can tell you all the things you have to look forward to as a single man."

Jack was on the verge of agreeing, thinking that he really didn't want to go back to his depressing little flat right now. But the conversation with Vanessa was replaying on a loop in his mind—and one bit was sticking out, getting louder and louder each time.

She was in a bit of a temper, the way only certain things can fire you up.

"Actually, do you know what?" he said decisively. "I've got plans."

"Have you?"

Jack tried not to be offended by the shock in Ed's voice. "Yeah."

"You didn't have plans when I asked yesterday."

"Well, call me spontaneous."

"Mate, no one has ever called you spontaneous in your life." There was a pause. And then, "Does this have anything to do with that woman who showed up a few weeks ago? The hot redhead who you spent the whole weekend with and then pretended was a figment of my imagination?"

How? How had Ed guessed it in bloody one? "Ah . . . maybe. How did you . . . ?"

"Because, Jack . . . You are not spontaneous, but you asked her out on the spot."

Jack shook his head as he turned in to Balham station. From here to Clapham—and from Clapham to Windsor. "Well, if it makes you feel any better, the spontaneity was three years in the making."

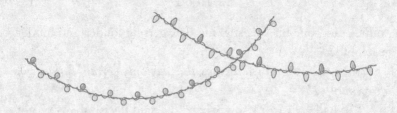

Chapter Seventeen

Within two hours, Jack was standing outside a sixth-form college, feeling like a total idiot. He was hovering near a bench on the grass on the outskirts of the car park, trying not to look odd or out of place, but feeling too uncomfortable to go into the school and ask for Holly. It didn't help that the building itself looked like it could be some sort of bloody country hotel, with big pillars on either side of the entrance to what he presumed was reception, a clock tower extending above, the red brick of the rest of the building bright in the June sunshine. A far cry from the secondary school he'd attended in Plymouth.

It was four thirty P.M., and the end of the school day: Hordes of teenagers were swarming out of the building and heading toward the car park. No sign of any teachers, though. Maybe they had a different finishing time? He had no idea how it worked. He'd never paid that much attention to what his own teachers had done—he'd put his head down, worked hard to get the grades, but generally got out of there as soon as possible at the end of each day, like everyone else.

He was just thinking that maybe he should give up, when he saw her, coming out between the pillars, the sunlight glinting off her hair. He felt the flash of heat running down his spine, told himself it was just the warmth of the summer's day. She was walking side by side with a woman with chestnut-colored curls, the kind that bounced when she walked, and a skinny man with blond hair that was thinning out on top. It was Holly he couldn't stop looking at, though. She was wearing a short-sleeved bright-blue shirt and a black skirt, with white pumps. Her arms were bare, though she was still as pale as when he'd seen her in March. There was no reason, none at all, for the completely teacher-appropriate outfit to look sexy, yet somehow it did. It was the color, he thought. The way it offset that quick, vibrant way she always moved, making her seem somehow . . . electric.

He didn't have to wave or shout to get her attention. He saw it, the moment she clocked him. He saw her stumble, tripping over her own feet as she came to a stop. Saw the way her eyes widened, then flickered to either side of him, as if looking for an explanation. He straightened, coming out from beneath the shade of the nearest tree, stepping from the grass to tarmac in between two parked cars.

The woman with the curls had stopped at almost the exact same moment and spun her head to look at Jack. Her eyes narrowed, assessing him, before she turned back to Holly, saying something in a low tone. The man had been slower on the uptake but had now stopped too, frowning back at Holly, who still showed no sign of wanting to approach Jack.

Taking a slow, careful breath, tasting the warm summer air and breathing in the smell of freshly mown grass, Jack started toward her.

Holly watched him carefully as he approached. He tried not to think of the last time he'd seen her, of how she'd run from his office—and how he'd done nothing to stop her. She lifted her chin when he drew near enough to speak to. Preparing for a confrontation, probably.

"Hi, Holly," he said, keeping his eyes level on hers, even though she refused to hold his gaze for long. The man and the woman on either side of her, however, were both staring at him. Sweat pricked the back of his neck, but he kept his posture casual.

"What are you doing here?" she asked, not quite a snap but definitely leaning in that direction.

He tried for a smile. "You're not the only one who can track someone down and show up unannounced."

"Ah," the woman with the curls said, as Holly's lips tightened.

"That was different."

He cocked his head. "How?"

"Errr . . ." the man interjected. "Hi?"

"Hi," Jack said, offering him a polite smile.

The woman with the curls raised her eyebrows. But she did not look pissed off, like Holly, or confounded, like the man. More curious. "Jack, I take it?" She held out a hand, her handshake firm, confident.

"Jack?" repeated the man, looking at the woman with the curls. "Who on earth is . . . ?" But he trailed off, seeming to realize he was being rude. Jack hadn't thought of what to do if there were other people here. Which in hindsight was stupid—it seemed obvious that there was a very good chance there would be other people with her since she was at work. This was why he generally shied away from the impulsive—it was usually better if you had a plan, stuck to it. Less opportunity for things to go wrong.

"Can we talk, Holly?" At least his voice was level—that was something.

They were getting a few curious looks from the teenagers—

the ones who were straggling behind, having stayed on late. The woman with the curls seemed to notice that too, and when she spoke her voice was brisk, used to taking charge. "Daniel, I think Holly and Jack need to have a chat, so why don't you and I get going? No, come on," she said, as Daniel began to protest. "I'll drive you. Unless . . ." she added, giving Holly a searching look, "you haven't finished prepping for parents' evening tomorrow? Because you know we need to be in top form, after last time."

An out, Jack recognized. Whether or not this small, take-charge woman was actually Holly's boss, she was offering Holly an out, should she need it.

Holly hesitated, and for a moment Jack thought she'd take it. Then she huffed out a breath. "No, it's all right. I'll talk to him."

"Right. Come on, Daniel." She whispered, "See you later, babe," before putting a hand on Daniel's back and marching him off across the car park.

Holly wound her fingers around the handle of her tote bag on her shoulder, then moved to the side of the car park, underneath the shade of the trees once again. Jack followed her, welcoming the slightly cooler air.

Holly took the bag off her shoulder, dumping it in front of her feet on the grass unceremoniously. Then, without preamble, she asked, "What are you doing here, Jack?"

He ran a hand across the back of his neck, feeling pressure rise up in his chest—the need to get it right. "I wanted to apologize."

Holly was frowning. Though, actually, maybe she'd never stopped frowning since she'd seen him. Not a great sign. "So you showed up at my school?" She shot him a dry, cutting look. "Seems a bit over the top."

He forced himself to stay even despite her tone—after all, he was the one coming to her this time. "Again: pot, kettle." He said it with a little smile in his voice, to try to steer the conversation away from more antagonistic directions.

"That analogy doesn't even make sense—kettles aren't black, and my pots are silver."

He felt his lips twitch up ever so slightly. "You never answered my message."

"No," she agreed. "I didn't think there was anything more to say. You made yourself perfectly clear."

"Well, that's the thing. I . . . Can we talk, please? Go somewhere . . . else? Maybe somewhere we can sit? Or walk?"

She hesitated. "I'm not sure that's a good idea."

"I'm not married, Holly," he said quietly. It was dancing around the issue, really, but it was something. She looked at him for a long moment, and he felt more words start to spill out despite his attempt to stay clear and rational. "Well, I mean, I was, but I'm divorced. Vanessa, my wife—ex-wife—cheated on me and we separated in October and we were already halfway through the process by the time I saw you again and . . ." He stopped himself, took a breath. "The point is, I'm divorced. Back in March, when Vanessa came to the office, it was only because she needed me to sign something, to get the last bit of paperwork done."

She was still looking at him, her eyes assessing. "If that's true," she said eventually, "then why didn't you say so before?"

"Because I'm a dick," he said, and it got a small smile from her. "And because I was angry, and I thought it was easiest, to let you believe it."

She nodded slowly. "And now you want to, what, set the record straight? After telling me, if I remember correctly, to get out of your face?"

He winced, ashamed of himself for his words, and this time he didn't think he stopped it from showing.

She sighed. "OK, we can go somewhere."

"We can?"

She gave him a look. "Why did you come, if you didn't think I'd say yes?"

He gave a sheepish shrug. "I hadn't really thought that far ahead."

She cocked her head, her hair spilling to one side. This time, there was something lighter in her eyes. "Well, I can understand that, at least. Come on," she said, picking up her tote bag and starting across the car park, fumbling in her bag for keys. "I'm not inviting you back to my flat, but I know somewhere we can go."

And, following behind her, Jack allowed himself a small smile.

Holly parked the car up against a line of evergreen trees, and Jack released his hand from the seatbelt, flexing his fingers as he unbuckled it. He saw Holly glance at his hand, knew she'd noticed it. He still wasn't very good at being a passenger in a car, even so many years later. Driving, he was fine with—you were in control when you were driving. He wasn't *scared*, exactly, when he was a passenger, but he'd got into a habit of holding the seatbelt, and he always felt a bit tense, even if he only realized it when he saw other people noticing. You'd think he'd have got over it by now, but he couldn't quite shake it.

"You're taking me to a castle?" Jack asked, before she could say anything about it. They couldn't see Windsor Castle from the car park, but Jack had caught a glimpse of it on the way in.

"It was the first place I thought of."

"The first place you thought of was a castle?" Jack asked, shooting her a little smile as he got out of the car.

She emptied her tote bag on the backseat of her car, then shoved her phone and keys in it before slinging it over her shoulder, much lighter now. "Well, this is Windsor. And besides, I'm not taking you to the castle, I'm taking you to the *grounds*," she said, putting on a grand voice as she locked her car—a little green Clio. "Abi has a membership to the park so she gets free parking, and I can use it too."

"Who's Abi?" Jack asked, following Holly.

She glanced up at him as they walked. "The woman from the car park. My friend."

"Ah." It was a reminder of how little they knew each other. And then of how much he'd overreacted to her telling him about Emma—because yes, he still thought she should have told him earlier, rather than pretending to know nothing about him, but they'd only met up twice in London, a little over four hours in total, so it wasn't like she'd betrayed some kind of trust after months of dating.

Jack matched his stride to Holly's as she headed for the entrance. He saw the sign—*Windsor Great Park, The Savill Garden*. He'd never been here—to the castle or the gardens. She led him through a glass building where a small crowd of people were milling around, and, after taking care of all the admission details, he followed her out at the other side. She seemed to do everything at speed, and he couldn't help admiring the constant energy fizzing off her, like a background hum. The type of energy that made you feel it too, just by being near her.

She shot him a glance and he looked away from her, putting his thumbs through the belt loops in his jeans as he scanned the garden. Though "garden" was hardly an appropriate word for the scale of this place. He wasn't really sure where to look first—there was no end in sight, and the way the different paths wove out in front of them hinted at various corners to explore. It was bright green and full of color, and though there was no shortage of people milling about, some with binoculars around their necks and wearing impressive sunhats, Jack could still hear the hum of insect life in the bushes to his left.

"There are different bits you can visit," Holly said. "Like the summer garden, the spring wood, the autumn wood." She frowned. "I'm not sure if there's a winter wood. I guess winter's not a good time for gardens." She seemed to think about that for a moment, then shrugged. "Still, let's go this way." She struck out confidently, heading for a path through a woodland area, and Jack followed, his brain calculating the way the garden must have been put together. It was a cool idea, to organize it around the seasons—presumably each part of the garden would come alive at different times, so that there was always something to enjoy.

"So," Holly said, and Jack immediately looked at her. She was looking straight ahead, though. "The divorce is official?"

"Yes." Jack hesitated. "As of today."

Holly visibly jolted, like she'd walked into something. "Today! Jack, what—?"

"I got the piece of paper today," Jack said, his voice firm. "But it's just a piece of paper. It turns out that it's not that easy—or quick—to just 'get' a divorce."

"I suppose that's because it should mean something," Holly muttered.

Jack winced. "Yeah. I suppose so." And wasn't that an echo of what Vanessa had said? That if it was right, it shouldn't have been so easy to walk away from?

"Sorry," Holly said on an outward breath. "Not my place."

"That's all right. Maybe I deserved it."

Holly turned right, down a grass path, perfectly mown, the green vibrant under the blue sky. The herbaceous borders were impressive—different colors and plants all offsetting each other perfectly, in a way that made him wish he could stop to study it properly. He looked away from the plant life, though, and at Holly instead.

"I'm sorry, for not explaining properly." She kept walking. "And I'm sorry if . . . I shouldn't have lashed out like that, when you brought up Emma. It was just a shock. And it's something I don't really like to be reminded of."

She said nothing for a while, her lips pursed. He felt the prick of sweat on his palms, forced himself not to say anything into the silence. She wouldn't have come with him, if she hadn't wanted to listen.

"I'm sorry too," she said eventually. "I shouldn't have sprung it on you like that." She shot him a look. She was good at those looks, he was learning—the ones that made you want to cringe or back away. "Though I did try to apologize then, too."

"Yeah. I know. I'm—"

"Sorry?" she asked sweetly, and he let out a short, dry laugh. "Yeah."

"Well, there we are then." Was that the end of that, then? Done and dusted? His palms were still prickling, though, like there was tension in the air between them, even if neither of them wanted to admit it.

Holly hesitated at the end of the path, then struck off to the left. He wasn't sure if she had somewhere in mind, or if she just didn't want to stand still for too long. This path had another herbaceous border, full of various shades of purple, from lilac to deep black currant. He could hear the sound of two kids laughing, a few other voices washing over them, but the silence between him and Holly was building.

"This is what I used to want to do," he said into the quiet between them. She looked up at him in question. "For a job, I mean."

She frowned. "Hang out in gardens?"

He laughed quietly. "Landscape gardening. I love being in

gardens, always have. I love it on the micro level—you know, getting your hands in the soil, nurturing something, seeing it grow. Figuring out what works best for each individual plant and why. And I love looking at the big scale of it too." He gestured to their surroundings. "Designing something that can be enjoyed by other people, yes, but that also helps promote diversity of species." He sighed. "We are destructive by nature, us humans, and it's a tiny thing, really, but a good landscape gardener can both help think about the design and help to regain some of what's lost, too."

Holly was watching him. "Emma said she used to garden with you," she said, her voice low and careful.

He'd been prepared for Emma to come up this time, but it still caused a spasm in his gut, hearing her name. "Yeah," he said. "Yeah, she did."

There were a lot of memories of his childhood that had grown hazy—something which, when he'd been forced to see a therapist after the crash, he'd been told was normal: After trauma, memories can fade. He regretted it—especially that he'd lost parts of his dad, when he had so little to cling on to in the first place. Only ten years, and of that, only around five he had any sort of recollection of. But he still had memories of Emma, like it or not. He could remember the two of them in the garden, both with their hands dirty, Emma sitting on her knees, leaning back, and Jack crouching over the plant they'd just planted.

"I want it to grow now," he'd said, his voice demanding.

"Well, that's the thing about plants—they rarely do what we want just because we want them to. We have to learn how to give them what they need instead."

Jack had scowled at that, just as his dad had come out into the garden. He hadn't realized his dad had come over. He remembered it—the excitement of seeing him, after a few days of being asleep by the time he'd come home. They'd lived a few doors away from Emma, and his dad must have come to pick him up.

"Richard," Emma had said, straightening up. "I thought you were working late today."

"Got off early," his dad said with a grin. "But don't let me stop you."

"You could help," Emma said pointedly.

His dad headed for the patio, pulled out one of those wicker chairs Emma had let Jack choose from the gardening center, and slouched into it. "Nah, I'll just watch. This way you can learn to do it, Jack, and I won't ever have to bother."

He'd never really got the interest in the garden, his dad, but he'd bought Jack a trowel for Christmas one year, then suggested he take it in to school, next time one of the boys in his class called gardening "girly."

Holly was still watching him. There was no point, he supposed, in trying to skirt around the subject—it was hanging over them, whether he liked it or not.

"How is she?" He could hear the grate of his voice as he spoke. "Emma?"

Holly hesitated. "She's refusing chemo." Her face was tight as she said it—she clearly cared about Emma. He wanted to know how they'd met. Had she gone back to the café one day? The way he'd gone back there, before the service for his dad, wanting the reminder of childhood trips there for cake? He couldn't ask that, not right now.

Instead he asked, "Why?"

"Because she doesn't like the side effects, and apparently it's not one hundred percent effective anyway."

His frown deepened. "What type of cancer is it?"

She gave him one of those looks, and he knew why—he should have asked this the first time around. "Pancreatic cancer."

He nodded, trying to digest the information. He couldn't

imagine it. The Emma he'd known had been healthy and active, and tough—in a way that made you think she'd always just be there. He wasn't sure he could picture her as an old, ill woman—wasn't sure he wanted to. But people survived cancer all the time, didn't they? Ed's uncle had had cancer last year, and while he hadn't yet been given the all clear, Ed said he was past the worst of it and had a good prognosis. And if anyone could survive it, surely Emma—the Emma he remembered, anyway—could, because she was too damn stubborn not to. Though he didn't think that refusing chemo would increase the chances of her survival.

"They'll kick us out of here soon," Holly said. He wasn't sure if that was a way of her voicing disapproval, or of ending the conversation between them. She turned to walk away, but when he didn't immediately follow because he was trying to think of something to say, something to keep her there, she glanced back at him. "Come on," she said, jerking her head to get him to come with her. "This isn't the only cool bit to see."

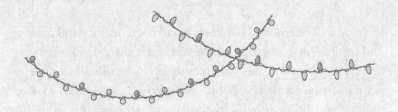

Chapter Eighteen

Holly led him back the way they'd come and through the glass building again, but instead of heading toward the car, she led him onto a tarmac path on a perfectly mown, seemingly endless lawn, a line of trees running down each side—a mix of horse chestnuts, oaks, and London planes, their leaves that brilliant early summer green. Jack didn't have to turn to look at the castle behind him—he could feel the presence of it, like it was alive, watching everyone.

"I think I remember reading about this. This is the Long Walk, right?" Holly nodded. "So I'm pretty sure they replanted these—the trees, I mean. They used to be elms until the Dutch elm disease in 1980. Which means the trees are only around forty years old."

"Only?"

Jack shrugged. "Not a long life, for a tree—they'll be here standing long after us, if no one tears them down."

They kept walking. The sun was getting lower now, turning the sky a faint pink.

"Why didn't you pursue it?"

He glanced down at Holly. "Huh?"

"Gardening. Or landscape gardening, whatever. Why didn't you ever try to do it as a job?"

"Well, it's not that easy a career path. Hard to get into it, hard to make money. Not very . . ."—he waved a hand in the air, looking for the right word—"secure, I suppose."

"But if you love it, then isn't it worth it?"

Jack looked at her pointedly. "I could ask you the same thing."

"What do you mean?" But she said it too quickly, and looked away, straight up through the trees, along the long, straight path.

"You love art—why did you give it up?"

She said nothing for so long, he didn't think she was going to answer. When she did speak, her voice was so low, he had to strain to hear it. "I was in a car crash. Three years ago."

He sucked in a breath.

She continued, still staring straight ahead. "It wasn't half an hour after we bumped into one another. It's why I never called—I meant what I said, I did lose the cup with your number on it."

He was staring at her now, he realized—but she wouldn't look back at him.

"My sister was in the car," she whispered. "She was pregnant, I don't know if you remember?" She didn't wait for an answer. "Anyway, I was driving."

His heart stuttered.

"I got distracted by my phone, and another car came straight at us. I braked, but not in time, so we crashed. And my sister miscarried."

"I . . ." But his throat felt thick, and he had to swallow. "Jesus, Holly, I'm so sorry."

"She hasn't spoken to me since that day." Her tone was even, but her face was pale and she was staring hard at the concrete in front of her. "My sister. Because she blames me." Holly came to a stop, turned to face him, and lifted her gaze to his—her green eyes made greener out here. "So I know what it's like." Her voice lifted, became louder, firmer. And something sparked in those eyes of hers. "To be the one responsible. I know what it's like to be blamed."

He thought of what he'd said to her, in March. That Emma had *killed* his dad. The word he'd used, the way he'd said it. He hadn't thought—he would never have been able to guess. Was this what had drawn them together, his grandmother and Holly? He couldn't think how, but it seemed impossible—two car crashes, both of them driving, both of them losing someone. "I'm so sorry, Holly," he said, his voice quiet. "But . . . But if the other car was coming at you, was it really your fault?"

She cocked her head. "Couldn't you say the same about Emma?"

He took his time to answer, not wanting to say the wrong thing. "She ran into something," he said slowly. "She crashed into a tree at the side of the road. It's not the same thing."

But there had been another car, hadn't there? It had been winter, dark and rainy outside, and he could remember the incoming car lights, the sound of a horn. He still wasn't sure of the order of things. He'd had nightmares about it, over and over, for months afterward, and it had become difficult to separate what had actually happened from what was made worse by the dreams. But he did remember Emma swiping the keys out of his dad's hands as they came down the stairs together that day.

"I'll take those, Richard, don't you think?" Then Emma had winked at Jack. "Come on, my boy, don't want to be late. I want to hear if you're as good as your dad keeps telling me you are." She ruffled his hair when she reached him, seemed to sense his nerves, even though he said nothing. "Don't worry. I'm tone deaf anyway, so I'll think it's brilliant no matter what."

"What does tone deaf mean?" Jack asked.

"It means you don't want to listen to her singing in the shower," his grandad had said, getting up from where he was sitting in the living room and joining them all. He'd tended to do that, his grandad—stay out of the way, wait in the background. Jack barely had any memories of him. He hadn't even gone to his funeral. It was something he'd felt uncomfortable about, afterward, but he'd been at university when he got the news. His mum had found out about the funeral and though she hadn't been going, she'd wanted to tell him, just in case. He'd used the excuse of being too busy, of not being able to make the trip on short notice. But really, he hadn't wanted to go down that rabbit hole—hadn't wanted to open up the past when he was successfully starting his adult life. He really should have gone, he thought now.

Maybe it was that, the lurking guilt, that made him say, a touch defensively, "She chose to drive. My dad wanted to drive and she . . ."

A flash of the incoming headlights again. Of his dad, in the passenger seat, complaining about Emma not going fast enough, of his mum telling him to *shhh*. He remembered kicking the back of Emma's seat, nerves and frustration getting the better of him. Remembered Emma's voice. "Don't do that please, Jack. It's distracting."

He was grateful when Holly's voice pulled him out of the memory. "That doesn't change the fact that it was an accident."

Holly turned to look back at the castle and he mirrored her, looking out at the stone turrets. Then she folded her legs underneath her and sat where she was on the grass, placing her hands behind her and leaning back on her palms. Jack copied her. He tried—and failed—not to feel pleased, at the fact that she was settling in to talk to him.

"I invited her, you know," he said quietly, after a moment.

"To the ceremony I was planning that day." She didn't ask which day. They kept circling back to it, one way or another. "I invited Emma and she didn't come," he repeated. "She ever say anything about that?"

He'd kept his tone casual but though he'd mentioned it to make a point to Holly, to prove that he wasn't the bad guy here, he realized he actually wanted to know the answer. He *wanted* there to be a reason—a reason, not an excuse—that explained why Emma hadn't been there. Because it had been an olive branch. He'd sent the invitation to Emma via post, since even though he didn't have a phone number, he still knew where she lived—and she'd proven that she didn't care enough to come.

"No," Holly said. "She's never said." She bit her lip. "That doesn't mean . . . We don't . . ." She huffed out one of her impatient breaths. "She doesn't like talking about it that much."

"What *do* you talk about?"

"I don't know. Other things. Art. It's kind of hard to explain. If you got to know her, you'd get what I mean." She paused. "I think you'd like her, you know."

He frowned—because Emma was his grandmother and he *had* known her. But perhaps that was the point. A child relationship was different from an adult one, and maybe that was part of the reason it was so difficult—because how did you even begin to form that, when there was so much missing in between?

Holly's phone buzzed, and she fumbled in her bag for it. She read a message, glancing at Jack quickly before typing a reply and then shoving the phone back in her bag. And he knew. He just *knew* who had texted her, even before she said, a little pointedly, "That was Emma. We're having lunch in a few days."

He nodded slowly, not sure of what to say. How often did they check in with each other? he wondered. He couldn't really fathom it: the thought of his grandmother, the one he'd cut so completely from his life, talking to this woman sitting next to him. He opened his mouth, not really sure of what he was going to say. But then a shape jumped out several meters ahead of them, and Jack made a startled sound. "Is that a deer?"

It was. It had antlers and everything. And it was right *there,* in front of everyone. "That's so cool!" He was grinning, though he schooled his face when he clocked Holly watching him, looking amused by his delight.

"They live here," Holly said. "You're such a city boy."

It was a teasing tone, and he felt lighter, hearing it. She was impressing him too, how easily she'd softened once they started to talk through things—maybe not completely, but still. He'd been bracing for the temper he'd seen back in March, but maybe she was the type to flare with anger and then let it go just as easily. Or maybe she was good at hiding it, though he didn't think so. But he wanted to know. It surprised him how intensely he wanted to dig beneath the layers and figure her out.

"Hey, I was a country boy, once upon a time." He looked out at the trees again. "It must be amazing in autumn here," he murmured. "All these trees changing colors, all at different times."

"It is," Holly agreed. "I brought my students here in autumn last year to paint the landscape and capture the colors changing for just that reason."

He ran his hand through the warm grass. "Do you ever paint here?"

"No. Not really my thing, painting. I'm OK at it, but not brilliant. Not enough to . . ." She trailed off, tucked a strand of hair behind her ear.

It was Jack's phone that beeped this time, and he slipped it out of his back pocket automatically.

"Feel free to take it," Holly said.

"No, it's an alarm," he said, switching it off as he spoke.

"An alarm? Regularly get up at six P.M., do you?"

He rolled his eyes. "A reminder, then, not an alarm. It's my half-sister's birthday next week, so I'm reminding myself to get her a present."

"Half-sister?"

"Different dad," he explained. But now he felt like a dick, for calling attention to it specifically. She was his sister, wasn't she? Half or not.

"Oh right, of course." Holly paused for a moment and he remembered that she had already known about his dad's death when he'd told her about it, but she quickly covered up any awkwardness by asking, "So what are you going to get her?"

"No idea." Jack spread his legs in front of him, supporting himself on his hands, sunlight warm on his face. "A voucher? Amazon voucher? She can get whatever she likes then."

Holly did a sort of nod-shrug thing and he tapped one finger on the grass.

"She's going to be fourteen—what did you want when you were fourteen?"

"I hate to tell you this, but not all fourteen-year-old girls want exactly the same thing. And unless she wants a DIY pottery set, I don't think I'm your marker."

"Right, you're right." He paused for a moment. "They're having a family celebration this weekend—separate from her birthday party with all her *actual* friends, or so my mum tells me—but I might not go to it, which buys me a bit more time, I suppose."

"Why wouldn't you go?"

"Just . . . I don't know." He couldn't think of the right way to phrase it. "It's sort of . . . my mum's family. No," he corrected quickly. "I don't mean that, obviously they're my family too, but there's sometimes this awkwardness. I can't quite explain it, but I'm never quite sure if they want me there or not. There's such an age gap between my siblings and I, it just feels a bit like I don't quite belong."

Holly pursed her lips. "If it were my sister," she said slowly, "I'd give anything to be invited to her birthday again." He watched it, the way the pain flashed across her face, even as she picked up a strand of grass, started to play with it. She offered him a quick glance. "I'm just saying."

And it made him feel ridiculous. Because she was right—he *should* go. And because he couldn't imagine what the guilt Holly was so clearly carrying around would be doing to her. He was surprised he hadn't noticed it, hadn't somehow *felt* it, back in March. But then that made him think of the guilt other people were carrying around, and that made his throat feel tight.

"Well," Holly said briskly, "usually I'd say you can't go wrong with a voucher as a present, but it's also pretty impersonal, so if it were me I'd go for something that's a bit different. I don't know your sister at all, and it sounds like you might not know her that well either—no judgment there," she added quickly, "but like, a cool phone case—an arty, recycled one, you know, because she'll probably have a phone she's obsessed with, or a trip somewhere for her and her friends—a spa or something. Or a piece of art." She wrinkled her nose. "Obviously I would say that, but it's something you can keep—and it can decorate her room. You'd have to guess at what she'll like on the art front—but something cool and colorful generally goes down well with that age group, if my students are anything to go by."

"Thank you," he said.

She shrugged, the action almost careless, though he knew it couldn't be, not really. Not if she was thinking about her own sister, and the birthdays she had missed. "You're welcome."

He watched her, trying to think of something to say, as she brushed her hair away from her face again. The strand of grass she'd been fiddling with got stuck there and he shifted automatically, leaning toward her and reaching up to pull it gently from the tangle of red. She stilled, and her gaze snapped to his in a way that made him briefly freeze too. His hand was still there, resting against her jawline now, her skin soft, a line of freckles running across her cheeks—something that hadn't been there in the spring.

For a moment their gazes held. His heart sprang into action, thudding against his ribs, making him very aware of every beat, every breath. He heard it from her, too, the shift in her breathing. She reached up, placing a hand over his, and his skin sparked at the contact. But she took his hand in hers, lifted it away from her face.

"I don't think we should go there," she whispered.

He pulled his hand away from hers. "Right," he said, his voice gruffer than he would have liked. "Right, I'm sorry." There was no point in playing it cool. She'd be able to read it—just as he could read it in her too, the way her eyes had sharpened, the intense stillness of her body. But she was right. It wasn't a good idea, to go there.

"I'm sorry I can't," she said, looking him very directly in the eye. "I'm friends with Emma. It would feel . . ."

"I know," he said, sighing as he looked back out toward the castle. Weird, is what it would feel. For him, too. He couldn't kiss her, when she was texting his grandmother. His grandmother, who had cancer. His grandmother, whom he'd spent years blaming for the worst moment of his life.

"Do you think you'll speak to her at some point? Emma?" Holly was watching him like she knew the thoughts that had been running through his mind.

He waited before answering, trying to let it all settle a bit. "I'll think about it," he said eventually. "I just . . . I need to figure some things out, Holly. I've got nearly twenty years of emotions I've got to sort through first."

"I'll text you her number," she said immediately. "Then you

at least have it if you . . . Sorry. I'm interfering again." She offered a self-deprecating smile. "Apparently that's my thing."

He huffed out a laugh. "I've noticed."

She gave him a playful prod in the ribs, and though he appreciated the attempt to keep it light, he had to stop himself from grabbing her hand, pulling her close. He remembered what it had felt like, to have her in his arms, feel her energy vibrating there. Remembered the smell of her, spicy somehow, like cinnamon.

Holly grabbed her bag, then pushed to her feet. "I need to head home. Do you want to walk back with me? I can give you a lift somewhere if you need?" No suggestion of dinner, or drinks, or extending their time together. No, she was very clearly signaling to him that their time was up.

But he nodded, got to his feet too. A walk back with her, then they'd go their separate ways. It was the sensible thing to do—and at least the air was clear between them now, more or less. And he tried, he really did, to feel glad about that. After all, Emma was the only connection between them—a connection he hadn't even wanted. Without that, Holly was practically a stranger. Just a woman he'd met in a café three years ago.

And had thought about ever since.

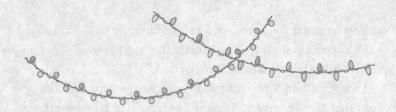

Chapter Nineteen

It was Derek who answered the front door when Jack rang the bell, Mia's present clutched under one elbow.

"Jack!"

"Derek!"

They clapped each other awkwardly on the back, their tones full of the false bravado they'd moved on to after the slightly sullen stage of Jack's teenage years, and never quite moved past.

"Come in, come in," Derek said, gesturing Jack in through the door then leading him through the house and out to the back garden. The garden was the selling point of the house, in Jack's opinion. Not that they did a lot with it—the grass was mown in neat lines, and there was a patio complete with barbecue and plastic chairs and tables, along with a trampoline at the end, from when Mia and Theo had been little. Jack had always thought they could do so much more with it—they had the space to really get some color and layers in, maybe some delphiniums, hardy geraniums for the base of some taller plants, even some climbing roses for the fence at the back. But his mum had never been big into gardening, and apparently Derek wasn't either. Jack had always envied them this green space, something he didn't have in London.

"Can I get you a beer, Jack?" Derek asked.

"Sure."

Derek crossed the patio for a cooler, which Jack couldn't help smiling at—they were doing the barbecue properly, stocking up a cooler so they didn't need to head indoors to the fridge. The way Derek looked then—wearing a T-shirt with a dog on it, a little round around the edges, big arms on show, reminded Jack of his dad a little. A memory came to him then, of his mum and dad in their little kitchen on the other side of Devon, and his mum making a comment when his dad swiped a sausage from the frying pan.

"You making fun of my dad-bod, Rose?" his dad had asked, wiggling his eyebrows for comic effect.

"I'm only saying, it might do you good to cut back a bit."

His dad had caught Jack's eye, then winked. "Jack doesn't mind, do you, Jack? Makes for a good punching bag, all this flab."

"Jack, you made it!" His mum's voice pulled him back to the sunny garden. She was walking over to him, complete with a sun hat and sunglasses, Pimm's in hand, wearing a floaty summery dress, looking tanned and happy. He smiled at her, gave her a kiss on the cheek. "I'm so glad you could come," she said, giving him a one-armed hug, then pulling back to look at him. "Was the drive awful?" She'd changed her hair, he noticed now—it was always blonde, but it was now cropped to her shoulders.

"It was all right," Jack said. Though he'd felt the mounting pressure, the way he always did, as he crossed the border into Devon.

Derek headed away to take up residence behind the smoking barbecue, grabbing one of the utensils and holding it up in preparation to start flipping burgers.

"Mia!" his mum called down to the end of the garden. Mia was sitting with another teenage girl on the trampoline, both of them cross-legged and showing no intention of jumping on the thing. She took after his mum in her looks: Her blonde hair was straighter and longer and a little darker, probably because it was without the highlights his mum put into hers, but she had the same round face, and the same eyes—hazel, as opposed to Jack's darker brown.

"Mia!" his mum shouted again, and this time both girls looked up. "Come and say hello to Jack."

Mia threw a slightly sulky look at them but got up nonetheless, and she and her friend sauntered up the garden toward them.

"Hi, Mia," Jack said, then immediately cringed. His voice was too bright. She wasn't a dog, for God's sake.

"Hi," she said, exchanging a look with her friend—just as skinny as Mia, with dark hair and a long fringe that partly obscured her face.

"Ah, happy birthday."

"Thanks." Another look at the friend.

"This is Jess," his mum said, indicating said friend, who looked up at Jack through thick eyelashes when she was introduced.

"Right, so, Mum, can me and Jess go out tonight?" Mia twirled a lock of hair around her finger. "Sadie's having a party."

"No," his mum said, so firmly it made Jack wince—that tone hadn't changed since he was a kid. "It's a family day."

"But it's my birthday!"

"It's not your birthday until Thursday, and you're having your party next weekend so don't try that on me."

She took a sip of her Pimm's while Mia scowled at her and Jack rubbed the back of his neck awkwardly. It was unfamiliar to him, this kind of family dynamic. Maybe it was the kind he might have had, if his dad hadn't died. If he and his mum hadn't been trying to pick up the pieces after the fact.

Mia turned to walk away, but Jack called her back. "Hey, Mia! I got you a present." He held the package out to her, and her scowl softened slightly as she took it from him.

All of them leaned in closely as she unwrapped it. Even Jack, and he'd bought the bloody thing. He watched her face carefully as she discarded the wrapping paper on the floor, which his mum bent to pick up, and held up the painting. He'd gone for Holly's suggestion in the end, unable to come up with anything else. She pursed her lips as she looked at it, then nodded. "This is cool," she said, and Jack let out the breath he hadn't realized he'd been holding. She held it up higher. "What's it supposed to be?"

"That's up to you, I think," Jack said, shoving a hand in his jeans pockets and rocking back on his heels. It was an abstract piece—again, Holly's idea—with a black background, bold reds and oranges splashed across the page. It had reminded him of Holly's fire, but also of that teenage feeling of impossibility, of being trapped in your own body.

"It's . . . angry, I think," she said, frowning in a contemplative way. "But also kind of hopeful?"

Jack smiled. "That's what I thought, too." It was why he'd liked it—the angry fire being offset by lighter yellows, just rising out on top, tempering the harshness of it and suggesting that the anger may perhaps only be fleeting.

She looked up at him and smiled too—not a full smile, but still. And he couldn't help but think of Emma in that moment, of how she'd given him his very first painting—the Mirabelle Landor card, the one he still had. The one he'd been carrying around with him when he met Holly that day in the café. He'd been carrying it almost like a talisman, because he'd been wondering if he might see Emma at the memorial.

What would Emma make of Mia? For some reason, he could

imagine Emma taking her under her wing, the way she'd apparently done with Holly, and the way she'd done with him when he was a kid. She'd been so much *cooler* than other grandmothers—so matter of fact, the way she'd spoken to him like he was an adult, which had made him think he could talk to her, no matter what.

He hadn't called her. It was all very well for Holly to tell him to, but it was easier said than done, with the weight of what had happened between them.

"So how are you, Jack?" his mum asked, once Mia and Jess had headed up to Mia's room to decide where to hang the painting. "How have you been, since the . . . ?"

"I'm fine," he said with a little shrug.

"No chance of getting back together, then?"

His mum had liked Vanessa. She was impressed by her, in part, he thought—Vanessa was pure glamour, and the embodiment of a life that his mum had never really had. Not that they'd spent a lot of time together—Vanessa was part of his London life, his adult life, which his mum had only made fleeting appearances in.

"Have you been getting out there? Meeting anyone new?"

He thought of Holly, of the way they'd shouted at each other in March. Thought of the way she'd looked in the castle grounds, humming with energy. How they'd left things, on an understanding that nothing could happen between them.

"No," he said. "There's no one new."

"Burgers are up!" Derek called.

Jack headed to the barbecue at the same time as Theo slouched over. Theo looked a bit like him, Jack realized with a little jolt—it wasn't something he'd ever noticed before. Like Mia, Theo had their mum's lighter hazel eyes, but they had the same face shape, and Jack had had the same scrawny figure growing up—something he'd lamented at the time.

"Hey, Theo," Jack said, and got a grunt in reply. He racked his brains for something to say. His mum had disappeared inside now to get the girls, and Derek was plating up the burgers. "How's school?"

Theo gave him a look.

"Sorry, that was lame."

"Yeah," Theo agreed.

"Wait, but haven't you just finished your GCSE's?" Jack asked.

"Got my last exam on Tuesday. History. I'm revising." He held up his phone as if to prove it, then took the burger that Derek was handing him and reached for the ketchup.

"How have they gone?"

He shrugged. "All right."

Jesus, talk about drawing blood. Had it always been this tough to talk to him? Then again, he had nothing to compare it to. Theo had been two when Jack had moved out and Mia hadn't even been born yet. He did remember Derek trying to engage him in conversation when he was sixteen, back when he and his mum had first started dating. He'd undoubtedly been even worse than Theo was now.

"What are you doing for A levels?" Theo made a face and Jack raised his eyebrows. "What?"

"I didn't want to go back for A levels," Theo said grudgingly. "But Mum's making me."

"Well," Jack said diplomatically, "I suppose they're useful if you want to go to university or whatever."

Theo conceded with a kind of half-shrug as he took a bite of his burger. Then he looked down at Jack's shoes, and spluttered, coughing up some bun. "Hey, are those LØCI shoes?"

Jack looked down at his feet, the gray-and-white high-tops he was wearing. "Ah, yeah, I guess so."

"I would love some, but Mum says they're too expensive."

"Well, they *are* pretty expensive, I guess."

"So does that mean you're rich?"

Jack laughed. "Not really. My job's all right but London's expensive, so it sort of balances out."

"I want to move to London," Theo said, his voice managing to be wistful even over a mouthful of burger.

"You do?"

"Yeah. Do you like it there?"

"Ah . . ." Jack took the burger Derek offered as he thought about that. "Well, if you love it, you love it and there's nowhere else, but if you don't . . ."

"I'm guessing you don't, then," Theo said shrewdly.

"I'm glad I went," Jack said by way of a non-answer.

"Well, it's got to be better than here," Theo muttered.

And Jack could remember that feeling. There were beautiful spots around here, especially on the coastline on a nice day, but there were also rough parts, and it could feel far away from anything. When Jack had first moved here, he'd preferred the Devon he'd grown up in—the countryside, all that open space, rather than the suburban feel of this place, and while he'd had friends and grown to like hanging out on the beach on a nice day, daring each other to swim even when it was cold, trying to get into one of the many student haunts before they were old enough, really he'd always been waiting to leave. To get away, start his life, leave the past well and truly behind. He was surprised that Theo hated it so much, though. He smiled slightly. "Not keen on it here then?"

"It's all right." It was said with another careless shrug, but there was something lurking there below the surface.

"Well, you can come visit me in London sometime, if you like."

Theo frowned at him—they were almost the same height now—and Jack felt the back of his neck grow hot.

He rubbed at it. "I mean, if you want to get a feel for the place or whatever. Have you been?"

A headshake.

"Well, I could show you around. See if it's somewhere you like, for the future."

Theo smiled then, and it added a vulnerability to his face. "Yeah, OK. When?"

"Ah . . ." Jack hadn't expected that—he'd expected Theo to turn him down, ask what they'd do, what they'd talk about.

He was stupid, he realized, for not having made more of an effort before now. He thought of what Holly had said to him in Windsor Park. *If it were my sister, I'd give anything to be invited to her birthday again.* Holly had lost it, that sibling connection, and was still clearly grieving for it.

"Come whenever," he said decisively. "I'll take some time off—we can go to all the sites."

"I'm not really into museums," Theo said in a warning tone.

"That's OK, me neither. London has more than museums."

"The shops?" He said it with another glance at Jack's shoes.

"Ah yeah, I guess."

"And clubs." Theo's voice turned sly and Jack laughed.

"Nice try. The most you can hope for is a beer with a meal one night."

"Fair enough. That's more than Mum lets me have." Jack looked over at his mum, who'd come back out onto the patio now, and she glanced away so quickly, Jack felt sure she'd been watching him.

Theo took another burger, then slouched off, getting out his phone and staring down at it.

"He's being bullied at school," Derek said quietly as he added sausages to the barbecue, along with slices of eggplant that were definitely Jack's mum's doing. "He doesn't talk about it much—we had to hear about it from the teacher in the first instance—but some of the boys are being quite nasty, sounds like. We asked him if he wanted to change schools—he gets quite good grades and I think he could move for sixth form—but he said that would be worse, so . . ." Derek blew out a breath. "Anyway, I'm glad he's got you to talk to—might help to have someone other than me and Rose."

Jack nodded, not knowing what to say. He hadn't known. He would make more of an effort, he told himself again. He should be there for Theo—and Mia—if they ever wanted or needed him. And even if they didn't, wasn't it his job, as their big brother, to find a way to connect?

"Mum!" Jack turned to see Mia coming out the back door, Jess in tow. "There is no popcorn. You said you'd get popcorn."

"You haven't even had a burger yet, and we've got cake in a bit."

"But Jess and I *need* popcorn."

"On the scale of needs that ranks pretty low," his mum said dryly.

"And those fruit cooler things, too," Mia carried on, folding her arms now. "The ones at the farm shop down the road. *Please* can you drive us? If we have to stay here all day and night then we need to stock up on supplies."

"We are having a family celebration for you, Mia," his mum said, and again, her tone, the gritted teeth, was all so familiar, that it made him smile. "Besides, I can't drive. I've had too much to drink."

"You've had one glass of Pimm's!"

"That's still too much for me. I'm a lightweight."

Mia turned to study her dad, who shook his head without even making eye contact, then looked at Jack. Her gaze scrutinized him, in a way that made Jack want to look away. He saw Mia's eyes light up—weak link. "Jack can take us," she said decisively.

"I, ah . . ." He swallowed. "I can, I guess."

His mum let out an exasperated sigh. "Fine."

"Great," Mia said brightly. "We'll just go and get changed."

"Why on earth do you need to get changed?" his mum asked.

"Because we might see someone!" Mia called over her shoulder as she and Jess scampered upstairs again. Jack's mum looked at Derek, who held up his hands in a *don't ask me* gesture.

Jack pulled his keys from his pocket and started to head through the house to wait by the front door.

His mum followed him. "Be careful, won't you?"

He turned to look at her. Did the accident still linger with her, the way it did with him? They'd all been in the car that day. He didn't remember it, that moment of impact, but he knew that his dad hadn't been wearing his seatbelt and had gone straight through the window when Emma swerved, crashed. He was the only one who had died, though his grandad had been unconscious for several hours and Emma had a concussion and bruises from the airbag. Jack had a cut across his neck from the seatbelt but he and his mum had been relatively unscathed. He could remember his mum running around to his side of the car, getting him out, shielding him with her body. Could remember the way she shook as she held him. He only had a vague sense of the chaos after—the sirens, police, ambulance, people handing out blankets. It hadn't seemed real. Still didn't seem real, somehow.

"I'll be careful," he said. "I always am."

His mum nodded, something unspoken passing between them.

He hesitated for a moment before saying, "Emma has cancer." He watched her expression. By unspoken agreement, they never talked about Emma. Her eyes flickered, but otherwise her expression stayed neutral. "Did you know?" he pressed.

"No." She pulled a hand through her hair. "No, I didn't

know. I don't run in those circles anymore, you know that." She paused. "How did you find out? Did she tell you?"

"No. I don't speak to her anymore either." Both he and his mum, blaming Emma. Because she was driving. Because she'd taken the keys and swerved and hit the tree. He had a flash of that night again. Of Emma's voice, on edge already, because they were late and his dad was making that known. Of his legs, smacking against her seat.

I told you not to do that, Jack!

He closed down that particular part of the memory, the way he always did.

"So how did you find out?"

"I . . . I heard it through the grapevine."

"Is it serious, do you know?"

"Well, it's cancer." A non-answer, both because he didn't know, and because he didn't really want to think about it. "Do you . . ." He broke off, started again. "Do you think I should get in touch with her?"

"That's up to you," she said carefully. "She's your grandmother." There was the tiniest inflection on *your*—the fact that he was related to Emma, and she was not.

"This girl, the person who told me. She reckons I should call Emma, says she wants to see me. But she never tried to get in touch herself, did she? When we moved, she could have tried, so I don't see why *now* I should . . ."

His mum winced at that. "Jack . . . Look, what happened that night . . . It broke things to a point that I didn't know how—and I'm not sure I wanted—to repair. I know you know that—you were there. But we all . . . It was something terrible, to come back from, and we all tried to deal with it in the best way we could. For me, that meant starting afresh. But Emma . . . she handled things differently." She took a breath, as Mia and Jess started down the stairs. "I can't tell you what to do there—I haven't spoken to her in a very long time, but I—"

Mia bounded up to them, Jess a step behind. "Ready!" she announced, and Jack opened the front door obediently.

He gave his mum's arm a friendly squeeze as Mia and Jess headed out in front of him toward his car. "Sorry," he said. "I shouldn't have brought it up."

"Come *on*," Mia cried.

So he went, and when they got to the shop he ended up agreeing to buy them way more than they'd originally asked for, hanging around for a good twenty minutes longer than was necessary.

When they got back home, Mia and Jess got out of the car with all the bags, but Jack stayed sitting there for a little longer. After a few moments, he took out his phone and brought up Holly's message with Emma's number. He took a breath, and then called it, feeling his heartbeat quickening with each ring.

It went to voicemail. He could leave a message, but what would he say? How did you even begin, in a voicemail? So he hung up. It was probably for the best. He had his own reasons not to want to open up that can, after all. Besides, maybe it was a sign—that what was in the past should stay there.

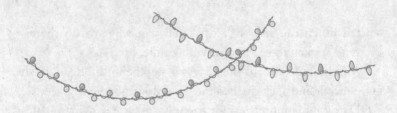

Chapter Twenty

"Who's having the risotto?"

"That's me," Holly said, smiling up at the waiter as he put it down in front of her.

"The house salad, no dressing?"

"Me," Abi said, the lack of enthusiasm in her voice almost comical. She was on the obligatory pre-wedding diet, having started months too early, in Holly's opinion.

The waiter placed the pasta dish in front of Emma and the pizza with an inordinate number of toppings in front of Pam. The four of them were in an Italian restaurant on the outskirts of Bristol, a meeting point between Windsor and Devon. None of them knew the area well, so it had been a bit of a punt, and so far seemed decidedly average, in Holly's opinion. Still, it was nice to see them, and she was pleased that Abi had finally got to meet Emma.

"More Prosecco?" asked the waiter, picking the empty bottle out of the wine cooler and holding it up in question.

"Oh, I should think so, darling," Pam said, draining the remainder of her glass. "Emma and I will drink it, even if the young'uns are being boring, won't we, Emma?"

"I'm driving," Holly protested.

"And I'm dieting," said Abi, prodding a limp-looking lettuce leaf with her fork, and earning an eye roll from Pam, as the waiter disappeared off to get another bottle.

"I only bothered to go on a diet for my first wedding day and that was the shortest marriage of them all," Pam said, as if this proved some kind of point.

"Well, I'm hoping my marriage will *not* be short," Abi said, picking up her sparkling water. "And therefore worth the diet."

"We all hope that, darling," Pam said.

Emma had been rather quiet since the starters had been taken away, and she'd barely touched the bruschetta she'd ordered, claiming that it was too dry. Holly kept sneaking looks at her, trying to figure out if she looked grayer than the last time she'd seen her. She certainly looked thinner, though she was wearing a nice bright dress today, which somewhat disguised that. Her hair seemed to be thinner, too—though again, that was difficult to be sure of, because she'd actually, to Pam's delight, been to the hairdresser for a blow-dry just the other day.

The waiter brought a new bottle of Prosecco over to the table and topped up Pam's and Emma's glasses. Holly gave Emma's glass a distrustful look. "Should you definitely be drinking?" she asked, though regretted it when she got a *look* in return. "I'm just wondering!" She'd been doing some research into pancreatic cancer online, though she was trying not to go into full-blown Doctor Google mode.

"It's hardly going to make things worse," Emma said, in a way that didn't feel wholly convincing. "And besides, I've got to make the most of things, while I can."

"What do you mean, while you can?" Holly asked sharply. Both Pam and Abi glanced at her, but she ignored them.

Emma sighed. "My girl, I'm just saying that when you get to my age, in my condition, you learn to enjoy the little things." Holly opened her mouth to ask more, but Emma spoke loudly over the top of her. "How's the wedding planning coming along, Abi?"

Abi coughed as she tried to swallow her salad too quickly. "Oh, good. I think I'm nearly there with everything."

"Already?" Pam asked. "Gosh, you're very organized."

Abi shrugged. "Being organized makes me feel calmer about the whole thing." Holly raised her eyebrows at that as she shoved a forkful of risotto into her mouth, and Abi gave her a guilty grin. "Most of the time."

"Abi's latest worry is why James hasn't written his speech yet—with four months still to go."

"Write it for him, darling," Pam said wisely. "That's what I did for Jim, and he's the one I'm still married to. And you, Holly?" Pam asked, looking at her over a slice of pizza. "How's the dating scene?"

"Ah . . ."

It was stupid, that her mind went immediately to Jack. She'd never even *dated* him, for God's sake. But she had seen him without Emma's knowledge, not once but twice now. And that thought made her stomach squirm, even as her mind wanted to remind her of the way his fingers had felt, tugging grass from her hair.

"I'm taking a break right now," she said, focusing deliberately on getting more risotto onto her fork. Even as she felt Abi shoot her a glance, like somehow she knew exactly where Holly's mind had just gone. "It's not been that long since Daniel and I broke up."

That earned a "Hmph" from Pam. "You've got to get back out there, darling."

"Oh, give her a break," Emma said, with a wave of her hand.

"Not everyone can be a serial dater like you. I wasn't," she added, almost as an afterthought.

Holly watched Emma's expression, trying to gauge it, but Emma became suddenly very interested in her Prosecco. She didn't talk a lot about her family or her past. Perhaps because it was too painful, thinking about what had once been, or what could have been if things had gone differently, if the accident hadn't happened. Holly hadn't been able to coax the fact that Emma was driving out of her yet. At first, she'd felt like she needed to get her head around it and then it felt like the kind of thing you shouldn't do over the phone—and this was the first time she'd seen Emma in person for a while. And she couldn't exactly have the conversation in front of Abi and Pam.

Emma was picking at her food now. Holly could have sworn she'd only eaten about two pieces of penne. "Aren't you hungry, Emma?" she asked.

"It's just a little cold," Emma said, by way of a non-answer.

"Well, that's no good," Abi said firmly. "Let's get the waiter over here." She straightened, opening her mouth to call out, and Holly knew she'd have her stern teacher voice prepped and ready.

"No, no," Emma said quickly. "Don't bother him. Besides, I had a big breakfast." She sighed, put her fork down. "I'll just pop to the loo, if that's OK." She waved a hand at them all as she stood. "Talk among yourselves."

Holly watched Emma going, assessing the way she was walking. The problem was, she hadn't known Emma *before* she'd got ill, so it was hard to tell whether she was worsening or not. Pam was watching her too, Holly realized. Even Abi was, which for some reason Holly found more worrying—like Emma was so obviously ill that Abi had tuned in to it. Silly, she told herself. She'd told Abi about the cancer.

"How's she doing, Pam?" Holly asked, keeping her voice low.

Pam considered, picking up her Prosecco but not drinking.

"She's . . . Well, I don't think she's doing as well as she pretends to be." It was carefully phrased, and Holly wondered how much Pam knew. Was Emma fobbing her off with half-answers too? Or did Pam know more than she was letting on, and just not want to tell Holly?

"Has she talked to you about what the doctors are saying?" Holly asked.

Another hesitation. "Not really. She isn't sleeping well, though; she's let that slip a few times. And I think there's some pain—but she's still only taking the over-the-counter painkillers."

Holly frowned, and Abi opened her mouth to say something, but Emma was coming back out of the ladies now, and all three of them went studiously back to their food.

Emma sat down and narrowed her eyes at them. "What are you all sitting here muttering about?"

"Nothing," Holly said quickly.

"You're a terrible liar."

"We were just saying thank God you're making a bit of an effort with your outfits these days," Pam said, adopting a lofty air. "I haven't seen the holey cardigan in a while now."

"Well, don't you worry. I've still got it at the back of the closet for special occasions."

They were all quiet for a moment, and Holly took a breath, squared her shoulders. "Emma," she started, but again she was cut off.

"Can't we just have a nice lunch, my girl? Aren't I allowed a little distraction from my cancer-riddled body?"

Holly winced at the word *riddled*, but she bit her lip, nodded. She was being selfish. She wanted to know the ins and outs of what Emma was going through, what the doctors had said about the cancer, because *she* wanted to know. But Emma was the one with the illness; Emma was the one who had to live with it, who had to decide on treatment options. So Emma was right: She should be allowed some distraction.

"So, I've been thinking about my honeymoon," Abi said brightly, and Holly gave her a grateful little smile.

"Oh goody," Pam said, pushing her half-eaten pizza away from her. Holly clocked the longing look Abi gave it. "That's the best bit. What's the short list?"

"We've been thinking about the Caribbean, but it's expensive, or Bali, but it's so far, or maybe a city like Venice, but is it a cliché to honeymoon in Venice?"

"I had my first honeymoon in Venice," Pam said with a smile. "It's a cliché for a reason."

"I've always wanted to go to Venice," Emma said. There was no real longing or envy there; it was just matter-of-fact.

Pam's eyebrows shot up. "You've never been?"

"No. Not everyone has had a life of luxury like you."

"Well, you should go!" Pam exclaimed.

"What, on my own? I don't think it's a city for that." There was a vulnerability there, hidden under the dry exterior. Holly thought again about Jack, about the fact she'd failed to persuade him to talk to his grandmother. They hadn't spoken since he'd come to Windsor. And that was a good thing, she told herself. She couldn't be his friend if he continued to blame Emma for everything without even talking to her. *Especially,* said a sly voice in her mind, *as you don't want to be just his friend, do you?*

"Lily and I used to talk about going too," Holly said, dragging herself back to the conversation. She and Emma exchanged a look, one of pure understanding. And next to her, Abi reached out, squeezed Holly's hand. She had people who cared about her, she reminded herself. She had people who didn't hate her for what she'd done.

"Well, then you both must go," Pam said, sitting back in her chair like that had settled things.

Emma scoffed. "Must we?"

"Yes. Autumn's the best time for it—not as hot, fewer tourists."

"I have to work around term time for holidays," Holly said mildly.

"Well, you can't go in October half term," Abi said, her voice stern. "That's my wedding."

"Oh really? You should have mentioned it."

"It'll have to be summer, then," Pam said. And somehow, it seemed agreed. Pam was even getting out her phone, looking up flights. Emma didn't protest, and neither did Holly. Because really, why the hell not? And if it was something Emma wanted to do, then they should do it.

It was all done lightly, and they started chatting about what Emma and Holly should do in Venice, before going on to think of more and more extreme ideas for Abi's honeymoon. Not one of them mentioned the idea that Emma might be able to go to Venice next year instead.

AUGUST

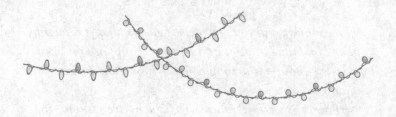

Chapter Twenty-one

Dear Lily,

I'm writing to you from Venice—can you believe it? It is amazing! I think I want to live here. Though maybe I'd get fed up with all the tourists. Do you think there are still tourists in winter? Maybe I could live here in winter, find a job teaching English or something.

We talked about coming here ages ago, do you remember? I think it was just before you met Steve, so I wasn't even out of school yet. But we planned this whole European adventure, saying that we'd stop off at all the big cities before spending two weeks on the beach and you'd soak up the sun while I learned to surf—even though I'd objectively be terrible at surfing, which you quite rightly pointed out.

What happened to that plan? I think I got distracted with my art, and worrying about how I was going to *make money, and you met Steve. I guess I always thought there'd be time to do it in the future. I suppose that just goes to show—you should never take your future for granted.*

Emma is getting worse. That's why we're here, together, in Italy. Not that anyone has said that out loud, but Pam told me back in June to book the tickets and get going, before Emma got too sick to do it. Emma won't talk to me about it. And I'm scared, Lily. I'm scared that she's more ill than she's telling me, or that the doctors have told her something that she's keeping from us.

Sorry. I know you don't want to be hearing about that. I suppose it's easier to get my thoughts straight this way, by writing them down. You used to tell me to do that, do you remember? When I couldn't figure out how to apologize to mum and dad about whatever I'd done, you'd tell me to write it down first, so that I'd know what to say.

But now is not the time for apologies—I've written those a thousand times over. So right now, I'm going to put this pen down, and go and enjoy Venice with my friend. Even if I can't be here with you, I want to try and make the most of it—because you never know when things might change, just like that. If anyone knows that it's us, right?

Love,
Holly

Holly picked up her Aperol Spritz, the cool beads of condensation welcome against her skin, and raised her glass to Emma, who was sitting opposite her. "Cheers."

Emma smiled and returned the gesture, but picked up her water rather than the spritz Holly had ordered her.

Holly relaxed into her chair, her back sticky with sweat, even though it was early evening. Venice in August was *hot*, just as Pam had warned them. Hot and busy.

It was also, Holly thought while taking a sip of her drink, absolutely incredible. One of the things she loved about it was how you could be surrounded by tourists one moment, around St. Mark's Square, for instance, and then you could wander down a little alleyway between buildings and find yourself completely alone, like you'd discovered some kind of secret passageway. Everywhere you looked you wanted to take a photo—the whole place was an artist's dream, and Holly had found her fingers itching more than once, desperate to pick up some clay.

Right now, though, they were sitting at a café along the waterway, near a stop for one of the gondolas. Holly had insisted they go on one, sitting down and getting punted around, seeing Venice from the Grand Canal and other waterways, even though Emma had wrinkled her nose about it being for "sucker tourists." Dusk was settling in now, and Holly loved how the city looked in the changing light—the way the water deepened in color, how the beautiful stone buildings seemed to absorb some of the fading sunlight.

Holly studied Emma over the rim of her glass. She'd seemed especially tired over these last few days, though she had waved it off whenever Holly had asked her about it. The latest on her cancer was that she was in "observation mode," which meant she was going for regular check-ups with her doctor but wasn't, as far as Holly could tell, actually *doing* anything about the cancer. Emma had phrased this as a good thing, telling Holly that if the doctors weren't worried then she shouldn't be either, and if it was just a case of "waiting and seeing," then that's what they should do. But Emma's face was pale, despite the heat and sun, almost yellowy in color, and she was too thin—thinner than when Holly had seen her in June. She hadn't eaten much the whole time they were here, either, claiming the rich food was making her stomach funny, but Holly had looked up pancreatic cancer and knew that the tumor could press on the nerves in your abdomen and cause stomach pain. So she'd decided over the last few days that when she got back, she was going to make Emma go to the doctor with her, so that Holly could ask these questions for herself. And if Emma refused, well, she'd just lie and tell her she was taking her to an art gallery or something—if she was the one driving, there was nothing Emma would be able to do about it.

Emma took another sip of her water, looking out at the canal.

"Emma?" Holly asked.

Emma looked over at her, shadows under her eyes.

"Are you—?"

Emma waved a hand in the air. "I'm fine, I'm fine. Just tired— nothing a slice of tiramisu won't fix."

Holly's phone buzzed and she looked down to see Abi replying to the photos she'd sent with a line of heart-eyes emojis. Holly smiled, then looked up again.

"Abi," she said in answer to Emma's questioning look.

"How's she doing? Wedding's in about six weeks, that right?"

"Yep." And thank God Emma had agreed to come as her plus one. Fine, maybe it was unconventional to have an eighty-year-old woman as your date to a wedding, but it would make her feel better about being single.

"This is glorious," Emma said, leaning back contentedly against her chair. She sounded so sincere, it made Holly feel a bit better. And despite having been worrying about Emma, Holly felt relaxed in herself. Next week, the summer holidays would be over and she'd be back at work with new classes. But right now, she felt all loose and content. And by the looks of things, maybe Emma felt the same after all—which had been the whole point of this. Pam had been right—it had been a good thing, for them to come together.

Holly slipped her phone back into her handbag—a little green one she'd found in the RSPCA charity shop in Windsor. Her fingers brushed over a mask as she did so, and she brought it out, setting it on the table to look at it.

Emma smirked. "You didn't even want to make one, if I remember rightly."

"Well, I was wrong, wasn't I?"

The Venetian masks were traditional here, ranging from the ones for tourists that you could take home for presents—Holly had already bought one for Abi—and the beautiful, delicate ones escalating in price. Emma had arranged a session at the back of a small shop for them to make their own—and Holly was sure it was to make a point, to get her using her artistic skills again, in some small way. But she had loved it. And she was so proud of it. She'd gone for bold blues and silver around the eyes, capping it all off with three long feathers.

"Think you'll ever find an excuse to wear it?" Emma asked, nodding at the mask.

"Well, a girl can dream of a masked ball, can't she?"

Emma smiled. "It was nice, to see you like that."

"Like what?"

"Like an artist. I've not really seen it before, but I knew you had talent—you can tell just by looking at you."

Holly rolled her eyes. "You can't tell that just by looking at someone."

"*You* might not be able to, but I can. It's not an appearance," she continued, raising her voice over Holly's attempt at a protest. "Not a physical trait—not what someone wears or how they do their hair or anything. It's an expression. That hunger—the need to create, to do something. You either have that, or you don't."

"Do you?" Holly asked, genuinely curious. "I mean, I know you find art and you can spot talent in other people, or so you say, but do you have that . . . need?"

Emma was quiet for a moment. "I used to want to paint," she said, softly. "But I could never find the time—a lousy excuse, I know. And then everything happened and, well, it felt *wrong* of me, to still want to have that for myself."

Holly nodded. She could say that it hadn't been wrong, but she knew that feeling all too well. They both went quiet, listening to the chatter of tourists. A police boat went past on the waterway, complete with siren and everything, sending waves lapping over the edges of the canal.

"I wonder what Lily would have made of it here," Holly mused, looking out at the water. Though she realized as she said it that she wouldn't necessarily know if Lily *had* been here—she might have come with Steve sometime in the last three years. She hadn't seen any evidence of it on social media, but then Lily was slightly sporadic with that.

"You talk to her recently?" Emma asked and Holly shook her head. "You still writing to her?"

Holly gave a noncommittal shrug. She sort of wished she hadn't told Emma about the letters. There was no judgment from Emma, but still, it was something deeply personal, something that had felt silly to admit out loud.

She'd once written a letter to Lily when they were little. She'd taken one of Lily's dolls, claiming that Lily didn't play with it anymore, and painted the doll's face. Lily had gone mental when she'd found out, and had refused to let Holly into her room. So Holly had written Lily a letter to say sorry and slipped it under the door.

Lily had scowled when she'd opened the door, the letter clutched in her hand. "Why can't you just apologize face-to-face like a normal person?"

Holly's lips had trembled, but she'd held herself steady. "I didn't mean to ruin her." She'd meant to make her *better,* but she wasn't sure she should say that to Lily. "I thought she'd like having face paint on. And it will wash off."

Lily wrinkled her nose. "I suppose so."

Holly had given Lily a sly look. "Want to paint the others' faces too?"

Lily scowled again. "No." Then she huffed, looked down at her feet. "I can't do it as well as you."

"Yes you can!"

"No I can't. I'm older, and I can't do it as well as you."

Holly had thought about that for a moment. "Well, maybe. But you're better at most things. Like math, and French, and . . ." She searched in her mind, thinking of what Lily loved. "And making all the dresses and the food and everything. You're better at *taking care* of them." It had been a punt, but it had worked. Slowly Lily nodded.

"I am better at that."

Holly grinned. "So we can paint their faces?"

And finally, Lily caved. "Fine. Come on, then."

"You want my advice?" Emma said in the present.

"Do I get a choice?"

"Mend things now, before it's too late. Let it go on too long, and you might run out of time." Holly heard the slight bitterness in her voice.

"Have you heard anything from Jack?" she asked tentatively. She'd wanted to ask ever since she gave Jack Emma's number in June. Had thought he might at least send Emma a message. She'd wanted to ask Emma about Jack inviting her to the memorial too—maybe the invite had never made it to her, for instance. But she couldn't do that without revealing she'd spoken to Jack, so she was kind of stuck.

Emma had said nothing about Jack, so Holly wasn't surprised when she said, with a slight frown," No, why would I have?"

"No reason," Holly said quickly. "I just wondered."

"Hmm." Emma gave her a suspicious look.

"Emma?" Holly said after a beat. "Would you want to call him? If I could . . . track him down, I mean?" She ignored the worm of guilt wriggling its way through her stomach lining. It wasn't an outright lie, just . . . the absence of a time frame. And if Emma said yes, that would make it OK, right?

But Emma's lips tightened—not a good sign. "Maybe you ought to try fixing your own family situation," she said, "rather than keep pushing into mine."

Holly winced. "That's not fair," she said, her voice almost a snap—because actually, maybe there *was* something in it. "I—"

"You're right," Emma said, shaking her head. "It wasn't fair. I'm sorry. I'm just—I'm feeling a little tired at the moment. It's getting to me." She sighed, pushing back her wavy gray hair. "Look, Holly, there's something I haven't told you about that day. Something I should have said a while ago."

Holly's stomach tensed, but she said nothing, waited for Emma to continue.

"The car crash, the one that killed Richard." She took a deep breath. "I was the one driving. That's what drove us all apart—that's why Jack doesn't want to see me."

Holly tried to school her face into something appropriate, though she wasn't sure what that would be—shock? She aimed for shock, but Emma narrowed her eyes. "You knew."

"No, I—"

"My girl, you have many fine qualities, but lying is not one of them. How did you find out? Did you look it up?"

Holly squirmed. She should tell her. Tell her that she tracked Jack down in London, that she'd seen him in Windsor too, that she had his goddamn phone number saved on her mobile. She shouldn't be lying to Emma like this. Well, actually she shouldn't have got involved in the first bloody place—though, in all fairness, if she hadn't hunted Emma down after getting her letter then they wouldn't be sitting outside under the Venetian sun sipping an Aperol Spritz right now.

"No," she said slowly. "I didn't look it up."

"Then what—"

"Why didn't you tell me?" Holly interrupted quickly. "Why didn't you tell me, when I told you about Lily?"

Emma sighed. "Holly, you were basically a stranger when we first had that conversation."

"But I told *you*," Holly pressed. "And fine, OK, you didn't want to say anything then, but why not later?"

The lines around Emma's mouth grew white. "It's not something I like to own up to. It's not something I like to remember. Richard, *my son,* died, and I was the one driving. If anyone can understand that, it's you."

Emma gave her a very level look, one that made Holly's chest tighten. Because that's what she'd thought—it was why she thought Emma *would* have told her. But she saw it the other way too, now—Emma thought she'd understand why she wouldn't want to talk about it, because, while Holly had told Emma, there were many people she would never tell. Even Daniel didn't know the full story of what had happened that day.

"And that," Emma continued, her voice a little softer, "is why I'm telling you now." Holly nodded, felt her eyes sting, and blinked rapidly to cover it up.

"But you are deliberately avoiding answering the question," Emma continued, more briskly now, leaning forward and bridging her fingers on the table. "I want to know how—"

But Holly was saved from the interrogation by the sound of Emma's phone. Both of them looked down to where it sat on the table to see Pam FaceTiming.

Emma lifted her phone and jerked her head at Holly to indicate she should come round to her side of the table. Holly got up, walked around, and crouched down in front of the screen to see Pam sitting in her living room, on her plush cream sofa, holding a glass of red wine in a way that seemed dangerous.

"Oh, it looks gorgeous!" Pam was saying. She must have moved her phone a bit farther away, as her face became smaller. "Hello, Holly, don't you look glowy?" Given Holly never tanned, she thought "glowy" was a pretty good compliment. "Come on, then," Pam said. "Tell me everything—make me jealous."

Holly leaned over Emma's shoulder as they both proceeded to fill Pam in on their trip, Holly obediently grabbing her Venetian mask off the table and holding it up when Emma told her to. "And we're going to Burano tomorrow," Emma was saying. "You know, the place where they make all the lace."

"Oh yes, I've been there. It was excellent—beautiful houses." Pam, as far as Holly could tell, had been everywhere. "I bought some lovely lingerie there."

"Well, I don't know about lingerie," Emma said, "but I do want something beautiful and lacy to take home with me."

Holly continued to join in the conversation, though she was only half concentrating. Her mind was on Jack, on the fact that he still hadn't called Emma. She couldn't help the rush of disappointment, even as she'd told herself, repeatedly, not to think of him, that she'd done all she could there—and that getting involved any further would be a mistake. She could call him, in theory. She could press him on the subject further, because she wanted him to connect with Emma again. If it had *only* been that, then maybe she would have called, despite the fact it would make her even more of an interfering busybody. But the problem was, there was a selfish desire there too. Because she wanted to see him again, for herself.

And that, she told herself firmly, was why she absolutely must *not* call him.

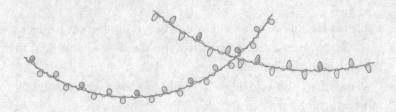

Chapter Twenty-two

One of the staff at the hotel—a petite woman with long dark hair—smiled at Holly and Emma as she brought over two coffees. Emma had tried to ask for Earl Grey but had to settle for coffee when they told her they didn't have any. It was early morning—she and Emma were deliberately getting up first thing so they could do something touristy in the morning and then spend the hottest part of the day lying down somewhere cooler, in true Mediterranean fashion—and they were currently sitting in the small courtyard where they'd had breakfast every day. It was a little boutique hotel, slightly off the beaten track—somewhere Emma had found, having insisted that Holly leave all the big arrangements of the holiday to her. It was perfect—Holly was pretty sure it was full, but there were only around ten rooms in total, so it never felt overwhelmingly busy, and they'd never had to fight for space in the courtyard, which was just stunning. There were a handful of stone tables with iron-backed chairs, all around a three-tiered fountain that lit up in the evening. There were plants all around the edges, climbing up the walls—big green leaves and a climbing purple flowering plant that Emma had told her was wisteria.

The waitress set the drinks down next to the basket of fresh pastries and brioche and a platter of fresh fruit. "Grazie," Holly said—about the only word of Italian she'd managed to pick up. Once the woman had gone back inside, Holly went back to staring at her phone.

Emma made a *tch* sound in the back of her throat. "No point staring that hard at it, my girl. Either you're going to call or you're not—looking at it won't make any difference."

Holly bit her lip, glancing down at her screen again—at Lily's number. Then she looked up at Emma. "Is this your way of reminding me to sort my own family situation out?"

Emma winced. "I shouldn't have said that."

"Maybe you were right," Holly muttered, tapping her fingers on the table next to her phone. But how did you call someone after so long without saying a word to them? And because it had been so long, it felt like a text wouldn't cut it—it would have to be a proper conversation, or nothing at all. Which was perhaps how Jack felt, Holly reasoned. Was that why he hadn't called Emma?

Emma took a sip of her coffee, then made an impatient noise. Holly frowned at her. "What is it?"

"Nothing. I'm just going to need to excuse myself. Again."

"Is there anything I can—"

But Emma flapped her away. Holly watched her leave the courtyard, heading for the hotel reception, where there was a rather plush bathroom with golden taps and fancy sinks and everything. Then she rolled her shoulders. *Come on, Holly.* Emma was right—staring at her sister's number was not going to accomplish anything.

She pressed the call button quickly, trying to stop her brain from whirring too much.

"Hello?"

Holly sucked in a breath at the sound of her sister's voice. She'd answered! She'd actually answered. The word was cautious, like she wasn't sure who would be at the other end of the line. Holly had kept the same number, though, so if Lily wasn't sure, that meant she had deleted her number. She felt sweat prick her palms and flexed her fingers on the phone.

"Lily?" The word sounded sticky. "It's . . . It's Holly." Her heart was beating fast, and she felt too hot, even though it was early and she was in a light summer dress.

"I know," Lily said. Her voice was guarded, careful, and Holly couldn't work out how to take that.

"I just . . ." Holly closed her mouth, swallowed. Tried again. "How are you?"

"How am I?" Lily seemed baffled by the question. Holly couldn't work out what her sister was thinking—or what the right thing to say was. They used to be able to read each other so well, could answer questions before the other one even asked—how had that all disappeared?

"Yes. I . . ." She could feel herself about to go into babble mode, just to fill the space between them. "I wanted to call you because I'm in Venice."

"Venice?" Still in that same baffled tone. But she was talking to her! For the first time in three years, that was Lily's voice at the end of the phone. She hadn't hung up. Where was she right now? Holly wondered. In her kitchen, maybe, getting ready to go to work?

"Yes, Venice," she said, trying not to speak too quickly. "And I remembered—"

"Holly," Lily interrupted. "Why did you call me?"

"Like I said, I—"

"Lily Jenkins?" There was a voice at Lily's end of the line, a voice that sounded a little distant, and very formal.

"Lily?" Holly asked. "Who was that?"

"No one," Lily said, and her voice was sharp. "This actually isn't a great time, Holly—did you really just ring for a chat?" The words were brisk, rushed. It could not be clearer that, athough she'd answered the phone, Lily did not want to be talking to her.

"Yes, I . . ." She swallowed again. "I wanted to see how you were," she said softly.

There was a quiet that stretched on too long. A quiet in which Holly counted five heartbeats.

"Why did you answer?"

Lily said nothing still, and Holly felt something hot in the back of her throat.

Her own tone turned sharp. "If you didn't want to talk to me, why did you answer?"

Emma was coming back into the courtyard now, her gait stiff. She was grimacing, though when she saw Holly looking at her, she eased her face into a smile.

"Because I thought it might be something important," Lily said—and it cut through Holly.

"And what, seeing how you are isn't important?" She shouldn't do that, shouldn't make her voice defensive, like she was ready to lash out. She should be calm. "Lily, I—"

But she didn't finish. Because Emma was stumbling in the middle of the courtyard. Stumbling, then falling.

Holly dropped her phone onto the table as she stood and lurched toward Emma. She got there just in time to catch her shoulders, to break the fall before she hit the stone. She threw one hand out to catch the both of them. And then they were both on the ground, Holly sitting, Emma in a crumpled heap. She wasn't moving and her eyelids were closed.

"Emma?" Holly's voice was high and scratchy. She shook Emma's shoulders, got no reaction. "Emma!" She looked around wildly, saw the waitress from earlier, staring at them wide-eyed. "Get help!" Holly shouted, and the woman lurched into action.

She heard the message being relayed, caught snatches of Italian. *Svenuta . . . aiuto . . . ambulanza*. The last one stuck with her. Ambulance. Someone was calling an ambulance, someone was sorting it.

She moved Emma's head so it was pillowed in her lap. When she took her hand, she saw that her own was shaking. "You'll be OK." She tried to keep her voice from trembling. She needed to be calm, strong. Emma would need her to be. She'd just fainted, that was all. It was only the heat; it was enough to get to anyone. "You hear me? You'll be OK." And she tried, very hard, to believe what she was saying.

Holly's phone was pressed to her ear, sweat dripping down her back. She'd come out of the cool, air-conditioned, and very hospital-like waiting room to make the call, and was now pacing along the long red carpet, next to big stone pillars, the mullioned windows showing a glimpse of the city outside. The hospital was a former fifteenth-century monastery, the man behind the reception desk in the waiting room had told her. It was probably in an attempt to distract her, and certainly, when she'd followed the paramedics wheeling Emma on a stretcher into the grand stone building with its mosaic floor, she had initially panicked that they were taking them the wrong way because, until you got to the main bit inside, the hospital looked like another tourist attraction.

The paramedics hadn't spoken English, so she'd been unable to ask them what was going on as they strapped an oxygen mask over Emma's face, got her onto the stretcher, and then onto a yellow boat, the word *Ambulanza* on its side. Then Emma had been taken away from her, through white doors where she wasn't allowed to follow, and none of the doctors had explained what was going on. The man at reception had been a lifesaver so far, had explained that they needed to run some tests, and had asked her to call a next of kin.

So now that was what she was doing, dialing his number for the second time because he hadn't answered the first time around. Maybe he didn't want to speak to her. Maybe he'd continue to ignore her and she'd have no way of getting ahold of Emma's *next of kin*. She hadn't actually asked why they needed that—would they refuse to tell her anything, because she wasn't related to Emma? Or did they just think Emma would *need* a family member here—and was that because this was something really serious? Was she going to . . . ? But no. She could not think that.

Come on, she pleaded silently, her breath coming in short sharp bursts, her feet unable to stand still. *Answer.*

And then he did!

"Hello?"

"Jack? It's Holly." She stopped walking, clutched the phone tighter to her ear.

"I know. I'd almost given up hope I might hear from you again." It was said with an almost carefully light tone.

"Jack, I . . ." But she couldn't stop the sob from coming, racking through her tightly wound body.

"Holly?" Jack's voice changed, became more urgent. "Holly, what's wrong?"

She pressed her lips together to try to stem the sobs. "It's Emma."

There was a silence.

"What about Emma? Is she . . . ?" An audible swallow. "What's happened?"

"She's in hospital. We're in Venice and—"

"Venice? Venice, Italy?"

"No, Venice, Scotland." But she snapped because she was

stressed, and freaking out, and that was not Jack's fault. "Sorry. I'm sorry. Look, she collapsed. And we're in hospital and they won't tell me anything and I can't understand most of it anyway but they told me to call her next of kin and I think that's you and—"

He cut off her babbling with a much calmer voice. "OK. OK. Is she . . . Where is she now?"

"I don't know. They won't let me see her." Tears sprang to her eyes and she blinked them away. "But she collapsed, Jack. And she's not well, I know she's not, but they won't tell me anything. Maybe they have to speak to you? If it's . . . You know, if it's bad." Her voice was quiet, barely more than a whisper.

"Jesus, OK. Look, hang on." There was a pause and she could hear nothing, just the hum of chatter outside somewhere. Then, "Holly? I'm on my way."

"You're what?"

"I'll come to Venice—the Italian one. I'm going to get the next flight I can. I'll be there today, OK?"

"You're coming? Here?"

"Yes." His voice was firm, and Holly felt relief slide through her.

"Thank you," she breathed.

"Look, why don't you go back to wherever you're staying, text me the address and I'll . . ."

"No," she said sharply. "I'm staying here. At least until I can see her, check she's OK." She wouldn't let her mind consider the option that she *wasn't* OK.

"All right," Jack said, and though he was clearly trying to stay calm—stay calm for *her*—there was a tension there, rippling under the surface of his voice. "I'll see you soon, OK?"

"Yes," Holly said, and she moved to a stone pillar, closed her eyes, and rested back against it. "I'll see you soon."

Chapter Twenty-three

It was late afternoon by the time a nurse came out to find Holly and told her—in Italian, though she got the gist after a couple of repetitions—that she could see Emma.

The nurse led her down a gray-floored, white-walled corridor—the monastery bit was definitely lost in this section—and into one of the rooms. Holly balked in the doorway. It was a single room, just one bed. The smell of antiseptic lingered in the air and there was the sound of a machine beeping quietly in the corner. It was air-conditioned, but Holly still felt heat rising in her chest. The last time she'd been in a room like this, it had been Lily on the hospital bed.

She stepped farther into the room as the nurse smiled and left her. *Emma,* she told herself firmly. She crossed to where Emma was lying, a tube hooked up to her, her purpling eyelids closed, her skin holding a yellow tinge that extended to her bare arm under the hospital gown someone had changed her into. It was Emma, not Lily, who needed her right now.

Holly glanced around, saw two little wooden chairs in the corner of the room. She picked one up, moved it next to Emma's bed. As she sat down, Emma's eyelids flickered open.

"About time you got here," Emma croaked.

Holly let out her breath on a whoosh and felt a heavy weight lift from her body. Emma was OK. "Well, I would have been here earlier, but I took advantage of the time alone and slipped out to do some shopping. You know, Gucci was calling . . ." But the joke was ruined by her shaky voice.

Emma grunted. "You found Gucci in the nearest charity shop, did you? I guarantee it's a fake."

She shifted, then grimaced in pain. Holly felt a breath get stuck in her throat.

Emma blinked up at her, then reached out to take one of Holly's hands. "I'm OK, my girl."

Holly pressed her lips together. "I've been so scared," she whispered.

"I know; I'm sorry. But I'm OK, I promise. Just trying to add a bit of drama to your life, that's all." She paused. "Did they take me on one of those boat ambulances and everything?"

Holly nodded, not trusting herself to speak.

"Well, there's a story you'll be able to tell when you get back, going on an ambulance boat in Venice. And at least one of us was conscious for it."

Holly gave Emma's hand a gentle squeeze. She seemed so fragile. It was strange—Emma was an old woman, and she'd been diagnosed with cancer before Holly had even met her, but—Emma hadn't ever *seemed* frail, not in the ways that mattered. But now . . .

"What's wrong?" Holly whispered. "Did they tell you? Did you understand? Is it the cancer?"

Emma sighed. "Well, I think it all comes back to that, in the end."

"But why did it make you collapse?" Holly pressed.

"It's just making me tired, that's all."

"That's *all*? Emma, we need to talk about this. You can't keep pretending it isn't happening. . . . This is—"

But she didn't finish. Because the door to Emma's room was opening again. Emma, facing the door, reacted before Holly did. So Holly saw it: the slight frown that played across her forehead, the way that froze in place for just a moment. Then the whoosh of breath, her turquoise eyes blinking rapidly, as if they were checking what was in front of them. And then she felt Emma draw her hand from hers slowly.

So Holly knew, before she turned. But she still felt her own heartbeat flare as she stood and faced Jack.

They were quiet. Jack and Emma were looking at each other, Emma now struggling to try to sit up, Jack very pale. Holly's body was tense as her gaze flicked between the two of them. She didn't know what to do. She hadn't thought this far ahead. She'd just wanted Jack here, and even then, she hadn't dared to believe he would come.

It was Jack who broke the silence. "Hi, Memma." His voice was small, quiet. His hands were shoved into his pockets and his shoulders were hunched, uncertain.

Holly heard Emma let out a sob, felt her own eyes filling in response, the strain of the whole damn day getting to her.

"Jack?" Emma was still struggling to get upright, and then she let out a half huff, half sob. "For God's sake, Holly, give me a hand, will you?" And Holly let out a sound between a laugh and a cry as she bent to rearrange Emma's pillows and help her into a sitting position.

"I'll leave you to . . ." She gestured between them, keeping her eyes downcast, not wanting to look at Jack in case he was regretting coming, and not wanting to have to answer any of Emma's questions.

She stumbled over her own feet as she walked too quickly to the door—*of course* she bloody did. But as she reached it, she felt Jack's hand grab her wrist. Felt her pulse thrum in response—even now, in a situation like this. He moved his hand to clasp hers, fingers twining together briefly. Then he squeezed gently—whether to offer her reassurance or comfort or because *he* needed reassurance or comfort, she wasn't sure.

She looked up. For a moment their gazes met, held. She squeezed his hand back, before leaving the room and closing the door behind her.

It was after seven P.M. by the time Jack and Holly left the hospital together, a small rucksack slung over Jack's shoulder. They'd been allowed to stay outside of normal visiting hours, but only for today, the doctor had told them—tomorrow, they had to come in the morning if they wanted to see Emma, and they were recommending she stay in the hospital for the next two days. Which meant they'd probably miss their flights, Holly realized—they had been due to fly back to London the day after tomorrow, giving her a few days to get ready for the start of term. *Later,* she told herself. She'd figure that out later.

Holly blinked as they came out onto the street outside the hospital. It was quieter here than around St. Mark's Square, but there were still plenty of people milling about—on their way to dinner, or making their way to look at some of the architecture after the heat of the day had died down.

"Are you hungry?" Jack asked.

Holly looked up at him, and fought a sudden, inappropriate urge to laugh. Jack was here, in Venice. It was all so weird.

"Yeah." She blew out a breath. "God, yeah, I really am."

They wandered for a while, taking random lefts and rights, perhaps the way you only can in Venice, and found themselves on one of the quieter streets, one where you could pretend that the city was home to you and only a handful of other people. There were tables outside a little restaurant, candles on each one, low music coming from inside an arched stone entrance. It was much less busy than the restaurants Holly had been to so far—only five small tables outside, three of which were already taken, all by parties of two. Jack came to a stop and raised his eyebrows to Holly in question, and she nodded.

A waiter came out, smiled at them. "Please," he said, gesturing toward one of the two free tables.

Holly and Jack sat opposite each other, the candlelight flickering between them in the dimming evening light. The waiter gave them each a menu, which was all in Italian—no pictures or English translation like the restaurants she and Emma had eaten at. Holly stared at the menu blankly, not even turning the pages.

The waiter came back almost right away with water and a basket of bread and breadsticks, which Holly immediately latched on to. God, she was so hungry—she hadn't eaten since the fruit at breakfast, which now felt like a very long time ago.

"To drink?"

Jack and Holly glanced at each other. "Wine?" Jack asked, and Holly nodded, glad he'd suggested it. She could really do with a glass, after that day. "Red?" She nodded again.

He looked up at the waiter. "Ah . . ."

"Red wine?" the waiter repeated, his English laced with a strong Italian accent, but better than Holly's Italian by far. "The house, it's good."

"The house red sounds great," Jack said.

"And to eat?"

Jack gestured at Holly, who shook her head helplessly.

"You need more time?" the waiter asked.

"No," Holly said quickly. She didn't need time; she needed

food. She stared down at the menu again, but all the words seemed to blur together. She looked up at Jack, and he must have seen the slight panic there, because he lurched into action, picking up his menu and pointing, ordering a few things, reading out the Italian. The waiter nodded and took the menus away.

Holly raised her eyebrows. "You speak Italian?"

"Ah, no."

"So what did you just order?"

Jack gave a guilty shrug. "No idea. I suppose we'll find out."

Holly gave a tired snort, just as the waiter came back out with a carafe of red wine and two glasses. He poured them one each, then smiled as he left them to it.

Jack held up his glass. "Well, cheers, I guess."

They clinked glasses, though Holly found she couldn't keep the eye contact as she took a sip. There was something a little too intimate about the way he was looking at her. The wine was delicious—by far the most superior she'd had since being here. She turned her attention to her breadstick, munching down and enjoying the satisfying *snap* it made each time she bit into it.

She realized she was eating so quickly that crumbs were falling on the table, and she wiped them away, looked up at Jack guiltily. "Sorry," she mumbled.

He laughed a little, though it didn't quite reach his eyes. "Don't be. Eat. Sorry, I should have thought about it and brought you food on the way." He frowned. "How long were you there, in the hospital?"

Holly brought her hands to her temples, massaged. "Not sure. Since breakfast." She dropped her hands and took a sip of her wine. Then she made herself look at Jack directly, at the candlelight warming the depths of his dark eyes. "Thank you, for coming."

"I should be thanking *you*," he murmured. "So, thank you,

for calling me. Thank you, for being with her, for looking after her." He rubbed his hands over his face.

She couldn't really imagine what it must be like, seeing Emma after all this time. She could theorize—she could try to think what it would be like if she were to see Lily, for instance, but it would all be the wrong sides, because Jack was the one who'd been blaming Emma; Jack was the one who hadn't wanted to see her. Yet he'd come when it had mattered, in the end.

"Are you . . . OK?" she asked tentatively.

"Yeah." He blew out a breath. "Yeah, I guess. I just . . ." He sipped his wine, and Holly suspected he was buying time to think. "I've spent so long, holding on to this . . . grudge, and I don't know what to do. Seeing her . . . Well. I don't know how to move forward." He shook his head. "I'm not sure how to take this . . . what to do now, what to say, or—"

"One step at a time," Holly said gently. Then, because she sensed he needed it, she reached out, placed a hand over his on the table. The table was so small, it was hardly a stretch. "Don't think too far ahead," she continued. "Even if . . . Even if you can't find a way to move on or forgive her for what happened"— she didn't offer up an opinion as to whether that would be right or wrong, kept her voice judgment-free—"the fact that you're here, that you cared, that you came . . ." She swallowed. "It will mean so much to her, Jack."

"Yeah," Jack said after a pause. "Yeah, OK. One step at a time."

Holly opened her mouth, then bit her lip, hesitated.

Jack smiled, just a little. "You want to know what we talked about."

Holly glanced at him, then away, drawing her hand back. "You don't have to tell me," she said quickly.

"Honestly? We didn't talk about much. She cried a bit. I

cried a bit." He grimaced, like he hadn't meant to admit that. "She kept saying thank you for coming, and it made me feel so damn guilty and I . . ." He heaved in a breath. "Then she asked me whether I still liked gardening, and that subject managed to tide us over for a bit."

She laughed quietly. "That sounds like Emma."

"I guess the hard stuff will come," Jack said with a sigh.

Holly nodded slowly. "Yeah, I guess."

The waiter came out with the food at that point—a burrata and tomato salad, an eggplant and mozzarella pasta dish, and gnocchi with what looked like candied walnuts mixed in. Holly's stomach rumbled at the smell as the waiter put down the dishes, along with two side plates in front of each of them. A sharing deal, then. Good, it meant she could have everything. She fell on the food immediately, serving herself as much as she could fit on the little plate, and didn't talk for a good few minutes as she ate. The food, like the wine, was incredible—each mouthful bursting with flavor so that she wanted both to linger over the taste and to eat as quickly as she could. The candied walnut gnocchi in particular made her tastebuds sing—the sweetness offset by a buttery saltiness, with a grating of Parmesan to top it off. Jack, too, seemed content to just eat, and it was only when Holly was on her second plateful that she managed to stop long enough to talk again.

"So, how *is* the gardening dream coming along?" she asked. Better, perhaps, to keep it light for the time being. There would be plenty of time for more serious conversations later, she was sure.

"Well, currently nonexistent, but I've told my mum I'll redo her whole garden, so that'll be fun."

Holly cocked her head. "I can't work out if you're being serious."

"Oh, I am," he said with a little smile. "Having a whole garden to do what I want with? That is definitely my idea of fun."

"And how are your sister and brother?"

"They're good. Theo—my brother—came to stay with me a few weeks ago, and he is definitely more in love with London than I ever have been." He speared a piece of gnocchi. "How's your scary friend? Abi, right?"

"Oh, she will *love* that you think she's scary. It will literally make her day."

They kept talking, and she found herself relaxing into the conversation, found that she was able to forget, briefly, about the day she'd had as she enjoyed the wine and the food and Jack's company. It felt easy, in a way it hadn't really done with him before—perhaps because there had always been Emma's presence between them each time they'd spoken. And now that was reversed, because they were both here *for* Emma, together.

When they'd finished and paid for dinner, Holly led the way back to the hotel, having to rely on her phone to get them there in the maze of the city. She felt better for having eaten and for walking in the evening air, though her body tensed as they drew nearer to the hotel. Here she was, about to settle in for the night, while Emma was in hospital, alone. Not that they'd had any choice about that—they'd *had* to leave her—but still, she must be so scared, even if she refused to show it.

Holly was quiet as she headed into the reception, Jack behind her. It was dimly lit, the lamps offering a low glow, and their footsteps echoed on the polished stone floor.

Jack let out a low, quiet whistle. "Well, this is pretty fancy."

Holly smiled. "Yeah. It was Emma's pick." But saying her name made Holly's eyes fill with tears, and even as she tried to blink them away, she could feel the heat as one of them escaped to trace a path down her face. "Sorry," she said, lowering her face to look down at her white pumps. But now that they'd started, the tears were only coming faster, even as she tried to wipe them away.

"Hey, it's OK." Jack's hand was gentle as he cupped her elbow. "Come on. Which room are you in?"

She led the way up the red carpeted stairs, then past wooden shuttered windows along to her room on the first floor, two doors down from Emma's. Her hands were shaking, and Jack had to take the key, unlock the door for her. She walked inside, putting her key down on the dresser. Then, to her alarm, she started sobbing. Big, wracking sobs that took hold of her body, making her feel like she might collapse right there onto the fancy rug and never get up again.

Jack was next to her in an instant, arms coming around her. She went into them without question and pillowed her head on his chest as she continued to cry, unable to stop. He stood there, stroking her back gently.

"I'm sorry," she sobbed, her breath hitched. "I don't know what's wrong with me."

"Nothing's wrong with you," he said, still stroking her back.

"It's just . . . I called my sister earlier and it was . . . Well, it was not good and she still hates me and then Emma and I—"

"Shhh," he said gently. "It's OK. You're OK." He maneuvered them so they were sitting on the end of the bed, Holly curled into his lap, still crying against his T-shirt. And he just held her. Held her and said nothing, letting her cry it all out.

Eventually, her sobs subsided into a few gentle hiccups. As she grew quiet, she grew aware of where she was, and what she was doing. Sitting on Jack's lap, curled up like a toddler, her face buried against his shirt, which was now wet from her tears. She drew back and peered up at his face.

His hands were stroking her back, a comforting caress, but as their gazes met, they grew still. She bit her lip. What must she look like? They were so close, their faces inches from each other. He seemed to realize it at the exact same moment—she could feel his heart kick into gear alongside hers, could sense the way his breathing shifted. He ran one of his hands to her waist, brought the other to her jaw, and gently wiped away the one remaining tear on her face with his thumb. He kept his hand there, cupped against her face, and her skin heated.

"Sorry," she whispered again.

"Don't be." And the way he was looking at her did not make her feel like she was red and blotchy—though surely she must be. His fingers curled in at her waist, and she felt an answering pulse of heat. But then he dropped his hand away from her face and eased back, with what little space he had, given she was still sitting on his lap.

"Well," he said, his voice a little raspy, "I guess I better go and see if they've got a room for the night. Or know of anywhere that might have one."

She felt her breath come out on a whoosh as she stood up, too quickly, too awkwardly. He stood too, didn't look at her as he started toward the door.

"Jack?" She spoke before she could think too much about it. "Why don't you stay here for the night?"

He turned to face her.

"Just to sleep, I mean," she added quickly. "It's only that I doubt you're going to be able to get a room. It's August in Venice and this place was booked months ago, and I suppose you could use Emma's room but that might be . . ."

He grimaced, nodded. Then he hesitated before saying, "OK. Yeah. If you're sure?"

"I'm sure." She wondered if he guessed that she didn't want to be alone tonight. She left him fumbling around his tiny rucksack and headed to the en suite bathroom to brush her teeth, wash her face—which *was* red and blotchy—and change into her pajamas. She tried not to feel self-conscious about the fact that they were her skimpy summer ones—shorts and a tank top—as she came back into the bedroom.

Jack had stripped down to his boxers and a fresh T-shirt and was lying on the bed. He was concentrating on his phone, a bit too intensely for it to be entirely real, Holly thought as she crossed the room and clambered up on the bed next to him. With the air-con on she'd still only needed a sheet over her at night but now, with the heat of Jack's body next to her, she doubted she'd need even that. There were red curtains you could pull around the bed, but Holly left them untouched, feeling it might create an intimacy that neither of them would be able to handle. She fluffed up her white pillows instead and lay down with her head just skimming the wooden headboard. Neither of them said anything, though Holly heard Jack put his phone down on the table next to him.

"OK if I switch out the light?" she asked, feeling the need to whisper.

"Sure."

She reached out and flipped the switch on the wall next to her—it was one of the fancy rooms where you could control all the lighting from the bed as well as the doorway. The blinds over the stained-glass windows were still open, but night had well and truly fallen, and the room descended into darkness. Even now, tired after the day she'd had, she could feel the weight between them, the way it made her skin prickle, every inch of her aware of every inch of him. Maybe it had been a bad idea, asking him to stay—how was she supposed to sleep?

"You OK?" Jack murmured.

"Yeah." She turned on her side, facing away from him and trying to get comfortable. But she moved too much and her side collided with Jack's elbow. She made a face into the dark. "Sorry."

He laughed softly, then ran a hand down the length of her arm. It was all she could do not to lean into him, to purr at the touch. He kept his hand there, a soothing presence. Slowly, she felt herself settle, felt her eyelids droop closed. He shifted, just a little, so that his arm dropped over her stomach, curling her into him. She heard his breathing slow, deepen. Felt her own match it. And with him there, his arm around her in comfort, she drifted into sleep.

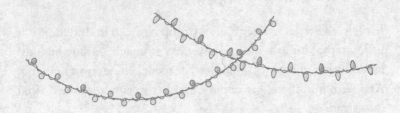

Chapter Twenty-four

"She's fine, Pam, honestly," Holly said as she and Jack walked down a line of bright, colorful houses next to the canal on the island of Burano. Jack was walking a little way away from her, giving her space for the call but no doubt still able to overhear every word.

"Tell me again—what happened, exactly?"

So Holly explained again how Emma had seemed over the last few days, how she'd collapsed, been rushed to hospital. Emma had told Holly not to call Pam, but Holly knew she would want to know. Emma would no doubt tell her off for it later, for worrying her friend, but Emma also needed to accept that other people cared about her, and that it was OK to share her worries with those people. Holly had tried to tell Emma as much this morning, when she and Jack had visited the hospital, but had been brushed off in classic Emma style.

"Did the doctor tell you why she collapsed? Why it was so bad?"

"Not really," Holly hedged. "And Emma won't tell me anything, either. But it's got to be . . . Do you think this means she's much worse than she's been telling us?"

Pam sighed, and for the first time since she'd met her, Holly thought she sounded tired. "In all honesty, my darling . . . Yes. I think it's pretty bad."

"Do you know something?" Holly asked sharply, earning a quick look of alarm from Jack.

"No," Pam said slowly. "I don't *know* anything. But at our age, there are certain signs you learn to look out for."

Holly let that sit for a moment. But she didn't push. She was trying to tell herself there was no use guessing, that she needed to speak to someone with the answers—a doctor, if Emma was refusing to be honest about her condition.

"She's trying to protect us, I think," Holly said quietly.

"Yes. There's a lot of that at our age, too. And Emma . . . She's got that tendency more than most. But, darling, she might just not be ready to face up to things herself yet, either. That's what I think, anyway. And I decided that, as her friend, I would give her the space. Though I suppose we're all going to have to have a sit-down very soon and find out what exactly is going on."

"Yeah," Holly said quietly. And Emma would have reason not to want to face up to things, wouldn't she? Because there were things in her life that were still unfinished. She snuck a glance at Jack, who was making a show of looking down the canal now.

"Jack's here," Holly said, as quietly as she could. If Jack heard his name, he didn't react.

"Is he, now? That's interesting. I take it that was your doing?"

"Well, I—"

"Well done, darling. I'm glad you didn't listen to the boring people who say meddling is bad."

Holly felt a smile pull at her lips. "Abi doesn't like meddling."

"Course she doesn't, she's sensible. And nothing wrong with that—we all need a sensible friend. But you and I, we are not sensible, now, are we?"

"Ah . . ." She wasn't really sure how to answer that. Or how, exactly, Abi would feel, being described as "sensible." "I'm sorry, Pam," she said after a moment, "but I think I have to go."

"Of course you do. I bet you're entertaining Jack, aren't you? And I'll bet anything he's a looker."

"He's . . . ah . . ."

"Course he is. Now, you tell Emma that she should call me the moment she's able to, OK? I'll text her myself, but no harm in you telling her too."

"I will," Holly promised.

"Good girl. And if you need anything—and I mean anything—money, flights, whatever, you call me, yes?"

"I—"

"Promise?"

"I promise."

"Well, then." Holly heard it—the slight waver in Pam's voice. Felt an answering swell in her own throat.

"I'll call you tomorrow with an update."

"Thank you, my darling. Now go and buy Emma something lacy, won't you? And with regards to that grandson of hers—"

"I'm being careful," Holly said quickly. "Don't worry."

"Oh gosh, are you? How incredibly boring, that's disappointing."

Holly couldn't help it—she laughed.

When she hung up, Jack glanced back at her.

"Sorry about that," she said. "It's just I had to tell her and—"

"Don't worry about it. Honestly." But it hung between them for a beat—the fact that it was Holly, not Jack, filling in Emma's friend.

"I don't remember a Pam," Jack said with a slight frown, like he was trying to dig up some memory.

"I think she moved there about ten years ago."

"Ah. Well, that would explain it then."

Again, another beat between them. One which Holly covered up by saying brightly. "Well, I think it's time to do some shopping, don't you?"

"I do love shopping," Jack said, deadpan. "Especially for lace." Holly gave him a look, and the corner of his mouth quirked up.

He followed her into one of the stores along the canal, looked around while Holly tried to find something she liked.

"What do you think?" Holly asked, holding up a long white skirt, the bottom adorned with lace.

"Ah . . ." Jack ran a hand across the back of his neck, looking a little alarmed at having been asked his opinion. "For you or Emma?"

Holly's eyebrows pulled together as she looked back at the skirt. "Me," she said, thinking that should be obvious—the skirt was far too floaty for Emma. "But if you had to ask, then maybe not." She put it back and glanced along the rack at the small boutique shop, the wind from the fan fluttering her hair. "I doubt any of this would look good on me anyway—everything's too *white*." She glanced behind her, worried that the shopkeeper had overheard her, but she was distracted by two other tourists, women in their forties, at a guess, who looked like they were grateful to be inside, where there was a fan.

"Or red, or black," Jack said, pointing out two dresses.

"Yes, but they're not traditional." Surely, if she was going to buy a lacy something from an island known specifically for its lace, it had to be white.

"Well, get white then," Jack said with a shrug, perusing the shelves absentmindedly. "White looks good on everyone."

"It so does not: You can't wear white when you're as pale and pasty as me." Bright colors suited her best—like the cobalt-blue strappy dress she was wearing right now. Usually, she liked it that way, but right now her inability to wear white felt like a serious shortcoming.

Jack glanced over at her. "You're not *that* pasty."

Holly huffed as she looked along the line of clothes again. "Way to flatter a girl."

"Want flattery now, do you?" He grinned, lightness coming into his face. "Because I'm pretty sure I could do a whole lot better than 'tanned,' as far as compliments go."

She rolled her eyes but couldn't stop the smile. She picked up a white lace shift dress from the end of the rack, held it up critically. "Would Emma like something like this, do you think?" she asked, not really as a genuine question, more just musing out loud.

"I don't know," Jack said, in a tone she couldn't quite read. Because he didn't know? Because he wished he *did* know? Or because he was wondering, like she was, if Emma was going to be OK—*really* OK—in the long run?

They'd been to visit her that morning, the two of them getting up and going to the hospital in a way that had felt very intimate, even if they didn't so much as hold hands the whole way there. Emma had given them explicit instructions—they were not to sit around waiting for her to get the green light. Emma and Holly had missed their Burano trip yesterday, *but Jack, take Holly, will you?* she had said. It had felt very fragile, the space between Emma and Jack. Emma was doing her best, Holly could tell, not to make it a big thing, not to make Jack feel awkward, and actually, in her opinion, she was playing it right—allowing them both the pretense of normality. It was what Holly had tried—and failed—to do with Lily. Jack had matched that, allowing Emma to set the tone. There was something there still, though—some tension that had not yet broken.

Holly put the shift dress back and held up a wrap, one that tied at the waist. "Actually, maybe something like this," she said, deciding to copy Emma and try for some normality.

Jack looked up, then did a sort of shrug-nod thing. "Yeah. I like that better."

Holly studied it, then glanced back to the shift dress. "Are you sure?"

He raised his eyebrows. "Are you asking for my expert opinion?"

Holly wrinkled her nose. If Emma hated it, she'd just tell her that Jack picked it out—Emma was hardly going to fault Jack right now, was she? She also picked out something for herself— a white playsuit with three-quarter-length sleeves and a tie at the middle—and after paying they left the shop, thanking the owner.

Holly sighed as they walked back along the canal. "I keep thinking I should be doing something more useful."

"I know," Jack said quietly. There was nothing; they both knew that. But it didn't stop Holly from feeling useless.

"How long, do you think . . . ?" She didn't want to say the rest of the sentence out loud. Because saying it out loud would make it real.

"I don't know," Jack said quietly. "I suppose I need to book in some visits to the doctor, when we get back." Holly didn't miss the implication there—he was planning to stick around.

"Well, I think that's me done," Holly admitted. The back of her neck was pricking with sweat, and her feet were starting to feel swollen. She needed to get back to the hotel, shower, and lie down. "We could get a quick drink before heading back to the water bus?" It wasn't actually called the water bus—she couldn't remember the official name—but that's what it was: the boat that everyone used to get around the islands that made up Venice. It had been packed on the way out: so many people off to explore. Then she frowned. "I didn't look at what time the return journeys are, though."

"I did," Jack said as they stopped at the nearest café, right at the edge of the water.

"Of course you did." She saw an empty table and made a beeline for it.

One eyebrow quirked up. "Are you mocking me?"

She gave a solemn headshake. "Never."

He chuckled quietly. "I'll get some drinks—what do you want?"

"A Coke, thanks." What was it about hot weather and being abroad that always made you want a Coke?

"So," Jack said when he came back with two bottles, "I came up with a better idea."

Holly took the drink, and a greedy gulp. "Better idea than—"

"Than the vaporetto."

Right, that was what it was called. "And that would be . . . ?"

He only held up a finger, indicating she should have patience.

"*What?*" she demanded. "What's the idea?"

But she didn't have to wait long to find out. Soon enough, a sleek looking wooden speedboat pulled up next to the café, in the designated area of the water that seemed to have been designed specifically for that purpose. Jack immediately stood, offering his hand to Holly. She laughed but shook her head. "Jack, those things are really expensive." She knew, because she and Emma had asked—they'd been overtaken by one on the way from the airport and had looked enviously at the private boat and its two passengers, who seemed so comfortable and *smug*, but when they'd found out the cost, they'd immediately deemed the water taxis way out of their budget.

"It's on me," Jack said.

"You can't—"

"Too late," he interrupted. "I'll probably have to pay either way now."

She hesitated, glancing at the water taxi and the man who was waiting behind the wheel.

"Come on—when in Venice?"

And really, she was hardly going to argue, was she? Especially not when she really *did* want to take one and see if it was as good as that couple had made it look.

The driver held his hand out when she approached and helped Holly onto the boat—which was a good thing, since she stumbled as she stepped on, causing Jack to laugh quietly behind her. The two of them headed for the back of the boat as it reversed out of the parking bay. There was an undercover bit with seating, but Holly opted to stand up, leaning against the railings—and holding on for good measure—and Jack stayed with her.

They sped up and Holly couldn't help the whoop of laughter as she felt the wind tug through her hair. And fine, the smug couple had been right to look smug, because this was *so* much better than the water bus. She just about resisted the temptation to throw her arms out and catch the wind.

Jack's head was bowed toward her, looking at her rather than across the water. He looked so damn sexy in sunglasses, his dark curled hair windswept in a ruffled, bedhead kind of way. She couldn't quite see his eyes behind the dark frames, but she could tell that he was watching her.

"What?" she asked.

He smiled. "Nothing. Just like hearing you laugh, that's all."

She felt the jump in her stomach, then couldn't help laughing again when the boat swept around the corner—even if a tiny part of her felt guilty for laughing. And even as a bigger part of her wished Emma could be here to enjoy this with them.

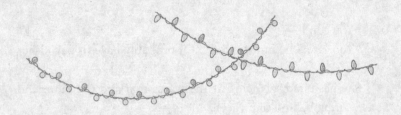

Chapter Twenty-five

Back at the hotel, Holly checked her phone for the time, trying to calculate how many hours there were before she could see Emma again. Another fourteen—she still had to get through the night before they were allowed back.

As if Emma was somehow sensing her worry from afar, a text popped up.

I'm ok. I'm going to sleep so I'm awake and perky for when you come to visit tomorrow— mainly because I want to have words with you for going behind my back and calling a certain someone.

Holly felt her lips twitch.

Would you rather I sent him back home?

The reply was almost instantaneous.

He's still here then?

It broke her heart a little, the idea of Emma worrying about that.

Yes. Shall I tell him thanks for coming all this way, but actually he best be off home?

I'm not going to rise to that.

Are you ok—honestly? Can I do anything?

I'm ok—honestly. And there's nothing you can do right now, and I need to sleep anyway. Keep exploring Venice with Jack and then at least you'll have something interesting to tell me tomorrow.

"What are you smiling at?"

Holly looked up to see Jack standing by the window—a window which offered just the tiniest glimpse of the beauty of Venice. "Emma," she said, putting her phone down, then suddenly wondering what to do with her hands. They'd been mid-conversation when they'd got back to the hotel, and had just carried on talking as they climbed the stairs, heading to Holly's room, neither of them questioning it. But now what?

"She has her phone on her?" Jack asked.

"Sure. It's not a prison. A monastery, once upon a time, but not a prison."

Jack nodded, looking back out at the street below. Holly wondered if he'd message her, let her know he'd still be here tomorrow, was still planning to stay. But that was for him to decide, and she was trying to be less pushy.

"So, what do you want to do now?" Jack asked.

"I don't know . . . We could grab dinner somewhere?" *Obviously, Holly.* Because what was the alternative—they didn't eat? But maybe he'd want a break from her, the chance to clear his head a bit. She opened her mouth, ready to suggest that, but he beat her to it.

"OK, well, don't laugh, but I *may* have googled the top ten things to do in Venice."

"Of course you have."

It earned a grin.

"When, exactly?"

"When you were trying on your lacy thing."

"Right. And?"

"Venice Jazz Club came pretty high up. I put our names on the list, if you want to go?"

"Jazz?" Then she shrugged. "OK. Why not?" It would be good to have the distraction, in any case. "Just let me shower and change." Then she frowned at him. "Actually, do you want to shower too?"

"Yeah, but you go first. Or I could go first and then leave you to have the room?"

She hesitated, then nodded. "Yeah, OK." Because politeness be damned—getting ready while he was in the en suite would be far too awkward and distracting. It had been bad enough this morning, grabbing her clothes to change in the bathroom, after having woken up with his arm still around her.

He showered and she tried to compose a text to Abi to tell her what was happening. Though she wasn't sure how, exactly, to explain that Jack was in her hotel room in Venice, taking a shower in her bathroom, without it sounding completely weird.

She looked up when the door clicked open. And there he was, a towel tied around his waist, hair all damp and ruffled, his bare chest right there on show. She forced herself to look up at his face. "That was quick."

"Just trying to get out of your hair."

She nodded, suddenly unsure of what to say. *Jesus,* what a body. Her eyes traced the contours of his chest of their own accord, moving from there to his arms—and why did arms suddenly become even more sexy, when they were attached to a naked body?

She realized what she was doing and snapped her gaze back to his, registering the subtle curve of his lips as he suppressed a smile.

"I'll get dressed, leave you to it," he said. She picked up her towel off the bed, and he moved into the room at the same time as she stepped toward the bathroom. She was very, *very* aware that he was naked, that all it would take was one tug on the towel. She looked up and their gazes met. She felt something pull inside her, though she told herself not to be stupid as she took another step toward him, to where he'd gone still, watching her.

She tilted her face up to him. "Thank you, for today."

"You shouldn't be thanking me." His voice was low, like liquid dark chocolate, smooth and impossibly sexy.

"Well, I am." Then, marveling at her own self-control, she stood on tiptoes to press a kiss to his cheek. She felt the way his body tensed as she eased back and she tried to take a breath as she started to move around him to the safety of the bathroom.

But he grabbed her hand to stop her, and she felt the electric flare of her pulse. She looked up at him.

"I came here for Emma," he said, quietly.

And she frowned—because that was obvious.

"I have been trying to figure out a way to . . ." He shook his head. "I should have got in touch before now. With Emma, I mean. Should have found a way to . . ." He blew out a breath. "The point is . . . it shouldn't have taken you calling me to tell me she was in hospital."

Because he looked like he needed the comfort, she reached out, cupped his face in her free hand.

"I came for Emma," he repeated. "But I also . . ." He swallowed, Adam's apple bobbing. "I mean, when I heard your voice . . ." She felt the huff of his breath on her hand. "I'd be lying if I said I didn't come for you too, Holly."

She felt the spark at his words, the way her heart thudded against her chest. So she didn't let herself think too hard about it as she leaned in, pressing her lips to his. Gently, something soft and sweet. But he reached up, placed his hand over hers, and deepened the kiss, just a little. Her eyelids fluttered closed. She could smell the shower gel the hotel provided, could taste mint on his tongue. He pulled away gently, their faces still close, his dark brown eyes boring into hers. She let out a shaky breath and pulled back farther, before she acted on what her body was telling her to do right now.

"I'll see you downstairs?" His voice was still low, and just rough enough to make her belly stir.

She nodded, stepped away. And when she turned the shower on, she turned it down cold.

Holly sat next to Jack at a small table—there were only around ten in the club, creating an intimate atmosphere, one that was only added to by the bottle of red wine between them. The music was amazing, and not at all what Holly would have expected. Admittedly, she didn't have much experience with jazz, but she'd imagined something a bit boring. But this was the type of music to set you alive, to make you smile or bring a lump to your throat. The way the instruments spoke to one another, the way the musicians were able to work with one another with no sheets to read from, relying only on their own ear or talent or whatever—well, it made Holly wish she'd learned to play an instrument.

"I think I might be a converted jazz fan," she whispered to Jack, and he smiled at her.

"Me too."

They had barely looked at each other all evening, Holly keeping her attention resolutely on the band. Or at least, trying to *seem* like all her attention was on the band, when really it was on the way Jack's knee was pressed against hers under the table— had been since they'd sat down after the short interval. He was in jeans—not having taken the time to properly think through the best clothes to pack in his hurry to leave for the plane—but she was in the playsuit she'd bought, the white lace skimming three quarters of the way down her arms but leaving her legs bare. Bare—and all the more sensitive for it.

They couldn't really speak above the music—not without being rude and shouting—and somehow that only added to the thrumming in her body, her nerves pulsing in time with the flickering candlelight.

When the second set ended, Holly and Jack clapped along with everyone else, and something like relief slid through her. Not that she hadn't enjoyed it—she'd loved it. Could imagine Lily loving it too.

Together Jack and Holly headed to the bar to pay, and promised to come back if they were ever in Venice again. The sun had set by the time they stepped outside—reinforcing her belief that Venice at night was just as beautiful as Venice in the day. The buildings glowed with the light of the street lanterns and the water glimmered in answer, giving the whole place a magical, mysterious feel, like you couldn't be quite sure what was waiting for you around the corner.

Jack shoved his hands into his pockets as they walked back to the hotel over the Rialto Bridge, the chatter of tourists humming around them. Holly looked straight ahead. She'd thought it would be easier, out here in the open air, but she still felt it, that pull toward him, and had to flex her fingers by her sides with the effort not to touch him. Did he feel it too? He'd kissed her back in the hotel room earlier, and she'd read something there, had been sure he'd wanted her. But when she snuck a glance at him, his face was so neutral, it was impossible to tell.

They made it back to the hotel in record time, both of them walking at speed. When they headed into the reception, Jack pulled a hand through his hair. "Shit, I didn't do anything about a room."

"That's OK," she said, and was impressed with how even her voice sounded. "You can share with me again—then we'll make a plan when we see Emma tomorrow."

Emma. Was she OK? Hopefully she was asleep by now. Hopefully they'd give her something for the pain, something that meant she'd get some proper rest.

Quiet descended between them as they climbed the stairs. Holly let them into the room, deliberately not looking at Jack. It was different from yesterday, the air between them thicker. And unlike yesterday, when he'd sat on the edge of the bed and let her cry on his lap, today the bed felt like this big presence, taking up all the space between them.

Jack shut the door with a quiet click and Holly moved away to place her bag on the chair in the corner of the room—as far away from him as she could get. But he reached out, placed a hand gently on her arm. "I'm not sure it's a good idea for me to stay here again tonight," he said, his voice a low rumble.

Holly frowned and tried to push away the sting of rejection. It wasn't rejection if she hadn't made a move, was it?

"Why not?" she asked.

His lips twisted into a small, self-deprecating smile. "Because I don't think I can sleep if I'm lying next to you all night." Though there was a touch of lightness in his voice, his gaze was very direct on hers, enough to send something hot shooting through her body.

She turned, and though he'd dropped his hand from her arm,

she placed both her hands on his chest, feeling the muscle through his shirt. It was a relief, to be able to touch him, to finally give in to it. She cocked her head up at him. "Who said anything about sleep?"

He was very still. "You told me we shouldn't go there, last time," he said, his voice slow and careful. Windsor—he meant Windsor, when he'd reached for her, and she'd backed away.

She shook her head. "That was then. This is now." And really, who was she kidding? The moment he'd suggested the jazz club, she'd known it would happen. Maybe even before that, though she'd refused to let her mind go down that route—because to call it *inevitable* made it feel too much like *fate*.

His hands came to her waist and beneath her playsuit, her skin burned. "I don't want to take advantage of you. You've had a rough couple of days, and I—"

She pressed a finger to his lips, felt the whisper of his breath on her skin. "Jack. Trust me when I say that you are in no way taking advantage of me." She leaned in to kiss him, felt his hands slide down her body, his fingers dig into her hips. He returned the kiss, and she could feel it, the effort it took to be gentle, how his body vibrated with it.

It was she who deepened it, wrapping her arms around his neck and pulling his head down toward her. Self-control had never been her strong suit, in any area of her life, and right now, she wanted this. She needed it, something real and all-consuming, and she was not going to let herself think past that.

Jack murmured an oath against her lips and hooked one arm around her, the other going to her hair, his tongue meeting hers, changing the angle of the kiss and chasing away the gentleness. She gasped when his teeth caught her bottom lip.

He moved to kiss her neck, teeth lightly scraping her skin, and she groaned, arching her back to allow him better access as a shiver ran down her body.

"Fuck, Holly," he murmured against her neck, and the sound of his voice all low and husky like that made her toes curl.

She tugged his shirt out of his jeans, ran her hands up his torso. It wasn't enough. She wanted *more*. "Let me," she said, tugging at the shirt. "Just let me . . ."

Laughing a little breathlessly, he pulled his shirt over his head, and she ran her hands down that glorious chest, before moving them around to feel the muscles on his back. His eyes stayed on her the whole time, and she thought she might burn with the intensity of it.

He leaned in to kiss her again, then moved her back toward the bed. His thigh came between her legs, and even that was enough to make her feel swollen. He tugged at her playsuit and it was her turn to laugh that same breathless laugh. "Playsuit. *So* not attractive to get off. I should have thought this through."

He grinned, and it was the grin she realized she was growing to love—mischievous and quick and a bit cocky, all things that only came out in those unguarded moments. "Planning this, were you?"

She let her breath out on a hiss when his teeth scraped against her jawline. "Oh God, you have no idea."

He ran his hands up her thighs, his fingers skimming just under the shorts of her playsuit. "I think I do. I really think I do."

She managed to get out of the playsuit—ungracefully, in a way that made them both laugh. At least she'd thought through the underwear combination. His eyes dipped, taking the time to travel up the length of her body, in a way that made her nerves quiver. His hand skimmed over the top of her bra, down her sides, and she felt that liquid pull, one that made her grab at him, pulling him with her when she lay down on the bed.

Her pulse flared at the feeling of him on top of her, and she fumbled with the belt on his jeans, heard the buckle, the slither of the belt.

Her breath was coming in shudders now as his fingers dipped below the cotton of her panties. He kissed her stomach, then lower, and she ran her fingers through his gorgeous dark hair, groaning when his tongue took the place of his fingers.

He grinned up at her, and she pulled him to her, running her hands down his body, feeling the bulge beneath his boxers. It was only then that something occurred to her, and she stopped, biting her lip as she looked at him. "Jack. Do you have a condom?"

He stilled, stared back at her. "No."

"You don't?" Her voice came out as a squeak.

"Well, I wasn't exactly planning that kind of holiday."

She laughed, but it was a restless, frustrated laugh. He pressed his forehead against hers. She could still feel the thrumming inside her body, the way her hips lifted, begging despite herself. He kissed her neck, tongue teasing. "Jack," she said, her voice pleading.

He linked his fingers through hers, lifted her hands above her head. "Don't worry," he murmured, and kissed her lips again, more searchingly now. "There are plenty of things we can do without a condom."

And as her body arched beneath him, she realized that those things were going to keep them *very* busy until morning.

Chapter Twenty-six

Holly glanced up at Jack as they walked down the line of stone pillars, toward the main entrance of the hospital. He *seemed* relaxed enough. But then, he was very good at keeping any big emotions hidden, which made it all so frustrating. And not just because she was wondering how much tension he felt about Emma, but also because she was wondering how he felt about last night. Because it had been incredible—even if a little frustrating. And when she'd woken, her hair tangled and messy on the pillow, one leg trapped between his thighs, she'd just felt . . . content. Even when she'd crept out to shower, leaving Jack looking all sexy and rumpled in the sheets, she hadn't felt the need to scrabble around for clothing or anything, and he'd made things easy as they got ready, chatting to her like normal.

But stepping into the grand hospital building, *now* it felt awkward. Like they'd done something wrong—because this was Emma's grandson, for God's sake, and Emma had been here, in hospital, while they'd been . . . She snuck a glance up at him again, and this time he saw her doing it, offered her a little smile.

Then he hooked an arm around her, pulled her to his side and kissed the top of her head. Like he knew what she was thinking and was trying to reassure her. She tried not to think about how easily she fitted against his side, how right it felt to have his arm around her.

Jack dropped his arm away as they approached the reception desk. "Ah, we're here to see Emma Tooley?"

The man behind the desk pushed up his glasses, looked at the computer screen, then gestured for them to go on through, all without speaking. Though maybe that was because of the Italian-English barrier.

When they found Emma's room, there was a doctor coming out—a woman in her forties or fifties, long dark hair with a tinge of gray pulled back in a low ponytail over her white coat. "Good," she said briskly, "you're here." The way everyone had to speak English to them made Holly feel a bit embarrassed—why hadn't she learned a few languages, just in case?

"Is she OK?" Jack asked. And now Holly could see the tension, skirting in around the edges.

The doctor blew out a breath. "Well, as OK as she can be, given the circumstances, I would say. But perhaps you can talk to her." She glanced between Holly and Jack. "Even at this stage there are still options, and after the recent episode perhaps she—"

"What do you mean?" Holly interrupted sharply. "What stage?"

The doctor frowned. "It's stage four. You knew this, yes?"

Holly felt Jack's body stiffen next to hers and automatically reached out to lay a hand on his arm at the same time as she shook her head wordlessly. *Stage 4.* It echoed around her mind, seeming less and less real each time. Because Emma couldn't have stage 4 cancer. People with stage 4 were really ill, terminal, even, and Emma, she was . . . But even as she tried to deny it, she knew that this was what they'd been skirting around for months now, none of them willing to admit it. *Emma* not willing to admit it.

"I'm sorry," the doctor was saying. "I assumed . . ." She cleared her throat, an efficient sound. "The best thing is to get her back home, then talk to her doctors there. Make a plan. There is only so much we can do here, and it is no use in me talking through the options, because it is not me treating her."

"We have a flight this afternoon," Holly said, her words feeling numb on her lips.

Jack looked down at her, a slight frown creasing his forehead. She hadn't told him, she realized. The last few days had felt suspended in time, waiting for what would happen next, and she hadn't thought to bring up her return flight, because it had seemed irrelevant.

"Hmm," the doctor said. "Well, we still need to clear her, do some tests, make sure she is safe to fly. So I'm not sure about today, but tomorrow, or the day after, yes?"

"Yes," Jack said. "We can rebook the flights, I'm sure."

Holly nodded, still feeling numb. *Stage 4.*

"I'll leave you to see her. But perhaps you can talk some sense into her. As I've said, best to talk to your doctors back home, but there are things you can do to make it . . ."—another throat clear—"more comfortable."

Holly watched the doctor leave, her ponytail swishing in time with her quick walk. Had she been alone, she wouldn't have moved, but Jack was opening the door to Emma's room and she knew she had to follow.

Emma looked up at them both as they stepped inside, and her expression twisted.

"So," she said. "They told you."

Jack was now holding himself so stiff, Holly thought something might snap. But she didn't dare touch him—she didn't want Emma to notice, to ask about it, not when—

"Why didn't you tell me?" she asked, stepping toward Emma, tears burning the back of her eyes.

"Because there's nothing you can do," Emma said flatly. She glanced at Jack. "Nothing anyone can do."

"But surely there are treatments," Holly said quickly. "Things that can help prolong—"

"Let's not talk about this," Emma said, her voice firm.

And that was her go-to, wasn't it? Let's not talk about it, let's pretend it's not happening. Could Holly really judge that tactic, though? Was there a right way to deal with something like this? Would she deal with it any better?

Dying. Emma was dying. She couldn't comprehend it. They were on holiday in Venice, for God's sake.

"How was yesterday?" Emma was saying. Jack was still standing, frozen in the doorway. "Did you go to Burano?"

"Yes," Holly said, "but—"

"Did you buy me something nice? Don't tell me you forgot. I was banking on some lace."

"Emma, we—"

"And Jack."

Jack jolted at the sound of his name.

"I barely asked you anything yesterday. Tell me. What's been happening? There's so much I want to know." Emma's no-nonsense tone faltered here, something deeper and more pleading coming through. "Are you still in London?"

Jack moved closer to Emma's bed, standing at the foot of it, while Holly stayed beside Emma's head. "I shouldn't have left it this long, to get in touch."

"So, we're talking about it, then," Emma said. She closed her eyes briefly.

She looked so tired. So *old*. She *was* old; Holly knew that. Logically, she knew it. But Emma just didn't seem it—she still seemed so vibrant, so *alive*.

Emma opened her eyes and indicated the chairs next to her. "Come and sit down, I don't want to have to look up at you."

Jack moved to take one of the chairs next to Emma, as if he was thankful to have an order to obey, and Holly bit her lip. "Should I—"

"No, you stay," Emma said. "You're the reason he's here, aren't you?"

Holly winced.

"Oh, don't start with that again, I'm not going to bite your head off."

"Well, that would make a first," Holly muttered as she took the second chair, earning a wink from Emma and a small smile from Jack.

"Look," Emma continued, addressing Jack, her turquoise gaze sharp on his, "this goes two ways. You are not to take all the blame, just because I'm, well . . ." She puffed out a breath. "I didn't get in touch either, even after this one's prodding."

Holly felt her chest growing hot at the reminder that she was caught in the middle here—even if that was totally and completely her own fault.

"Even after I sent the letter, I—"

"What letter?" Jack asked with a frown.

"The Dear Stranger letter," Emma said with an impatient wave of her hand.

"The what?"

Now Emma looked at Holly. "You didn't tell him."

"Ah, no. I didn't go into much detail about how we met." She could feel Jack's gaze on her too, now. Somehow the whole why of it all, the letter that had brought Holly into Emma's life in the first place, just hadn't come up—Jack hadn't asked, and she hadn't thought to tell him.

Emma gave Holly a raised-eyebrow look, then glanced between the two of them. There was something in that glance—something which suggested she knew more than she was letting on. "Right, well, we can circle back to that. The point is, after it all happened, after the crash . . ." Emma's face tightened. "I understood why you and your mum blamed me. I blamed me too. I was driving, and it doesn't matter if another car was there."

"Another car?" Jack repeated, his voice sounding far away. He'd told Holly Emma had hit a tree, she remembered. "I sort of remember, but I don't . . ." He shook his head. "I can't remember all of it."

"Well, that's a small blessing," Emma said quietly. "It's a curse, remembering. I've lost a few things, memories going hazy with age—but I've never forgotten that night."

"There was another car?" Jack repeated. "That's why you swerved?"

"Yes."

Holly felt twitchy. Like she shouldn't be here, witnessing this—even as another part of her wanted to stay, to understand. But the heat rising in her chest was more than either of those things—because the whole conversation, it was making her think of *her* crash, of the car that had come at them. Of the car behind. Of what might have happened, if there hadn't been another stranger on the road that day, ready to call an ambulance when they saw the accident.

"Mum said it was your fault," Jack said, and his voice sounded thick.

"Well, it's easier to have someone to blame," Emma said quietly. "I was still the one driving. I . . ." But she glanced at Holly and swallowed whatever she was going to say.

I was still to blame, was that it? But if she was to blame, then so was Holly.

"And maybe it would have panned out differently, if there was someone else behind the wheel." The lines around Emma's mouth tightened. "I've replayed the scene often enough, wondering."

Holly was staring down at her lap now, trying to breathe slowly. She shouldn't be the one to cry here. She needed to hold it together. This was not the time to think about her own crash, about Lily. This was about Emma.

"I've dealt with the whole thing horribly," Jack said, still in that same strained voice. "And now—"

"You've dealt with it in a way that got you through it," Emma said, and though she was clearly trying for her usual matter-of-fact voice, there was a gentleness there that Holly had only heard occasionally. "And I should have tried harder," Emma continued, tiredness creeping into her voice. "I shouldn't have let you and your mum turn me away."

Holly peeked up to see Jack frowning at Emma. "What do you mean, let us turn you away? You never tried to get in touch, afterward."

"Of course I did. When you left, I was constantly ringing your mum, wrote her a few letters for good measure. But she said she didn't want to see me, and she said *you* didn't want to see me, and I could hardly blame either of you, so I . . ." She trailed off at the look in Jack's eye and Holly found herself holding her breath.

"She said you wanted space. She never said . . . I thought you'd given up. I thought you didn't want to see me."

Holly couldn't stand it, the way his voice sounded like it was about to break. She reached out, laid a hand on his. He flipped his palm, linked his fingers with hers.

Emma followed the action with her eyes, but she didn't comment. "I always wanted to see you," she said. "But maybe I did give up."

"I tried to get in touch, about the service I was holding for Dad. It was just before Christmas, nearly four years ago now. I wrote to you about it. You never came."

Emma's eyes were shining with tears. "I was in the car, driving there. But an accident had happened in an intersection along the way. I couldn't get by, and the crash looked pretty bad."

Holly's heart started to thud. Christmas, nearly four years ago. Jack in the café because he was headed to the memorial. A crash that happened not far from there.

She pulled her hand away from Jack's. "Where?" she breathed, and both Jack's and Emma's gazes snapped to hers. "Where was the crash?"

When Emma named the road, Holly stared at her. Did they hear it, that ringing? "You couldn't get past?" Holly repeated, and her voice was shaky.

"No. And not just that . . ." She swallowed, and the action looked painful. "I had to get out—I had to see if there was anything I could do. I called the ambulance and they told me not to get too close, because it might be dangerous, but I waited, to make sure. I saw them get everyone out of the cars and into the ambulance. It was OK, though, in the end," she continued, her tone reassuring, clearly having clocked something in Holly's expression. "They were all OK—I called the hospital to check."

"You called the ambulance?" The thudding of her heart felt painful now. The ambulance had arrived so quickly. It was something she'd heard her mum thanking the hospital for.

Jack was watching her. "Holly, what—?"

"It was my crash," she whispered. "That's why you didn't get to the service. It was because of me."

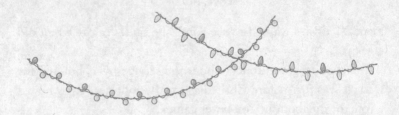

Chapter Twenty-seven

Both Jack and Emma were staring at her.

Holly licked her lips, her mouth dry. "The crash I told you both about," she said, and now her palms felt sticky. "The one with Lily."

"I know what you mean," Emma said, the no-nonsense tone back. "I'm just . . . processing." She stared at Holly for a good long moment. Holly's ears were ringing, the noise almost deafening. Her heart was thudding, sending little bolts around her body. So many threads, pulling them together—the connections between her and Emma and Jack. All of them had had accidents in the past, had all lost something because of that. It was the reason she had been drawn to Emma, the reason she felt such kinship. And now this . . .

Fate, fate, fate. It chanted around her mind, Lily's voice and her own merging together. *Stop it,* she told herself. *There's no such thing as fate.* Because what purpose would fate serve? Why would fate send that driver swerving around the corner? Why would fate cause Lily to lose her baby, her chance at motherhood? Why would fate rip her sister from her, and why would it bring Emma into her life, just as Emma was dying, so that she'd have to lose someone she cared about all over again?

Holly got to her feet, backed away from the bed. "I need some air," she said, and it was no more than a scratchy whisper.

Behind her, Emma was saying something, and she registered Jack's low voice in reply, but she couldn't hear properly over the thudding of her heart, that damned ringing in her ears. She walked quickly to the door, yanked it open and fell into the corridor, letting the door shut behind her and leaning back against the nearest white wall. Her brain was whirring, trying to make sense of it all, but she couldn't untangle the threads. It was too much, all too much.

The door opened again, and Jack stepped out. Seeing her slumped against the wall, he took a step toward her. Was it her, or was it very careful, that step? He kept a distance between them, too—was that deliberate?

His dark gaze met hers. "Are you OK?"

She hesitated. "Are you?"

"I don't know. This is . . ."

"I know." She closed her eyes. "It's a bit much."

"Yeah."

There was a beat of silence between them, broken only by the sound of a door opening somewhere down the corridor, of chatter swelling and then fading. When Holly opened her eyes again, Jack was staring at Emma's closed door.

"I'm not really sure what to do," Jack said. "What do you do, when you find out . . ."

"I don't know." She felt her lips trembling and bit down on them. "Jack, I . . ."

"It wasn't your fault." How had he known that she was about to apologize? For being the reason Emma didn't make it to the service that day, the reason Jack and Emma hadn't reunited three years earlier. "None of it. OK? It's just . . . Jesus, I don't know what it is."

Fate, fate, fate.

Holly took a breath. Because even if *that* wasn't her fault, a part of it still was. "I tracked her down. After I got her letter, I tracked her down, and then I tracked *you* down, and I've been trying to—"

"If you hadn't, maybe I never would have known. Maybe I never would have had the chance to . . ."

To what? Holly wondered. To understand? To say goodbye?

"I can't believe that after all of this, I'm supposed to be getting on a flight in a few hours," she said, feeling the weight of that settle on her. "I'm supposed to fly back today, because term is starting and I need to prepare and—"

"It's fine. You go. I'll stay with Emma. I'll figure it out."

That wasn't what she'd meant, but his words were so final that she wasn't sure she could argue the fact. "You will?"

He blew out a breath. "Yeah."

"What about *your* job?"

He shrugged. "They won't care; it's only an extra couple of days." He rubbed his hands over his face. "Or maybe they will care, and I'll get lucky and they'll fire me." He dropped his hands and tried for a smile, but though his lips curved, it didn't meet his eyes. "It'll be fine, Holly."

Again that same firm, certain voice. But he was wrong—because it wouldn't be fine, would it?

Stage 4.

Jack's expression changed, became more serious. He took a step toward her. "Holly, I . . ."

She took a breath, bracing herself, though for what she wasn't quite sure.

"I really like you."

Holly bit her lip as she looked at him, tried to read his expression. She wasn't even sure what she wanted to see there. Her brain was too muddled with everything that was going on.

"But all of this . . ." Jack continued. "It just feels like—"

"Too much?" Holly suggested, her voice quiet.

"Yeah," Jack said on a sigh. "No," he corrected quickly. "I don't mean . . ." He ran a hand across the back of his neck. "It feels impossible, doesn't it, that we bumped into each other in that bloody café, and somehow our lives are . . ."

"Connected?" It felt silly, saying it—but it was also true.

Jack nodded. "Yeah. And because of all that, it feels like if we . . ." He reached out to take her hand. "If we give it a go, whatever this is between us, I think we should give it the best shot we can."

Holly's stomach was fizzing with something—nerves, maybe. And Jack's hand felt warm, comforting on hers. The only steady thing around her right now. "So you're saying . . . ?"

"I'm saying, not right now."

"Not right now?" Holly repeated.

"Yeah. Emma, she's . . . I owe it to her, to try and make up for . . ." He shook his head. "I need to try and make sure she's OK, or . . . well, you know what I mean. I need to try to figure this all out and I don't want to promise you something and then be distracted. When the time comes for this—for us—I want to be able to be all in with you. Is that OK?"

She reached up, cupped his face with her hand. "Yeah. That's OK. Emma's what's important here."

And it was true, wasn't it? She couldn't start something with Jack, whatever *something* might end up being, when they'd just found out Emma had stage 4 cancer. What if it ended badly, for instance, and they broke up, and that caused more stress for Emma? They should both be focused on her right now, not on each other and all the things that come with figuring out a new relationship.

Jack reached up to lay his hand over hers. "I mean it, though."

She frowned. "Mean what?"

"I like you. A lot."

Something hot sparked in her stomach, but she smiled, kept it easy. "I like you too." And it was safe to say that. She liked a lot of people, no big deal.

Liar, a voice in the back of her mind whispered. She chose to ignore it. Because really, it was better this way, wasn't it? It wasn't rejection she felt right now, but *relief.* Relief that he'd made the decision, that he was stepping away before anything serious could happen. Before she could really tumble. It was safer—because if he wasn't really hers, then she couldn't lose him. Especially not when Emma . . .

Stage 4.

Holly drew her hand away from Jack's face. "I'd better go and check out, get my stuff."

"OK. I'll stay here, try to talk to the doctors, figure out a plan."

Holly nodded. "I'll come back before I go to the airport to check on Emma again."

"OK. I'll see you soon, then." He hesitated, like he might be about to kiss her. Instead he stepped back.

"Yeah. I'll see you soon."

She turned, trying to keep her emotions at bay as she headed out of the hospital, back into the buzz of Venice. It was the right thing to do, to step back from Jack. She'd have to put it from her mind, how it had felt, spending time with him, how it had felt being with him last night, waking up to him. He was right—Emma was what was important. Somehow, they needed to figure out how to be there for Emma, how to help her through this. How to come to terms with it themselves.

And really, if she was being honest with herself, there were other things she needed to sort out too, before she thought about

a relationship. Because the little sense of relief she'd felt in deciding to wait with Jack, maybe it meant that Daniel had been
right—maybe she wasn't really ready. She felt the tiniest squirm
of guilt at that. Maybe she'd been unfair, lashing out at him—
because maybe he'd seen what she hadn't, seen the fact that she
couldn't give him her whole heart. Because how could she give all
of herself in a relationship when a part of her was stuck in the
past? When a part of her had never got over what had happened,
and the way she had lost Lily. So Holly supposed Emma was
right too; she needed to try to sort her own family situation out.
She just wasn't sure how to do that yet.

Regardless, there was no getting away from the fact that her
and Jack's lives were intertwined now, whatever they decided. So
she'd have to figure out a way to push her feelings aside, to not do
anything stupid. And she would, she told herself firmly. Whatever happened, however much they saw each other over the coming months, she could be a grown-up about the whole thing and
keep herself in check. She'd do that, for Emma.

OCTOBER

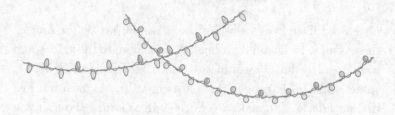

Chapter Twenty-eight

Jack stuck his hands in the pockets of his jeans as he walked, wishing he'd brought a better coat. It was October, but there was a bite in the air, a warning of winter just around the corner. It might be one of the last warmish days, Jack mused, though he didn't mind winter, with its cold, bright days and sheets of frost in the morning.

Next to him, Theo had his shoulders hunched as he walked. He was wearing the black-and-green sweater that he'd bought— or, more accurately, that *Jack* had bought, to promises from Theo that he'd pay him back once he had a job—on the shopping expedition they'd been on in London. Theo had refused to wear a coat as they'd left the house, but Jack had a suspicion the hunched shoulders were less about the chill in the air and more about the enforced family day out—to a National Trust property, no less.

It had been their mum's idea—Theo and Mia were on half term, so she'd invited Jack down for a Day Out (the capitals weren't implied; she'd actually written it like that in her text) at Buckland Abbey, a big old estate where someone important had once lived. Derek was working, so it would just be the four of them. Once, Jack would probably have said no to this: He would have dreaded the awkwardness, feeling like he didn't fit in. But something had changed in the last six months. Maybe it was just that he'd decided to make an effort—and as it turned out, if you made an effort then other people did too. He'd spent so long assuming he didn't belong with his family anymore, that he had to forge his own path, away from them, and away from where he grew up, but, really, that had been something he'd decided—it had never been forced on him.

The Abbey was impressive—old stone with plants creeping up the sides of it. They'd wandered through the house, his mum pretending to be more interested in the history of it all than Jack knew was really the case, and had passed an old barn where people were making cider with apples from the gardens. Theo and Mia had been all for trying it, but their mum had said no, so that was that. Now they were out in the gardens, and this was the bit that Jack liked best—probably the reason his mum had invited him in the first place. He loved gardens in autumn—everyone was always on about the beauty of spring and summer, but autumn could hold its own too, with roses coming into their second bloom, apples ripening and falling, and all the golden and red colors as the leaves turned.

"So," Jack asked Theo, "how's the new school?"

"It's all right." But there was an easiness about the way he said it, with none of the tension Jack had seen when he'd asked Theo about his old school. Derek had mentioned the new school to Jack, and Jack had floated the idea with Theo when he'd come to visit in the summer.

"Why do you think it might be worse?" Jack had asked.

"Well, OK, maybe not worse, but not better, and at least I know how to handle . . . them."

"It might be better."

"Might not."

"Yeah, I suppose it's about weighing up the risks and bene-fits, then."

Theo had given him a scarily knowing look, for a sixteen-year-old. "Is that why you're still in London—because the risk outweighs the benefit or whatever?"

"I don't know what you're—"

"Sure, because you're the only one who can hand out life advice." Theo had grinned then and it had made Jack laugh. But the upshot was that Jack, along with his mum and Derek, had convinced Theo to try it—and so far, he seemed happier.

Jack glanced behind them, down the gravel path that ran be-tween the Tudor knot hedges, and paused to wait for their mum to catch up. Despite being the one who'd suggested coming here, apparently, Mia was lagging even farther back. She'd seemed completely checked out so far, constantly looking at her phone and glancing around as if worried someone would see her here and call her out for being uncool. Jack remembered that feeling well from being a teenager and was eternally grateful he'd never have to relive it.

Jack's mum came up beside them and frowned back at Mia, who had now come to a stop. "Mia!"

Mia jumped and looked up. "Why does it *matter* if I'm slow?" she called back. "We're not trying to get anywhere, are we?"

Their mum gave Mia a look, and then started walking again, chin tilted up, making a big show of looking around the gardens, which, Jack could see, were pretty boring for the average teen-ager. Theo slouched off after their mum, but Jack stayed back to wait for Mia.

"Maybe if we do a quick turnaround," he said when she

caught up, "I'll float the idea of getting back early so we can have curry in front of Netflix rather than the hour-long walk she has planned around the grounds."

Mia glanced up at him. "Really?"

"Yeah, I'll—"

"Mia!"

Mia jumped again at the sound of her own name, not coming from their mum this time but from a teenage boy, who was coming up behind them. The silent panic was written all over Mia's face.

Jack frowned—was she being bullied too, like Theo? He dropped his voice to a whisper. "Who is . . . ?"

"Liam," Mia whispered back, and she blushed. Ah, OK.

"Mia," said the boy again, as he came closer. He was skinny, in the way that most teenage boys are, his face still boyish, brown hair sticking up all over the place. He was wearing a Kate Bush T-shirt—why?—over baggy trousers that Jack thought looked totally ridiculous. And when, exactly, did Jack get so *old*?

"Hey," the boy said. "I was calling your name."

"Oh," Mia said, just about managing not to stutter. "Sorry. I didn't hear you." She briefly caught Jack's eye, and he gave her the shadow of a wink.

"I didn't know you were coming here today." So that explained it, then.

"No, well, last-minute plan," Mia said, reaching up to toy with a lock of her hair. She glanced at Jack. "This is my brother," she said, and Liam gave Jack the once-over in a way that was almost comical. Jack couldn't help returning the favor, though—Mia clearly liked the kid, but that didn't mean he was a good guy. Although maybe he didn't have the right to go all protective big brother on her yet.

Jack started to back away, but Mia shot him a slightly panicked look that made him stall.

"So. How's your half term been?" Liam asked.

"All right."

Jesus, this was painful. Was this what teenage flirting had been like when he was one? Probably it was, actually, especially at Mia's age, when you were only just figuring out how to talk to one another.

When neither of them said anything more, Jack spoke, unable to stand the awkwardness. "You into Kate Bush?" he asked Liam.

"Yeah. She's epic. Why, do you know her?" As if she was some kind of indie musician that no one had heard of. But it made Jack think of something.

"Not really. But she's in *Stranger Things*, right?"

"Right," Liam agreed, proving Jack's hunch right. "You watch it?"

"Not really. I only watched one episode, because Mia made me." Not actually true, but he did know Mia had won a long-fought battle with their mum to start watching the show recently, because everyone was going on about it.

Mia did the jolting thing again—was she going to do that every time her name was mentioned?

Liam looked at her. "You're into *Stranger Things*?"

"Of course," Mia said, and there was a touch of her eye-roll in there.

And then they were off, actually talking, and this time Mia did not look at him as he backed away. He saw his mum and Theo waiting, not far up the path.

"Who's that?" his mum asked immediately when he reached them.

Jack shrugged. "Friend from school, I guess."

"Sucker," Theo muttered under his breath.

Jack's phone buzzed and he slid it out of his jeans pocket. His heart did that familiar lurch thing when he saw her name.

Really, he should learn to get a fucking grip. They'd agreed in Venice that it wasn't sensible to go down that route. And he was trying, he really was, to think of her as a friend. To send *friendly* messages. When they'd first started texting it had all been about Emma, checking in with each other on how she was doing when one or the other of them saw her. But as the weeks had gone on, they'd ended up just chatting or, as today, sending random GIFs. Right now there was one of a woman sitting on a rock in a pretty dress, getting smashed repeatedly by a wave and looking all bedraggled afterward.

Me in the bridesmaid dress Abi picked out.

His lips twitched into a smile as he tried to think of something funny or clever to say back. He wasn't any better than that Liam dude, was he? He started to type back *I'm sure you look great,* then stopped, wondering if that was friend-appropriate. Well, obviously it *was* friend-appropriate, just not when he was currently imagining just how great she would look.

"Mia!" his mum called, oblivious to first love, and got an "I'm *coming*" back, though when Mia joined them again she was smiling—and she reserved a bigger smile just for him. He'd take it. Maybe there was still a way to go with her, to figure out their relationship, but he'd get there, one way or another.

As Theo and Mia set off—Mia leading the way now and Theo ribbing her for it—Jack's mum came up side by side with him, linking her arm through his.

"So, how's the job?" she asked.

"Ahh . . ."

"Oh dear."

"What?"

"Jack, that's the same 'Ahh' as when I asked you if Katie Evans had been over while Derek and I were away that one night."

Ah, Katie Evans: his first proper crush. Jack gave her a shifty look. "I sort of . . . quit."

"What? You quit your job?"

"Yeah."

"Why? I thought . . . It's a good job, isn't it?"

"Yes, it's a good job." The way his mum was looking at him right now said it all. He thought about the stream of messages he'd got from Ed, immediately after.

You're QUITTING???

Why didn't you run this important life
decision past me?

What is the PLAN? Surely you have a plan.

Don't think this means you can get away
without a leaving do. There WILL be drinks in
Soho.

"It's a good job," Jack repeated, "but for someone else. I just . . . I need a change." Though what, exactly, that change would entail, he hadn't quite figured out. Still, he was trying to take things one step at a time, like Holly had said in Venice.

She studied him for a moment. "Well. I suppose I know a little about that."

It was as good an opening as any. "I've been speaking to Emma." No need to go into the specifics—his mum didn't need to know about Venice. "She's . . . She's not well."

His mum became very focused on the gravel beneath their feet, but he could feel her attention laser-focused on him.

"It's stage four pancreatic cancer."

He felt her grip tighten on his arm.

"I thought I should tell you, in case you . . . ." But he trailed off, because that sounded like some kind of superiority bullshit, when he'd only spoken to Emma for the first time two months ago. "Not that you have to do anything," he carried on quickly. "I don't mean . . . I just thought you might want to know."

"Stage four?" Her voice was constricted. "So she . . ."

"Yes."

"When?"

"We don't know." Jack had gone with her to the hospital once they'd returned from Italy, had refused to let Emma shake him off, and had got the full story—or as much of it as the doctors could give him. And it turned out they couldn't give him a straight answer—she could have four months or she could have four years. The cancer had spread from the pancreas, surgery wasn't a viable option and she was refusing chemo. And even if she *did* consent, that would only buy her a little extra time—there was no curing her.

His mum took a slow breath. "I don't know if I can go down that road again. I'm sorry—that probably sounds heartless. If I could change anything, you know, but it's . . . And Emma and I, we were never close. I appreciate you telling me, though."

"You don't have to explain it to me," Jack said, giving his mum's hand a gentle pat. "Although . . ." He might as well go there, now he'd started the conversation. "Why did you tell Emma I didn't want to see her after the accident?"

His mum's eyebrows shot up. "Because you told me that."

"I did?"

She gave a small, birdlike nod, glancing up the path to see where Theo and Mia were before looking up at Jack again. Her gaze was a little guarded, Jack thought. "I remember one night, after we'd moved, you were . . . you were upset." She swallowed, like she was trying to swallow down a painful memory. "You were crying in your room and I didn't know what to do."

Jack could remember, but only vaguely. The memories in the

year after the accident had a tendency to blur into one big mass, a feeling of being lost and lonely, and of not knowing how to talk to his mum because she was lost and lonely too. Maybe that's where the distance between them had started—not after she married Derek, but after they'd moved.

"I didn't know what to do and I was overwhelmed and even though it was my decision to move, it meant I had no one nearby and so . . ."

"You suggested calling Emma." He could remember that now, the way his mum's voice had quavered. *What about speaking to Memma? Would that help?*

"You always had such a good relationship with her," his mum continued. "Richard and I used to joke about it. Do you remember you ran away from home once?"

Jack smiled a little. "Right, because you wouldn't take me to see *Matrix* or something."

"*X-Men.*"

"*X-Men,* right."

"Because you were too young," she said pointedly.

Jack laughed at that: the fact that she'd still bring it up, the fact that she was having the very same debate with Mia over *Stranger Things*.

"And so you packed a bag—you wouldn't be one to leave without thinking it through—and the whole time you were up in your room packing Richard was *convinced* you wouldn't go through with it, but then you left the house. We had a whole ten minutes of utter panic before Emma rang us and said you were there but that she was pretending not to call us and if we came round and revealed we knew where you'd gone she'd refuse to babysit for the next two years and we could see how we did with Mary Gregory down the road—she was the fourteen-year-old who used to babysit and there were a fair few stories about what she got up to when the parents were out."

Jack felt another smile pull at his lips. "That sounds like Emma."

"The point is, when you felt like you wanted an escape from us, you always had her."

He could remember that day—showing up at Emma's with his rucksack and crisps, just in case she wasn't there and he got hungry waiting for her to come home. Emma had told him to come in and he'd explained the whole saga to her. And what she'd said was, "Well, I've known people to run away for less." Then he'd told her his mum had said he was too young to go and see *X-Men* in the cinema, and she'd said, "Age is just a number, but sadly the rest of the world is a little ruled by that, so how about I send Grandad out for pizza and a blockbuster film instead."

"So you tried to call her, when I was upset," Jack said, circling back around.

"Yes. But you didn't want me to call her: It made you cry even more and you were saying it was her fault and you didn't want to speak to her."

He grimaced, not really at the childishness of the words but at the fact he'd held on to them for so long.

His mum squeezed his arm, where they were linked. "You were just a boy, Jack, and you'd been through something awful. You were not to blame."

The memory of his feet, kicking Emma's seat in front of him, flashed in his mind.

Don't do that, Jack.

"I shouldn't have blamed her," Jack said quietly.

"No, *I* shouldn't have. And I shouldn't have pulled you out of your life like that, even if I thought it was for the best. I couldn't face the reminder of it." His mum's voice turned pleading now. "I loved your dad. I know we argued, and he had his faults, like we all do, but I loved him. Afterward, I couldn't keep that relationship with Emma and also feel like I could move on. I needed to start afresh. I'm sorry I allowed you to not talk to her, that I encouraged that, to protect myself. I just thought that was the only way we'd heal."

Jack sighed. "I've been blaming her for so long, holding on to that as some kind of . . ." He shook his head. "I don't know." He supposed it had been a way to make himself feel better, in some weird way, a way to channel the grief outward. "I kept thinking, if someone else had been driving, if *Dad* had been driving, then it might not have happened." He glanced at her. "I heard you say that, once. Talking to someone on the phone."

Her face pinched together. "I shouldn't have said that. I didn't mean it." She let go of his arm, pulled her hand through her blonde hair. "Your dad had had a drink that night, Jack. That's why Emma took the keys."

He stared at her as they walked, then dropped his gaze as Mia and Theo came into view, waiting for them around the corner. He lowered his voice. "He was drinking?" He remembered how Emma had swiped the keys—"I'll take those, don't you think, Richard?"—and it clicked into place. And as the knowledge settled on him, he felt any remaining resentment fade away.

"Yes. It wasn't like he was always drinking and driving," she said quickly. "I wouldn't want you to think . . . It was just, he'd had a hard week at work, and it was near Christmas, and he'd had a glass of wine without really thinking about it. So Emma, she took the keys, because she hadn't had anything to drink, and she thought it was safer that way. Just one of those things. Something that shouldn't have meant anything, but . . ." She broke off. "I'm sorry. I should have encouraged you to get in touch with Emma sooner. I shouldn't have taken you away from her—and her away from you. I think I assumed that somewhere along the line, we'd be ready to go back, but then I started to find my own life here and—"

"And then you met Derek." Jack said it with a smile, so she'd know he didn't mean it as a bad thing. The opposite, in fact—he was glad that she'd found a way to come back from something awful, where other people might have drowned from it.

"And then I met Derek." She came to a stop, took his hand in both of hers. "But that never meant there wasn't room for you too, Jack."

"*Mum!*" Mia shouted from up ahead. "Now *you're* the one being slow."

Jack laughed quietly as his mum squeezed his hand once more. "The point is, you have a family here, Jack. And we will always be here, whenever you need us."

Chapter Twenty-nine

Jack carried two cups of tea—Earl Grey, because that was all Emma ever seemed to have in stock—through from the little kitchen. The first time he'd been back here as an adult, it had felt like slamming into something hard and unyielding. It was spookily similar to how it had been when he was a kid. Well, except that the garden was unloved and overgrown now, something he was working on.

Emma looked up at him as he came into the living room. She was sitting on her little sofa, flicking through an old newspaper on the glass coffee table. "Your mum called me yesterday, incidentally."

Jack fumbled the mugs, nearly spilled the tea. "She did?"

"Yes. She wanted me to know that she was sorry, that kind of thing. I take it that's your doing." It wasn't really a question, and she only half glanced up at him from her newspaper, holding out her hand for the tea.

He handed her the mug. "Ah . . . Well, not exactly, but probably, by way of getting her to think about it."

"Thank you." Her voice was the brisk, efficient one he'd once known so well, but there was a layer of emotion under the surface—one she wasn't always as good at hiding as she thought she was.

"Yeah. Sure." He took a sip of his tea for something to do.

"Don't look so awkward—we've not got time for that."

He frowned. "Don't make jokes about that."

"Well, I think I'm entitled to—" But she was cut off by the sound of the front door opening and someone stomping in.

"You know, you really should lock the door."

That voice—he knew that voice. His heart leaped—actually leaped—at the sound of it.

"Anyone could just walk right . . ."

She trailed off as she came into the living room. Her red hair was damp and she was wearing a tightly fitted bottle green sweater, which made her eyes sing. Eyes that were currently staring right at him.

"Jack." The sound of his name on her lips, after so long not seeing her, sent a ripple through him.

"Holly." He didn't mean her name to come out like that, all whisper-like. Jesus.

"Emma." Emma said her own name, bringing both Jack and Holly's attention to her.

"You didn't tell me Holly was coming," Jack said accusingly. Though he supposed it made sense—if it was Theo and Mia's half term, it might also be Holly's. But he wasn't prepared for it. They'd been messaging, but they hadn't actually *seen* each other since Venice.

"Didn't I?" But he didn't buy the innocent tone, not when she went back to oh so casually flicking through her newspaper. Neither he nor Holly had told Emma the ins and outs of their . . . encounters . . . but Jack was pretty sure Emma had cottoned on anyway.

Holly cocked her head, recovering before he did. "Is it that bad, to see me?"

"No," he said quickly. "No, of course not . . . Sorry, I—"

"Don't worry," she said, clearly trying not to laugh.

How was she this casual? Had she known he'd be here? Or maybe it was only him. He felt like his skin was on fire around her, but maybe she'd got over it—whatever "it" was.

Holly was looking at Emma, scanning her from head to toe. He knew that look, because he did it too, every time he saw Emma. So he knew that Holly was checking to see what the damage was, checking for any visible signs of the illness attacking Emma's body. But the problem was, the signs weren't all visible.

"So," Holly said, moving to sit next to Emma, while Jack was still just *standing* there, like a complete lemon. "Are we still going shopping for your wedding outfit?"

"Yes, yes, but you only just got here—give an old girl a chance. Let me finish my tea first, will you?"

Holly drummed her fingers on her thigh, and Jack saw now how she was holding herself very straight. So, not feeling totally as laid back as she'd made it seem, then? Though he couldn't quite figure out if that was a good thing.

Holly seemed to sense him looking and glanced over at him. "Want to come shopping too?" she asked. "Maybe you can help me convince Emma to spend more than twenty pounds on a wedding day outfit."

"There's just no *point* in spending money, if I'm only going to—"

But Holly cut her off with a glare. He got it. Holly might be more forceful than he was on the matter, but he hated it too: Emma's little reminders that she was dying, that she might only have months left to live. *Months—or years*. It's what he told himself, as often as he could. But it was the uncertainty that was the worst thing—for her as well, he was sure.

Jack crossed to Emma's little armchair, trying to avoid sinking into it completely as he sat down. "I'd love to, but I don't think I can face hours in a shopping center."

Holly rolled her eyes. "We will not be *hours*."

"Well, I won't be," Emma muttered.

"That is so unfair. I wasn't hours when we were shopping in Venice, was I, Jack?"

Their gazes met then, and he saw her eyes change, the exact moment he felt something tighten in his gut. At the memory of that day, after Burano. Of the jazz club, and what had happened after.

Holly flushed and Jack cleared his throat, clocking the suspicious look Emma was giving them.

"So, ah, how's Abi doing then, Holly?" he asked, changing the subject to something safer.

"Yes, and how are the wedding toppers coming along?" Emma piped up.

Holly shrugged. "OK, I guess."

Emma narrowed her eyes. "You are still going to do them, aren't you?"

"Of course I am," Holly said with an offended huff.

"Good."

"I wouldn't let Abi down like that."

"Of course—nothing to do with the fact you actually enjoy it."

"I don't—"

"Ah," Jack said, raising his hand like a school kid as he interrupted the argument. Both Holly and Emma looked at him. "What are you talking about?"

"Oh, Holly is making little sculptures for the top of her friend's wedding cake."

"Really? You didn't tell me that."

Another suspicious look from Emma. Dammit. But they

were allowed to talk, weren't they? It would be weird, all things considered, if they hadn't been talking.

"They are not *sculptures*," Holly said. "They're—"

"You know," Emma said, talking over Holly and flicking through the newspaper on the coffee table, even though there was no possible way she could actually be reading it, "maybe creating sculpture wedding toppers will be your thing."

"My thing?"

"Yes, like Mirabelle Landor and the cards. Do you know, she started from nothing? She had no experience in the industry and then—"

"Then you found her?" Holly used a falsely sweet voice, one that made Jack chuckle.

"It has nothing to do with that," Emma said, sniffing.

"Are you ever actually going to *introduce* us to Mirabelle Landor?" Jack asked. "Or just use her as a point to try and win arguments?"

"Yes," Holly agreed. "Quite. I think I'd like to meet her; she's clearly made such an impression on you."

"She's an example of a woman following her dream and making it work as a business. What's not to love?" Emma said with a vague air. "She's what *you* could be," she added, looking at Holly, "if you ever gave it a go."

Jack looked at Holly with raised eyebrows. "She give you a Mirabelle Landor card too?"

"You did," Holly said. "Ah, in the café, I mean," she added quickly, a tinge of red creeping into her cheeks again. She shrugged, though she didn't quite pull off the nonchalance. "It's a cool painting—I still have it."

"In the café? What do you mean, in the café?" Emma's eyes turned sharp.

"Nothing," Holly said quickly.

But Jack remembered. He'd been carrying around the card

Emma had given him for his birthday, the one she'd written in. He'd been carrying it, because he'd been preparing to see her—maybe hoping to, despite everything. And he'd bought another of Mirabelle Landor's cards on a whim, and then given it to Holly.

She still had it. She'd held on to it, all this time—even after the crash.

Emma opened her mouth, clearly about to press the issue, but Holly beat her to it. "Anyway, Abi is freaking out at the moment because one of the guests has canceled last minute and now the seating plan is all messed up, and she's already paid for all the food for them."

"Inconsiderate, canceling last minute," Emma sniffed.

"Yeah. She's looking for someone to replace them, actually, so the money's not wasted. At this stage, I wouldn't put it past her to ask a random stranger off the street."

"Jack could come," Emma said, as if it were the most natural suggestion in the world for him to gatecrash Holly's friend's wedding.

"Ah . . ." Jack said, glancing at Holly for instruction. She was still looking at Emma, but he could see all the different emotions playing across her face as she clearly tried to think of the right thing to say. He loved that about her, he realized. The fact that she wore everything so openly, even when she tried not to. Liked. He *liked* that about her.

"I'm sure Jack has plans for Friday," Holly said eventually.

"Jack never has plans," Emma said—not entirely untruthfully. Especially now he didn't have work to hide behind. So unless Ed dragged him out somewhere, which was harder to do now he was spending more time down in Devon, he tended to spend his time with Emma, or making lists of possible places he could apply to for jobs.

Holly looked down at the coffee table, clearly still unsure of what to say, then frowned at some brightly colored leaflets there. "What are these, Emma?"

"Oh nothing, just some light reading."

But Holly was paling as she picked them up.

"Don't worry," Jack said quietly. "She won't be going into one." Emma had been making noises about going into a hospice recently, but Jack was determined not to let her. He was planning to move down here, once he'd worked out his notice. And fine, yes, he was trying to make up for not having been in touch, trying to alleviate his own guilt, but so what?

"Jack," Emma said with a long-suffering sigh, "I know I look robust right now, but it may get a lot worse than this and I just think having the option—"

"No," Jack said bluntly.

Holly bit her lip as she stared at the leaflet in her hand.

"Care to weigh in on this?" he asked, harsher than he'd meant to. But he wanted her to back him up.

"Not about this."

"Ah, see, this one's got her head screwed on," Emma said, patting Holly's knee.

But Holly put the leaflet back on the coffee table and took a breath. "Emma, I've been doing some research into pancreatic cancer and—"

"I stand corrected," Emma said with a sigh.

"And I—"

"You think you know better than the doctors, do you?"

"No, I just—"

"Holly, I've made up my mind."

Holly shot Jack a helpless look and he grimaced in solidarity. He'd tried too.

"I don't want to have some awful treatment that will make

me feel sick and give me all sorts of terrible side effects, only to add on a few extra months of what may well become a very debilitated existence because of those same treatments."

"But it might be longer than that!"

"Not a lot longer," Emma said firmly.

Really, she might have been discussing how long to bake a bloody cake, rather than how long she had left to live. He supposed that was how she was getting through it—being practical. He supposed that was how *he* was getting through it, too.

"I would rather have quality over quantity—and right now I am able to be at home, I can do pretty much everything I've always done, and I am not constantly back and forth to the hospital, which, by the way, is miles away. You won't change my mind on this, my girl, and quite frankly it's not your decision to make, so let's move on once and for all, shall we?"

Holly stared at Emma, then glared at Jack, as if it were somehow his fault. "Back me up here, will you?"

He shook his head slowly. Because Emma was right: It was her decision. The hospice, no, but this . . .

She glared at him again, before looking back at Emma. "You're giving up."

"I'm not, Holly. I'm accepting and choosing to enjoy what I have left, which I'm far more likely to do *without* chemo." She smiled a little. "Death is inevitable, my girl, so all we can do is choose how to face it."

"But it doesn't have to be now," Holly insisted.

"It's not now."

Holly shot Jack another look. "Don't you have anything to say?"

"It's her choice," he said softly.

Holly's lips tightened. She stood up off the sofa, nearly losing her balance in the process, and stormed out of the living room.

Emma only jerked her head at Jack—a silent instruction. He got to his feet and followed, found her in the kitchen.

"What are you doing?" he asked.

She was filling the kettle with water. "What does it look like I'm doing?"

He grabbed her arm as she crossed the kitchen, still with that angry, storming stride. "I wasn't trying to hurt you. I don't like this any more than you do."

She looked like she was going to say something horrible at that, but she managed to bite back whatever it was as she pulled her arm from his grip. She set the kettle on to boil and crossed her arms tightly. "I can't believe we are here, talking about the end of her life."

He felt the wince run through him but did his best to control it—one of them needed to be the level-headed one here. "There is time, yet. And we both know things can change in an instant. She is still here, still enjoying life—and I say we try to enjoy it with her too. It's not the end of the road yet."

"I might die getting hit by a champagne cork before the road naturally ends anyway," Emma shouted from the other room. "Twenty-four people a year do."

"You've made that up," Holly shouted back.

"I have not."

"Aren't you supposed to be deaf at your age?"

"Well, that says something about your ability to hold a hushed conversation, doesn't it?"

Holly looked back at Jack, and there were tears in her eyes.

He couldn't help it. He couldn't stand seeing her like this. So he crossed the kitchen, put his arm around her. He felt her stiffen, briefly. Then she sighed, her body relaxing a little as she rested her head against his chest. He stroked a hand down her hair, still tangled from the wind outside, felt her loosen just a bit more.

"It's not fair," she muttered.

"I know."

She sighed again before pushing back away from him and dashing a tear from her cheek. Then she squared her shoulders. "Fine. I can get on the bloody enjoying life bandwagon." The way she said it, through gritted teeth, was so at odds with the words, that it made him smile.

"You don't have to sound so excited about it."

She got a mug down from the cupboard and scooped some instant coffee into it. Then she glanced back at him. "But if that's what we're doing, then Emma's right—you can come to the damn wedding."

Chapter Thirty

Dear Lily,

I'm going to Abi's wedding tomorrow. I know you don't actually know Abi, which is completely bizarre, but I'm excited about it. Excited—and nervous, because I want it to be perfect for her. I'm also nervous because Jack is coming. I'm going to have to be really careful not to be alone with him, and not to drink too much and definitely not to dance with him. Though come to think of it, the dancing might not be much of an issue—seeing me dance will probably put him off me.

It's making me think a lot about your wedding, about the night before, when you couldn't sleep, do you remember? I stayed up with you, because you didn't want to be alone in the hotel room—you said it felt weird without Steve. You were so worried you wouldn't sleep at all and you'd look all puffy for the wedding day, and you made me talk to you nonstop. I can't remember what I talked about—nonsense babble, I'm sure. But it worked, and you fell asleep before me. It makes me wish I could go back to that night—go back and appreciate how easy it was, between us.

I've also been thinking of when I called you, while I was in Venice. I remember the way I heard your name over the phone and do you know what it sounded like? I only realized when I was back from Venice, because I was so distracted with what happened after Emma collapsed. But it sounded like a waiting room. That sort of formal voice, calling your name. I realize it could be anywhere—lots of places have waiting rooms, I suppose. But the one thing I keep coming back to is a doctor's surgery. Were you at the doctor's, or is that just me, catastrophizing? I wish you'd tell me what's going on. I think Mum would tell me, if it was something serious. I hope she would.

I wish you could tell me what I can do to make things better between us, Lily. I asked Mum what to do at first, and she told me to give you space. But I've tried that. And I've tried getting in touch with you, even just through Mum and Dad, but they've always said you're not ready.

I wish you'd reply to these letters—but that's never going to happen, is it?

Because I can't even work up the courage to send them.

Love,
Holly

Under the grand marquee, Holly sat on a table at the edge of the black-and-white-squared dance floor, watching as Abi and James started their first dance to an Irish song, sung in Gaelic, one that Holly didn't recognize. Abi had told her that she'd never heard it either, before she and James listened to *I'm not kidding, babe, literally two* thousand *songs*. Given the wedding was in Ireland— about an hour away from Dublin at Clonabreany House, a brilliant manor house with grounds for miles—and there seemed to be a disproportionate number of Irish wedding guests, Holly supposed an Irish first-dance song made sense. It worked, too— there was a live band, with the female singer now singing fluently in Gaelic, the violins and bass backing her up effortlessly. The music was slow and soft to start, and James, looking incredibly dapper in his tux, the stubble grazing his chin a little more neatly than usual, took Abi into his arms like she was the most precious thing in the world.

They'd had the actual ceremony in the woods on the grounds, Abi and James saying their "I do"s under sunlight filtering through golden leaves, the sun just warm enough to keep the chill autumn air at bay. After that they'd moved to this gorgeous white marquee, where four chandeliers hung from the ceiling, along with white and silver paper lanterns. Each round, white-clothed table was adorned with white and purple flowers, along with a multitude of glassware for the many different drinks on offer, and the candles in the center of each one now flickered as the light outside began to fade.

The music changed, becoming a little quicker, more upbeat, and James spun Abi in a circle. Abi had been nervous about this dance, Holly knew—she thought it would be awkward, getting up in front of everyone—but now the nerves must have gone completely. The old adage of a bride glowing on her wedding day definitely made sense when you looked at Abi. She'd taken some of the pins out of her chestnut hair after the ceremony, as the hairdresser had told her to, and her curls now bounced around her shoulders. Her dress suited her perfectly—long-sleeved, rising high around the neck and dipping low down her back. It was an off-white color that suited her skin tone, and her shoes completed the picture or at least would until Abi switched into the pumps she had brought along for when her feet started to hurt.

After another few seconds, Abi broke away from James and gestured to the room at large, encouraging people to get to their feet and join the dancing. Abi caught Holly's eye and jerked her head, and Holly got to her feet obediently. She scanned the marquee quickly. Emma had been sitting next to her all afternoon and had proved a useful buffer between Holly and the overly interested Rob, one of James's ushers—a cousin, according to Abi—who was now leaping to his feet enthusiastically. Emma had gone to the loo after dessert had been served and while everyone was waiting for the next thing to happen. Holly couldn't see her anywhere, but she did see Jack, who was sitting at a table in the middle of the marquee, his back to the entrance, where white drapes were tied neatly at the sides, ready to be dropped if it got too cold. Beyond that, it was still just light enough to see the gardens and the stone house they'd all used to get ready in that morning.

Jack met Holly's gaze almost instantly, like he'd been watching her, the now-familiar jolt running through her. Abi had said she would try to adjust the seating plan so he could sit with Holly and Emma, but honestly, her friend had been nearing breaking point and rearranging the seating plan had seemed like too much to ask. So after the ceremony, where Jack and Emma had sat together, with Holly up at the front in her pastel green bridesmaid's dress, Jack had gone to his assigned table and Holly and Emma to theirs. With that and her bridesmaid duties, she'd barely spoken to him. Not that it had stopped her stealing glances at him whenever she could. Because, Jesus, did he look good in a tux.

"Emma?" she mouthed, to explain why she was looking over at him.

He gave a cursory glance around the marquee. "I'll look," he mouthed back, and gestured for her to go to the dance floor, to Abi. Holly nodded. He'd find her, make sure she was OK. She was sure that was part of the reason he'd agreed to come—making up for lost time with Emma. Not that Emma was holding any sort of grudge. It was odd: Despite the fact that she surely couldn't be feeling well, despite the fact that she was living with the knowledge that her life would come to an end soon, Emma was clearly happier than she'd been in a long time.

Holly made a beeline for Abi, who was now bouncing around with her sister. It gave Holly a pang—she and Lily had been like that at Lily's wedding, the only other time Holly had been a bridesmaid.

Abi clasped Holly's hands as she reached her. "Did I look awful? I bet I looked awful."

"You did not look awful," Holly said immediately. "In fact, I don't think I've ever seen anyone dance so well in real life—you've been keeping that talent hidden."

Abi laughed and waved Holly away, but her whole face beamed, her very eyes seeming to glow. She pulled Holly and her sister into a hug, two green dresses against Abi's white. "I love you both so much."

"Don't go getting emotional on us yet," said Abi's sister, with a wink at Holly. "There's still the cake and the—"

"The cake!" Abi exclaimed. "They said we should do that after the first dance." *They* were the owners of the manor, who had run through the whole thing with Abi beforehand and who were, according to Abi, better than ten wedding planners.

"I don't think it matters if you don't stick exactly to schedule," Holly said, but Abi was already pulling her off the dance floor, grabbing James as they went.

"You should be at the front," Abi said firmly. She let go of Holly and went to stand with James behind the beautiful four-tiered wedding cake—the traditional white icing, but with hand-painted flowers around the edges of each layer. It really was gorgeous. Holly knew that each layer was a different flavor—had heard quite a lot about those flavors, about how Abi and James had disagreed over whether one layer should be white chocolate and passionfruit or white chocolate and blueberry.

And there, on the very top of the cake, stood the two wedding toppers Holly had made—a mini-Abi and a mini-James. She'd had a photo of Abi and James in front of her as she'd sculpted, getting out her smallest scrapers and scoring tools to add detail to their tiny faces. The first two attempts had been terrible; her hands had been shaking too much. The third was bad too, but only because she'd had some wine in an attempt to calm herself down. So what was now atop the cake was the fourth attempt. They were the first sculptures she'd done since the crash. She wasn't sure if that's why Abi had asked her, to give her something she couldn't say no to—but she suspected so. Either way, she was glad she'd agreed—it had proven she *could* still do it, even if it was only something small and silly like this. But there was something else there too, something that sat deep and sad in her core—because she'd made the wedding toppers for a cake once before.

Did Lily still have them? she wondered. She'd promised to keep them forever, in pride of place above the fireplace in her and Steve's flat. But maybe she'd thrown them out, at the same time as she'd thrown Holly out of her life.

She felt a hand, cool and papery, squeeze hers as Abi and James held the knife together and sliced, to much applause. "They're beautiful," Emma said quietly.

Holly felt Jack come up on her other side, but she didn't turn to look at him—she didn't want to let on how in tune to him she

was, how her body was constantly aware of where his was in re-
lation to hers.

"Care to dance?" It wasn't Jack asking her but Rob, the usher
whom Emma had been so effectively blocking all night, holding
out his hand as people either headed straight for the cake or
moved back onto the dance floor. His accent held an Irish lilt, but
it was less strong than some of the accents she'd heard today, so
maybe he was visiting, like James. He had an air of James about
him, too—a little more stubble and a little broader around the
chest, but the same red-brown hair, and tall enough that she had
to tilt her head back to look up at him. He was attractive enough,
she supposed—if it weren't for the way he was leering at her
right now, his cheeks flushed from all the red wine he'd drunk,
his lips stained brown. Not his fault—it was a wedding, after
all. Although maybe the leering was his fault.

"Oh, I can't, I'm so sorry," she said, doing her best at a meek,
apologetic smile. "I told you about my foot, remember?"

Rob, looking disappointed, drew back his hand, but Jack,
who had clearly tuned in to the conversation, piped up from next
to her. "What about your foot?"

Holly glanced at Jack. "I broke it in a skating accident a few
years ago," she said, trying to sound casual.

"Did you?"

"Yes," Holly said, the word a bit too emphatic to be totally
believable. She quickly added, "I told you about it, remember?"

Though Jack's lips quirked at the corners, he gave a solemn
nod. "Ah yes. At the Somerset House ice rink. And it started as
such a beautiful day . . ."

"I thought you said you broke it in Germany?" Rob asked
suspiciously.

Why—*why* did he have to pay so much attention to her lies?
She could feel her cheeks growing warm. "I ah . . ."

"That's because she broke it twice," Jack said easily.

"Right," Holly agreed. "Balance is not really my strong suit."

Rob was looking between Jack and Holly. "Why do you keep skating, then?"

"Because I love it," Holly said very seriously. "I love all the . . ."—she gestured a hand in the air—"ice."

"Can't get her away from icicles, either," Jack said, deadpan.

"Icicles?" Rob repeated.

"Yeah. She has a little book where she sticks photographs of them."

"You do?"

Holly shot Jack a look, but there was no going back now. "I do," she said, making it sound like she was admitting an embarrassing secret. "I also really like ice cubes." In for a penny . . .

"Right," Rob said dragging the word out.

"And ice cream," Jack said.

Holly made a *pfft* sound. "As if. That's hardly real ice, now, is it?"

Jack broke his serious expression to grin, and Rob turned to him. "And you are?"

"Jack. Old friend." He held out his hand and, after a suspicious look at it, Rob shook it.

Rob looked back at Holly. "If you change your mind, I'm sure I can hold you up while you sway." He did that leering thing again.

"Thanks. I'll let you know."

"So, ice skating, huh?" Jack said when Rob walked away. "Never would have guessed."

"Oh, I'm quite the pro."

"Clearly not, what with your multiple broken ankles."

Holly couldn't help smiling—though it faded slightly as she glanced around the room, saw Emma sitting down again, sipping some water.

Jack squeezed her hand. "I'll go." He nodded over her shoulder, and Holly saw Abi coming toward her. "You have friend duties."

"Here," Abi said, thrusting a plate in her hand. "You did the toppers—you have to eat some of the actual cake."

Holly laughed, took the plate and nibbled a bit of cake, though in all honesty she was still completely full from the three-course meal.

Abi wasn't scrutinizing how much of the cake she was trying, though. Instead she was watching Jack walk over to Emma.

"Don't tell me," Holly said with a sigh. "I'm being careful."

Abi's gaze shot to Holly. "I didn't say anything!"

Holly just raised her eyebrows.

"OK, fine, but that's not what I was thinking."

"No? No more telling me not to get burned, like with Daniel? Although really, in hindsight I think maybe I was a bit unfair with Daniel, so maybe I'm not the one who—"

"I didn't mean Daniel!" Abi exclaimed. She tucked a strand of perfectly curled hair behind her ear, her new wedding ring now sitting side by side with the sparkling engagement ring.

"Oh really?"

Abi hesitated. "I meant Lily."

Something hot shot down Holly's throat and she immediately jumped to defend her sister. "Lily didn't—"

"She did. I'm not saying I don't understand why she felt the way she did—though never having actually met her I'm taking a few leaps—but the way she handled it, after the accident, the way she blamed you . . ." Abi shook her head. "That's the burn I was talking about."

Holly didn't know how to respond. It didn't feel right, for Abi to be saying this—because of course Lily blamed her; Holly had always understood that.

"I don't mean to upset you," Abi continued. "It's just, I've seen the way you've tried to pull yourself together, and I wish . . .

I wish that you didn't still think you don't deserve amazing things, because of what Lily said or thinks." She smiled, and jerked her head toward Jack's back. "And actually, I wasn't going to say be careful. I was *going* to say that maybe I was wrong— maybe that guy right there is one of those amazing things you should start telling yourself you deserve."

"Well," Holly said, puffing out her cheeks. "That's a bit of a turnaround."

Abi gave her arm a friendly squeeze. "But, Hol, make sure you know what you're getting into, if you go there. Make sure you're . . . ready."

Holly bit her lip. It came too close to what she'd been thinking herself. "You don't need to worry," she said, trying to sound casual. "He came here so he could help look out for Emma."

Abi rolled her eyes, and the expression was so comical, it got a laugh out of Holly. "If you believe that, you're a total dolt."

Abi's aunt and uncle came over at that moment, and Holly slipped away, toward the table where Jack was now helping Emma to her feet. Holly didn't like seeing it, the way Emma needed that help more each time she saw her. But right now, she was determined not to let that show. She'd regretted her outburst at Emma's house the other day, almost immediately after it had happened. Because Emma was right—of course it was her choice, whether to put herself through the grueling cancer treatments, only to add a few more months on to her life. It was selfish. Holly was upset because *she* didn't want to lose Emma, not so soon after she'd found her.

So Holly plastered a smile on her face as she reached the table. "Heading up to dance, Emma? I'm pretty sure I saw Abi's grandad chatting you up in between courses earlier."

"Ah, if I were ten years younger . . ." Emma wrinkled her nose. "Actually, no, not even then. Not my type—too unkempt."

Holly laughed, while Jack placed a supportive hand on Emma's shoulder.

"Where are you going?" Holly asked.

"It's well past my bedtime, I'm afraid." Emma took both of Holly's hands in her own. "But it's been a wonderful day. Abi is lovely, and it means more than you know that you invited me. I never thought I'd go to a wedding again and, well . . ."

Jack dropped his hand away from Emma's shoulder. Was he thinking of his own wedding day, and the fact that Emma hadn't been there? Evening had well and truly set in now, and the estate took on a different feel under the night sky. Instead of being peaceful and serene, it felt almost magical, like anything could happen out here, in a hidden corner, with only the stars as witness.

"I'll walk you to your room," Jack said, and got an impatient huff from Emma.

"I am perfectly capable of getting there myself, thank you." They were all staying on the estate—not far to go. "Stay. Drink. Dance. Party. It's a wedding, for God's sake." And with that and one final, dismissive hand wave, she shuffled off down the gravel path toward the old stone courtyard, where ninety rooms were waiting to welcome tired wedding guests, leaving Jack and Holly standing on the grounds together, the music from the band reaching out from the marquee.

She should go back inside. It was the smart thing—the *safe* thing—to go to where there was light and noise and dancing. She wasn't ready to admit to herself why she didn't move. Why she stayed standing in the garden, under the moonlight, with Jack.

A soft breeze pulled through her hair, which Abi's hair and makeup artist had managed to tame more than she ever could herself, threading it into a soft plait down her back. She wrapped her arms around herself, the tiniest shiver rolling through her as the wind caressed her skin.

"You cold?" Jack asked, immediately shrugging out of his jacket.

"A little, but it's OK. It's nice." She looked away from the marquee, toward the woods and the rolling countryside she could no longer see.

"What is it?" Jack asked.

"Nothing," Holly said. She glanced at him, saw his expression, patiently waiting. "It's just . . . last time I was at a wedding, I was with Lily. My sister. It was her wedding, I mean."

He nodded. They'd not talked much about Lily. She supposed they hadn't had enough time together to really get into it. There were always more pressing things to discuss. "Were you close?" he asked softly.

"Yes. But then . . . Can you be that close to someone and then cut them off like that?" She realized, too late, that the same could be said of him and Emma. "I'm sorry. I didn't mean—"

"No, it's OK. With Emma, there was a whole host of stuff going on, and I'm not trying to make it OK, but I was a kid and—"

"So there's no hope for me and Lily?" She'd meant for her voice to come out jokey, but it just sounded sad—and a little bitter.

"No, that's not what I'm saying." He walked away a few steps, then turned back to face her. "I wonder, though, if maybe you should take some of the determination you had for me and Emma and apply that to Lily."

Holly frowned. "What do you mean?"

"Well, you went out of your way to help Emma—to find her, first off, and then to find me. And, well, maybe you could try that hard with Lily. I don't mean that as a judgment," he said quickly.

"I just meant, if you wanted to, I think you're more than capable of—"

"I called her. In Venice. I called Lily." She sounded defensive, even as she tried not to.

"Yeah. But it's hard, when it's sprung on you, when you don't have time to figure out what to say, how to say it. What to feel, even. These things . . . Well, it's never easy on either side, is it?" He hesitated. "I just can't help wondering if you blame yourself a little, and that's why you don't fight as hard as you could."

"I do blame myself," Holly said, wrapping her arms tighter around herself and looking down at the ground, at the gravel underfoot.

"Have you ever thought that maybe Lily might blame herself too?"

She dashed away a tear that had escaped, despite her best efforts. Then she shook her head, and gave herself a little mental shake, too. "Sorry. I didn't mean to cry." Though she'd done it a fair amount around him already, hadn't she?

"That's OK." He gave her a wry smile. "Weddings bring up all kinds of emotions."

She hesitated for a beat. "Your wedding?"

He rubbed a hand along the back of his neck. Even with the light from the marquee, he was still too far away for her to make out his expression clearly, so she stepped toward him, off the gravel and onto grass, her heel sinking softly underfoot. "Vanessa and I . . . We sort of just fell into it. She was my friend from university and we moved to London around the same time and it just seemed like we should give it a go, you know?"

She nodded, because it seemed like she should. He looked right at her then, the moonlight catching his face so that she saw the glint of his eyes. She loved those eyes—the depth of brown.

"But it wasn't right, Holly. I don't look back at my wedding and feel sad or angry. I don't even wish things had been different. We tried, and it didn't work, and there's not much I can do about that now." He made a face, changed the tone a little. "Well, when I'm at my most level, that's what I tell myself—I won't pretend I'm always perfect."

"Gosh, really?"

"Hey, no one said you're perfect either."

"I don't know what you mean," Holly said primly. "I'm perfect in every way."

He grinned, though it was only fleeting. "The point is, that part of my life is over and I need to figure out how to live the rest of it—because you never know, right?"

Holly nodded. You never knew.

They went quiet for a moment, and the music shifted, another Irish song coming on after Katy Perry.

"Want to go back in and dance?" Jack asked.

"I can't. What if that guy sees me?"

"I hate to tell you this, but he probably knew you were lying."

"Probably is different from definitely. Besides, no one likes having rejection rubbed in their face."

"Dance with me here, then." And the way he said it, like it was the most reasonable of suggestions, made it impossible to say no. So she took his hand when he held it out, allowed him to pull her to him.

"I meant what I said," she murmured against his chest. She'd forgotten just how good he smelled, all rustic pine and wood. "I don't have the balance or coordination to dance well."

He laughed softly. "As if I hadn't noticed that."

But pressed against him, one of his hands in hers, the other at her waist, she did not feel clumsy. She felt almost graceful, letting him guide her body, not really thinking about where or how to put her feet, thinking only of the way his hand felt in hers, the way her skin pulsed against his touch under the thin fabric of her dress. She'd been pressed against him like this before—but now it was worse, because now her body remembered what it had been like to have nothing but skin between them, to have his chest above hers, to feel his mouth on her neck. Something in her core pulsed and she tilted her head up, found his gaze there, waiting for her.

His thumb circled on the back of her hand. "I know this is complicated," he said, his voice low, "and maybe it can't go anywhere. But how about we have tonight?" He spun her away, gently, before pulling her back to him, making her breath catch. "Just tonight," he murmured again, before bringing his mouth to hers.

And really, there was no question of doing anything else but kissing him, of running her hands up his back and into his hair, of reaching up on her toes so she could match the intensity with which he was now kissing her. There was no use pretending. She wanted him. She wanted *him* and no one else.

So she took his hand, leading him away from the marquee, down the gravel pathway and toward the stone courtyard. It was stupid, anyway, to pretend she hadn't considered this possibility, hadn't prepared for it, just in case. Hadn't *hoped* for it.

His room was before hers, and they headed to it without question, Jack fumbling with the key a little and making Holly laugh before dragging her inside.

"Thank fuck for that," he said, his mouth against hers as he closed the door, pressed her against it. She laughed again, though it turned to a gasp as he bent to kiss her neck. She dug her fingers into his shoulders, those goddamned impressive shoulders, and a pulse went through her as his hands skimmed down her sides, then ran up her thighs, setting her skin alight. Her dress was bunched at her hips, and she reached down and pulled it up, over her head. He drew back, his eyes even darker than usual, and his gaze scorched her as it traveled slowly over her. He ran his thumbs down her sides, slowly, tortuously, before making her let out an embarrassing squeal as he grabbed her hips and literally lifted her off the ground, pressing her farther into the door. She hooked her legs around his waist, tilting her head back as he went for her neck again.

"I feel like this is a bit one-sided," she said, her voice halfway to a gasp as he flicked open her bra strap. He laughed against her neck, his breath hot. But she managed to get her hands under his shirt, felt him shudder at the feel of her palms on his stomach.

And when there was nothing but skin between them, when he took her to the bed, finally laying her down, his expression turned softer. He reached up, brushed her hair away from her face. "I take it back," he murmured. He kissed her one more time before sliding into her, making her gasp. "You are perfect."

No, she wanted to whisper back, *you are*. She didn't say it, though, even if it *felt* perfect in that moment, even as she buried her face in his neck to stop herself from crying out.

But there were tears on her face when he pulled away: because of Lily, because of Emma, but most of all, in that moment, because she wanted him and it couldn't last longer than tonight.

Chapter Thirty-one

Holly woke, bleary-eyed and with sunlight filtering through the blinds, to the sound of her phone vibrating somewhere in the room. Jack's side of the bed felt cool. Had he snuck out somewhere, while she'd been asleep? Taking the *just one night* to extremes? It made her heart spasm uncomfortably, even as she tried to push down the sensation. Her phone vibrated again and, swearing silently, she threw the duvet off, scrabbling around for her bag, discarded last night, along with her dress, and retrieved it.

Then she stared at the name on the caller ID.

Lily.

Lily was calling her, right now.

She stared at it again for another ring, then, with a shaking finger, lifted the phone to her ear.

"Lily?" she asked, her voice a little croaky.

"Hey." It was not the same tone she'd heard in Venice. Now her sister sounded small, uncertain. "I, umm, saw the photos of Abi's wedding on your Instagram and it . . ." She cleared her throat. "Well, I've been thinking of you."

There were a million questions Holly could be asking right now, but all that actually made it out of her mouth was "You know who Abi is?"

"Well, Mum fills me in. And social media, you know."

There was a beat of silence between them as Holly moved to perch on the edge of the bed. Her heart was thudding gently in her chest—waiting. "Lily, I—"

"I'm sorry, Holly," she blurted out.

"You're . . . sorry?"

"About the last time you called. I shouldn't have . . . I didn't mean . . . There is a lot of stuff going on in my life right now, and I was stressed and then you called. And it was a bad time. I wasn't at home. I . . . I was at the doctor's, actually."

"You were?" So, she'd been right.

"Yes. I . . . There is some stuff . . . They've been doing a lot of tests over the last two years and, well, it doesn't look like I'll be able to get pregnant."

"Oh, *Lily.*" Holly felt her stomach tighten. Lily's hopes of being a mother, gone. No wonder her sister hadn't been able to talk to her.

"No, now's not the time, I'm just trying to explain why I was so short with you. When you called, I was at the doctor's, and I knew what they were about to tell me, and it just made me think . . . It reminded me of that day, and what I lost."

Because of you. Holly could hear the words—even if Lily's voice did not now hold the same icy blame as it had in the hospital all those years ago.

"It's no excuse. And it wasn't *you,* Holly, but I didn't know how to deal with it all, and when I saw your number come up, I thought it must be because something terrible had happened, because why else would you be calling? And then you just wanted to *talk* to me and I didn't know how to . . ." She took a breath, and it sounded shaky. "But I'm here, looking at the cake toppers you made for me, like the ones on Abi's cake, and—"

"You kept them?"

"Of course I did."

Quiet descended between them again, but it was less awkward this time. Dimly, Holly could hear a man's voice out in the corridor outside her room. Jack, she thought, and her heart leaped a little.

"I don't know what to say," she admitted. "I've wanted to talk to you for so long, wanted to hear your voice, and now I . . ."

"I know," Lily whispered.

"You know?"

"Of course—you don't think I've wanted to speak to you too?"

"Well, no," Holly admitted. "I thought you never wanted to speak to me again, actually."

"Oh, Holly, I'm so sorry. I didn't . . ." She took another breath and it was hitched this time. "It's my fault—so much of it is my fault. There's a lot we have to talk about."

"I know. I'd like to talk to you about it all someday." The fact that Lily *wanted* to talk about it gave Holly hope.

"Will you meet up with me? Mum and Dad too, if you don't want to see me alone."

"I don't mind seeing you alone," Holly said, her voice sounding distant. She was still trying to take it all in. Lily wanted to see her. Lily was worried that *she* wouldn't want to meet.

"Really?"

"Of *course,* Lily."

"Shall I . . . Shall I send you some dates?" Lily's voice was hesitant.

"Yeah. Yes, please do that."

Holly heard another hitched breath. She knew that sound—Lily was trying not to cry.

"Lily, I—"

"I have to go. Sorry. I do want to talk to you. I do. I know I haven't . . . Mum said . . ." Another breath. "I just . . . Let's talk in person, OK? I don't want to do this over the phone."

"OK." God, could she really not say anything else?

"I'll see you soon," Lily said, her voice firm.

"I hope so," Holly whispered back.

She sat there, staring at her phone after she hung up. Her emotions felt like they were swirling in her stomach, unable to settle on just one. It was only the sound of Jack's voice again that made her look up. She could hear it clearly through the door, now that she was no longer distracted by her own phone call.

"Vanessa, I have to go." *Vanessa.* His wife. Ex-wife. "Look, you're just having a moment, don't worry about . . . OK. Look, I'll call you later. OK. Bye."

Suddenly aware that she was still naked, Holly sprang up from the bed, finding her discarded bridesmaid dress and slipping back into it, wishing they'd chosen her room over his, so she could have her clothes—and a toothbrush. She'd just managed to get the dress on when Jack came back inside.

"Hey," he said with a smile. "You're up. I didn't want to wake you."

Holly nodded, but when he stepped toward her, she stepped back.

His eyes turned a little wary. "What is it?"

"Nothing." She pulled a hand through her hair—the plait having come undone last night, now back to its usual tangled form. "Who were you on the phone to just now?"

He hesitated. "What did you hear?"

"Nothing," she said again. Then she rolled her shoulders.

She was an adult, for Christ's sake—she could have the conversation. "I heard you say 'Vanessa,' that's all."

He nodded slowly.

"So you called her?" Holly pressed. "Vanessa?" There was something so *wrong* with that—calling his ex-wife after sleeping with her.

"No! No, of course not. She called me."

"Oh."

"She was upset, needed someone to talk to."

"Oh," Holly said again.

"Look, Holly, I promise it was nothing. She is just going through a rough patch with this guy she's seeing and she was upset and she called me because it's what we always used to do, way before we were even together. We were friends first, and I think she's trying to get back to that."

"Does she want to get back together with you?"

"No," he said. "I told you, it wasn't right. I promise you, Holly," he said, his voice firm, gaze direct on hers. "There is no chance of Vanessa and me getting back together, none whatsoever."

Holly nodded slowly, allowing that to settle. She felt strangely vulnerable, there in the corner of his room in her clothes from the night before, while he looked fresh-faced, dressed in smart black jeans and a dark-blue shirt. She angled her body away, opened up the blinds for something to do, letting in cool sunlight. What time was it, even? She had to be at the wedding breakfast at eleven.

"Holly? Did you hear me? Please look at me."

She turned, her back to the green wall of the hotel room. She knew, logically, that it made sense. But she could feel a protective barrier coming up around her heart—because she also knew that she couldn't get hurt again. Maybe Abi was right—maybe it had started with Lily, the fact that the person she'd assumed would always be there had turned away from her so completely, leaving her broken. Regardless, she didn't want to go through it again. She didn't want to get close to someone, only to have them leave her again. And she didn't want to fall for someone so completely that she wouldn't be able to put herself back together when they left.

And Jack . . . It was worse with Jack. Because there was Emma to think about too. If she went there, with Jack, and then Emma died, what happened then? What if Jack couldn't be around her, because she was a reminder of what he'd lost? Hadn't Lily said as much, on the phone?

"I suppose it doesn't matter," Holly said, keeping her voice careful. "It was just last night, right? That's what you said."

Jack made a face, then stepped closer to her. "I don't want it to be just last night."

Holly tensed. "What do you mean? You said, in Venice—"

"I know. But I think I was wrong. Or at least, I think that's wrong *now*. I think we should try."

Even though it was what she wanted to hear, Holly didn't feel ready to hear it yet. "I don't know, Jack." And something in her tone made his expression tighten.

"You don't even want to try?"

"That's not fair."

"Isn't it?"

"You don't get it!" Holly's voice rose, and she tried to take a soothing breath. "You don't know what it's like to be the cause of someone's unhappiness and—"

"I do get it, Holly!"

"Yeah, right," Holly said scornfully. "The only way you can get it, really get it, is if you've—"

"Been through it?" Jack asked, his eyebrows raised. "I don't actually think that's true—I think if you have enough empathy, you can get it if you try to. But I *did* go through it." He swallowed. "I was the reason Emma crashed, the reason my dad died."

Holly's arms dropped to her sides. "What? What do you—?"

"Talking through things with Emma, it's made me remember things I think I'd purposefully forgotten. We were late," Jack said, and though his voice was calm, Holly could hear the edge of something simmering there. "It was this stupid school concert thing and we were running late, and I was worried and impatient and . . . and honestly I was just young and being a kid." He closed his eyes. "I was annoying Emma. I was kicking the back of the driver's seat, the way kids do. I'd been told not to do it, but I didn't listen. I kept kicking, harder and harder because I was frustrated and trying to, I don't know, get the car to go faster? And Emma, she was getting frustrated too—obviously, because it was distracting as she was trying to drive. And she turned, snapped at me not to do it, and that's when the car came the other way. So she wasn't looking at the road, and she had to swerve, and she hit the tree and . . ." He blew out a long, slow breath, and finally opened his eyes again, something swimming in the depths of them.

Holly looked at him for a long moment, trying to figure out what to say. "Emma never said . . ."

"I think Emma's probably blamed herself enough for the both of us. Or maybe she forgot why she swerved, what with everything that happened after. But I remember. I've stopped shutting it out now that I've seen how not dealing with it robbed me of so much time with Emma.

"It was part of the reason I didn't want to see her again, afterward. At least at first. I was scared that it was all my fault. So it was easier to blame her, like my mum was doing. But it wasn't her fault. I was just being a coward." He moved to the edge of the bed, and sat down, staring at his lap. And without really thinking about it, she went to sit down next to him.

"You were just a kid, Jack. You can't blame yourself." She put her hand on his, offering comfort.

"I don't. Not anymore. I know I was young and I know that it wasn't me kicking the seat that made her crash, that no one is solely responsible. Logically I know all that. Logically, I know an accident is just that, an accident. But at the time, I didn't. At the time, I was looking for someone else to blame. And then I just held on to that, in a way I really shouldn't have." He flipped his hand over, linked their fingers together. "You were the one who made me confront that. And now I'm wondering . . ." He trailed off, took a breath. "Well, maybe I can help you to see it too. That your crash wasn't your fault, even if your sister blamed you, even if you blamed yourself."

She tensed, tried to pull her hand away, but he held tight.

"Maybe that's the reason we met," he murmured, his eyes on her face. "So we could help each other to see that."

"I don't believe in stuff like that," Holly whispered. "I don't believe in fate."

"Really?" Jack asked, with a hint of a smile. "Even after all this?" His reached for her face and his thumb caressed her cheek, softly. "Give me a chance, Holly. Give *us* a chance. What have you got to lose?"

Everything, she thought.

Holly swallowed a lump in her throat. "I can't, Jack. You were right, before. It's too complicated, and—"

"Now's not the time?" he asked, with a small, sad smile.

"Yes. No. I mean, I just don't think we should go there. I can't risk . . ." But it sounded pathetic to finish that sentence out loud, so she didn't. "Besides," she said briskly, "we don't even know if it would go anywhere. You barely know me, Jack."

He dropped his hand away from her face, and her skin registered the lack of warmth.

She bit her lip. "I mean, we barely know each other."

He looked at her for a long moment, and she felt herself flush under his gaze. "OK."

Her heart jolted. "OK?"

"OK, we won't go there."

It should have been a relief. It *was* a relief. She was just waiting for her heart to catch up with her on that. "OK. Good."

"If you need some time, to figure some things out, then that's fine."

"Yes, I— Wait. Time?"

"Yes. It's unfair, to expect you to be on my timeline. There were things *I* needed to figure out, after Venice, so it's only right that you get the chance to do the same. And if it's never the right time for you, that's OK too. I don't want you to feel any pressure or expectation—just know that I'm here if you need me."

She frowned at him, not really sure what to say.

He stood, kissed the top of her head, a friendly, easy gesture. "I think you should talk to Lily. For what it's worth."

Her frown increased, and she opened her mouth to say something, to argue back automatically.

He laughed at her expression. "I'm not saying you *have* to. I'm only doing what you did, to me."

There was too much truth in that to properly argue, so she wrinkled her nose.

"But if and when you are ready, Holly, I'll be here. OK?"

Her heart was beating fast as he turned away from her and walked into the en suite shower room. Right. His room. It was *his* room—she was the one who needed to leave.

"And by the way," he added, almost conversationally, glancing back at her over his shoulder, "I do know you."

"Huh?"

"You said we barely knew each other, but I do know you. I know the way you fall even when there is nothing to trip over. I know how you hate brushing your hair more than I thought anyone could hate something as minor as that. I know how you light up when you talk about teaching, even if you've convinced yourself it was a backup career, and how you have something more, this kind of glow, when you're thinking about sculpting something. I know you speak without thinking sometimes, but that even when you're angry, you have kindness there." He smiled, a little sadly. "I know how you are still hurting, from what happened to your sister. I know you are scared, to really let someone in. But I also know you've already done it—with Emma—because I see the way you are with her. And I *know* you can do that again, with someone else. If you want to."

Holly was holding her breath, unable to look away from his dark gaze.

"I know all of that and more. And I love it all, Holly."

And with that, he shut the bathroom door behind him, leaving her to get slowly to her feet. Her body was trembling, her heart stuttering. But what could she do? She wanted to cry, to open the door to the bathroom and run to him, let his arms come around her, breathe in the scent of him. But her reasoning stood. So she walked carefully to the bedroom door to let herself out. And she only paused for a second before she closed the door behind her.

DECEMBER

Chapter Thirty-two

Holly checked her phone for the millionth time, shifting in the booth as she did so. Less than a minute since she'd last checked—the phone still said 5:53. And Lily wasn't due until six. She'd got to the pub that Lily had suggested at five forty-five, figuring it was better to be there early, so that she could see her sister arrive and wouldn't have to do that awkward, uncertain scan of the room if she arrived second. But now that seemed like a bad idea—because now she was here, worrying that Lily wouldn't show, having already drunk the glass of sauvignon she'd ordered.

Holly knew this area well, having lived here as a teenager, and she recognized this pub, though it had been under a different name when she'd been here—a different name, and a much grubbier feel. Now it had all the charm of an English country pub, right in the middle of Hammersmith. Low wooden beams, slate floors, and rustic, mismatched tables. It was decorated for Christmas—next to the crackling fire, there was a tree in the corner, with presumably fake wrapped presents under it. Instead of flowers there were Christmas wreaths on each table, and green tinsel and golden bells were decorating the wooden bar. Candles flickered on the windowsills by the entrance, threatening to go out each time someone walked in and brought a rush of cold air, and there was the smell of mulled wine lingering in the air.

Holly checked the time again. Five fifty-four.

It had taken them a bit of time to find a date to meet. They had both been so busy, and wanted to wait until they had a chance to speak without feeling stressed or distracted. So they'd settled on meeting in December, on a weekday, after Holly's school broke for Christmas. December the twenty-third—the day before Christmas Eve. Holly's mum had clearly got wind of it—Holly had received a text from her, asking Holly to come round and say hello afterward. She imagined it was only thanks to her dad that her mum wasn't here now, sitting at a nearby table and watching to see what happened when her two daughters saw each other for the first time in four years.

Holly looked up at the next rush of cold wind. Her heart gave a painful thud.

She looked exactly the same. She'd seen photos of her on Facebook, but it was different, in real life. She was wearing jeans and a blue polo shirt with little threads of silver, a nod to the festive season.

Holly stood up, a little clumsily, her palms clammy.

Lily saw Holly and smiled—though it looked a bit strained. She crossed the pub, stepping around the queue at the bar. When she made it to Holly's table, the two of them just looked at each other.

Holly had the sudden urge to cry. Should they hug? It felt too awkward to hug. Should she say something? What should she say?

Lily put her handbag down on the chair opposite Holly—the

moment for hugging now gone. Then she looked at Holly, her hazel eyes overly bright. "I'll get us drinks, yes?"

"I can get—"

"Don't be silly, I'm already up." So was Holly, but maybe Lily needed a beat. "They do a great mulled wine here, if you fancy?"

Holly tried to match Lily's light tone. "Sure, sounds great."

She sat back down as her sister went to the bar and was quickly ushered to the front of the queue. Of the two of them, Lily had always had more natural charm.

Holly smiled when Lily returned and put the mulled wine down in front of her—in a tall latte glass with a little handle, a slice of orange, and a decorative cinnamon stick poking out of the top. She took a sip, felt the spices warm her tongue.

"You were right—this *is* great."

"It's their own recipe," Lily said as she sat down. "I managed to get it from them, though I can never replicate it *quite* as well at home. It's got all the usual spices like cinnamon and cloves and everything, but instead of brandy they use cognac, and they also add—" She shook her head. "I'm so sorry. I'm babbling. I just . . . I can't believe you're really here."

"Me neither," Holly murmured.

Lily took a breath, and Holly felt her shoulders tense. "Holly. I'm sorry."

"What? Why are *you* sorry?"

Tears filled Lily's eyes. "I'm sorry for what I said, four years ago."

"No, I'm sorry, Lily. I never even got the chance to say—"

"Exactly. You never got the chance, because I didn't let you. I just . . ." She lifted a hand to smooth down her hair and Holly saw it was shaking. When she spoke again, she addressed the table. "I didn't know what to do. When I lost the baby . . . I was not OK."

Holly felt the ugly punch to her heart, but Lily plowed on, clearly determined to say her piece.

"I spiraled. I didn't get out of bed for weeks; I lost my job because I couldn't function. I had to go on medication."

Holly placed her hands around her mulled wine, needing to take some of its warmth. She hadn't known. She'd assumed Lily would be struggling, of course she had—that was what had made it all the more difficult, because she knew her sister was in pain and she wasn't allowed to be there for her. But whenever she'd asked her parents, she'd always got a vague answer in response.

"At first, I needed someone to blame," Lily continued, her voice unsteady. "But it shouldn't have been you." She was still looking at the table, rather than at Holly.

She sounded like Jack. Holly thought about what he'd said at Abi's wedding, about there being a reason they had met, so that they could each learn to see the other side of the story.

"I will spend the rest of my life regretting what I said in that moment and how I let things go on for so long."

"So you don't . . . You don't blame me now?" She closed her eyes as she spoke. She didn't want to see her sister's face, if the answer was not the one she hoped for.

"Of *course* not, Holly."

Holly's eyes opened, and saw Lily's, shining with tears.

"It was not your fault. There was nothing you could have done. I realized that a long time ago. I just didn't know how to tell you that. Even through my pain, I remember the look on your face and the hurt in your eyes when I told you to get out of my hospital room. And I put it there, and I didn't know how to cope with that. And I'm so, so sorry I let you believe that it was your fault for so long, that I didn't reach out before." She took a breath. "I didn't know what to do, how to fix things."

A small smile crept over her lips as they exchanged a look at that, and Holly knew Lily was thinking the same—of all the years Lily had told *Holly* to fix things.

"I thought *you* would hate *me,* for the way I'd treated you. I thought it was why you never came around anymore. And I was still trying to get pregnant, and it wasn't working, and I was distracted. I shouldn't have been, but I was. So I let it go on. And on. And the longer it went on, the harder it was to see a way to reach out to you."

Both of them, unsure how to reach out to the other. Could they have had this moment sooner, if Holly hadn't been so scared too? But she pushed that thought aside—because they were here now.

"I'm sorry too," she said eventually. "I'm sorry I didn't call you. I thought you hated me."

Lily dashed at a tear on her face. "I hated *myself,* for what I'd said to you. But I never hated you, Holly."

"I thought, in Venice—"

"I'm sorry," Lily said again. "That was bad timing." She tried for a smile, but it crumpled. "I actually tried to call you back, later that day, but it said the line was engaged."

"You did?" Lily nodded and Holly shook her head, trying to recalibrate what she'd thought over the last few years. "That was . . . Well, there was a lot going on that day."

Lily frowned in question.

"I'll fill you in at some point. But can I ask? The doctor . . ."

Lily grimaced and picked up her mulled wine. "I don't really want to get into it."

"Right. Right, sorry, of course not."

Lily reached out, took Holly's hand on the table. "Not because of you, Holly. But because it's still not . . . easy . . . for me to talk about. But I think we're going to adopt." She tried for a smile.

"Yeah?"

"Yeah. We've started the process. It can take a bit of time, but it's what we want to do."

"Well," Holly said, trying to smile too. "I'll keep my fingers crossed for you, in that case."

Lily smiled. "Thank you." She pulled her hand back gently. "So, now that that's all out of the way . . . what are you doing for Christmas?"

Holly laughed at the ridiculousness of this. But she appreciated the attempt at normality. Maybe that's what they'd have to do for a little while—pretend, until they didn't have to pretend anymore.

Holly thought about Lily's question. She thought of the unopened Dear Stranger letter waiting for her at home. Of the one she'd already written and sent out this year. All the same as last year—with one big difference.

"I'm spending it with a friend of mine, in Devon." She had mentioned all the time she'd have on Christmas Day, trying to be jokey, and Emma had frowned at her. "Aren't you coming here, then?" And that was that. Holly hadn't spoken to Jack about it, though. Had barely spoken to him at all, since the wedding.

"Well," Lily said, "Steve and I are spending Christmas with his parents, but we'll be at Mum and Dad's for Boxing Day, if you wanted to come along . . ."

Holly stared at her sister, her heart thumping a little more heavily than usual. "Really? Do you think they'd want me there though?"

"Are you kidding? Of course they'd want you there! Holly, they'd be over the moon."

"I'm not so sure that's true," she said quietly. And when Lily just looked at her, she elaborated. "They never invite me round. Never really seem to want to see me at all after the accident."

Lily frowned. "That's because *you* never want to go round.

You always have some excuse, something else you're doing. Mum stopped asking, she told me."

"She did?"

"Yes. She was upset with me about it, actually," Lily said, with a sad little smile. "She was telling me off, for driving you away. It was just once, and she apologized after, but I think she really did blame me for it."

"She blamed *you*? I thought she blamed *me*."

"No! Of course not. It wasn't your fault, Holly."

Holly had been trying, very hard, not to cry, but now she could feel the tears, dripping off the end of her nose. In one smooth motion Lily came around to her side of the table and sat down next to Holly in the booth, putting her arm around her. Her big sister, comforting her like she used to when they were little.

"I'm so sorry, Hol. I should have been around. I shouldn't have pushed you away."

"We should have been around for each other," Holly said, her voice thick through tears.

"We are now, I promise."

Holly nodded. "Can I give you something?" she asked Lily.

"Holly, you don't need to give me anything. All I've wanted for years is to see you, and you've already given me that."

"I want to, though." After a brief hesitation, Holly reached into her bag, and brought out a bundle of letters, held together with an elastic band. She hadn't known whether she was going to give them to her, but it felt right now, that her sister should be able to read them, if she wanted to. That she should know how much Holly had thought about her over the last four years, even if she hadn't had the courage to face her.

"I wrote letters to you. Since the crash, I mean."

Lily's brow furrowed a little as she took the offered letters, staring at the blank envelopes.

"I wrote them, but I never sent them. I couldn't bring myself to. You don't have to read them," she said quickly. "But I wanted you to know, that I didn't just forget about you."

Lily took Holly's hand, squeezed. "Thank you. I wish I had letters to give you."

Holly smiled. "It was always more my thing than yours."

Lily laughed a little. "And I was always telling you off for doing it, wasn't I?"

"Yeah." Holly tried for a sly grin, one that she used to give Lily when they were little. "And since when did I ever listen to you?"

Lily's laugh was fuller this time, and she squeezed Holly into another hug. "I love you, you know. I'm sorry I've not been around to say that."

"I love you too," Holly whispered into her sister's hair. And if she'd been braver, maybe she would have got the chance to say that sooner.

It was what she'd been doing with Jack, she realized. She already knew that, of course, but it really hit her, in that moment. She'd kept pushing him away, too scared to take the risk that he might get close enough to hurt her. But look at Lily, look at Emma. She'd rather have them in her life, even if they did have the power to hurt her. And like it or not, Jack was already one of those people—she knew, deep down, that even if she did nothing, it would still hurt, if he walked out of her life forever.

Holly broke away from Lily when she heard her phone buzzing on the table. She slid it toward her and her heart performed a familiar little backflip. "Jack?"

"Holly? Hey, I'm sorry to call you out of the blue, it's just . . . it's Emma."

Holly froze, her fingers tightening their grip on the phone. "What about Emma? What's happened?"

"She had to go to hospital. I think . . ." Jack's voice was

raspy, not as smooth as usual. "I think you ought to get here, if you can."

"I'll leave now, I'll be there as soon as I can." She was on her feet before she'd even hung up.

"Holly?" Lily was standing too. "What's happened?"

"It's my friend . . . She . . ." But her brain wouldn't focus. Oh God, Emma. "I'm sorry. Lily, I have to go. This is terrible timing and I promise it's not you. I'm so happy to see you and I wish I could stay longer but it's my friend, she needs me. I'll call you soon, OK? I love you."

And with that, Holly took off out of the pub, trying very hard not to think about what this call might mean. Refusing to believe that this could be it, that she might miss the chance to say goodbye.

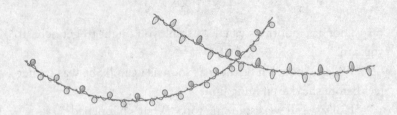

Chapter Thirty-three

Jack heard footsteps coming from down the corridor and turned to see Holly. He'd called her on impulse, the moment Pam had rung him to say she was taking Emma to hospital, and now he realized he'd probably completely panicked her.

He'd prepared for it, the squeeze to his heart, seeing her again, but hadn't expected it to be quite so painful. She was in a big green sweater and long brown boots, hair swept back into a ponytail, with tendrils of it misbehaving and creeping around to frame her face. Sparkly earrings glinted in the artificial hospital light as she strode toward him, her expression pinched and tight.

"She's OK," Jack said immediately, and he saw the breath Holly let out. Although "OK" was in the loosest sense of the word, he thought to himself. What he really meant was, this is not the moment. It is not the call you might have thought it was. He was sorry for scaring her like that. It was because *he'd* felt scared, when he'd got the call from Pam. And now he felt knackered—he'd been at the hospital for hours, waiting. Surely Holly must be exhausted too, having driven all this way.

"Can I go in, see her?" Holly asked, nodding toward the door. Clearly, someone at reception had told her where to find them.

"Yeah. There's a doctor in there at the moment and she was asleep, but—"

He broke off as the doctor in question came out. A man in his fifties, with the posture of someone used to being listened to. Giving Holly a cursory glance, the doctor stepped up to Jack.

"We've got the situation under control. She had an attack of diabetic ketoacidosis, which is why she nearly passed out—her friend did the right thing, bringing her here. But she'll be OK."

"Diabetic what?" Jack repeated blankly. "But she's not even diabetic."

"She is, I'm afraid," the doctor said briskly. "Diabetes is a common side effect of pancreatic cancer. She may have been living with it for a while, or she may not have known. I can talk it through with her when she wakes up, make sure she knows what to do to try and avoid a future episode. But it might also be time to think of hospice care, to help manage the other side effects. If she gets an infection, it's possible the same thing will happen again. She's also in some pain, from the tumor. I've given her something to help with that, but it's something a hospice can help with longer term—or there are hospice nurses who can come to you, depending on where you live."

"Right," Jack said. He could feel Holly watching him and didn't know where to look. Emma had been preparing for this, but it was he who would have to learn to deal with being unable to help her himself.

The doctor checked his watch—some gold designer type. "Best she spends the night here, but she should be able to go home tomorrow." Jack let out a breath. She'd be home in time for Christmas at least.

The doctor left, and Jack became acutely aware of Holly,

standing so near to him he could almost smell her, that cinna-mon spice, above the bleach and tangy metal smell of the hospi-tal. He had no choice—he had to look at her now.

"Sorry to get you down here like this," he said. "I just . . . I wasn't sure . . ."

"That's OK. I'm glad you called." She took a deep breath, and he could tell she was gearing up to something. "Jack, I—"

But he wasn't sure he was ready for whatever conversation she was about to start. At least, not if it was going in a bad direc-tion. "Are you staying down here for Christmas?" he asked, even though he knew the answer already.

"Yes. If that's OK?"

"Of course. We'd love to have you." He sounded so formal—why the hell did he sound so formal?

"We?"

"Yeah. I'll be there too. I wanted to spend Christmas with her before . . ." He couldn't bring himself to finish that sentence.

"Of course." They exchanged a glance, both of them smil-ing a little at the way she repeated his words back to him.

She frowned. "I don't know where to stay tonight, though. I didn't know you'd be there and I'd kind of planned on crashing in Emma's guest room again like last year. I didn't think it through, I'm sorry."

"You'll stay at Emma's of course."

"Won't you be there?"

What did that mean? That she didn't want him there? They'd barely spoken since Ireland. It had felt wrong, to text her, after his little speech—because he meant what he'd said, he didn't want to put pressure on her. He'd said his bit, and now it was up to her. He'd told himself he'd deal with it, either way. But he hadn't realized that the waiting would be so difficult. And what if she decided she didn't want to be with him, but didn't clue him in on that? Which would be perfectly reasonable: She didn't *owe* him anything.

He realized she was looking at him, a slight frown on her forehead. Right. She'd asked a question. "Ah, no. I've actually got my own place around here at the moment."

"Really?"

"Yeah." He hesitated for a moment. "I, ah, got a job. Well, it's more of a volunteer situation, which is fine for now."

"Where? Doing what? Garden stuff?"

He felt his lips tug into a smile at the way she said that—*garden stuff*. "Yeah. At Buckland Abbey. It's near my mum, actually. A bit of a drive from here but doable. I'm helping in the grounds. It's not overly glamorous, but it's a start, a way to get some experience."

A start, to see if there might be a way to make his hobby his job—and if not, at least it had got him back to Devon. He'd wanted to come back here—not just for Emma, but for his mum, his brother and sister. He'd run away when he left for university, and he'd never allowed himself to come back. But after making the decision to quit his job, it had just felt *right* to move back here. He felt like he could breathe again, away from the claustrophobia of London, even if Theo had told him that he was "completely mental" to give it all up.

"That's brilliant, Jack." She smiled at him, her green eyes lightening. He loved that smile. It gave him a pang, to look at it. What would happen, after Emma . . . ? Would they stay friends, even if Holly didn't want anything more? He wasn't sure he could do that, but he hated the thought of his life without her in it. It felt wrong, after all that had happened.

"Yeah. Yeah, it's pretty cool."

"Anyway. I'd better go in, see Emma."

He nodded. "Yeah. I'm going to go and grab some food, actually. But if you leave before me, there's a key, underneath Emma's . . . But you already know that."

She smiled again. "Yeah. It's a terrible hiding place."

"It really is."

He cleared his throat. "Do you need anything, before I go?" Holly shook her head and he rocked back on his heels. "I'll, ah, see you tomorrow, then?"

"Yeah. I'll get the mulled wine on." She hesitated, like she might say something more, then turned from him, toward Emma's room. He watched her go, that mane of hair rippling like flame. And he couldn't help it—he was glad she was here. Glad that she'd be there for Christmas. Not just for Emma's sake, but for his own, too. So if he could only have friendship from her, then that was what he'd take.

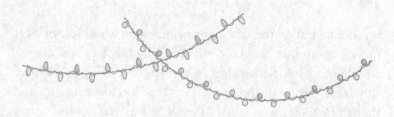

Chapter Thirty-four

"You're home!" Holly was standing in the doorway of Emma's cottage, arms spread wide as Jack and Emma got out of Jack's car.

"Don't make a fuss, my girl," Emma grumbled as she crossed the gravel driveway, her steps looking stiff and painful.

"It's Christmas Eve, I'm allowed to make a fuss." She jumped up and down on the balls of her feet as she waited for Emma and Jack to make their way into the house. She was wearing a big white sweater over leggings, but it still wasn't warm enough to combat the chill biting the air, one that brought a dampness which clung to her skin.

She only snuck a brief glance at Jack before ushering them both inside, then headed to the kitchen while Jack and Emma went into the living room. She'd done her best to make mulled wine, though it was nothing like the stuff in the pub, and was getting ready to cook a salmon dish for dinner, because that was one of the best dishes to make on Christmas Eve, according to BBC Good Food. She filled three mugs—no fancy latte glasses here—and managed to carry all three through at once.

Emma was on the sofa in the living room, her purple blanket tucked up around her. Jack was down by the fireplace, adding wood onto a low flame, already having got it going in the brief time she'd been out the room. He turned as she came in, and though he took the mug she offered, he was very careful not to touch her. What was that about? Had the whole waiting thing had a time limit on it?

Holly held out a mug for Emma too, then pulled it back a fraction when Emma reached up to take it. "Wait. Are you allowed sugar?"

Emma smiled a little. "Yes, my girl. Especially at Christmas." She winked. It was tired, but it was still there. She'd had her hair done recently, Holly noticed. It was still wispy, but it was cut neatly above her shoulders, and fell in soft gray waves, rather than its usual slightly unkempt style. It was more obvious now than in the hospital, and it brought a lump to Holly's throat, even as it made her want to smile. Emma, making an effort for Christmas.

And Christmas at Emma's cottage this year looked very different from last. There was a tree up in the corner—Jack's doing, no doubt—decorated in white fairy lights and silver tinsel, with a handful of presents underneath it.

Holly clinked her mug with Emma's, took a sip of her mulled wine. Emma patted the sofa next to her. "Come and sit down, my girl. Don't you have a meeting with a certain sister that you need to fill me in on?"

Jack glanced over to Holly at that and she felt the heat of his gaze on the side of her face. She hadn't told him she was going to see Lily—hadn't wanted to, in case it ended badly.

"In a minute," she said. "But first . . ."

She headed back to the kitchen, leaving Emma grumbling about unfinished sentences, and collected the two little clay models off the table—the two clay models she'd had the foresight to put in her car a few days ago, paranoid that she would forget them, the way she did with so many things, when she set off for Emma's for Christmas.

"Now, I know it's not actually Christmas yet. But I want to give you your present now." She held out her hand as she came back into the living room, then turned it palm up, the little sculpture sitting on top. It had taken her a few days to put it together. She'd kept it small, because that way Emma could take it with her, if she did end up having to move at some point.

It was the face of a woman. Of Emma. But it was Emma as Holly saw her. Fierce, and wise. A little cranky at times, but with a vulnerability there that she tried to hide. Someone kind, even if she pretended not to be. Most of all, someone who was loved. She nearly hadn't done it. She'd wanted to make something for Emma for her present, because she knew Emma would like that, more than anything she could buy. But she'd nearly given up on this idea and made a tiger instead. But seeing Emma's face as she took the sculpture from Holly—wide-eyed, almost awed—Holly knew she'd made the right decision. It wasn't always easy, to see yourself the way others saw you, especially in art—it was unforgiving, at times, even when the artist didn't mean it to be so. She should have known that if anyone could take it, it would be Emma. That if anyone could understand what she meant, what she'd poured into this, without saying anything, it was Emma.

Emma swallowed. "I don't have the words."

Holly bit her lip. "As long as you like it."

Emma looked up at Holly. "My girl, I don't think I've ever been as touched by anything in my whole life." She held out her hand and Holly took it, sliding onto the sofa next to her as she did. "I look like the version of myself I always wished I could be."

"That's the version of you I see," Holly said softly.

"It's beautiful." Holly looked up at the sound of Jack's voice, felt her cheeks warm from the way he was looking at it. Because he was looking at it the way she'd caught him looking at her, once or twice. The way he'd smiled at her, on that boat in Venice.

"I made one for you, too," she said, her tone a little cautious. She held out her other hand.

She hadn't done a face this time. She'd wanted to—she *still* wanted to sculpt that perfect face of his—but it had felt too personal and potentially too invasive, given everything that had happened between them. But she'd thought she might see him at Christmas, and had wanted to be prepared. So for him, she'd done a tiny little vase, small enough to fit comfortably in the palm of her hand—and too small by far for any real flowers, other than perhaps a single daisy. It had started as a joke—a vase for the garden lover, too small to be useful—and something fun, so that he wouldn't feel awkward about her giving him something. But then she'd spent *hours* painting the damn tiny thing, and that's where Jack came in. She'd painted the colors of him—green, of course, because of the countryside, starting from the bottom, and curling upward, like grass left to grow in an untouched meadow. Then purples and yellows, for the gardener in him, tiny little flowers there, if you looked closely enough. And all of it gave way to an orange glow—a sunset, she imagined. Something warm, something with heat, but also solid, unbreakable.

He took it from her, his fingers as gentle as Emma's had been. Then he looked right at her, and the corner of his mouth pulled up, the depths of his eyes warming. "I think I get this one."

She laughed, as something like relief washed through her, as he echoed their conversation at the gallery, one that felt so long ago now.

Jack put the tiny vase down carefully on the coffee table. "Well, if we're doing presents early . . ."

He crossed to the Christmas tree, bent down and picked up an envelope, then held it out to Emma.

Emma raised her eyebrows, but opened it obediently.

"It's a plot of land," Jack said, almost before she'd even opened the thing. "It's near where . . ."

"I know where it is," Emma said quietly.

Holly, of course, didn't know where it was they were talking about, but from their expressions, she could guess. Richard. This had something to do with Richard.

"Well," Jack said, "it's in your name. And it's protected. It's not much at the moment, but I'm going to work on it, if you agree. I'm going to make it somewhere welcoming for wildlife, somewhere positive, after what happened there. I hope you'll come out and see it too and give me your opinion on what we should do with it. I thought . . . Well, you were the one who got me into landscaping. So I thought maybe it could be something we share. And, well, I wanted it to be something that might last." He didn't say it, but Holly knew what he was thinking. He wanted this to be something that would last, because it might be the last gift he ever gave her.

Emma was silent for so long that Holly and Jack exchanged worried glances.

"Emma?" Jack nudged gently. "Are you—?"

And then, for the first time since Holly had met her, Emma let out a sob. She pressed her hand to her mouth, shook her head.

"Emma!" Holly said, reaching out to rub her arm.

"I'm sorry. Stupid. I just . . ." Another sob, and Emma wiped away the tear that escaped. "I didn't think I'd ever have this again. Christmas with family." She took Holly's hand, then reached up to take Jack's too. "I am so grateful to you both, for giving me this, one last time." She took one more shuddering breath, then adopted a tone that sounded much more like her usual voice. "Well, given you two are making me look bad, hand me that parcel from under the tree, will you, Jack?"

She pointed to one wrapped in gold paper, and Jack handed it over.

Emma took a breath. "Now. I meant to do one of these for each of you, but, well, it's taken me a little longer than I would have liked, what with . . . everything. So you can share this for now, and then decide on whose is whose when I've done the other one." She held the present out in the space between Holly and Jack.

Holly looked at Jack, who nodded, encouraged her to take it. She felt her fingers tremble unexpectedly as she opened it. It was a painting. A Mirabelle Landor painting. It was like the rainforest in the café, the one that Holly had been staring at when she'd bumped into Jack. The one that Emma had been looking at when she'd written the letter that had found its way to Holly. But it had differences. There were parts that were a deeper green, and some of the plants, to Holly's limited knowledge, looked like they didn't belong in a rainforest. There was a section of orange and gold, the warmth of the sun beating over the landscape.

"This is a Mirabelle Landor painting," she said, processing what she was holding with what Emma had said.

"Well spotted, my girl."

"But you just said you made . . ." Holly trailed off as the pieces started to come together.

She felt Jack shift closer to her, glanced at him to see him frowning down at the painting. "Those are ghost orchids." He was looking at the plants that Holly had clocked. "They don't really belong in a—"

"I know that," Emma said briskly. "But they're your favorite flowers, aren't they?" She turned to Holly. "And this is your bit." She gestured to the orange and gold shades. "Because you are a bit chaotic, but you bring warmth and hope—or at least you did to me."

Holly felt a lump form in her throat, and her vision blurred.

But despite that, she saw it, confirming what she thought she'd heard Emma say. The signature, in the bottom right-hand corner—where the name Mirabelle Landor was usually written.

Emma Tooley.

The handwriting was the same. She knew that, without having to check—because she'd studied her Mirabelle Landor cards enough to know.

She looked at Emma, her heart doing a funny little thump. "Emma . . . What does this . . . ?"

Jack was looking between them, his brow furrowed.

Holly pointed to the signature.

He read it. Stared. Then looked at Emma. "What?"

His voice was a bit too loud, and it made Holly let out a small little laugh.

"Tone it down a bit, my boy, otherwise Pam'll be round in a flash, and we're already spending all day with her tomorrow."

"But you . . . Is this . . . ?"

"Yes." Emma shifted on her seat. Uncomfortable, Holly realized. She was uncomfortable, letting them in on this secret.

"You're Mirabelle Landor?" she demanded.

"I am," Emma said, her voice calm, despite her posture. "Or she's me; I'm not really sure which way round it should be."

"You painted the card that you gave me?" Jack demanded. "When I was a kid?" The card he'd been carrying around on the day they'd met, Holly remembered.

"Yes."

"And you painted the rainforest? In the café?" Holly said, staring at Emma's face.

"Yes!" Emma huffed impatiently. "Not very quick on the uptake, you two, are you?"

"But . . ." Holly exchanged a glance with Jack and was sure her expression mirrored his—a particular kind of bafflement. "Why? Why did you never tell us? Why did you never tell *anyone*?

Or did you? Did you tell Pam? Because if you told her and neither of you—"

"Holly," Emma said firmly, and Holly wrinkled her nose. Right. She was overreacting—and Emma didn't deserve that.

"I'm sorry," she began again, trying not to speak as quickly.

Out of the corner of her eye, she thought she saw Jack shoot her a small smile.

"I just—"

"I know, my girl. Now, I don't want to spend forever dissecting this, OK? That's not why I told you. But to answer your questions, briefly: No, no one else knows. Pam doesn't know—though I wouldn't have put it past her to have guessed. I didn't tell you for the same reason I didn't tell anyone else—because I didn't want to own up to it. I painted the first one before Richard died," she said quietly, looking at Jack now as she spoke.

Holly glanced at him too, expecting a stiffness to show, but all he did was nod.

"Your card, the one I gave you, was one of the very first. A sort of trial, to see if I could do it, without having to put my name out there. But then, after Richard died . . ." She ran a hand over her face. "I didn't think I should *want* to paint. I felt guilty for it. But I couldn't quite stop myself. So I kept hidden behind a different name, and then it all became bigger: Mirabelle Landor became a bit of a *thing*, and I felt like I couldn't own up to it."

She dropped her hand to her lap. Tired. She looked so tired.

"But I wanted to tell you. Both of you," she said, glancing between them before letting her gaze settle on Holly. "But especially you, my girl. Because I know that you've been scared to start your art again, too. And I didn't want you to shy away from that part of you, like I've been doing my whole life." She turned the sculpture Holly had given her around in her hands, studying it. "Though I suppose I should have known you'd be stronger than me, in the end."

She looked up at them both, and her eyes were shining.

Holly reached out to place a hand on Emma's shoulder, but Emma waved her away.

"Anyway, enough about me. Can we move on now, please? I didn't tell you so I could be subjected to the Spanish Inquisition." She huffed out a breath. "It's a present, that's all." She sniffed. "Do you like it?"

A simple question, but Holly could hear the vulnerability under the surface—the first painting she'd put her name to.

Holly swallowed down her own feelings on the matter and laid a hand over Emma's. "It's beautiful. We love it." She glanced up at Jack.

"We do," he agreed, and Holly felt something stir at the way he'd gone along with the "we" so easily. "Memma, it's incredible."

"Well. Good. I also got you gin baubles, just in case," Emma said, brushing down imaginary lint off the skirt of her dress. "Now, I think it's about time for a refill, don't you?"

She held up her mug and Holly took it, headed for the kitchen.

It was only early afternoon, but already an evening winter glow was taking over the garden—pink skies and fading light. The garden, too, was very different from how Holly had seen it last time. It was winter, but even so Holly could see Jack had been at work—he'd made it look loved again.

She had to blink a few times as she looked out of the back door, to be sure she hadn't imagined the little flecks of white falling softly from the sky. She felt a bubble of delighted laughter rise up inside of her.

"Hey, guys, it's snowing!" She laughed again and, shoving on a pair of boots that had been left by the back door, she stepped outside. She lifted her hands, feeling the snow melting where it touched her skin, and turned a slow circle.

It didn't take long for Jack to come outside too. "Emma sent me to get you," he said, crossing his arms over his dark blue sweater. "She doesn't want you to catch a cold and then give it to her, apparently."

She smiled as she looked up at him, the white snow a shock against his dark hair. He didn't make any move to drag her back inside, though.

"Thank you for my sculpture," he said, his voice a gentle caress.

"You're welcome," she said. Her heart was starting up, the way it always did when it was just the two of them.

He took a step toward her, slid a small box out of the back pocket of his jeans. "I got something for you, too."

She hesitated, then took the box. She hitched in a breath as she opened it. It was a necklace. A green pendant hanging from a golden chain. Green and—was that gold, at its center? It seemed to pulse, like it was desperate to be worn.

"It's you," he said, still in that low, smooth voice. The one that never failed to make her skin heat. "The green and the gold and the fire. It's what I think of when I think of you."

"I love it," she murmured.

She held the necklace out to him, then lifted her hair and turned around in silent invitation. She felt the whisper of his touch on the back of her neck as he fastened the chain, gone before it was really there.

She turned back to face him. "I'm going to keep teaching."

His eyebrows shot up at the abrupt change in direction. "OK. Good to know."

"Wait, I'm going somewhere with this."

"OK . . ." Said more cautiously this time.

"I'm going to keep teaching, because you're right, I do love it. But I'm going to go part-time. I'm going to put some serious work into my art and see what comes of it. Maybe nothing, but I'm going to try—actually, properly try." She'd thought about it before, but the conversation with Emma made her feel sure it was the right thing.

"That's wonderful, Holly."

"Yeah. It is." She paused, then plowed on. "You know, you can make sculptures from anywhere." She said it casually, trying to disguise the way her heart stepped up a gear, as she put it on the line.

"I suppose that's true." The same casual tone, matching hers.

"And there are teaching jobs everywhere too."

"Also true."

She took a deep breath. Here was the leap. "I'm sorry for what I said at the wedding. You were right. I was closing myself off. Ever since Lily . . . You know, I spoke to her the other day. Realized I'd got a few things wrong." She shook her head. "I got something else wrong too." It would hurt. If she was wrong about this, if he didn't still feel the same. "I should have said yes. When you asked me to give us a go. And if you still want me, I want to try, too."

He looked at her in a way she wasn't sure how to read. "Holly, I—"

"No, wait," she said quickly, trying to keep the panic from her voice—the thought that he might say no making her feel as though her chest was being crushed in. "I'm not finished."

He opened his hands in invitation.

"I want to say, I was wrong about something else, too. Because I know you, Jack. I know the way you are never as happy anywhere as you are out in the countryside. I know about your impossible ability to keep what you're thinking off your face. I know your playful side, which only comes out now and then, but which is even more brilliant because of that. I know that you are generous, and I know how much you love your family, even when you've been unsure about how to handle that in the past. I know how much you care about your brother and sister, and how you will make sure you're always there for them." She reached out to touch his face, and he stayed very still. "I know that it hurt so much, when your dad died. I know that you ran from the past, because what other choice was there? And I know how brave you are, that you found a way to face it all again.

"I know all of that and more. And I love it all, Jack."

She saw the smile before it came, saw the way his dark eyes warmed. "You love it *all*, huh?"

She laughed, breathlessly and nudged him in the side.

He caught her wrist, pulled her to him, and she let out a long breath as he folded her against him.

"I was just going to say," he said, "that of course I want this, us. It's all I've been thinking about for months."

She smiled into his chest. "Really?"

"Yeah. But I'm glad you interrupted me. That was quite the speech, I would have hated to have missed it."

"Just returning the favor."

He rested her forehead against hers, their breathing matching in rhythm. Then she tilted her face up, and he kissed her, tentatively, like he couldn't quite believe it. And she kissed him back, allowing his woody scent to wrap around her, wrapping her arms around his neck to bring him closer.

She broke away, needing to say it, needing for him to know. "I love you, Jack Tooley."

And there it was, the smile—the full one, the one that lit up his whole face.

"This," she breathed as she traced it with one finger. "I want to sculpt this."

He laughed, squeezed her waist. "Why, when you've got the real thing right here?"

"Because then I'll always have you."

His arms tightened around her. "Don't say that. I want you

to sculpt it too, but not for that reason. Because I won't leave you. We found each other. I think we were always meant to find each other."

This time, she didn't contradict him.

"I won't leave you, because I love you too, Holly Griffin."

And the words were said with such promise that she found she could believe them.

They both started at the sound of Emma's voice. "Once you two have *finally* kissed and made up, could you come back inside and close the door? It's bloody freezing!"

Holly laughed, dashed away a tear that she didn't realize had escaped. And, then hand in hand with Jack, she headed back inside to welcome in Christmas.

One Year Later

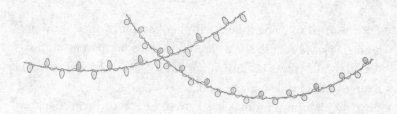

Chapter Thirty-five

Holly scrabbled around in her room for her keys, finally finding them on the windowsill, next to the decorative candle her mum had put out. It was the same room she'd had as a teenager—same single bed, different bedsheets. Down the hall, Lily and Steve were staying in Lily's old room, while Jack had had to settle for the sofa bed. All of them, spending the week before Christmas together, under one roof. And then, on Boxing Day, off to Jack's family.

Holly had to admit, she was pretty excited to give Mia and Theo their presents—she couldn't *wait* to see Mia's expression. She and Mia had bonded over art, and Holly was doing her best to encourage Mia to paint, something she was actually pretty good at. Jack had lamented the fact that Holly and Mia had bonded so instantly, when it had taken him a full year to win her around, but Holly knew he was pleased really.

She glanced up at the painting she'd hung above her bed. It had pride of place at home—a two-bed terraced house not far from Jack's family, where she and Jack now lived together—but she'd wanted to bring it here with her, for Christmas. She'd pretended it was because she'd wanted to show her parents and sister, but really it was because it felt like a piece of Emma, and she hadn't wanted to leave it behind.

The painting Emma had given her and Jack. Back at home—at *their* home—there was another one. Emma hadn't finished the second painting she'd wanted to do for them before she passed away. But they'd bought the painting from the café—the original rainforest one. The one with Mirabelle's signature, rather than Emma's.

This one, though, the one Emma had finally owned up to . . . this was the one Holly couldn't bear to part with. Especially as it was Emma who had given her the courage to really start pursuing her art again. Thanks to her encouragement, Holly had already been featured in two exhibitions, and she was slowly but surely starting to sell her art. She was even getting commissions, from people who wanted something specific, and she had her own website and everything.

But Emma wasn't around to see that anymore. She'd died earlier this year, back in March. She'd gone in her sleep, in the hospice, and it had been as painless as you could hope for, according to the nurse. Holly still found it difficult to believe she was gone. After only a year of knowing her, she'd cemented herself in Holly's life—in her heart—so fully, that it didn't feel like she could have dropped out of it as suddenly as she'd dropped in. Some people you know for a lifetime, but they never really make an imprint on your soul—and some people you only have to know for an instant to know they will be part of you forever. And Emma, of course, could be nothing but the latter.

She knew Jack still struggled with the loss too. She'd heard many more Emma stories in the last year, the ones he could remember from his childhood, and she delighted in every one. They were both still trying to accept what had happened—but they were also giving each other time—and support—to find their own way through the grief.

Holly had been worried, once, that Emma dying would be too much for Jack, that he'd push Holly away, that it would cause a fracture between them. But she'd been wrong—if anything, it had bound them more closely together.

After grabbing her keys, Holly found the other thing she'd come up to her room for—a letter—and ran back down the stairs. Their mum had gone all out with the Christmas decorations this year, so there was red tinsel wrapped around the white stair banister, and Holly could smell burnt orange as she reached the hallway, a product of her mum's "Christmas orange hot chocolate" experiment.

"Holly!" Her mum's voice sounded from the kitchen. "While you're out, could you pick up some milk? We don't have enough for the cauliflower cheese tomorrow." No doubt because she'd used it all up for the hot chocolate.

Jack came into the hallway at that moment, looking a little shifty. "Ah, your mum says—"

"I *heard*, Mum!"

"Well, answer then!"

Jack looked at the letter in her hand, and his expression turned a little odd. "That's the Dear Stranger letter, isn't it?"

"Yes."

"Hang on." He turned to start up the stairs himself.

"Jack, what?"

"Don't leave, OK? Two seconds." He jogged the rest of the way up to the second floor, to her room, where he was keeping his suitcase.

Holly stood in the hallway, waiting like a lemon, just as Lily and Steve came in through the front door, letting in a gust of cold wind with them.

"How'd it go?" Holly demanded immediately.

Lily smiled. "Well, I think. We'll know more soon."

Holly nodded. Lily and Steve had come back from a meeting with the adoption agency. It was a long, agonizing process, but they were on the road, and Holly was full of admiration for how her big sister was handling it.

Jack came bounding down the stairs just as Lily and Steve headed to the kitchen to fill their parents in.

"What's that?" Holly asked, nodding to a letter in Jack's hand.

"This," Jack said, with a meaningful pause, "is something Emma wanted me to give you, around this time—and ideally if I caught you sneaking off to send a Dear Stranger letter."

"A) I'm not *sneaking,* and B) it's—"

He kissed her quickly on the lips to stop her talking.

"Right," she agreed. "Not the point."

"It's from Emma," Jack continued. "I don't know what's in it. She wrote me a letter too."

"She did?"

He nodded.

She didn't ask why he hadn't shared it with her. His relationship with Emma was his own, and if the letter was meant only for him, then it wasn't her place to read it. Just like Jack wouldn't ask her what was in this one. Not unless she wanted to talk about it. So instead she took the letter and stared down at her name on the front.

"You don't have to open it yet," he said softly. "Not until you're ready. I'm just doing my part."

Holly nodded; the damn lump in her throat was back, making it difficult to talk.

"Right," Jack said, clapping his hands. "I'm off to work my charm on your mum."

Holly snorted and Jack's eyebrows shot up.

"Hey, it worked on you, didn't it?"

She smiled. "I suppose it did." She stretched on tiptoes to kiss him, lingering only briefly, in case someone walked in.

Leaving Jack with her family, she stepped outside, clutching the two letters. The bite to the air was cold, but bearable, and the sky was a bright, clear blue. The street was relatively quiet as she passed the houses, some with Christmas trees in the front garden, one with a flashing reindeer in the window. She headed for the nearest park, smiled to a woman out jogging with her dog. Then she found a bench and, ignoring the damp wood, sat down, and took out Emma's letter.

To my own personal stranger,

I hope I've timed this right and that you are reading this around Christmas. I thought it would be a bit much, having a letter from me right away, but it also feels right that we've come full circle, don't you think? It was a letter at Christmas that brought us together, after all.

Well, where to start? I suppose short and to the point is best—that was always more my style. So, thank you. In case I don't say it enough, thank you—thank you for tracking me down, and for forcing your way into my life despite my awful temperament. Thank you for offering me a lifeline, at a time when I was ready to give up. You have made my last year on this earth more than I could ever have hoped. You brought me joy, when I was sure there was none left to be had.

Thank you for bringing me Jack. I'd given up on him, too. I should never have done that, but I did. You saw that, I think. And because you are so brilliantly you, you refused to let it drop, and that is something that is both incredibly annoying and utterly wonderful. I'm sure you'll piss many people off with that tendency, over the years, but I for one hope you never lose that quality. Despite the fact I told you many times to butt out, I am eternally grateful that you didn't.

I have wondered, over the course of the last year and a bit, how it was that we came to find each other. How it was that you were the person to receive my letter. I have spent many years feeling bitter at the universe, for offering me a sour hand, for leaving me alone in my old age, with nothing but regret to fill the void—and so, I wonder, did the universe interfere somehow? I don't claim to think that the universe particularly cares about the fate of one old woman, but it does feel extraordinary, to have found you in this way. Maybe it was chance—or maybe the universe really does care about us all. Maybe we were all meant to find each other this year: you, me, and Jack—pieces of a puzzle that could fit together.

As for Jack—I imagine he's confessed this to you himself, but he is totally smitten with you, my girl. I have to say, I approve of his judgment.

I know, I know—this letter is overly sentimental, especially coming from me. But I wanted you to know, my girl, just how special you are to me—and will continue to be, long after I'm gone.

Please don't spend too long mourning me. Miss me, occasionally—I like the idea of having someone who cared for me enough to miss me—but don't mourn, if you can help it. I don't want you to be like me—I don't want you to spend your life mourning, instead of living.

But you won't be like me, I know that. You are far too clever, and far too sparky, to ever let that happen.

So all that's left to do is to say goodbye, Holly. It has been a pleasure knowing you, my girl. But I suspect it's not goodbye forever. Because if the universe cared

enough to throw me in your path and change the course
of both our lives, then I feel sure that it will allow us to
see each other again, one day.

Until then—
Emma

Holly felt the tears spark in her eyes, and hitched in a breath as she traced the words again. All the words she wished she could say back to Emma—because if Holly had been Emma's lifeline, then Emma had also been hers. She'd known, of course, that Emma had forgiven her, long ago, for tracking her down two Christmases ago—but there was still something special about her having written it down. Something special about coming full circle, with a final letter from the woman who had changed her life so completely.

This time, when she read the letter through again, she smiled a little. *Miss me, occasionally . . . but don't mourn me.* And she would try to find a way to do that. Try to find a way to hold Emma in her heart, to miss the brilliant things about her, to think of her, a little, every time she molded her clay, without letting the grief dampen Emma's memory.

And so she got to her feet once more, slipping Emma's letter inside her coat, and holding on to the remaining one in her hand. When she reached the nearest postbox, she looked down at the envelope one more time: her Dear Stranger letter, written to someone who might be feeling a little lonely, a little lost, this Christmas. She hoped whoever read it would find some comfort there, would feel some small hope, that things might be brighter in the future. She hoped they would feel a little less alone—as she had done, each time she'd received a letter like this. And she hoped that, whoever they were, there might be something waiting for them, just around the corner—after all, look at what had happened to her.

With that thought, she let the Dear Stranger letter slip through the postbox—the last one she would ever write. Because from now on, she knew that no matter what happened, she no longer needed the Dear Stranger club. And with that thought, she turned away—back to Jack, to her parents, to Lily. Back to her family, to celebrate Christmas.

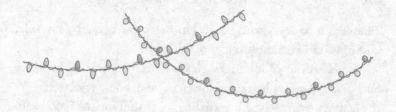

Acknowledgments

This is now my third book and I'm starting to feel that writing the acknowledgments is the final full stop on a novel—it means that it's really done! As always, my very talented editor, Sherise Hobbs, deserves huge thanks for her creativity, attention to detail, and enthusiasm, which gets me through the writing process! And on the U.S. side, Hilary Teeman and Caroline Weishuhn deserve huge love and thanks for their creative brainstorming, encouragement, and wise advice. I am hugely lucky to be able to work with such brilliantly talented editors.

There are so many people who work so hard to bring a book into the world. In the United Kingdom, thank you to Isabel Martin for keeping me on track, Emily Patience and Isabelle Wilson for pressing the book into many hands, and all the team at Headline who work so very hard. In the United States, I'm lucky to have such a creative, enthusiastic, and hardworking M&P team—thank you very much to Megan Whalen, Taylor Noel, and Melissa Folds for all that you do. As always, thanks so much to Rebecca Folland and now Grace McCrum on the rights front.

Thank you to my agent, Sarah Hornsley, for being by my side, and to Cara Lee Simpson for stepping in.

I feel so incredibly lucky to have been supported by other authors, bloggers, bookstagrammers, and book reviewers over the last few years—and it is that support that means I'm able to keep writing! So if you have read and reviewed any of my books, thank you so very much!

Finally thank you to you, reader, for reading this book. You are the reason that we are able to tell stories in the first place.

Love, Holly

EMILY STONE

A BOOK CLUB GUIDE

Questions and Topics for Discussion

1. At the very beginning of the novel, we get a glimpse into Holly and Lily's sisterly relationship as they drive to meet their parents for the holidays. Do you have a similar relationship with any of your siblings or cousins? How would you feel if that relationship suddenly came to a halt?

2. Holly and Emma ultimately meet as the result of a "Dear Stranger" letter-writing club, where the writers are encouraged to say what's on their mind during the holiday season. What do you think of the idea that talking to a stranger can sometimes be easier than talking to someone you know?

3. If you were in Emma's situation and Holly turned up at your front door, how would you have reacted? Would you have welcomed her, or would you have been taken aback. Why?

4. What did you think of Holly's decision to try to bring Emma back together with her grandson? How do you feel about the way she went about it?

5. What did you think of Jack's reaction when Holly told him

about Emma? Could you sympathize with where he was coming from?

6. Throughout the novel, we see Holly focusing on repairing Jack and Emma's relationship, all while feeling unable to take significant steps to repair her relationships with her own family. Why do you think that is?

7. Jack and Holly, although very different people, deal with their grief in similar ways. What do you think that says about humanity (or grief) as a whole? Do you think that some experiences are more universal than we might realize at the time we are going through them?

8. Similarly, we see that both Jack and Holly have to go on their own individual journeys before they can give each other the time and attention that they both deserve in a relationship. What do you think of their decisions to do so?

9. What did you think of the secret that Emma reveals at the end of the novel? Were you surprised? What do you think that says about her character?

10. Throughout the novel, we see Holly resisting the idea of fate, which her sister always pushed her to believe in more. How big a role do you think fate plays in this novel? How big a role do you think fate plays in real life?

EMILY STONE is the author of *Always, in December, One Last Gift,* and *Love, Holly.* She lives and works in Chepstow and writes in an old Victorian manor house with an impressive literary heritage.

Twitter: @EmStoneWrites
Instagram: @EmStoneWrites

Don't miss these other novels from
EMILY STONE

Follow Emily Stone on Instagram
@emstonewrites

DELL

Learn more at
PenguinRandomHouse.com

RANDOM HOUSE BOOK CLUB

Because Stories Are Better Shared

Discover

Exciting new books that spark conversation every week.

Connect

With authors on tour—or in your living room. (Request an Author Chat for your book club!)

Discuss

Stories that move you with fellow book lovers on Facebook, on Goodreads, or at in-person meet-ups.

Enhance

Your reading experience with discussion prompts, digital book club kits, and more, available on our website.

Join our online book club community!

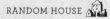 randomhousebookclub.com

Random House Book Club ™

Because Stories Are Better Shared

RANDOM HOUSE